GEN

WOODLAND

PAINTBALL ZONE

EIGHT OBSTACLE COURSE

LAKE

HEATRE

TRAINING HUT

TRAINING OFFICE

PITCHES

BASIC TRAINING COMPOUND

CRICKET FIELD

FARM
FIELD

D034415b

What's it all about? ... www.hendersonsboys.com

Robert Muchamore was born in 1972 and spent thirteen years working as a private investigator. He has written ten books in the CHERUB series.

The series has won numerous awards, including the 2005 Red House Children's Book Award. For more information on Robert and his work, visit **www.muchamore.com.**

Praise for the CHERUB series:
'If you can't bear to read another story about elves, princesses or spoiled rich kids who never go to the toilet, try this. You won't regret it.' *The Ultimate Teen Book Guide*

'My sixteen-year-old son read *The Recruit* in one sitting, then went out the next day and got the sequel.' Sophie Smiley, teacher and children's author

'So good I forced my friends to read it, and they're glad I did!' Helen, age 14

'CHERUB is the first book I ever read cover to cover. It was amazing.' Scott, age 13

'The best book ever.' Madeline, age 12

'CHERUB is a must for Alex Rider lovers.' Travis, age 14

THE RECRUIT
Robert Muchamore

Hodder
Children's
Books

A division of Hachette Children's Books

CHERUB: *The Recruit*

Copyright © 2004 Robert Muchamore
First published in Great Britain in 2004
by Hodder Children's Books
This edition published in 2008

1

A Catalogue record for this book is available
from the British Library

ISBN 978 0 340 988884 8

Typeset in Goudy by Avon DataSet Ltd,
Bidford-on-Avon, Warwickshire

Printed in Great Britain by
Clays Ltd, St Ives plc

The paper used in this book is a natural recyclable
product made from wood grown in sustainable forests.
The hard coverboard is recycled.

Hodder Children's Books
a division of Hachette Children's Books
338 Euston Road, London NW1 3BH
An Hachette Livre UK company

WHAT IS CHERUB?

During World War Two, French civilians set up a resistance movement to fight against the German forces occupying their country. Many of their most useful operatives were children and teenagers. Some worked as scouts and messengers. Others befriended homesick German soldiers, gathering information that enabled the resistance to sabotage German military operations.

A British spy named Charles Henderson worked among these French children for nearly three years. After returning to Britain, he used what he'd learned in France to train twenty British boys for work on undercover operations. The codename for his unit was CHERUB.

Henderson died in 1946, but the organisation he created has thrived. CHERUB now has more than two hundred and fifty agents, all aged seventeen or under. Although there have been many technical advances in intelligence operations since CHERUB was founded, the reason for its existence remains the same: adults never suspect that children are spying on them.

1. SCIENCE

James Choke hated Combined Science. It should have been test tubes, jets of gas and sparks flying all over the place, like he'd imagined when he was still at primary school. What he got was an hour propped on a stool watching Miss Voolt write on a blackboard. You had to write everything down even though the photocopier got invented forty years earlier.

It was last lesson but one, raining outside and turning dark. James was sleepy because the lab was hot and he'd been up late playing Grand Theft Auto the night before.

Samantha Jennings sat next to him. Teachers thought Samantha was fantastic: always volunteering for stuff, neat uniform, glossed nails. She did all her diagrams with three different coloured pens and covered her exercise books in wrapping paper so they looked extra smart. But when the teachers weren't looking Samantha was a total cow. James hated her. She was always winding him up about his mum being fat:

'James' mum is so fat, they have to grease the bath tub or she gets stuck in it.'

Samantha's cronies laughed, same as always.

James' mum *was* huge. She had to order her clothes out of a special catalogue for fat people. It was a nightmare being seen with her. People pointed, stared. Little kids mimicked the way she walked. James loved his mum, but he tried to find excuses when she wanted to go somewhere with him.

'I went for a five-mile jog yesterday,' Samantha said. 'Two laps around James' mum.'

James looked up from his exercise book.

'That's so funny, Samantha. Even funnier than the first three times you said it.'

James was one of the toughest kids in Year Seven. Any boy cussing his mum would get a punch. But what could you do when it was a girl? Next lesson he'd sit as far from Samantha as he could.

'Your mum is so fat—'

James was sick of it. He jumped up. His stool tipped over backwards.

'What is it with you, Samantha?' James shouted.

The lab went quiet. Every eye turned to the action.

'What's the matter, James?' Samantha grinned. 'Can't take a joke?'

'Mr Choke, pick up your seat and get on with your work,' Miss Voolt shouted.

'You say one more word, Samantha, I'll . . .'

James was never any good at comebacks.

'I'll bloody . . .'

Samantha giggled. 'What will you do, James? Go home and cuddle big fat Mommy?'

James wanted to see something other than a stupid grin on Samantha's face. He grabbed Samantha off her stool, bundled her up against the wall, then spun her around to face him. He froze in shock. Blood was running down Samantha's face. Her cheek had a long cut where it had caught on a nail sticking out of the wall.

James backed away, scared. Samantha cupped her hands over the blood and started bawling her head off.

'James Choke, you are in extremely serious trouble!' Miss Voolt shouted.

Everyone in James' class was making some sort of noise. James couldn't face up to what he'd done. No one would believe it was an accident. He made a run for the door.

Miss Voolt grabbed James' blazer.

'Where do you think you're going?'

'Get out my way,' James shouted.

He gave Miss Voolt a shove. She toppled backwards, limbs flipping helplessly in the air like a beetle turned upside down.

He slammed the classroom door and ran down the corridor. The school gates were locked, but he escaped over the barrier in the teachers' car park.

*

James stormed away from school, muttering to himself, getting less angry and more scared as it dawned that he was in the deepest trouble of his life.

He was twelve in a few weeks' time. He started wondering if he'd live that long. His mum was going to kill him. He'd definitely get suspended. It was probably bad enough to get expelled.

By the time James got to the little playground near his flats he felt sick. He looked at his watch. If he went home this early his mum would know something was up. He didn't have change for a cup of tea in the chip shop. The only thing to do was go into the playground and shelter from the drizzle in the concrete tunnel.

The tunnel seemed smaller than James remembered. There was graffiti sprayed all over and it smelled like a dog had peed inside. James didn't mind. He felt he deserved to be somewhere cold that smelled of dog. He rubbed his hands to get them warm and remembered when he was little.

His mum was nowhere near as fat in those days. Her face would appear in the end of the tunnel with a daft grin. She'd speak in a deep voice, *I'm coming to eat you up, James.* It was cool, because the tunnel had a killer echo when you were sitting inside. James tried the echo:

'I'm a total idiot.'

The echo agreed with him. He pulled his coat hood up and did the zip to the top so it covered half his face.

*

After half an hour sulking, James knew he had two options: stay in the tunnel for the rest of his life, or go home and get killed.

James stepped into the hallway of his flat and checked the mobile phone on the table under the coat rack:

12 MISSED CALLS
UNIDENTIFIED NUMBER

It looked like school had been trying to get hold of his mum pretty bad, but she hadn't answered. James thanked god, but wondered why she hadn't picked up. Then he noticed Uncle Ron's jacket hanging up.

Uncle Ron had turned up when James was a toddler. It was like having a loud, smelly rug in the flat. Ron smoked, drank and only went out to go to the pub. He got a job once, but it only lasted a fortnight.

James had always thought Ron was an idiot and his mum had eventually agreed and kicked him out. But only after she'd married him and given birth to his daughter. Even now James' mum had a soft spot for Ron. They'd never got divorced. Ron turned up every few weeks, supposedly to see his daughter, Lauren. But mostly he came when Lauren was at school and he was short of a few quid.

James walked into the living room. His mum, Gwen, was spread out on a sofa. Her feet were up on a stool and her left leg was bandaged. Ron was in an armchair, feet on the coffee table, toes poking out of his socks. They were both drunk.

'Mum, you're not supposed to drink with your pills,' James said, so annoyed he forgot his problems.

Ron straightened up and took a drag of his cigarette.

'Hey Jamie boy, Daddy's home,' Ron said, grinning.

James and Ron eyed each other up.

'You're not my father, Ron,' James said.

'No,' Ron replied. 'Your dad legged it the day he saw your ugly face.'

James didn't want to say about school in front of Ron, but the truth was eating at him.

'Mum, something happened at school. It was an accident.'

'Wet your pants again, did you?' Ron giggled.

James didn't want to take the bait.

5

'Listen, James, me darlin',' Gwen said, slurring her words. 'Whatever trouble you're in this time, we'll talk later. Go and get your sister from school. I've had a few too many drinkies and I'd better not drive.'

'I'm sorry, Mum, it's really serious. I have to tell you . . .'

'Just get your sister, James,' his mum said sternly. 'My head is pounding.'

'Lauren's big enough to come home on her own,' James said.

'She isn't,' Ron interrupted. 'Do what you're told. He needs my boot up his backside if you ask me.'

'How much money does he want this time?' James asked sarcastically.

Gwen waved her hand in front of her face. She was fed up with both of them.

'Can't you two stay in the same room for two minutes without fighting? James, go to my purse, buy something for tea on the way home. I'm not cooking tonight.'

'But . . .'

'Get out, James, before I lose my temper.'

James couldn't wait until he was old enough to batter Uncle Ron. His mum was OK when Ron wasn't around.

James found his mum's purse in the kitchen. A tenner was enough for his dinner, but he took two twenties. Ron would steal everything in the purse before he left, so James wouldn't get blamed. It felt nice stuffing forty quid into his school trousers. Gwen never left anything lying around that she didn't expect James or Ron to steal. She kept the big money upstairs in a safe.

2. SISTER

Some kids were happy to have one games console. James Choke had every console, game and accessory going. He had a PC, an MP3 player, Nokia mobile, widescreen TV and DVD recorder in his room. He never looked after any of it. If something broke he got another one. He had eight pairs of Nike trainers. A top-line skateboard. A £600 racing bike. When his bedroom was in a mess it looked like a bomb had gone off in Toys R Us.

James had all this because Gwen Choke was a thief. She ran a shoplifting empire from her armchair while she watched daytime soaps and stuffed chocolates and pizza. She didn't steal, herself. Gwen took orders and passed them down to thieves who worked for her. She covered her tracks, never going near stolen goods herself and switching mobiles every few days so the police couldn't trace her calls.

*

It was the first time James had been back to primary school since his last day as a pupil before the summer holidays. A few mums stood at the gate nattering.

'Where's your mum, James?' someone asked.

'Off her face,' James said sourly.

There was no way James was covering for her after she'd kicked him out of the flat. He saw the other mums exchange glances.

'I want Medal Of Honour for Playstation,' one of them asked. 'Can she get it?'

James shrugged, 'Course, half price, cash only.'

'Will you remember, James?'

'No. Give us a bit of paper with your name and phone number and I'll pass it on.'

The gaggle of mums started jotting things down. Trainers, jewellery, radio-controlled car. James stuffed the papers into his school blazer.

'I need it by Tuesday,' someone said.

James wasn't in the mood.

'If you want to tell my mum something, write it down. I won't remember.'

The kids all started coming out. Nine-year-old Lauren was last out of her class. She had her hands tucked in her bomber jacket and mud on her jeans from playing football with the boys at lunchtime. Lauren had blonde hair, same as James, but she kept asking her mum to let her dye it black.

Lauren was on another planet to most girls her age. She didn't own a single dress or skirt. She'd microwaved her Barbies when she was five and hadn't touched one since. Gwen Choke said if there were two ways of doing something, Lauren would always pick the third one.

'I hate that old bat,' Lauren said, when she got near James.

'Who?' James asked.

'Mrs Reed. She gave us sums. I did them in about two

minutes, and she made me sit still for the rest of the lesson waiting for all the dumb kids to finish. She wouldn't even let me go to the cloakroom and get my book.'

James remembered Mrs Reed had done the same thing when she was his teacher three years earlier. It was like getting punished for being clever.

'Why are you here, anyway?' Lauren asked.

'Mum's drunk.'

'She's not supposed to drink until after the operation.'

'Don't tell me,' James said. 'What can I do about it?'

'How come you got home early enough to pick me up?'

'Got in a fight. They sent me home.'

Lauren shook her head, but she couldn't help smiling.

'Another fight. That's three this term, isn't it?'

James didn't want to talk about it.

'What do you want first?' he asked. 'Good news or bad news?'

Lauren shrugged. 'Just tell us.'

'Your dad's indoors. The good news is Mum gave us money to get take-away. He should be gone by the time we get home.'

*

They ended up in a burger place. James got a double cheeseburger meal. Lauren only wanted onion rings and a Coke. She wasn't hungry, so she got handfuls of little milks and sugar packets and made a mess on the table while James ate. She tipped out loads of sugar, soaked it with milk, then shredded the paper wrappers and stirred it all up.

'What are you doing that for?' James asked.

'As a matter of fact,' Lauren said acidly, 'the entire future of western civilisation depends upon me making a smiley face with this ketchup.'

'You realise some poor sod has to clean all that up?' James said.

'Not my problem,' Lauren shrugged.

James tucked in the last mouthful of his burger and realised he was still starving. Lauren had hardly touched her onion rings.

'You eating those?' James asked.

'Have them if you want. They're stone cold.'

'This is all we've got for dinner. You better eat something.'

'I'm not hungry,' Lauren said. 'I'll make toasted sandwiches later.'

James loved Lauren's toasted sandwiches. They were mad: she got Nutella, honey, icing sugar, golden syrup, chocolate chips. Whatever sweet stuff was going, all poured on thick. The outside was crispy and the hot gloop was about three centimetres deep in the middle. You couldn't eat one without burning your fingers.

'You better clean up afterwards,' James said. 'Mum blew her stack last time you made them.'

*

When James turned into his road it was nearly dark. Two guys came out from behind a hedge. One of them grabbed James and knocked him against a wall, pulling his arm tight behind his back.

'Hello, James,' he said, his mouth up against James' ear. 'We've been waiting for you.'

The other guy grabbed Lauren and stuck his hand over her mouth to stop her screaming.

James' opinion of his own intelligence hit an all-time low. While he'd been worrying about getting in trouble with Mum, school and maybe even with the police, he'd forgotten something: Samantha Jennings had a sixteen-year-old brother.

Greg Jennings hung out with a gang of crazies. They were kings of the estate where James lived: smashing up cars, mugging people, getting into fights. If another kid saw them he'd look down at his shoes, cross his fingers and be happy if all he came away with was a slapped face and his money taxed. A good way to upset the gang was to beat up one of their little sisters.

Greg Jennings grazed James' face along the bricks.

'It's your turn now, James.'

He let go of James' arm. James could feel blood dribbling down his nose and cheek. There was no point struggling: Greg could snap him like a twig.

'Scared?' Greg asked. 'You ought to be.'

James tried to speak, only his voice didn't work and the way he was trembling seemed to answer anyway.

'Got money?' Greg asked.

James took out the rest of the forty pounds.

'Nice one,' Greg said.

'Please don't hurt my sister,' James begged.

'My sister has eight stitches in her face,' Greg said, pulling a knife out of his pocket. 'Lucky I don't go round hurting little girls, or your sister might have ended up with eighty.'

Greg sliced off James' school tie. Then he cut the chest buttons off his shirt and slashed up his trousers.

'This is just the start, James,' Greg said. 'We're gonna be seeing a lot of each other.'

A fist smashed into James' stomach. Ron had hit James a few times, but never that hard. Greg and his henchman walked off. James crumpled up on the ground.

Lauren walked over to James. She didn't have much sympathy for him.

'You got in a row with Samantha Jennings?'

James looked up at his sister. He was in a lot of pain and ashamed of himself.

'She got cut by accident. I only meant to scare her.'

Lauren started walking away.

'Help me up, Lauren. I can't walk.'

'Crawl then.'

Lauren went a few more paces before she realised she couldn't abandon her brother, even if he *was* an idiot. James stumbled towards home with his arm round Lauren's back. It took all her strength to hold him up.

3. WORSE

James stumbled into the hallway, one hand clasped over his stomach. He glanced at the display on his mum's mobile:

48 MISSED CALLS
4 TEXTS

He turned the phone off and stuck his head in the living room. The light was off, TV on. His mum was asleep in her chair and there was no sign of Ron.

'He's gone,' James said.

'Thank god for that,' Lauren said. 'He always kisses me and his breath's revolting.'

Lauren pushed the front door shut and picked a handwritten note off the doormat.

'It's from your school.'

Lauren read aloud, struggling with the messy handwriting:

'Dear Mrs Choke, Please contact either the School Secretary or myself urgently on one of the numbers below, con . . . Con something?'

'Concerning,' James guessed.

'Concerning James' behaviour at school today,' Lauren continued. 'Michael Rook, Deputy Head Teacher.'

Lauren followed James into the kitchen. James ran a glass of tap water and slumped at the table. Lauren sat opposite and kicked off her trainers.

'Mum will absolutely massacre you,' Lauren grinned. She was looking forward to seeing James suffer.

'Can't you shut up? I'm trying not to think about it.'

*

James locked himself in the bathroom. He was shocked by what the mirror showed him. The left side of his face and the ends of his cropped blond hair were blood red. He emptied his pockets and stuffed his wrecked clothes in a bin-liner. He'd hide them under the other rubbish later so his mum didn't find them.

Ending up in this mess made James start asking questions about himself. He knew he wasn't a very good person. He was always getting in fights. He was clever, but he never did any work so he got bad marks. James remembered all the times his teachers had told him he was wasting his potential and that he'd end up in a bad way. He'd sat through billions of lectures with his brain turned off. Now he was beginning to think they were mostly right and that made him hate them even more.

James unscrewed the cap on a tube of antiseptic, but realised it was pointless without washing off the blood first. The hot shower soothed his face and stomach as a red puddle whirled around his feet.

James wasn't sure if god existed, but he couldn't see how everything just got here without something making it. If there was ever a time to pray this was it. He wondered if you were supposed to pray while naked in the shower, but figured what the hell and pressed his wet hands together.

'Hello, God . . . I'm not always good. Not ever really. Just help me be good and stuff. Help me be a better person. Cheers . . . Amen. And please don't let Greg Jennings kill me.'

James looked awkwardly at his hands, not convinced about the power of prayer.

*

After the shower, James put on his favourite clothes: an Arsenal shirt and a pair of tatty Nike tracksuit bottoms. He'd had to hide them from his mum. She chucked out anything that didn't look as if it had been shoplifted the previous week. She never understood that it was cooler if some of your clothes were a bit on the shabby side.

After milk, two of Lauren's toasted sandwiches and half an hour playing GT4 with his duvet over him, James felt a bit better. Except his stomach killed if he moved suddenly and he wasn't looking forward to telling his mum what he'd done when she woke up. Not that she looked like waking up soon. She must have had loads to drink.

James crashed his car into the barrier and six cars whizzed past, leaving him in last place. He hurled the joypad. He always got that corner wrong. The computer-controlled cars went round like they were on rails, which made it seem like the game was rubbing it in. It was boring playing alone, but there was no point asking Lauren. She hated computer games. She only ever wanted to play football or draw.

James grabbed his mobile and called his friend Sam. Sam lived down the balcony and was in James' class.

'Hello, Mr Smith. It's James Choke. Is Sam there?'

Sam picked up the phone in his bedroom, sounding excited.

'Hey there, psycho,' Sam said, laughing. 'You are in *soooo* much trouble.'

That wasn't how James wanted the conversation to start.

'What happened after I left?'

'Man, it was the sickest thing ever. Samantha had blood gushing out of her face. Down her arms, everywhere. They took her in an ambulance. Miss Voolt hurt her back, she was crying and going: *This is the last straw. I'm taking early retirement*. Both the Deputy Heads and the Headmaster came in. The Headmaster saw Miles laughing and gave him a three day suspension.'

James couldn't believe it. 'Three days' suspension for *laughing*?'

'He was livid. You're totally expelled, James.'

'No way.'

'Yes way, psycho. You never even made it to your first half-term. That's got to be the record for getting expelled. Did your mum give you beats?'

'She doesn't know yet. She's asleep.'

Sam burst out laughing again, 'Asleep! Don't you think she might want you to wake her up to tell her you've been expelled?'

'She won't care,' James lied, trying to sound cool. 'So you wanna come over and play Playstation?'

Sam's voice got more serious, 'No, man, I've got homework.'

James laughed. 'You *never* do homework.'

'I started. The folks are pressuring me. Birthday presents hang in the balance.'

James knew Sam was lying but couldn't figure out why. Normally, Sam asked his mum if he could come and she always said yes.

'What? What have I done to upset you?'

'It's not that, James, but . . .'

'But what, Sam?'

'Isn't it obvious?'

'No.'

'You're a mate, James, but we can't hang out until this dies down.'

'Why the hell not?'

'Because Greg Jennings is going to totally mash you and if I'm seen with you I'll be dead as well.'

'You could help me stand up to him,' James said.

Sam thought this was the funniest thing yet.

'My skinny arse is not gonna make any difference against those guys. I really like you, James. You're a good friend, but at the moment being your friend is a suicide mission.'

'Thanks for your help, Sam.'

'Should have switched your brain on before you decided to stab the hardest kid in school's little sister on a rusty nail.'

'I never meant to hurt her. It was an accident.'

'Ring me back when you get Greg Jennings to believe that.'

'I can't believe you're doing this to me, Sam.'

'You'd do the same if it was me. And you know it.'

'So that's it. I'm a leper.'

'It's a toughie, James. Sorry.'

'Yeah.'

'We can talk on the phone. I still like you.'

'Thanks, Sam.'

'I better go. Bye, James. I'm really sorry.'

'Enjoy your homework.'

James ended the call and wondered about praying again.

*

James watched rubbish TV until he fell asleep. He had a dream where Greg Jennings stood on his guts, and woke with a jolt.

He needed to pee bad. The pain in his guts was fifty times worse than earlier. The first drop of piss hitting the toilet was red. James did a double-take. Bright red. He was peeing blood. After he'd been to the toilet the pain was mostly gone, but he was scared. He had to tell his mum.

The TV in the living room was still turned up loud. James flicked it off.

'Mum,' James said.

James felt weird. His mum was too quiet. He touched her hand. Cold. He put his hand in front of her face. She wasn't breathing. No pulse. Nothing.

*

James hugged Lauren in the back of the ambulance. Their mum's corpse was two feet away with a blanket on top. Lauren's hands clawed into James' back. James was freaking, but he tried to keep a lid on himself to stop Lauren getting worse.

When the ambulance arrived at casualty, James watched his mum get wheeled off on a trolley. He realised this was going to be his final memory of her: a bulging blanket lit by flashing blue bulbs.

James had to step off the ambulance with Lauren holding on. There was no way she was letting go. She'd stopped crying and was panting like an animal.

Lauren walked like a zombie. The driver led them through the waiting room to a cubicle. A doctor was waiting. She knew what had happened.

'I'm Dr May. You must be Lauren and James.'

James rubbed Lauren's shoulder to try and calm her down.

'Lauren, can you let go of your brother so we can talk?'

Lauren acted deaf.

'It's like she's dead,' James said.

'She's in shock. I'll have to give her something to calm down or she'll pass out.'

Dr May picked a syringe off a trolley and pulled up the sleeve of Lauren's T-shirt.

'Hold her still.'

As soon as the needle went in, Lauren went limp. James leaned her down on the bed. Dr May picked up Lauren's legs and covered her with a blanket.

'Thank you,' James said.

'You told that ambulance driver that you had some blood in your urine,' Dr May said.

'Yeah.'

'Did something hit you in the stomach?'

'Some*one*,' James said. 'I got in a fight. Is it bad?

'When you were hit your insides started to bleed. It's the same as a cut on the outside. It should heal itself. Come back here if it hasn't stopped by tomorrow night.'

'So what happens to us now?' James asked.

'There's a social worker coming to see you. She'll contact your relatives.'

'I don't have relatives. My nan died last year and I don't know who my dad is.'

4. CARE

James woke up the next morning in a strange bed with sheets that smelled of disinfectant. He had no idea where he was. The last thing he remembered was a nurse giving him a sleeping pill and walking towards a car with his head weighing a million tons.

He had his clothes on, but his trainers were on the floor. He took his head out of the covers and saw another bed with Lauren poking out of it. She was sleeping with her thumb in her mouth. James hadn't seen her do that since she was little. Whatever dreams Lauren was having, the thumb wasn't a good sign.

He got out of bed. The pill had made him dull, his jaw felt stiff and there was a weird ache in his forehead. The room was bright, even though the curtains were drawn. James slid a door and found the shower and toilet. He was relieved to see that his pee came out the normal colour. James splashed water on his face. He knew he ought to be upset about his mum dying, but he felt dead inside. Everything felt so unreal it was like sitting in an armchair watching himself on television.

James peeked out of the window. Tons of kids were running around. He remembered that one of his mum's favourite threats was to stick him in a home if he didn't behave.

A buzzer sounded when James went out of the room. A care worker came out of an office and offered him her hand. James shook it, a bit stunned by her purple hair and the metalwork hanging off each ear.

'Hello, James, I'm Rachel. Welcome to Nebraska House. How are you?' James shrugged.

'I'm really sorry about what happened to your mum.'

'Thank you, Miss.'

Rachel laughed.

'You're not at school here, James. They call me all sorts of rude things, but never Miss.'

'Sorry.'

'I'll give you the tour, then you can have some breakfast. You hungry?'

'A bit,' James said.

'Listen, James,' Rachel said, as she walked. 'This place is a dump and I know your life seems horrible now, but there are lots of good people here to help you.'

'Right,' James said.

'Our luxury spa,' said Rachel.

She pointed out of the window at a paddling pool filled with rainwater and cigarette ends. James smiled a bit. Rachel seemed nice, even though she probably used the same lines on every freak that ended up here.

'State of the art sports complex. Strictly out of bounds until homework is finished.'

They walked through a room with a dart board and two pool tables. The green felt was stuck down with carpet tape and there was an umbrella stand filled with tipless and split cues.

'All the rooms are upstairs. Boys first floor, girls second. The baths and showers are down here,' Rachel continued. 'We usually have trouble getting you lads into them.'

'My room has a shower in it,' James said.

'That room's the reception for new arrivals. You only get one night in there.'

They reached the dining room. There were a couple of dozen kids, mostly in school uniform. Rachel pointed everything out.

'Cutlery there, hot food at the bar, cereal and fruit juice. Make your own toast if you want it.'

'Cool,' James said.

He didn't feel cool. The room full of strange, noisy kids was intimidating.

'When you've eaten, see me in my office.'

'What about my sister?' James asked.

'If she wakes up I'll bring her to you.'

James got some Frosties and sat on his own. The other kids ignored him. New arrivals were obviously nothing unusual.

*

Rachel was on the phone. Her desk was stacked with papers and folders. A cigarette burned in an ashtray. Rachel put the phone down and took a puff. She saw James glance at the *No Smoking* sign.

'If they sack me they'll be six staff short,' she said. 'Do you want a cigarette?'

James was shocked to be offered a cigarette by an adult.

'I don't smoke.'

'Good,' Rachel said. 'They give you cancer, but we'd rather give them to you than have you stealing them from shops. Shift my junk, make yourself comfortable.'

James moved a pile from the chair with the least stuff on it and sat down.

'How do you feel, James?'

'I think the sleeping pill they gave me is making me groggy.'

'That'll wear off. I really mean how do you feel about what happened to your mum?'

James shrugged, 'Bad, I guess.'

'The important thing is not to keep it to yourself. We'll schedule some time with a counsellor, but you can chat to any of us house parents in the meantime. Even if it's three in the morning.'

'Does anyone know why she died?' James asked.

'As far as I understand, your mum was taking pain killers for an ulcer on her leg.'

'She wasn't supposed to drink,' James said. 'It's something to do with that, isn't it?'

'The pain killers and the alcohol mixed up put your mum into a deep sleep. Her heart stopped beating. If it's any comfort, your mother wouldn't have suffered.'

'What happens to us?' James asked.

'I don't believe you have any relatives.'

'Only my stepdad. I call him Uncle Ron.'

'The police found him last night.'

'They probably had him in a cell,' James said.

Rachel smiled. 'I sensed that the two of you don't get on when I spoke to him last night.'

'You spoke to Ron?'

'Yes . . . Do you get on well with Lauren?'

'Mostly,' James said. 'We row ten times a day, but we always have a laugh.'

'Ron was still married to your mum when she died, even though they lived apart. Ron is Lauren's father, so he gets automatic custody of her if he wants it.'

'We can't live with Ron. He's a bum.'

'James, Ron has very strong feelings that Lauren shouldn't be taken into care. He's her father. There's nothing we can do to stop him unless there is a history of abuse. The thing is, James . . .'

James fitted the pieces together for himself.

'He doesn't want me, does he?'

'I'm sorry.'

James looked down at the floor, trying not to get upset.

Being in care was bad. But Lauren getting stuck with Ron was worse.

Rachel walked around her desk. She put her arm round him. 'I'm *so* sorry, James.'

James wondered why Ron even wanted Lauren. 'How long can we stay together?'

'Ron said he'd come in later this morning.'

'Can't we stay together for a few days?'

'This might seem hard to understand now, James, but delaying the separation will make things worse. You'll still be able to visit each other.'

'He won't look after her properly. Mum does all the washing and stuff. Lauren's scared of the dark. She can't go to school on her own. Ron won't help her. He's useless.'

'Try not to worry, James. We'll make regular visits to see that Lauren settles into her new home. If she's not properly looked after, something will be done.'

'So what happens to me? Am I stuck here?'

'Until we find you a foster home. That means you go and live with a family that takes in children like you for a few months at a time. There's also a chance that you'll be adopted, which means another couple will look after you permanently, exactly as if they were your real parents.'

'How long does all that take?' James asked.

'We're short of foster families at the moment. A few months at least. Perhaps you should spend some time with your sister before Ron comes.'

James went back to the bedroom. He gently nudged Lauren awake. She came round slowly, sitting up and picking sleep out of the corners of her eyes.

'What's this?' Lauren asked. 'Hospital?'

'Children's home.'

'My head aches,' Lauren said slowly. 'I feel all queasy.'

'You remember last night?'

'I remember you telling me Mum died, and waiting for the ambulance to come. I must have fallen asleep.'

'They had to give you an injection to calm you down. The nurse said you'd feel weird when you woke up.'

'Are we staying here?'

'Ron's coming to pick you up later.'

'Just me?'

'Yeah.'

'I think I'm gonna spew,' Lauren said.

She covered her mouth. James sprang back, not wanting to get sprayed. 'There's a toilet in there,' he said, pointing.

Lauren dashed into the bathroom. James heard her throwing up. She coughed for a bit, then flushed the toilet. It went quiet for a minute. James knocked.

'You OK? Can I come in?'

Lauren didn't answer. James stuck his head round the door. Lauren was crying.

'What's my life gonna be like living with Dad?' she sobbed.

James wrapped his arms round his sister. Her breath smelled like puke, but James didn't care. Lauren had always just been there. James had never realised how much he'd miss her if she was gone.

Lauren calmed down a bit and had a shower. She couldn't face breakfast so they sat in the games room. All the other kids had gone to school.

The time until Uncle Ron arrived was painful. James wanted to say something amazing to cheer her up and make things right. Lauren looked down at the floor, banging her Reeboks on the chair leg.

Ron arrived with an ice cream. Lauren said she didn't want it, but took it anyway. She wasn't in any state to argue. James tried not to cry in front of Ron. Lauren was so choked up she couldn't talk.

'If you want to see Lauren, here's the number,' Ron said. He handed James a scrap of paper.

'I'm having the flat cleared,' Ron said. 'I spoke to the

social worker outside, they're taking you round later. Any of your crap still there on Friday goes in the rubbish.'

James couldn't believe Ron was acting nasty on a day like this.

'You killed her,' James said. 'You brought all that drink to the flat.'

'I didn't force it down her throat,' Ron said. 'And don't get your hopes up about seeing Lauren very often.'

James felt like he was about to explode. 'When I'm big enough I'll kill you,' he said. 'I swear to god.'

Ron laughed. 'I'm quaking in my boots. Hopefully some of the bigger lads here will knock some manners into you. It's about time somebody did.'

Ron grabbed Lauren's hand and took her away.

5. SAFE

James racked up the pool balls and blasted the white into them. It didn't matter where the balls went. He only wanted a distraction from the awful stuff going around his head. He'd been playing for hours when a jug-eared twenty-something introduced himself.

'Kevin McHugh. Dogsbody, former inmate.' He laughed. 'I mean resident, of course.'

'Hey,' James said, not in the mood for jokes.

'Let's get your stuff.'

They walked outside to a minibus.

'I heard about your mum, James. That's tough.' Kevin craned his neck, looking for a gap to pull out into the traffic.

'Thanks, Kevin. You lived here once?'

'For three years. Dad went down for armed robbery. Mum had a breakdown. I got on all right with all the staff here, so they gave me this job when I turned seventeen.'

'Is it OK?' James asked.

'It's not a bad place. Look after your stuff though, everything gets nicked. First chance you get, buy a decent padlock and stick it on your locker. Sleep with the key tied around your neck. Don't even take it off in the bath. If you've got cash we'll get you a lock on the way back.'

'Is it rough?' James asked.

'You'll be OK. You look like you can stand up for yourself. There's a few hard cases same as anywhere, just don't wind them up is all.'

*

The flat was a tip. A lot of valuable stuff had disappeared. The TV, video and hi-fi were gone from the living room. The telephone was gone in the hall and the microwave from the kitchen.

'What happened?' Kevin asked. 'Was it like this last night?'

'I half-expected this,' James said. 'Ron's been here and stripped the place. I hope he's left my stuff alone.'

James ran upstairs to his room. His TV, video and computer were gone.

'I'll stab him,' he screamed.

James kicked his wardrobe door. At least Ron had left the Playstation 2 and most other stuff. Kevin came in.

'You're not gonna be able to take all this,' Kevin said, looking at the piles of stuff. 'Your mum must have been loaded.'

'We'd better take as much as we can. Ron says the house is being cleared Friday.'

James had a thought. He asked Kevin to start packing his clothes in bin-liners and went to his mum's room. Ron had taken the portable TV and the jewellery box from the dressing table, but that was no biggie because Ron had stolen all the good jewellery years ago.

James opened his mum's wardrobe and looked at her safe.

There were thousands inside. Gwen Choke was a criminal; she couldn't keep money in the bank without people wanting to know where it came from. Judging by the tools on the carpet and the scratches around the safe door, Ron had made a fairly pathetic attempt to get in. He'd be back with better equipment.

James knew he'd never break open the safe. When it was delivered it took three guys to carry it up the stairs. There was no key; you dialled a combination of numbers with the big knob on the front. The only clue James had was that one time he'd walked in and surprised his mum while she was unlocking it. She'd been holding a Danielle Steele novel and it made sense that she would hide the combination inside the kind of book he and Ron wouldn't touch with a ten-foot pole. But what if she'd changed the combination since then? It was James' only chance to beat Ron to the money, so he was at least going to try.

Gwen had a handful of novels on a shelf over her bed. James found the Danielle Steele and flicked through the pages.

'Are you all right in there, James?' Kevin shouted from the other bedroom.

James was so tense he flew about a metre up in the air and dropped the book.

'Fine,' James shouted.

He picked the open book off the floor. There was a set of numbers written in the margin on the page in front of him. The book must have been opened to the same page hundreds of times. It sprung to the right place as soon as he let go. James felt luck was on his side for the first time in days. He scooted across the carpet and dialled in the numbers: 262, 118, 320, 145, 077. He grabbed the handle. Nothing happened. It wasn't going to work. The thought of Uncle Ron getting his hands on the money made James gag.

Then he noticed a sticker under the dial with instructions on how to use the safe. He read the first instruction:

(1) Dial the first number of the combination by turning the dial in an anti-clockwise direction.

James hadn't realised that the direction you turned the dial made any difference. He dialled in the first number and carried on reading:

(2) Dial the subsequent four numbers by turning the dial as follows: clockwise, anti-clockwise, anti-clockwise and clockwise. Failure to observe this procedure will result in non-operation of the mechanism.

He dialled the first four numbers.

'What are you playing at?' Kevin asked.

James spun around. Kevin was standing in the doorway. Luckily the open wardrobe door stopped him seeing the safe. Kevin seemed nice, but James was sure any adult who found out about the safe would make him give the contents either to the police or to Uncle Ron.

'Looking for stuff,' James said, convinced he sounded suspicious.

'Come and help me pack, James. I don't know what you want.'

'I'll be out in a minute,' James said. 'I'm just looking for photo albums.'

'Do you want me to help you look for them?'

'No,' James said, practically squealing.

'We've got fifteen minutes,' Kevin said. 'I've got to do a school run in an hour.'

Kevin finally went back to the other room. James dialled in the fifth number. The safe made a satisfying click. He read the third instruction before he pulled on the handle and couldn't help smiling:

(3) For security purposes, this sticker should be removed once you are familiar with the unit.

James swung the heavy door open. The inside of the safe was surprisingly small because the metal lining was so thick. There were four tall piles of cash inside and a tiny envelope. James took a bin-liner and shoved the money in. He tucked the envelope into his pocket.

James imagined Ron's face when he walked in and saw the safe open. Then he thought of something even better. He peeled the instruction sticker from the safe door and put it and the Danielle Steele novel inside. As a final touch, to make Ron extra mad, James took a framed picture of himself from his mum's bedside cabinet and stood it inside the safe so it would be the first thing Ron saw when he eventually broke it open. James shut the door, gave the dial a spin and replaced the tools exactly how Ron had left them.

*

James was in a slightly better mood when he walked back to his bedroom holding the cash. The room looked bare. Kevin had bagged up all the clothes and bedding that was usually strewn over the floor.

'I found the photo albums,' James said.

'Good. But I'm afraid you're gonna have to make some sacrifices, James. All you've got in Nebraska House is one wardrobe, a chest of drawers and a locker.'

James started hunting through the toys and junk on the floor. He was surprised how little he cared about most of his stuff. He wanted his Playstation 2, mobile phone and portable CD player, but that was about it. Everything else was toys and stuff that he'd grown out of. The annoying thing was, Ron had taken his TV so he had nothing to use the Playstation on.

Kevin crouched down looking at a Sega Dreamcast and a Nintendo Gamecube.

'Don't you want these?' Kevin asked.

'I only use the Playstation 2,' James said. 'Take them if you want them.'

'I can't take gifts from residents.'

James kicked the consoles into the middle of the floor.

'I don't want my stepdad to get the money from selling them. I'm not taking them with me. If you don't take them, I'll trash 'em.'

Kevin didn't know what to say. James slammed the heel of his trainer into the Sega. Surprisingly little happened, so he picked it up and threw it at the wall. The case smashed. It slid down the wall and dropped behind the bed. Kevin quickly bent down and rescued the Gamecube.

'OK, James, I tell you what. I'll take your Gamecube and the games and in return I'll buy your padlock for you on the drive back. Is that a deal?'

'Fair enough,' James said.

*

When they'd packed up the last few things and carried the bin-liners out to the minibus, James had a quick last look into every room of the flat he'd lived in since he was born. By the time he reached the front door he had tears on his face.

Kevin tapped the horn of the minibus. He'd already started the engine. James ignored him and went back one last time. He couldn't leave the flat without a memento of his mum. He rushed upstairs to her room and looked around.

James remembered that when he was a toddler he used to sit at his mum's dressing table after they'd shared a bath. She'd pull a pyjama top over his head then stand over him and brush his hair. It was before Lauren was born. Just the two of them, feeling tired and smelling of shampoo. James felt warm and sad. He found the battered wooden hairbrush and tucked it into the waistband of his tracksuit bottoms. Once he had the brush it felt easier to leave.

6. HOME

James realised he was stupid. He should have left a bit of cash in the safe. That way Ron would never know he'd been in there. Leaving the photo was a nice gag, but Ron would realise James had taken the money when he saw it. He might try and steal the money back. And if Ron was angry he'd make it ten times harder for James to visit Lauren.

*

Kevin found James a room and showed him the ropes. Like where the washing machines were and where he could get toiletries and stuff, then left him to unpack. The room had a bed, a chest of drawers, a wardrobe with a locker on each side and two writing desks under the window. The kid who lived on the other side had decorated his wall with Korn and Slipknot posters. There was a skateboard on the floor and boarder clothes hung neatly in the wardrobe: baggy cargos, a hooded top and T-shirts with Pornstar and Gravis logos on them. Whoever James' roommate was, he looked pretty cool. The other good thing was that the kid had a portable TV on his desk, meaning they could use the Playstation.

James looked at his watch. He reckoned there was about an hour until his room-mate got out of school. James got the cash out of the bin-liner. It was all £50 and £20 notes, separated into bundles by elastic bands. He counted a couple and realised each bundle was £1,000. There were forty-three bundles.

James thought of a way to hide the money in case Ron came after it. He had a portable cassette radio from the flat. It was wrecked; half the buttons had broken and the tape player didn't rewind. James had only taken it because Ron had stolen the good one with a CD player on it.

James rummaged through his bags of stuff until he found his Swiss army knife. He picked out the screwdriver and undid the back of his cassette player. The inside was all circuit boards and wires. James worked fast, taking the guts out of the player, unscrewing and snapping plastic, leaving only the bits you could see from the front, like the speaker and the slot where the tape went in. He stuffed all but £4,000 of the cash inside the hole, packing the money tight so it didn't rattle. He screwed the back on again and slid the radio cassette into his locker.

James took the four odd £1,000 bundles and hid them in obvious places: the back pocket of a pair of jeans, inside a shoe, inside a book. He peeled a hundred off the last bundle to use as walking-around money and taped the rest to the inside of his locker.

The idea was, if Ron tried to break into James' room he'd find £4,000 easily and never realise there was £39,000 more stuffed inside a cassette radio so crummy looking even Ron wouldn't steal it.

James filled the locker with the rest of his valuables. He banged it shut and put the padlock key on a cord around his neck. He couldn't be bothered unpacking anything else. He threw as many bags as he could in the wardrobe and kicked what was left under his bed.

Then he slumped on his bare mattress, staring at the wall. There were hundreds of pin holes and blobs of blu-tack where previous kids had decorated the walls. He wondered what Lauren was doing.

*

Just after four, James' room-mate, Kyle, came running in. He was a skinny kid, a bit taller than James, wearing school uniform. Kyle slammed the door and tried to get his key in the hole to lock it. James wondered what the hell was going on.

Kyle couldn't lock the door before another kid rammed it. This kid looked older. Same height as Kyle but twice the width. Kyle jumped on to his bed. The big kid bundled Kyle over and pulled him to the floor. He sat astride him and punched him a couple of times in the arm.

'You think you're so smart,' the thug said.

'Take it,' Kyle said.

Kyle took a couple of slaps in the face. The thug slid a diary out of Kyle's blazer and cracked him on top of the head with it.

'Touch my stuff again, doughnut, I'll smash your face in.'

He got off Kyle, kicked him in the thigh and walked out.

James sat up on his bed. Kyle tried to act like it was nothing but couldn't hide the pain as he raised himself on to his bed.

'I'm Kyle,' Kyle said.

'I'm James. How'd you upset him?'

'His diary fell out of his pocket this morning. I found it. Most of it's bogus, but he'd written this poem about a girl.'

James laughed. 'That big moose writes poetry?'

'Yep,' Kyle said. 'I read a couple of lines out in front of his mates. He took it badly.' Kyle was holding his face.

'You OK?' James asked. 'You took some serious beats.'

'I thought he'd grab the diary back, not try and kill me . . . One bit of the poem was great. *You give me a buzz that's like a bee. Even when I feel melancholy.* Isn't that cute . . . Man, is that what it looks like?'

'What?' James asked.

'That skateboard under your bed must have cost over a hundred quid.'

'You reckon?' James asked. 'I only used it about twice.'

Kyle started laughing. 'That board is a legend, James. Kids die to get their hands on them and you've used it twice. Can I see it?'

James shrugged. 'Whatever.'

Kyle seemed to forget his pain as he reached under James' bed and wheeled out the board. He sat back on his bed twisting it in his hands.

'Nice. Hard wheels, must be fast. Can I try it?' Kyle asked.

'Sure. I never use it. As long as I can use my Playstation 2 on your telly.'

'Playstation 2! We have Playstation 2 in this room? James, you're a little beauty. What games have you got?'

'I don't know. About sixty different ones,' James said.

Kyle rocked back on his bed and started kicking his feet in the air.

'Sixty games! I don't believe you, James. You must be the most spoiled kid in the world and you don't even realise.'

'What?' James asked. 'Don't kids in here have games consoles?'

'We get three pounds a week for pocket money. You see that Gravis shirt on the floor? Twenty-five quid. I had to save up two pounds for twelve weeks to get that. I had to steal my Stussy shorts from a shop at Camden Lock. Would have ended up with a security guard standing on my head if I didn't know a few moves.'

'You want to try the Playstation now?' James asked.

'After my homework,' Kyle said. 'I always do homework first.'

James laid back on his bed, wondering if Kyle was a swot. Someone knocked.

'Yeah?' James said.

It was one of the house parents, a bearded hippie type. He looked at James.

'I've sorted you a place at West Road School. You can start there in the morning. You'll have to come back at lunchtime. The counsellor wants to see you.'

James was miffed. He thought that his mum dying, and getting expelled, would get him off school for at least a couple of weeks.

'OK,' James said. 'Where's West Road?'

'Kyle,' the care worker said, 'can you find James a school uniform and show him to school tomorrow?'

'No worries,' Kyle said.

Kyle and James spent the whole evening together. After his homework Kyle took James down to dinner. The food wasn't the best but it was better than James got at home. Afterwards they set up the Playstation. While they played they told stories about stuff, like fights at school and how they ended up here. James was surprised that Kyle was thirteen and already in Year Nine. Kyle said he was good at everything except sports. He had a hard time because the rest of his class were bigger than him. James said the only things he was any good at were sport and maths.

Before they went to bed, Kyle took James to the laundry and found a box of school uniforms. James already had school shirts and trousers, but he needed a blazer with the West Road badge and a school tie. There wasn't much choice and everything was trashed. They found a blazer that fitted James OK and a school tie that was in threads.

*

Kyle fell asleep. James' head was too busy. Tomorrow was going to be the first day of a new routine: eating meals with all the other kids, going to a new school, coming home and spending time with Kyle. It wasn't the end of the world, but he wished Lauren was here.

James remembered the little brown envelope in the safe.

He'd forgotten until now. He scrambled out of bed and slipped his tracksuit bottoms on. He rummaged in the pockets. His heart skipped when he didn't find it straight away. He had to go somewhere light where he could look without anyone seeing. The toilet was the obvious place.

James locked himself in a cubicle and opened the envelope gently so he'd be able to reseal it. There was a key and a business card:

REX DEPOSITARY
Deposit Your Valuables with Total Discretion and Security
Individual Boxes in Eight Different Sizes

James flicked the card over. The address was on the back. It looked like his mum had another hidden stash. He put the key on the cord around his neck.

7. SHRINK

James had always been in mixed schools, but West Road was all boys. The lack of girls gave the place an air of menace. It was noisier and everybody in the corridor pushed harder than at his old school. It felt like something could go off any second.

A Year Seven got a hard shove from a Year Ten and knocked into James. The kid went down and yelped as the Year Ten stamped his hand. The kids were all heading somewhere. James had a map that made no sense whichever way he turned it.

'Nice tie, girlie,' somebody said.

James thought it was aimed at him. The tie was a wreck. He decided to steal one from some weed the first chance he got. The bodies were all disappearing into classrooms and within a couple of minutes James only had a few late arrivals for company.

A couple of nasty looking Year Ten kids blocked James' way. One of them had spiked hair and a Metallica T-shirt under his blazer. Both were wearing menacing-looking steel-toe-capped boots with fat laces dragging behind.

'Where you going, squirt?'

James looked up at them, thinking he was going to die before he even made it to his first class.

'Registration,' he said.

The Metallica kid snatched the map out of James' hand.

'Well, you're not going to make it,' Metallica said.

James braced himself for a boot or fist.

'Try using the side of the map that says main building, not annexe. It's over there.'

Metallica turned the map over and handed it back to James. He pointed at a yellow door up a corridor on the left.

'Thanks,' James said.

He hurried off. Metallica shouted after him: 'Take that tie off.'

James looked down at the tie. He could see it was tatty but why all the fuss?

*

James handed his form teacher a note. All the kids in his new class were staring at him as he looked for a seat. He sat at the end of a row, next to a black kid called Lloyd.

'You one of the little orphans from the council home?' Lloyd asked.

The kids sitting around James laughed. James knew first impressions counted. If he said nothing he'd look soft. His reply had to be sharp, but not so nasty it started a fight.

'How'd you know?' James said. 'I suppose your mum saw me when she cleaned our toilets.'

The group of kids laughed. Lloyd looked angry for a second, then he laughed too. 'Like your tie, sister,' he said.

James had had enough with the tie. He pulled it off and

looked. Then he looked at Lloyd's tie. It wasn't the same colour. Nor was anyone else's.

'What *is* this tie?' James asked.

'The good news, orphan,' Lloyd said, 'is that you have a West Road tie. The bad news is, it's from West Road *Girls* School.'

James laughed with the others. These kids seemed OK. He was angry Kyle had tricked him, though.

*

James left at lunchtime to see the counsellor. Her office was on the second floor of Nebraska. It had spider plants branching off everywhere. The counsellor, Jennifer Mitchum, was a rake, barely taller than James. She had veins poking out of her hands that James didn't want to look at and she sounded really posh.

'Would you feel more comfortable in the chair or on the couch?'

James had seen all the psychiatrist scenes on TV and felt he had to lie on the couch to get the full effect.

'Cool,' he said, settling himself down. 'I could sleep all night on this.'

Jennifer walked slowly around the room, lowering the blinds so it was almost dark. She sat down.

'I want you to be relaxed around me, James. Everything you say stays between us. When you talk, don't try and say the correct thing; say what you really think, and remember I'm here to help you.'

'OK,' James said.

'You said you could fall asleep on the couch. Have you been sleeping properly at night?'

'Not really. I have too much to think about.'

'What do you think about most?'

'I wonder if my little sister is OK.'

'It says in the file you're concerned about Ron's ability to look after Lauren.'

'He's a retard,' James said. 'He couldn't look after a hamster. I don't even understand why he wanted her.'

'Perhaps he loves Lauren, but found it difficult to express that while your mother was alive.'

James laughed. 'That's total rubbish. You'd have to meet him to understand.'

'If you see Lauren regularly that should help both of you feel better.'

'Yeah, but it won't happen.'

'I'll talk to Ron and see if we can set up a schedule of meetings. Perhaps you and Lauren can spend every Saturday together.'

'You can try, but Ron hates my guts. I don't think he'll let me see her.'

'What about your mother? How do you feel about her?'

James shrugged. 'She's gone. What can I do? I wish I'd been better when she was alive.'

'In what way?'

'I was always in trouble. Getting in fights and stuff.'

'What made you get in trouble?'

James had to think hard.

'I don't know. I always do stupid stuff without meaning it. I'm a bad person, I guess.'

'The first question I asked you was what you thought about most. You said you were worried about your sister.

Wouldn't a bad person always think about himself first?'

'I love Lauren . . . Can I tell you something I did?'

'Of course, James.'

'Last year at school. I got in this row with a teacher, so I stormed out to the toilets. This kid in the year below me was in there. I just laid into him. He didn't say one word. I just started beating him.'

'Did you know that what you were doing was bad at the time you were doing it?'

'Of course I knew beating someone up was bad.'

'So why did you do it?'

'Because . . .' James couldn't bring himself to be honest.

'When you were hitting that boy, how did you feel?'

James blurted it out, 'It was the best feeling. He was crying his eyes out and I felt fantastic.'

James looked at Jennifer to see if she was shocked, but her face was calm.

'Why do you think you enjoyed it?'

'I told you already. I'm sick in the head. Someone rubs me the wrong way and I go psycho.'

'Try and describe how you felt about the person you were hurting.'

'I owned him. There was nothing he could do, no matter how much I hurt him.'

'You went from a situation with your teacher, where you were powerless and had to do what you were told, into the toilet where you saw someone weaker than yourself and exercised your power over him. That must have been satisfying.'

'You could put it like that,' James said.

'It's a frustrating situation at your age, James. You know what you want but you have to do what you're told. You go to school when you're told, go to bed when you're told, live where you're told. Everything is controlled by other people. It's common for boys your age to enjoy sudden outbursts where they have control over someone else.'

'But I'll end up in loads of trouble if I keep getting in fights,' James said.

'I'll teach you some techniques to manage your anger over the coming weeks. Until then try and remember that you're only eleven years old and nobody expects you to be perfect. Don't think of yourself as being a bad person or that you're sick in the head. In fact, I want to do something we call Positive Reinforcement. I want you to repeat what I just told you.'

'Repeat what?' James asked.

'Say *I'm not a bad person.*'

'I'm not a bad person,' James said.

'Say *I'm not sick in the head.*'

'I'm not sick in the head.' James smiled. 'I feel like an idiot.'

'I don't care if you feel like an idiot, James. Take a deep breath, say the words and think about what they mean.'

James had thought that seeing the counsellor would be a waste of time, but he did feel better.

'I'm a good person and I'm not sick in the head,' he said.

'Excellent, James. I think that would be a positive note on which to end the session. I'll see you again on Monday.'

James slid off the couch.

'Before we finish, there is one detail on the notes from your school that made me curious. What's one hundred and eighty-seven multiplied by sixteen?'

James thought for about three seconds.

'Two thousand, nine hundred and ninety-two.'

'Very impressive,' Jennifer said. 'Where did you learn to do that?'

'I just can,' James shrugged. 'Right from when they first started teaching me numbers. I hate it when people ask me to do it, it makes me feel like a freak.'

'It's a gift,' Jennifer said. 'You should be proud of it.'

*

James went down to his room. He started doing some Geography homework but his heart wasn't in it. He switched on the Playstation. Kyle came in from school.

'How was your first day?' Kyle asked.

'Pretty good, no thanks to you.'

'That was a good gag with the tie,' Kyle said.

James jumped up off his seat and grabbed Kyle by his shirt. Kyle shoved James away, sending him crashing into a desk. He was stronger than James had expected.

'Jesus, James. I thought you were cool.'

'Pretty nice thing to do. First day at a new school and you make me look like a tit.'

Kyle threw his schoolbag down.

'I'm sorry, James. If I knew you were gonna have a tantrum I wouldn't have done it.'

James wanted to start a major row, but Kyle was the only kid in Nebraska he could even put a name to. He didn't want to fall out with him.

'Just stay out of my face,' James said.

James sat on his bed sulking while Kyle did his homework. After a bit he got fed up and went for a walk. He saw the kid in the Metallica T-shirt he'd met at school. He was in a corner with a gang who all looked pretty rough. James walked over to them.

'Thanks for helping earlier,' James said.

Metallica looked him over. 'No worries, man. Name's Rob. This is the gang. Vince, Big Paul and Little Paul.'

'I'm James.'

There was an awkward silence.

'You want something else, squirt?' Big Paul asked.

'No,' James said.

'Piss off then.'

James felt his face turn red. He started to walk away but Rob called him back.

'Hey, James, we're going out tonight. Wanna come?'

'Cool,' James said.

*

After dinner James went back to his room to change out of school uniform. Kyle had finished his homework and was lying on his bed reading a skateboarding magazine.

'You want to play Playstation?' Kyle asked. 'I'm sorry about earlier, James. It was mean to trick you on your first day.'

'You play it,' James said. 'I'm going out.'

'Who with?'

'Some guy called Rob.'

'You mean Robert Vaughn? The guy who wears a heavy metal shirt under his blazer?'

'Yeah, him and some mates.'

'Seriously,' Kyle said, 'don't hang out with those guys. They're mental. They go out stealing cars and shoplifting and stuff.'

'I'm not sitting in here watching you doing your homework every night. Get a life, man.'

James put his trainers on and walked to the door. Kyle looked offended. 'Hey, I warned you, James. Don't whinge to me when you land up in deep shit.'

'Use the Playstation whenever you want,' James said.

*

James sat on a brick wall at the back of an industrial estate. The gang were all older. Rob and Big Paul were fifteen. Vince was fourteen. He was the meanest looking, with bleached hair and a busted-up nose. Little Paul was twelve, Vince's younger brother.

They passed cigarettes around. James told them he didn't smoke. This didn't look cool but he thought it was better than pretending he smoked and coughing his guts up.

'I'm bored,' Little Paul said. 'Let's do something.'

They walked to a car park full of Fiesta vans and climbed through a gap in the fence. Vince and Rob walked along the row of vans trying the back doors to see if any were unlocked.

'Bingo,' Rob said.

A door swung open in his hand. Rob leaned in and took out a bag of tools. He put the bag down and unzipped it.

'Feel like causing damage, James?' Rob asked.

James reached in the bag and pulled out a hammer. The others all grabbed something.

James was nervous, but it was cool walking down the street in a gang carrying hammers and wrenches. A woman nearly got herself run over crossing the street to avoid them. James didn't know what they were looking for. Vince stopped when they found a flash Mercedes. The two Pauls walked into the road.

'Go,' Rob shouted.

Rob smashed his hammer through the back window of the Merc. The alarm started screeching. The others all joined in. James hesitated, then took out a side window, knocked off the wing mirror and made two big dents in the door with his hammer. In twenty seconds every panel was dented, the lights and windows all smashed. Vince led off, running up the road and taking a couple more car windows out along the way.

They ran on to a council estate, down a narrow alley and into a concrete square surrounded by flats. James was out of breath but fear kept him moving. A few more turns, over a fence and they were in a playing field. James' trainers slid in the mud. They all stopped, plumes of breath rising into the freezing air. James started laughing, even though he had a stitch burning down his side. Rob put his hand on James' shoulder.

'You're OK, James,' Rob said.

'That was *so* cool.' James laughed. The mix of fear, tiredness and excitement made his head spin. He couldn't believe what they'd just done.

8. BIRTHDAY

James felt like he was floating through his life. Every day was the same. Get up, go to school, come back, play football or hang out with Rob Vaughn and his gang. James never got into bed before midnight: he knew if he was exhausted he wouldn't lie awake feeling miserable about Lauren and his mum.

The only time he'd seen Lauren in the three weeks since his mum died had been at the funeral. The telephone number on the bit of paper Ron had given him didn't work. Ron had told Jennifer Mitchum that James was a bad influence. He didn't want him near his daughter.

*

'You stink,' Kyle said.

James sat on the edge of his bed rubbing his eyes. He didn't need to get dressed because all he'd done the night before was kick off his trainers and climb into bed wearing his football shirt and tracksuit bottoms.

'You've had the same socks on for days,' Kyle said.

'You're not my mum, Kyle.'

'Your mum never had to sleep in a room that stinks of your BO.'

James looked down at the blackened bottoms of his socks. They reeked, but he'd got used to the smell.

'I'll have a shower,' James said.

Kyle tossed a packet of Twix bars on to James' bed.

'Happy twelfth birthday,' Kyle said. 'Should have got you deodorant.'

James was pleased Kyle had remembered. It wasn't much of a gift, but five Twix was quite expensive for someone on three quid a week.

'You'd better clean yourself up, anyway. You've got to go to the police station today.'

James looked at Kyle. His hair was gelled down and his school uniform was immaculate, with the shirt tucked in and the tie done at the proper length, instead of ten centimetres long like most kids did it. James looked at the black under his nails, ran his hand through his gluey tangle of hair and couldn't help laughing about the mess his life was in.

*

Rachel was in a mood. Her car was overheating, the traffic was awful and there was no space in the police station car park.

'I can't park, you'll have to go in by yourself. Have you got the bus fare to come back?'

'Yeah,' James said.

He got out of the car and walked up the steps of the police station. He'd dressed in chinos and his best fleece, even combed his hair back after the shower. Everyone said getting a police caution was no big deal, but it didn't feel that way as James walked up to the desk and said his name.

'Sit,' the policewoman said, pointing at a row of chairs.

James waited for an hour. People came in and filled forms, mostly reporting stolen cars or mobiles.

'James Choke.'

James stood up. A fit-looking cop reached out and gave him a crunching handshake.

'I'm Sergeant Peter Davies, juvenile liaison officer.'

They went upstairs to an interview room. The sergeant got an inkpad and a piece of card out of a filing cabinet.

'Relax your hand, James. Let me do all the work.'

He dabbed the tips of James' fingers in the ink, then rolled each tip firmly against the card. James wished they'd given him a copy because the fingerprints would look cool pinned on his bedroom wall.

'OK, James, this is the caution. Any questions?'

James shrugged. Sergeant Davies began reading from a piece of paper:

'The Metropolitan Police have received information that on October 9th, while attending Holloway Dale School, you seriously assaulted one of your classmates, Samantha Jennings. During the assault Miss Jennings received a severe cut to her cheek, resulting in the need for eight stitches. During the same incident you also assaulted the class teacher Cassandra Voolt, who received injuries to her back.

'As this is the first criminal charge you have faced, the Metropolitan Police have decided to give you a formal caution if you admit to what you have done. Do you admit to the offences detailed above?'

'Yes,' James said.

'If you are found guilty of another criminal act before you reach the age of eighteen years, details of this offence will be given to the Magistrate or Judge and it is likely to increase the severity of the sentence you receive.'

Sergeant Davies put the piece of paper down and tried to sound friendly. 'You look like a decent kid, James.'

'I never meant to cut her face. I just wanted to make her shut up.'

'James, don't kid yourself into thinking it's not your fault Samantha got hurt. You can never predict what will happen in a fight. If you're stupid enough to start one, you're to blame for what happens whether you meant it or not.'

James nodded. 'That's true I suppose.'

'I don't want to see you here again, James. Will I?'

'I hope not,' James said.

'You don't sound sure. Do you know what sentence you would have got for what you did if you were an adult?'

'No,' James said.

'A young girl with stitches in her face, you'd be looking at two years in prison. That's not funny, is it?'

'No,' James said.

*

James was pleased the caution was out the way. Everyone was right; it was no worse than getting told off at school. He'd taken some money out of his locker and thought he'd buy himself a birthday present. He got a new game for the Playstation and a Nike tracksuit. Then he stuffed himself at the buffet in Pizza Hut. He made sure he didn't get back to Nebraska House until it was too late to go to afternoon lessons.

James put his new game on and lost track of time. Kyle came in and sat on the edge of his bed, the same as he did every day. Kyle felt something under the covers. He pulled them back and found James' Arsenal shirt.

'Why's your stinking football shirt in my bed?'

James knew he'd be furious. Kyle was a total girl when it came to cleanliness. When Kyle moved the shirt a new CD Walkman slid out on to the bed.

'James man, did you steal it?'

'I knew you'd say that,' James replied. 'Receipt's in the box.'

'This is mine?' Kyle asked.

'You've been whining about your old one since I got here.'

'Where'd you get the money, James?'

James liked Kyle, but he didn't trust him enough to say about the cash in his locker.

'Tied an old lady to a tree, beat her mercilessly and stole her pension,' James said.

'Yeah right, James. Seriously, where did you get sixty quid?'

'Do you want it? Or do you want to ask me stupid questions about it?' James said.

'This is sweet. I hope you didn't get yourself in any trouble. When I get my pocket money on Friday I'll buy you that deodorant you need.'

'Thanks, I think,' James said.

'So you want to do something tonight for your birthday? We could go to the cinema or something?'

'No,' James said. 'I said I'd go out with Rob and the gang tonight.'

'I wish you'd stop hanging around with those freaks.'

James sounded annoyed, 'You give me the same lecture every time.'

*

It was freezing cold sitting on the wall at the back of the industrial estate. After the first night all they'd done was hang around smoking. Big Paul had punched a public schoolboy's tooth out and taken his mobile and wallet, but James hadn't been with them.

The gang congratulated James on his first criminal offence. Vince said he'd been arrested fifteen times. He had half a dozen court cases coming up and was facing a year in a young offenders' prison.

'I don't care,' Vince said. 'Brother's in young offenders. Dad's in prison. Granddad's in prison.'

'Nice family,' James said.

Rob and Big Paul laughed. The look James got from Vince was scary.

'You say anything about my family again, James, you're dead.'

'Sorry,' James said. 'I was out of order.'

'Kiss the floor,' Vince said.

'What?' James asked. 'Come on, I said sorry.'

'He said sorry,' Rob said. 'It was only a joke.'

'Kiss the floor, James,' Vince repeated. 'I'm not saying it a third time.'

Fighting Vince would be suicide. James slid off the wall. He was worried Vince would jump on his back or kick him in the head when he crouched down. But what choice was there? James put his palms on the pavement and kissed the cold stone. He wiped his lips on his sleeve and stood up, hoping Vince was satisfied.

'You know what keeps out the cold?' Rob said. 'Beer.'

'Nobody will serve us round here,' Little Paul said. 'Got no cash either.'

'That off-licence up the road keeps the trays of twenty-four cans stacked up in the middle of the shop,' Rob said. 'You could run in, grab one and be halfway up the street before the tub of lard got out from behind the counter.'

'Who's gonna do it?' Little Paul asked.

'The birthday boy,' Vince said, laughing.

James realised he should have taken a beating; at least that way Vince would still respect him. Showing weakness to a guy like Vince was inviting him to tear you apart.

'Come on, man. I just got a caution this morning,' James said.

'I've never seen you do anything,' Vince said. 'If you want to hang out with us, you'd better be prepared for some action.'

'Fine, I'll go home. This is boring anyway,' James said.

Vince grabbed James and shoved him into the wall.

'You'll do it,' Vince said.

'Leave him, Vince,' Rob said.

Vince let go. James gave Rob a nod of thanks.

'You better do it though,' Rob said. 'I don't like being called boring.'

James wished he'd listened to Kyle.

'OK,' he said, now he had no choice. 'I can handle it.'

The gang walked to the off-licence. Big Paul gripped James' shoulder, making sure he didn't run.

'Be really quick,' Rob said. 'In and out, they'll never get you.'

James walked inside the shop, nervous as hell. The warm air was beautiful. He rubbed his freezing hands together and looked for courage.

'Can I help you, son?' the guy behind the counter asked.

James had no reason to be in an off-licence. The clerk knew something was up. James made a quick grab at the cans of beer. They were heavy and his frozen fingers didn't have much grip.

'Put those down, you little . . .'

James spun around and tore towards the door. He crashed into the glass. Vince and Big Paul were holding the door shut from outside.

'Let me out,' James shouted, hammering the glass.

The assistant lumbered around the counter.

'Please, Vince,' James begged.

Vince gave James an evil smile and flicked him off. James knew he was done for.

Little Paul was jumping for joy. 'You're busted, you're busted.'

The clerk grabbed James' hands and dragged him backwards. Vince and Big Paul let go of the door and walked off casually.

'Nice night in the cells, faggot,' Vince shouted.

James stopped wriggling. There was no point, the clerk was five times his size. He dragged James behind the counter and shoved him into a chair. Then he called the police.

*

They'd taken James' shoes and everything out of his pockets. He'd been sitting here three hours. Back to the wall, arms wrapped round his knees. James had expected the hard rubber mattress and graffiti but he'd never realised how bad a cell smelled. It was a mixture of disinfectant and everything nasty a body could pump out.

Sergeant Davies came in. James had hoped it wouldn't be him. He looked up nervously, expecting an explosion of rage, but the sergeant seemed to find it funny.

'Hello, James. Did you have a problem grasping the meaning of our little chat this morning? Fancied a few beers to celebrate getting off easy?'

The sergeant took James to an interrogation room. Rachel was there, she looked angry. The sergeant was still smiling as he put a cassette into a recorder and spoke his and James' names into the microphone.

'James,' the sergeant asked, 'bearing in mind that the off-licence you were arrested in has three video cameras inside, do you admit trying to steal twenty-four cans of beer?'

'Yes,' James said.

'On the video you can make out a couple of monkeys holding the door and not letting you out of the shop. Would you care to tell me who they were?'

'No idea,' James said. He knew he'd be dead if he grassed on four of the hardest kids in Nebraska House.

'Why not tell me, James? You wouldn't be here if it wasn't for them.'

'Never seen them before in my life,' James insisted.

'They looked like Vincent St John and Paul Puffin to me. Do those names ring a bell?'

'Never heard of them.'

'OK, James. I'm ending the interview.'

Sergeant Davies turned off the cassette recorder.

'Play with fire and you get burned, James. Hanging out with those two is more like playing with dynamite.'

'I messed up,' James said. 'Whatever punishment I get I deserve it.'

'Don't worry about this one, James. You'll go to juvenile court. The magistrate will probably give you a twenty quid fine. It's the bigger picture you want to look at.'

'What do you mean?' James asked.

'I've seen hundreds of kids like you, James. They all start where you are now. Cheeky little kids. They get a bit older. Spottier and hairier. Always in trouble, but still nothing serious. Then they do something really stupid. Stab someone, get caught selling drugs, armed robbery, something like that. Half the time they're crying. Or so shocked they can hardly speak. They're sixteen or seventeen and looking at seven years banged up. You might get off easy at your age, but if you don't start making better choices you'll be spending most of your life in a cell.'

9. STRANGE

This room was flashier than the one at Nebraska House. It was a single for starters. TV, kettle, telephone and miniature fridge. It was like the hotel when his mum took him and Lauren to Disney World. James didn't have a clue where he was or how he'd got here. The last thing he remembered was Jennifer Mitchum asking him up to her office after he got back to Nebraska House.

James burrowed around under the duvet and realised he was naked. That was freaky. He sat up and looked out of the window. The room was up high overlooking an athletics track. There were kids in running spikes doing stretches. Some others were getting tennis coaching on clay courts off to the side. This was clearly a children's home, and miles nicer than Nebraska House.

There was a set of clean clothes on the floor: white socks and boxers, pressed orange T-shirt, green military-style trousers with zipped pockets and a pair of boots. James picked the boots up and inspected them: rubbery smell and shiny black soles. They were new.

The military-style kit made James wonder if this was where

kids ended up if they kept getting in trouble. He put on the underwear and studied the logo embroidered on the T-shirt. It was a winged baby sitting on a ball. On looking closer the ball was a globe and you could see the outlines of Europe and the Americas. Underneath was a set of initials: *CHERUB*. James spun the initials in his head, but they didn't make any sense.

Out in the corridor the kids had the same boots and trousers as James, but their T-shirts were either black or grey, all with the CHERUB logo on them.

James spoke to a boy coming towards him.

'I don't know what to do,' James said.

'Can't talk to orange,' the boy said, without stopping.

James looked both ways. It was a row of doors in either direction. There were a couple of teenage girls down one end. Even they were wearing boots and green trousers.

'Hey,' James said. 'Can you tell me where to go?'

'Can't talk to orange,' one girl said.

The other one smiled, saying, 'Can't talk,' but she pointed towards a lift and then made a downward motion with her hand.

'Cheers,' James said.

James waited for the lift. There were a few others inside including an adult who wore the regulation trousers and boots but with a white CHERUB T-shirt. James spoke to him.

'Can't talk to orange,' the adult said before raising one finger.

Up to now James had assumed this was a prank being played on the new kid, but an adult joining in was weird.

James realised the finger was telling him to get out at the first floor. It was a reception area. He could see out the main entrance into plush gardens where a fountain spouted water five metres into the air. The sculpture in the centre was the winged baby sitting on a globe, like on the T-shirts. James stepped up to an elderly lady behind a desk.

'Please don't say *Can't talk to orange*, I just—'

He didn't get to finish.

'Good morning, James. Doctor McAfferty would like to see you in his office.'

She led James down a short corridor and knocked on a door.

'Enter,' a soft Scottish accent said from inside.

James stepped into an office with full height windows and a crackling fireplace. The walls were lined with leather-bound books. Doctor McAfferty stood up from behind his desk and crushed James' hand as he shook it.

'Welcome to CHERUB campus, James. I'm Doctor Terrence McAfferty, the Chairman. Everybody calls me Mac. Have a seat.'

James pulled out a chair from under Mac's desk.

'Not there, by the fire,' Mac said. 'We need to talk.'

The pair settled into armchairs in front of the fireplace. James half expected Mac to put a blanket over his lap and start toasting something on a long fork.

'I know this sounds dumb,' James said. 'But I can't remember how I got here.'

Mac smiled. 'The person who brought you here popped a needle in your arm to help you sleep. It was quite mild. No ill effects, I hope?'

James shrugged. 'I feel fine. But why make me go to sleep?'

'I'll explain about CHERUB first. You can ask questions afterwards. OK?'

'I guess.'

'So what are your first impressions of us?'

'I think some children's homes are much better funded than others,' James said. 'This place is awesome.'

Doctor McAfferty roared with laughter. 'I'm glad you like it. We have two hundred and eighty pupils. Four swimming pools, six indoor tennis courts, an all-weather football field, a gymnasium and a shooting range, to name but a few. We have a school on-site. Classes have ten pupils or fewer. Everyone learns at least two foreign languages. We have a higher proportion of students going on to top universities than any of the leading public schools. How would you feel about living here?'

James shrugged. 'It's beautiful, all the gardens and that. I'm not exactly brilliant at school though.'

'What is the square root of four hundred and forty-one?'

James thought for a few seconds.

'Twenty-one.'

'I know some very smart people who wouldn't be able to pull off that little party trick,' Mac smiled. 'Myself included.'

'I'm good at maths,' James smiled, embarrassed. 'But I never get good marks in my other lessons.'

'Is that because you're not clever or because you don't work hard?'

'I always get bored and end up messing around.'

'James, we have a couple of criteria for new residents here. The first is passing our entrance exam. The second, slightly more unusual requirement, is that you agree to be an agent for British Intelligence.'

'You what?' James asked, thinking he hadn't heard right.

'A spy, James. CHERUB is part of the British Intelligence Service.'

'But why do you want children to be spies?'

'Because children can do things adults cannot. Criminals use children all the time. I'll use a house burglar as an example:

'Imagine a grown man knocking on an old lady's door in the middle of the night. Most people would be suspicious. If he asked to come in the lady would say no. If the man said he was sick she'd probably call an ambulance for him, but she still wouldn't let him in the door.

'Now imagine the same lady comes to her door and there's a young boy crying on the doorstep. *My daddy's car crashed up the street. He's not moving. Please help me.* The lady opens the door instantly. The boy's dad jumps out of hiding, clobbers the old dear over the head and legs it with all the cash under the bed. People are always less suspicious of youngsters. Criminals have used this for years. At CHERUB, we turn the tables and use children to help catch them.'

'Why pick me?'

'Because you're intelligent, physically fit and you have an appetite for trouble.'

'Isn't that bad?' James asked.

'We need kids who have a thirst for a bit of excitement. The things that get you in to trouble in the outside world are the sort of qualities we look for here.'

'Sounds pretty cool,' James said. 'Is it dangerous?'

'Most missions are fairly safe. CHERUB has been in operation for over fifty years. In that time four youngsters have been killed, a few others badly injured. It's about the same as the number of children who would have died in road accidents in a typical inner city school, but it's still four more than we would have liked. I've been Chairman for ten years. Luckily, all we've had in that time is one bad case of malaria and someone getting shot in the leg.

'We never send you on a mission that could be done by an adult. All missions go to an ethics committee for approval. Everything is explained to you, and you have an absolute right to refuse to do a mission or to give it up at any point.'

'What's to stop me telling about you if I decide not to come here?' James asked.

Mac sat back in his chair and looked slightly uncomfortable.

'Nothing stays secret for ever, James, but what would you say?'

'What do you mean?'

'Imagine you've found the telephone number of a national newspaper. You're speaking to the news desk. What do you say?'

'Um . . . There's this place where kids are spies and I've been there.'

'Where is it?'

'I don't know . . . That's why you drugged me up, isn't it? So I didn't know where I was.'

Mac nodded. 'Exactly, James. Next question from the news desk: Did you bring anything back as evidence?'

'Well . . .'

'We search you before you leave, James.'

'No then, I guess.'

'Do you know anyone connected with this organisation?'

'No.'

'Do you have any evidence at all?'

'No.'

'Do you think the newspaper would print your story, James?'

'No.'

'If you told your closest friend what has happened this morning, would he believe you?'

'OK, I get the point. Nobody will believe a word I say so I might as well shut my trap.'

Mac smiled.

'James, I couldn't have put it better. Do you have any more questions?'

'I was wondering what CHERUB stood for?'

'Interesting one, that. Our first chairman made up the initials. He had a batch of stationery printed. Unfortunately he had a stormy relationship with his wife. She shot him before he told anyone what the initials meant. It was wartime, and you couldn't waste six thousand sheets of headed notepaper, so CHERUB stuck. If you ever think of anything the initials might stand for, please tell me. It gets quite embarrassing sometimes.'

'I'm not sure I believe you,' James said.

'Maybe you shouldn't,' Mac said. 'But why would I lie?'

'Perhaps knowing the initials would give me a clue about where this place is, or somebody's name or something.'

'And you're trying to convince me you wouldn't make a good spy.'

James couldn't help smiling.

'Anyway, James, you can take the entrance exam if you wish. If you do well enough I'll offer you a place and you can go back to Nebraska House for a couple of days to make up your mind. The exam is split into five parts and will last the rest of the day. Are you up for it?'

'I guess,' James said.

10. TESTS

Mac drove James across the CHERUB campus in a golf buggy. They stopped outside a traditional Japanese-style building with a single span roof made of giant sequoia logs. The surrounding area had a combed gravel garden and a pond stuffed with orange fish.

'This building is new,' Mac said. 'One of our pupils uncovered a fraud involving fake medicine. She saved hundreds of lives and billions of yen for a Japanese drug company. The Japanese thanked us by paying for the new dojo.'

'What's a dojo?' James asked.

'A training hall for martial arts. It's a Japanese word.'

James and Mac stepped inside. Thirty kids wearing white pyjamas tied with black or brown belts were sparring, twisting one another into painful positions, or getting flipped over and springing effortlessly back up. A stern Japanese lady paced among them, stopping occasionally to scream criticism in a mix of Japanese and English that James couldn't understand.

Mac led James to a smaller room. Its floor was covered

with springy blue matting. A wiry kid was standing at the back doing stretches. He was about four inches shorter than James, in a karate suit with a black belt.

'Take your shoes and socks off, James,' Mac said. 'Have you done martial arts before?'

'I went a couple of times when I was eight,' James said. 'I got bored. It was nothing like what's going on out there. Everyone was rubbish.'

'This is Bruce,' Mac said. 'He's going to spar with you.'

Bruce walked over, bowed and shook James' hand. James felt confident as he squashed Bruce's bony little fingers. Bruce might know a few fancy moves but James reckoned his size and weight advantage would counter them.

'Rules,' Mac said. 'The first to win five submissions is the winner. An opponent can submit by speaking or by tapping his hand on the mat. Either opponent can withdraw from the bout at any time. You can do anything to get a submission except hitting the testicles or eye gouging. Do you both understand?'

Both boys nodded. Mac handed James a gum shield.

'Stand two metres apart and prepare for the first bout.'

The boys walked to the centre of the mat.

'I'll bust your nose,' Bruce said.

James smiled. 'You can try, shorty.'

'Fight,' Mac said.

Bruce moved so fast James didn't see the palm of his hand until it had smashed into his nose. A fine mist of blood sprayed as James stumbled backwards. Bruce swept James' feet away, tipping him on to the mat. Bruce turned James on to his chest and twisted his wrist into a painful lock. He used his other hand to smear James' face in the blood dripping from his nose.

James yelled through his gum shield, 'I submit.'

Bruce got off. James couldn't believe Bruce had half killed him in about five seconds. He wiped his bloody face on the arm of his T-shirt.

'Ready?' Mac asked.

James' nose was clogged with blood. He gasped for air.

'Hang on, Mac,' Bruce said. 'What hand does he write with?'

James was grateful for a few seconds' rest but wondered why Bruce had asked such a weird question.

'What hand do you write with, James?' Mac asked.

'My left,' James said.

'OK, fight.'

There was no way Bruce was getting the early hit in this time. James lunged forward. Trouble was, Bruce had gone by the time James got there. James felt himself being lifted from behind. Bruce threw James on to his back then sat astride him with his thighs crushing the wind out of him. James tried to escape but he couldn't even breathe. Bruce grabbed James' right hand and twisted his thumb until it made a loud crack.

James cried out. Bruce clenched his fist and spat out his gum shield. 'I'm gonna smash the nose again if you don't submit.'

The hand looked a lot scarier than when James had shaken it a couple of minutes earlier.

'I submit,' James said.

James held his thumb as he stumbled to his feet. A drip of

blood from his nose ran over his top lip into his mouth. The mat was covered in red smudges.

'You want to carry on?' Mac asked.

James nodded. They squared up for a third time. James knew he had no chance with blood running down his face and his right hand so painful he couldn't even move it. But he had so much anger he was determined to get one good punch in, even if it got him killed.

'Please give up,' Bruce said. 'I don't want to hurt you badly.'

James charged forward without waiting for the start signal. He missed again. Bruce's heel hit James in the stomach. James doubled over. All he could see was green and yellow blurs. Still standing, James felt his arm being twisted.

'I'm breaking your arm this time,' Bruce said. 'I don't want to.'

James knew he couldn't take a broken arm.

'I give up,' he shouted. 'I withdraw.'

Bruce stepped back and held his hand out for James to shake it. 'Good fight, James,' he said, smiling.

James limply shook Bruce's hand. 'I think you broke my thumb,' he said.

'It's only dislocated. Show me.'

James held out his hand.

'This is going to hurt,' Bruce said.

He pressed James' thumb at the joint. The pain made James buckle at the knees as the bone crunched back into place.

Bruce laughed. 'You think that's painful, one time someone broke my leg in nine places.'

James sank to the floor. The pain in his nose felt like his head was splitting in two between his eyes. It was only pride that stopped him crying.

'So,' Mac said. 'Ready for the next test?'

*

James realised now why Bruce had asked which hand he wrote with. His right hand was painful beyond use. James sat in a hall surrounded by wooden desks. He was the only one taking the test. He had bits of bloody tissue stuffed up each nostril and his clothes were a mess.

'Simple intelligence test, James,' Mac explained. 'Mixture of verbal and mathematical skills. You have forty-five minutes, starting now.'

The questions got harder as the paper went on. Normally it wouldn't have been bad but James hurt in about five different places, his nose was still bleeding and every time he shut his eyes he felt like he was drifting backwards. He still had three pages left when time ran out.

*

James' nose had finally stopped bleeding and he could move his right hand again, but he still wasn't happy. He didn't think he'd done well on the first two tests.

The crowded canteen was weird. Everybody stopped talking when James got near them. He got *Can't talk to orange* three times before somebody pointed out cutlery. James took a block of lasagne with garlic bread and a fancy looking orange mousse with chocolate shreds on top. When he got to the table he realised he hadn't eaten since the previous night and was starving. It was loads better than the frozen stuff at Nebraska House.

'Do you like eating chicken?' Mac asked.

'Sure,' James said.

They were sitting in a tiny office with a desk between them. The only thing on the desk was a metal cage with a live chicken in it.

'Would you like to eat this chicken?'

'It's alive.'

'I can see that, James. Would you like to kill it?'

'No way.'

'Why not?'

'It's cruel.'

'James, are you saying you want to become a vegetarian?'

'No.'

'If you think it's cruel to a kill the chicken, why are you happy to eat it?'

'I don't know,' James said. 'I'm twelve years old, I eat what gets stuck in front of me.'

'James, I want you to kill the chicken.'

'This is a dumb test. What does this prove?' James asked.

'I'm not discussing what the tests are for until they're all over. Kill the chicken. If you don't, somebody else has to. Why should they do it instead of you?'

'They get paid,' James said.

Mac took his wallet out of his jacket and put a five-pound note on top of the cage.

'Now you're getting paid, James. Kill the chicken.'

'I . . .'

James couldn't think of any more arguments and felt that

at least if he killed the chicken he would have passed one test.

'OK. How do I kill it?'

Mac handed James a biro.

'Stab the chicken with the tip of the pen just below the head. A good stab should sever the main artery down the neck and cut through the windpipe to stop the bird breathing. It should be dead in about thirty seconds.'

'This is sick,' James said.

'Point the chicken's bum away from yourself. The shock makes it empty its bowels quite violently.'

James picked up the pen and reached into the cage.

*

James stopped worrying about the warm chicken blood and crap on his clothes as soon as he saw the wooden obstacle. It started with a long climb up a rope ladder. Then you slid across a pole, up another ladder and over narrow planks with jumps between them. James couldn't see where you went from there because the obstacle disappeared behind trees. All he could tell was that it got even higher and there were no safety nets.

Mac introduced James to his guides, a couple of fit-looking sixteen-year-olds in navy CHERUB T-shirts called Paul and Arif. They clambered up the ladder, the two older boys sandwiching James.

'Never look down,' Arif said. 'That's the trick.'

James slid across the pole going hand over hand, fighting the pain in his right thumb. The first jump between planks was only about a metre. James went over after a bit of encouragement. They climbed another ladder and walked along more planks. This set were twenty metres above ground. James placed his feet carefully, keeping his eyes straight ahead. The wood creaked in the breeze.

There was a one and a half metre gap between the next set of planks. Not a difficult jump at ground level but between two wet planks twenty metres up, James was ruffled. Arif took a little run up and hopped over easily.

'It's simple, James,' Arif said. 'Come on, this is the last bit.'

A bird squawked. James' eyes followed it down. Now he saw how high he was and started to panic. The clouds moving made him feel like he was falling.

'I can't stand it up here,' James said. 'I'm gonna puke.'

Paul grabbed his hand.

'I can't do it,' James said.

'Of course you can,' Paul said. 'If it was on the ground you wouldn't break your stride.'

'But it's not on the bloody ground!' James shouted.

James wondered why he was standing twenty metres up, with a headache, an aching thumb, plus dried blood and chicken crap all over him. He thought about how rubbish Nebraska House was and what Sergeant Davies had said about his knack of getting in trouble landing him in prison. The jump was worth the risk. It could change his whole life.

He took a run up. The plank shuddered as he landed. Arif steadied him. They walked to a balcony with a hand rail on either side.

'Brilliant,' Arif said. 'Now there's only one more bit to go.'

'What?' James said. 'You just said that was the last bit. Now we just go down the ladder.'

James looked. There were two hooks for attaching a rope ladder. But the ladder wasn't there.

'We've got to go all the way back?' James asked.

'No,' Arif said. 'We've got to jump.'

James couldn't believe it.

'It's easy, James. Push off as you jump and you'll hit the crash mat at the bottom.'

James looked at the muddy blue square on the ground below.

'What about all the branches in the way?' James asked.

'They're only thin ones,' Arif said. 'Sting like hell if you hit them though.'

Arif dived first.

'Clear,' a miniature Arif shouted from the bottom.

James stood on the end of the plank. Paul shoved him before he could decide for himself. The flight down was amazing. The branches were so close they blurred. He hit the crash mat with a dull thump. The only damage was a cut on his arm where a branch had whipped him.

*

James could only swim a couple of strokes before he got scared. He'd had no dad to take him swimming. His mum had avoided the pool because she was fat and everyone laughed at her in a swimming costume. The only time James had been swimming was with his school. Two kids James bullied on dry land had pulled him out of his depth and abandoned him. He'd got dragged out and the instructor had had to pump water out of his lungs. After that James refused to get changed and spent swimming lessons reading a magazine in the changing rooms.

James stood at the edge of the pool, fully dressed.

'Dive in, get the brick out of the bottom and swim to the other end,' Mac said.

James thought about giving it a go. He looked at the shimmering brick and imagined his mouth filled with chlorinated water. He backed away from the pool, queasy with fear.

'I can't do this one,' James said. 'I can't even swim one width.'

*

James was back where he'd started, in front of the fire in Doctor McAfferty's office.

'So, after the tests, should we offer you a place here?' Mac asked.

'Probably not, I guess,' James said.

'You did well on the first test.'

'But I didn't get a single hit in,' James said.

'Bruce is a superb martial artist. You would have passed the test if you'd won, of course, but that was unlikely. You retired when you knew you couldn't win and Bruce threatened you with a serious injury. That was important. There's nothing heroic about getting seriously injured in the name of pride. Best of all, you didn't ask to recover before you did the next test and you didn't complain once about your injuries. That shows you have strength of character and a genuine desire to be a part of CHERUB.'

'Bruce was toying with me, there was no point carrying on,' James said.

'That's right, James. In a real fight Bruce could have used

a choke-hold that would have left you unconscious or dead if he'd wanted to.

'You also scored decently on the intelligence test. Exceptional on mathematical questions, about average on the verbal. How do you think you did on the third test?'

'I killed the chicken,' James said.

'But does that mean you passed the test?'

'I thought you asked me to kill it.'

'The chicken is a test of your moral courage. You pass well if you grab the chicken and kill it straight away, or if you say you're opposed to killing and eating animals and refuse to kill it. I thought you performed poorly. You clearly didn't want to kill the chicken but you allowed me to bully you into doing it. I'm giving you a low pass because you eventually reached a decision and carried it through. You would have failed if you'd dithered or got upset.'

James was pleased he'd passed the first three tests.

'The fourth test was excellent. You were timid in places but you got your courage together and made it through the obstacle. Then the final test.'

'I must have failed that,' James said.

'We knew you couldn't swim. If you'd battled through and rescued the brick, we would have given you top marks. If you'd jumped in and had to be rescued, that would have shown poor judgement and you would have failed. But you decided the task was beyond your abilities and didn't attempt it. That's what we hoped you would do.

'To conclude, James, you've done good. I'm happy to offer you a place at CHERUB. You'll be driven back to Nebraska House and I'll expect your final decision within two days.'

11. GO

James was shut in the back of a van for the first part of the drive back to Nebraska House. Even though he was knackered and the driver wasn't allowed to talk, he couldn't sleep. After a couple of hours the driver stopped at motorway services. They both drank nasty tea and used the toilet. James was allowed in the cab for the rest of the journey. He read the first road sign he saw; they were near Birmingham, heading towards London. It wasn't much of a clue about where CHERUB was. James reckoned they'd already gone more than a hundred kilometres.

It was three in the morning when James arrived back at Nebraska. The entrance was locked. James rang the doorbell and waited ages. A house parent shone a torch in James' face before unbolting the door.

'Where on earth have you been?'

It hadn't occurred to James that CHERUB had taken him without telling anyone. He scrambled for an excuse.

'I went for a walk,' James said.

'For *twenty-six hours?*'

'Well . . .'

'Get to bed, James. We'll deal with you in the morning.'

Nebraska looked even dingier after CHERUB. James crept into his room, but Kyle woke up anyway.

'Hey, Einstein,' Kyle said. 'Where've you been?'

'Go back to sleep,' James said.

'I heard about your adventure in the off-licence. Ten out of ten for being a dumbass.'

James gave his nose a blast of some pain relief spray CHERUB had given him and started undressing.

'Can't say you didn't warn me,' James said.

'Vince is crapping himself,' Kyle said. 'He reckons you grassed him up and they've moved you to another home for protection.'

'I never grassed,' James said. 'I've got to get him back though.'

'Don't mess, James. He'll cut you up if you give him an excuse.'

*

Rachel shook James awake.

'What are you still doing here, James? It's ten-thirty. You should be in school.'

James sat up and rubbed his face. His nose was tender. At least the headache was gone.

'I didn't get in until gone three this morning.'

'Bit young to be out clubbing, aren't you?'

'I just um . . .'

James still couldn't think of a decent excuse for turning up at 3 a.m.

'I want you in school uniform and out of the door in twenty minutes.'

'I'm tired.'

'Whose fault is that?'

'I'm sick,' James said, pointing at his nose.

'Fighting, I suppose?'

'No.'

'How then?'

'I think I must have slept in a funny position.'

Rachel started laughing.

'James, I've heard some excuses in my time, but a swollen nose and a black eye from sleeping in a funny position is the worst ever.'

'I've got a black eye?'

'A shiner.'

James explored the tender area under his eye with his fingers. He'd always wanted a black eye, they looked cool.

'Can I see the nurse?' James asked hopefully.

'We don't have a nurse here. There's one at West Road School, though.'

'Please let me off school, Rachel. I'm dying.'

'You've been here for three weeks, James. You've been cautioned by the police, arrested for stealing beer, we've had a complaint from school about your behaviour in class and now you disappear for a day and a half. We're pretty lax here, but we have to draw a line somewhere. Get your uniform on. If you want to complain, go and see the superintendent.'

*

James was putting his schoolbooks in his backpack when Jennifer Mitchum came in.

'Aren't you too tired for school, James?'

'Rachel's making me go.'

Jennifer locked the door and sat on Kyle's bed.

'Those tests are exhausting, aren't they?'

'What?'

'I know where you were, James. I was one of the people who recommended you.'

'The last thing I remember is being in your office upstairs. Was it you that gave me the injection to make me sleep?'

Jennifer smiled. 'Guilty as charged . . . So have you thought about joining CHERUB?'

'It's so much better than here. I can't see any reason not to go.'

'It is a fantastic opportunity. I thoroughly enjoyed my time there.'

'You were in CHERUB?' James asked.

'Back in the Stone Age. My mother and father died in a gas explosion. I was recruited from a children's home, just like you.'

'You went spying and everything?'

'Twenty-four missions. Enough to earn my black shirt.'

'What's that?' James asked.

'Did you notice everyone at CHERUB was wearing different colour T-shirts?'

'Yeah. Nobody would talk to me because I was wearing orange.'

'An orange shirt is for guests. You need clearance from Mac to talk to a guest. The red shirt is for younger kids being educated on the CHERUB campus. When they reach ten years old they can do basic training and become agents if they choose to. The pale blue shirt is for trainees. When you qualify you get the grey shirt. After that, you can go *dark*, which means you get awarded the navy T-shirt after an outstanding performance on a mission or missions. The real high flyers get awarded the black shirt, which is for outstanding performance over a large number of missions.'

'How many?'

'It could be three or four really outstanding missions, it might take ten. The Chairman decides. The last shirt is the white one, that's for staff and old girls like me.'

'So you still work for CHERUB?' James asked.

'No, I work for Camden Council, but when I see someone like you I make a recommendation. I'd like to give one warning before you decide, though.'

'What?'

'Life on the campus will be hard to begin with. You have to learn a lot of skills and CHERUB needs you to learn them before you're too old to use them. Everyone will seem better than you at everything. How do you think you'll cope with that?'

'I want to try,' James said. 'When I got arrested the other night the policeman said kids like me get out of their depth and end up in prison. It freaked me out when he said it because that's *exactly* what always happens. I never try to get in trouble, but somehow I always do.'

'So would you like longer to think, or shall I ring CHERUB and tell them you're coming?'

'I've got nothing to think about,' James said.

*

James was being picked up at three, leaving tons of time to get packed. He felt a bit sorry for Kyle. He was a nice kid who deserved more from life than a crummy room at Nebraska

House and three quid a week pocket money. James peeled two £50 notes out of his wad and stuck them under Kyle's bedcovers. He scribbled a quick note.

> *Kyle,*
> *You've been a mate. Moving to another home.*
>   *James.*

Kyle came in the door. James panicked; he was crap at making excuses.

'What time's our pick-up?' Kyle asked.

'What?' James asked.

'You heard. When's the bus to CHERUB?'

'They recruited you as well?'

'When I was eight.'

'I don't understand,' James said.

Kyle started pulling everything out of his wardrobe.

'Four months ago I was on a mission for CHERUB in the Caribbean. I put something I shouldn't have been touching back in the wrong place. The bad guys noticed, got suspicious and disappeared. Nobody knows where. Two years' work for a dozen MI5* agents down the toilet. All thanks to me.'

'What's that got to do with you living here?' James asked.

'I wasn't exactly the golden boy when I got back to CHERUB, so they sent me on a recruitment mission.'

'Here?'

'Bingo, James. Stuck in this dump trying to find another kid to join CHERUB. Jennifer thought you looked the type

---

*MI5 is the adult branch of British Intelligence.

when she saw your school record. She made sure you got this room so I could evaluate you.'

'So what you told me about your parents and stuff was lies?'

Kyle smiled. 'Hundred per cent fiction, sorry . . . You wanted to get Vince back. Did you have a plan?'

'You said stay away from him.'

'I hate him,' Kyle said. 'He was in a foster home and picked a fight with a seven-year-old. Threw him off a roof and broke his back. The kid's in a wheelchair for the rest of his life.'

'Jesus.'

'You know where they keep the spare sand for the kiddies' pit?' Kyle asked.

'Under the stairs.'

'Get two bags. I'll meet you outside Vince's room.'

'It'll be locked,' James said.

'I can deal with that.'

James struggled upstairs with the sand. Kyle had picked Vince's lock and was already in his room.

'I thought *you* were a slob until I saw this,' Kyle said.

Vince and his little brother Paul weren't big on housekeeping. There were dirty clothes, magazines and CDs everywhere.

'It's a normal boys' bedroom,' James said.

'It's not going to be for long. Start tipping the sand everywhere, I'll find some liquid.'

James put sand in the beds, drawers and desks. Kyle smuggled catering size bottles of Pepsi out of the kitchen. They shook each bottle up so it exploded when the lid came off. When they finished everything was soaked in gritty brown sludge.

James laughed. 'I'd love to see his face.'

'We'll be long gone. Want to see what's in his locker?'

Kyle pulled a metal object out of his pocket.

'What's that?' James asked.

'It's a lock gun. Does most locks. You'll learn to use it in basic training.'

'Cool,' James said.

Kyle slid the gun into Vince's padlock and wriggled it until the metal door sprung open.

'Girlie mags,' Kyle said.

Kyle tipped the magazines on to the floor.

'Hang on.'

'What?' James asked.

'Look at these.'

There was a row of savage-looking knives in the bottom of the locker.

'I'll be confiscating these,' Kyle said. 'Get me something to wrap them in.'

'Everything's soaked.'

'I don't care,' Kyle said. 'I can hardly walk down the corridor with that lot in my hand.'

James found a sweatshirt under Paul's bed that only had a bit of sand on it. Kyle bundled up the knives.

'OK, James, how long to pick-up?'

'Twenty minutes.'

'Twenty minutes too long,' Kyle said. 'I hate this dump.'

12. NAME

James sat in Meryl Spencer's office wearing CHERUB uniform with the pale blue trainee T-shirt. Meryl was James' handler at CHERUB. She'd won a sprint medal for Kenya at the Atlanta Olympics and taught athletics on campus. Her legs looked like they could break rocks.

Meryl held James' safety deposit key in the air over the desk between them.

'Not many kids come in with one of these,' Meryl said.

'I got it when my mum died,' James said. 'I don't know what's inside the box.'

'I see,' Meryl said suspiciously. 'We'll keep the key safe for you. What about the cash Kyle found in your room?'

James was prepared for questions about his cash. He'd realised Kyle had been through all his stuff when he saw him crack Vince's locker.

'It was my mum's,' James said.

'How much is there?' Meryl asked.

'There was four thousand. But I've spent a couple of hundred.'

'Just four thousand?'

Meryl reached into her desk drawer and pulled out a green circuit board and a tangle of electrical wires. James recognised them from when he'd ripped them out of his cassette player.

'Oh,' James said. 'You know about that?'

Meryl nodded.

'Kyle found the insides of the tape player in the bin the day he met you. He found the hidden cash and we worked out that it was from your mother's safe. You even left some lying around in obvious places to deceive Ron if he came after it. Everyone here was impressed when they realised what you'd done. It's one of the reasons you were invited to join CHERUB.'

'I can't believe you found all that out about me,' James said.

Meryl burst out laughing.

'James, we struggle to find stuff out about the international drug smuggling cartels and terrorist groups. Twelve-year-old boys are less tricky.'

James smiled uneasily. 'Sorry I lied. I should have realised.'

'You see that track outside my window?' Meryl asked.

'Yeah,' James said.

'Next time you lie to me, you'll be running laps around it until you're dizzy. Play it straight with me, OK?'

James nodded.

'So what happens to my money? Will you hand it in to the police?'

'Lord no,' Meryl said. 'The last thing we want is the police asking questions about you. Mac and I discussed it before you arrived. I think you'll find we've come up with a reasonable solution.'

Meryl got two little red books out of her desk.

'Savings accounts,' she explained. 'Half for you. Half for your sister when she turns eighteen. You can withdraw thirty pounds a month if you want to, plus a hundred on your birthday and at Christmas. Does that sound fair?'

James nodded.

'What's your sister's name?'

'Lauren Zoe Onions.'

'And your name?'

'James Robert Choke.'

'No, your new name,' Meryl said.

'What new name?' James asked.

'Didn't Mac ask you to think about a new name?'

'No.'

'You can keep your first name if you want, but you have to take a new surname.'

'Anything I like?'

'Within reason, James. Nothing too unusual and it has to match your ethnicity.'

'What's ethnicity?' James asked.

'Your racial origin. It means you can't call yourself James Patel or James Bin Laden.'

'Can I think about it for a while?'

'Sorry, James. There are forms to fill out. I need a name.'

James thought having a new name was cool, but his mind was blank.

'Well, who's your favourite pop star? Or your favourite footballer?' Meryl asked.

'Avril Lavigne is OK.'

'James Lavigne then.'

'No, I've got it,' James said. 'Tony Adams, the old Arsenal player. I want to be James Adams.'

'OK. James Adams it is. Do you want to keep Robert as a middle name?'

'Yeah. But can I be James Robert Tony Adams?'

'Tony is an abbreviation of Anthony. How about James Robert Anthony Adams?'

'Sure,' James said.

James Robert Anthony Adams thought his new name sounded classy.

'I'll get Kyle to show you your room. Basic training starts in three weeks if you pass your medical and learn to swim.'

'Learn to swim?' James said.

'You can't start basic training until you can swim fifty metres. I've put you down for two lessons a day.'

*

Kyle took James upstairs to the living quarters.

'Bruce Norris said he wants to see you.'

Kyle knocked on a door.

'It's open,' Bruce shouted from inside.

James followed Kyle into Bruce's room. One wall had shelves stacked with trophies. The other was a mass of gory martial arts posters.

'Mental posters,' James said.

'Thanks,' Bruce said, getting off his bed and putting out his hand for James to shake.

'I wanted to make sure you're not holding a grudge against me after the test.'

'No worries,' James said.

'You want a drink or something?' Bruce asked, pointing towards his fridge.

'He's not seen his own room yet,' Kyle said.

'Is he on this floor?' Bruce asked.

'Yes,' Kyle said. 'Across from me.'

'Cool,' Bruce said. 'I'll see you at dinner.'

James and Kyle went outside.

'He's a bit scary,' James said. 'It's weird being in a room with someone who could kill you with their bare hands.'

'Most kids here could kill you in two seconds flat, me included. Bruce is hilarious. He acts all macho, but he's a total baby sometimes. After he finished basic training and got his grey shirt he heard all the little red shirt kids were going on an Easter egg hunt. They wouldn't let him go so he burst into tears. He laid in his room and cried for like, three hours. And you'll never guess what else.'

'What?'

'He sleeps with teddy.'

'No way.'

'I swear to god, James. Bruce forgot to push his door shut one night and everyone saw it. Little blue bear in the bed with him.'

Kyle stopped at a room with a key in the door.

'There you go.' Kyle said. 'Home.'

James' stuff was in bags on the floor. Everything in the room looked new. A decent sized TV and VCR. A computer, kettle, microwave and mini fridge. The double bed had a thick duvet and a pile of pressed CHERUB uniform on top of it.

'I'll leave you to turn it into a tip,' Kyle said. 'I'll call you when it's time for dinner.'

James swished open his curtains and saw kids playing football on Astroturf. All ages, boys and girls. Nobody was taking it seriously. Little kids got carried on bigger kids' shoulders.

James fancied joining in, but he was more interested in his new room. There was a telephone beside the bed. He picked up, wondering who he could call, but he got a recorded message: *Dial out privileges are currently suspended.*

The computer looked new and had a flat LCD monitor and Internet access. James realised the best thing of all: for the first time in his life he had his own bathroom. There was a thick towelling dressing gown hanging on the door, piles of different size towels and flannels. The bath was big enough for James to lie flat in. For some reason, he decided to stand in it fully clothed and try out the shower, soaking himself.

He stepped out of the tub and looked at all the unopened bottles and packets: soap, shampoo, electric toothbrush, deodorant, even a box of chocolate bath bombs.

James laid on his bed and sank into his duvet. He rocked the mattress gently, smiling uncontrollably to himself. It was hard to imagine the room being any cooler.

*

Dinner should have been good. The food was top: choice of steak, fish, Chinese or Indian and wicked desserts. James sat with Bruce and Kyle and a whole group of other kids. They all seemed nice and James thought the girls looked cute in their CHERUB uniforms. The downer was, as soon as they saw James' pale blue trainee shirt everyone started telling horror stories about basic training: being cold and muddy, not getting enough to eat, smashed bones, stitched up cuts, being forced to exercise until you either puked or fainted. It sounded bad.

*

James stood in the food store. There were snacks and soft drinks piled on the shelves.

'Take whatever you want for your fridge.' Kyle said. 'It's all free.'

James looked miserably at the goodies and didn't say anything.

'They shitted you up, didn't they?' Kyle said.

James nodded. 'Is it as bad as they all said?'

'I can't sugar-coat it,' Kyle said. 'Basic training is the worst hundred days of your life. That's the point. Once you've been through it you're not scared of much else . . . At least it doesn't start for three weeks.'

James walked to his room. A timetable had been slid under the door while he was at dinner. Tomorrow he had a medical, a dentist appointment and two swimming lessons.

13. NEEDLE

His alarm went off at 6 a.m. James noticed that a set of swimming shorts and a map had been put on his desk while he was asleep. Nobody else was about this early. James walked to the canteen where a couple of teachers were eating breakfast. He found a newspaper and looked through the sport pages while eating cereal. The map was easy to follow, but James hesitated when he read the sign on the pool door: *Learning Pool. Children Under Ten Only.*

James stuck his head round the door. The pool was empty, except for a girl of about fifteen who was swimming laps. When she saw James she swam to the side and propped her elbows on the edge.

'Are you James?' she asked.

'Yeah.'

'I'm Amy Collins. I'll be teaching you how to swim. Go in the back and get changed.'

James undressed. He noticed Amy's black CHERUB T-shirt on the bench and her bra and knickers on a hook. James had worried his instructor would be some tough guy shouting and bawling at him. Seeing Amy's undies made James realise that making a fool of himself in front of a girl was even worse. He stepped out of the changing room and stood by the steps at the shallow end of the pool.

'Come up this end,' Amy shouted.

James walked along the twenty-five metre pool, nervously reading the depth markings. The deep end levelled off at three and a half metres.

'Stand with your toes curled over the edge,' Amy said.

James shuffled up to the edge. The bottom looked a long way off and the chlorine smelled like the time he nearly drowned.

'Take a deep breath. Jump in and hold the air until you come back up to the surface.'

'Won't I sink?' James asked.

'People float in water, James. Especially if their lungs are full of air.'

James crouched down to jump. He could almost feel the water blocking his mouth.

'I can't,' James said.

'I'm right here to catch you. Don't be scared.'

James didn't want to look soft in front of a girl. He raised his courage and leapt in. The quiet when his head went under was eerie. James' feet touched the bottom of the pool and he pushed himself upwards. As his face broke the surface he let out a gasp and thrashed his arms. He couldn't see Amy. He felt the same terror as when his classmates had nearly drowned him.

Amy grabbed James and with a few powerful kicks she

pushed him to the edge of the pool. James clambered out and doubled over, coughing.

'Well done, James. You've learned the most important lesson: you float back to the surface when you jump in the water.'

'You said you'd catch me,' James said.

He tried to sound angry, but he let out a big sob in the middle of the sentence.

'Why are you upset? You did really well.'

'I'm never gonna learn to swim,' James said. 'I know it's stupid, but I'm scared of water. My nine-year-old sister can swim, but I'm too scared.'

'Calm down, James. It's my fault. I wouldn't have asked you to do that if I'd known you were so frightened.'

Amy took James back to the shallow end. They sat with their feet dangling in the water while Amy tried to calm James down.

'You must think I'm a wimp,' James said.

'Everyone is scared of something,' Amy said. 'I've taught loads of kids to swim. You may take longer to learn than someone more confident, but we'll get through it.'

'I should have stayed where I was,' James said. 'I'm not good enough for a place like this.'

Amy put her arm around James. James was uncomfortable at first. He felt too old for a cuddle, but Amy was nice.

*

'Get down off the treadmill,' the doctor said. His German accent made him sound like an extra from a World War Two film.

James wore shorts and trainers. Sweat dripped out of his

hair and streaked down his face. A nurse started peeling off the sticky patches on his chest. They were all wired up to a machine. The doctor touched the machine and a half-metre long strip of paper shot out. He stared at the paper and shook his head.

'Do you watch a lot of TV, James?'

'I suppose,' James said.

'You just ran one kilometre and you're exhausted. Do you play any sport?'

'Not much,' James said.

The doctor pinched a roll of fat on James' stomach.

'Look at that flab. You're like a middle-aged man.'

The doctor untucked his shirt and slapped a six-pack stomach.

'Like steel,' he said. 'And I'm sixty years old.'

James had never thought of himself as fat before. But now that he looked, he *was* a bit soggy around the middle.

'When does your basic training start?' the doctor asked.

'Three weeks. If I learn to swim.'

'You can't swim either? Pathetic! No need to swim in front of the television, I suppose, James? I'll send you down to the athletics department. Get you to do some running. No puddings, no chocolates. The good news is, apart from too much puppy fat, you seem fine. Now, injections.'

The nurse pulled a plastic tray with hundreds of syringes lined up on it out of a fridge.

'What are all these?' James asked, alarmed.

'CHERUB can send you anywhere in the world at a moment's notice. You have to be vaccinated. Influenza, Cholera, Typhoid, Hepatitis A, Hepatitis C, Rubella,

Yellow Fever, Lassa Fever, Tetanus, Japanese Encephalitis, Tuberculosis, Meningitis.'

'I'm having all those now?' James asked.

'No, that would overload your immune system and make you sick. Only seven injections today. Then five in two days' time and another four in a week.'

'I've got to have sixteen injections?'

'Twenty-three actually. You'll need some booster jabs in six months.'

Before James could comprehend the full horror of this, the nurse wiped his arm with a sterile swab. The doctor tore the packaging off a syringe and jabbed it into James' arm. It didn't hurt.

'Influenza,' the doctor said. 'Thought I'd start you off with an easy one. This next one goes into the muscle and you may feel a teensy little pinch.'

The doctor pulled the cap off a five-centimetre needle.

'OOOOOOOOO WWWWWWWWW.'

*

James was sitting in the changing room in his swimming shorts waiting for his afternoon lesson. Amy rushed in. She threw a bag of school books on the floor and started unlacing her boots.

'Sorry I'm late, James. Got talking and lost track of time. How's your day been?'

'Awful,' James said.

'What's wrong with your voice?'

'Four fillings at the dentist. I still can't feel my tongue.'

'Does it hurt?' Amy asked, stepping out of her trousers.

'Not as bad as my arse where the doctor stuck two needles

in it. Plus he says I'm fat and unfit. I've got to run fifteen laps five times a week and I'm not allowed to eat desserts.'

Amy smiled. 'Not a good day, then.'

14. SWEAT

Fifteen laps of a 400-metre track is six kilometres. James had no time limit; he could walk it in about an hour but that was boring. He wanted to go fast. The first day he raced off and died after three laps. He staggered the rest of the way with his legs aching and it took nearly an hour and a quarter. Next morning James' ankles were puffed up and even walking was agony.

Meryl Spencer showed James warm-up and cool-down stretches and told him only to run every third lap, then gradually to move up; running a lap and a half out of every three, then two out of three, and so on until he could run the six kilometres without a rest.

The third day it rained so hard James could hardly see through the wet hair stuck to his face. Meryl and the other athletics coach hid in the dry. James figured nobody was watching and after thirteen laps went into the changing room where the other drowned-rat kids were diving under the shower.

'Was that fifteen laps?' Meryl asked.

James knew he was busted just from her voice.

'Come on, it's belting down, Miss.'

'You cheat, James, you start again. Fifteen laps. Get going.'

'What?'

'You heard me, James. One smart word and I'll make it thirty laps.'

By the end, James' lungs felt like they were going to explode. Kyle and Bruce thought it was superb when James told them what had happened. Amy said it was good to learn early that discipline at CHERUB was stricter than James was used to.

*

A fortnight later James was getting fitter. He could run two laps out of every three fast and jog the other one. It was Friday, lap fifteen. The pulse in his neck felt like it was about to burst. His body was begging him to quit, but James wanted to do his laps in under half an hour for the first time and he wasn't giving in so close to the end.

James overtook a set of identical twins on the final bend and sprinted to the line. He glanced at his stopwatch: 29:47. Twenty seconds inside his previous best. As James looked at the watch he put a foot down awkwardly and overbalanced. The track slashed the skin off his knee, ripped his T-shirt and grazed his shoulder. The pain from the cuts wasn't as bad as the pain in his lungs, but James didn't care because he'd broken half an hour.

James clamped his hand over his knee. The twins stopped to help.

'You OK?' one of them asked.

'Fine,' James lied.

James hadn't seen them before. He noticed they were wearing pale blue shirts.

'You two starting basic training week after next?'

'Yeah. We arrived last night. I'm Callum, this is Connor. You want us to help you back to the changing room?'

'I'll manage,' James said.

*

'It's my birthday today,' Amy said.

They were in the pool together. James' cuts were stinging from the chlorine.

'How old?' James asked.

'Sixteen.'

'I would have got you a card or something,' James said. 'You never said.'

'I'm having a little gathering. Just a few friends in my room this evening. Want to come?'

'Sure,' James said.

James was more excited about going to Amy's party than he would admit. He liked her a lot. She was funny and beautiful. He was sure Amy liked him, but like a little brother not a mate.

'You have to do something first though.'

'How far?' James asked.

'From the steps in the middle of the pool on that side, to the opposite corner.'

'That's almost a length.'

'Almost. You can do it, James. Your stroke is getting stronger. Basic training starts in nine days and if you don't make it, it's three months until the next course starts.'

'I'll have three months to learn to swim. That's not bad.'

'They'll put you in a red T-shirt,' Amy said.

'I'm twelve. Red is for little kids.'

'No, James. Red shirts are for kids who are not qualified for training. Mostly that's because they're too young. But in your case it will be because you can't swim.'

'I'll be two years older than anyone else in a red shirt. I'll be slaughtered.'

'James, I'm not trying to pressure you, but if you have to spend three months in a red shirt, your life won't be a lot of fun.'

'You *are* trying to pressure me,' James said.

'On the bright side, James, red shirt kids are allowed to keep a gerbil or a hamster in their rooms.'

'Well funny, Amy.' James laughed, but he knew this was serious. Kyle, Bruce and everyone else would wet themselves laughing if they put him in a red T-shirt. James started walking through the water towards the steps, determined to swim further than before.

He managed. Amy gave him a hug.

'You'll be OK, James.'

James wasn't so confident.

*

Amy's door was wedged open and you could hear her stereo as you stepped out of the lift. The room was crammed with people and more lined the corridor outside. Everyone was dressed in normal clothes. After two weeks on campus seeing people in olive trousers and boots, James had almost forgotten skirts existed.

Amy had on bright pink lipstick that matched her mini skirt. James felt self-conscious because everyone was older and he didn't know anyone. Amy spun around when she saw James. She had a cigarette in one hand and a can of beer in the other. She gave James a kiss on the cheek, leaving a blur of lipstick.

'Hey James,' Amy said. 'I don't think I'll be in any state for a swimming lesson tomorrow morning.'

'Is this the kid who can't swim?' a guy sitting on the floor asked loudly.

Everyone heard. James thought people were looking at him thinking he was a wimp.

'You want a beer, kid?' a guy sitting by Amy's fridge asked.

James didn't know what to say. If he said yes everyone might laugh because they thought he was too young. If he said no he'd look soft. James picked yes. Nobody laughed at him. James caught the can and pulled the tab. Amy grabbed it out of his hand.

'Don't give him beer, Charles. He's only twelve.'

'Come on, Amy,' Charles said. 'Let's get the little kid drunk. It's always a laugh.'

Amy smiled and handed James the can.

'One can, James,' Amy said. 'No more. And don't tell anyone we let you have it.'

*

Once James had sneaked two of Uncle Ron's beers and got a bit drunk, but this was way beyond that. Amy's girlfriends all loved James. They kept giving him more beer. James blushed when one of them kissed him. So they all kissed him until his face was a mass of lipstick smears. As they got drunker one of the girls decided it would be funny to give him a love bite. They tickled James until he gave in. He knew he wasn't much more than their drunken pet, but it was fun being the centre of attention.

Some of the kids on Amy's floor complained about the racket, so the party had to move outside. It was midnight now and pitch dark. James followed the noise from Amy's portable CD player.

'Wait for me,' James shouted. 'Busting to piss.'

James wandered into a bunch of trees. Suddenly there wasn't any ground under his trainers. His heart shot into his mouth as he lost his balance. He slid two metres down an embankment and crashed into a muddy ditch.

James dragged himself up, spitting nasty tasting water out of his mouth. His sweatshirt was ripped. He shouted for help, but the others couldn't hear over Amy's music. By the time James scrambled back up the embankment there was no sign of anyone.

Campus was bigger than James realised. He got totally lost trying to find the main building. He felt sick from all the beer and started to panic. When he finally sighted the changing room at the edge of the athletics track he was thrilled.

James peered in the window. The lights were off. He tried the door, it wasn't locked. James crept in. The heating was off but it was still warmer than outside. James rubbed his hands together to try and get some feeling back. He found a bank of switches and flipped on the light in the boys' changing room. He left the others off. Any light shining through the frosted windows might have caught someone's attention.

James looked at himself now he could see and was gutted. He'd put his best clothes on for the party. An almost new pair of Nike Air trainers and some Diesel jeans. The bottom of the jeans had mud soaked through them and the trainers were a wet mess, coated with mud. James knew the route back to his room from here, but there could be awkward questions if he got seen like this. He had to tidy himself up.

James kicked his trainers off to avoid marking the floor. He went into the boys' changing room. Fear of getting caught had sobered him up a bit. The changing room was a mess. There was sweat in the air and quite a few bits of clothing tossed about. James found a grey CHERUB T-shirt scrunched up under a bench. It smelled nasty, but it was less suspicious than walking into the main building in a torn sweatshirt. James pulled it on. There were no clean tracksuit bottoms to replace the muddy jeans, so James pushed his jeans down his waist and turned the bottoms up so the muddiest area looked smaller. All he needed now was some trainers that wouldn't spread mud everywhere. There were a few running spikes laying around, but they'd be no good indoors.

James stepped across the hallway into the girls' changing room. He hadn't been in here before, of course. The difference from the boys' room was amazing. It smelled fresh. There was a counter stocked up with toiletries and perfumes. Best of all, there were two pairs of trainers on top of the lockers. One pair was James' size but pink. The other pair was smaller, but James could easily hobble a couple of hundred metres through the main building in them. He squeezed them on.

He caught himself in the mirror and realised his face was filthy. He wished Kyle could see all the lipstick marks. James damped a towel, scrubbed his face and hands, gave the smelly T-shirt a blast with deodorant and gargled mouthwash to mask the smell of beer.

He did a final inspection: not bad. If anyone asked why he was out so late, James decided to say he couldn't sleep, went for a walk and got lost. The only thing that might be tricky was explaining why he was wearing the wrong colour T-shirt.

James stepped into the corridor. A hand clamped his ankle. James shot about a metre in the air with fright.

'Caught you in the girls' changing room, pervert.'

James didn't recognise the voice. Torch beams lit up his face. Amy and the girl who'd given him the love bite burst out laughing. They had changed out of party clothes into uniform.

'Why are you hanging around the girls' changing room, James?' Amy asked.

James panicked. It was so embarrassing.

'I couldn't go back in the main building all muddy, so I came in here to clean up.'

'We're pulling your leg,' Amy said. 'I saw the light was on. We've been watching you for about five minutes. When I realised you didn't make it back we came out looking.'

James smiled with relief. 'I really thought you were going to tell everyone I was a pervert.'

'We still might,' the love bite girl giggled.

'Next time you say only have one drink, Amy, I will. I swear.'

'What makes you think I'll invite you next time? I know a back way into the main building. Let's not hang around here.'

'You saved my life, Amy. Thanks.'

Amy laughed. 'If you turned up drunk after half the school saw you at my party I'd be in as much trouble as you.'

15. TOWN

James swore he'd never drink again. It was a rough night. Throwing up, head floating, dry mouth and a throat like sandpaper. Lucky it was only three steps to the bathroom. It was 3 a.m. before James settled into an uneasy sleep. He kept jerking awake from weird dreams where everything was spinning.

'James,' Kyle shouted.

It was 7 a.m., Saturday morning.

'Wake up, man.'

James sat up in bed rubbing his eyes.

'You got drunk, didn't you?' Kyle said.

'Ugh.'

'This room stinks of beer.'

'I feel like I'm dying,' James groaned. 'How did you get in here?'

'Picked the lock. I did knock first but you didn't answer.'

'Can't you leave me to die?'

'James, shut up and listen. There's a mission in London tonight. Nine of us are spending the day up there hanging out. You're not supposed to come, but it's all been thrown together at the last minute and it's a Dennis King production so we can smuggle you on to the train.'

'What's a Dennis King production?'

'He's one of the mission controllers,' Kyle explained. 'He's a sweet old guy, but he's a bit doddery and he'll never notice an extra kid tagging along.'

'I've got a hangover,' James said. 'And I'm sick of always getting in trouble.'

'Don't you want to visit your sister then?'

'How will we do that?' James asked, excitedly kicking off his duvet and swinging out of bed. 'Ron won't let me in the flat.'

'If Lauren's home, we'll find a way. I wanted to help you visit her when we were at Nebraska House, but I couldn't without breaking my cover. This is your only chance. Once you start basic training, you're cut off from everything for three months.'

'When are we leaving?' James asked.

'Twenty minutes. Have a quick shower, put on civilian clothes and get your butt downstairs.'

*

It was weird being back. London seemed dirty and noisy, even though James had lived here until a few weeks before. The kids all split up when they arrived at King's Cross station. A bunch of girls were going shopping in Oxford Street. Most boys in the group were going to Namco Station, a big amusement arcade opposite Big Ben. They all had to meet outside Edgware Underground at 6 p.m. for the mission. Bruce wanted to go to Namco, but decided to stay with Kyle and James once he heard what they were doing.

'You'll get bored,' Kyle said. 'We're just going to James' old neighbourhood to visit his little sister.'

'You might need me for protection,' Bruce said.

Kyle laughed. 'Protection from what, Bruce? Come if you want. Just don't whine all day if you get bored.'

Bruce had never been on the Underground before. He looked at the map and counted how many stops like a five-year-old. Ron lived behind Kentish Town station, a couple of streets from the estate where James used to live with his mum.

'What do we do?' James asked when they reached the flat.

'Ring the doorbell,' Bruce said.

'Ron won't let me in, dummy,' James said. 'I wouldn't need you guys if I could just ring the doorbell and get in.'

'Oh,' Bruce said. 'I could kick the door down.'

'Like his stepdad isn't going to notice somebody kicking his front door down,' Kyle said sarcastically. 'What's your sister likely to be doing if she's inside?'

'Either drawing in her room or watching TV,' James said.

'And Ron?'

'He'll have been out drinking last night. Probably won't be out of bed for another hour.'

Kyle stuck his lock gun in the keyhole. He turned the lock but the door wouldn't budge.

'Bolt on the inside,' Kyle explained.

'Ring the doorbell,' Bruce said again.

'We can't. I just told you,' James said.

'You and Kyle hide. I'll ring the doorbell,' Bruce said. 'You said your stepdad is probably asleep, so I bet your sister answers. If she answers I'll say what's going on. If Ron answers I'll tell him I've made a mistake.'

Kyle and James walked away. Bruce rang the bell. A few seconds later Lauren's eyes appeared in the letterbox.

'How many packets do you want?' Lauren asked.

'I'm a friend of your brother James. Is your dad awake?'

'You don't want cigarettes?' Lauren asked.

Bruce waved for James to come to the door. James crouched at the letterbox.

'Let us in,' James said.

'James,' Lauren grinned. 'You better not let Dad see you. Every time I mention your name he looks like his head's gonna explode.'

Lauren undid a bolt on the bottom of the door.

'Is Ron asleep?' James asked.

'Won't get up until the horse-racing starts,' Lauren said, opening the door.

'Hide us in your room,' James said.

Lauren led the boys into her bedroom. The room was divided by a curved wall built out of thousands of cigarette cartons.

'What's all this?' James asked. 'You started smoking?'

'Dad buys them cheap in France,' Lauren said. 'He smuggles them in and sells them. He's making loads of money.'

Bruce studied the wall of cartons. 'Did you build this?'

'Yeah,' Lauren said. 'I was bored so I started messing about with the cartons.'

Bruce laughed. 'It's brilliant.'

'She always messes with stuff,' James said. 'When she had chicken pox she got every CD and video case in our flat and used it to make a pyramid.'

Lauren sat down on her bed.

'So what are you up to?' James asked.

'I go round with the kids down the balcony a lot. Ron gives their mum money and she gets me from school and makes my dinner.'

'So you're doing OK?'

'Could be worse,' Lauren said. 'You been in any more trouble?'

'No,' James said.

Kyle and Bruce both grinned.

'Pants on fire,' Kyle muttered under his breath.

'So you want to go out or something?' James asked. 'Can you sneak out?'

'Easy,' Lauren said. 'Dad doesn't like me waking him up. I'll do a note to say I'm round a mate's house.'

*

James took Lauren shopping and got her some jeans she wanted in Gap Kids. They ate pizza and went ten pin bowling. James and Lauren versus Bruce and Kyle. It started getting dark, but they still had an hour to kill before they headed up to Edgware for the mission.

They ended up in the little swing park near James' flat. James hadn't been back there since he'd hidden in the tunnel the afternoon before his mum died. Kyle and Bruce mucked about trying to make each other dizzy on a roundabout. Lauren and James sat next to each other on the swings, swaying gently and dragging their trainers in the gravel. They both felt a bit sad, knowing that their day together was running out.

'Mum used to take us here when we were little,' James said.

Lauren nodded, 'She was good fun when she wasn't in a mood.'

'Remember when you used to climb up the slide, but you could never work out how to sit your bum down and push yourself off the top. I always had to climb up and rescue you.'

'No,' Lauren said. 'How old was I?'

'Only two or three,' James said. 'You know, I can't come back to London till after Christmas?'

'Oh,' Lauren said.

They tried not to make eye contact in case they made each other upset.

'That doesn't get you out of buying me a present,' Lauren said.

James smiled. 'Are you getting me one?'

'You can have a box of cigarettes if you want.'

'Well, well, well,' someone said. 'Haven't seen you round here much lately, James. Been hiding from me?'

It was Greg Jennings and two of his mates.

'I've been looking everywhere for you,' Greg said. 'I knew you couldn't hide that nasty little face for ever.'

The three boys squared up to James, all of them about twice his size. Greg put the toe of his trainer on the swing between James' legs.

'My sister has a scar on her face thanks to you. The only thing that cheered her up was finding out that your pig mother dropped dead.'

'Leave her out of this,' James said angrily, bunching up his fist.

'Oh no,' Greg said, putting on a high pitched voice. 'The little faggot's gonna hit me. I'm so scared!'

A small rock bounced off Greg's head.

'Hey turd,' Bruce shouted. 'Why don't you pick on someone your own size, like me.'

Greg turned round and couldn't believe such a skinny little kid was being so brave.

'Get out of here,' Greg said, pointing at Bruce. 'Unless you want your legs smashed.'

Bruce tossed another rock at Greg's head. James laughed. Greg gave James a slap then spoke to his two sidekicks.

'Snap that little idiot in half.'

James knew Bruce was a good fighter, but he was only eleven and the two guys sizing up to him were massive. Kyle was nowhere to be seen.

Bruce backed into the roundabout, holding his hands out meekly, acting scared. He grabbed the rails on the roundabout and sprung his whole body behind a two footed kick. One of the thugs crumpled up. Kyle jumped out from behind the roundabout and barged the thug over, then smashed him with an elbow that burst his nose and left him unconscious.

Meanwhile, Bruce had taken on the other one. The kid plucked Bruce off the ground. Bruce kicked him in the balls then put a sharp pinch on his neck. He'd been trained to target the main vein running up the side of the neck. It caused an instant build-up of blood in the thug's head. He passed out and hit the ground like a falling tree, with Bruce holding on. Bruce clambered out from under his victim and ran towards Greg Jennings.

Greg still had his trainer pressed in James' crotch. There was a weird look on Greg's face; like his brain wasn't believing what his eyes were seeing. Greg reached inside his coat. James realised he was going for a knife. He dived backwards off the swing and grabbed Lauren.

Greg pulled the knife. Bruce faced him off.

'I'll stick that knife in you if you don't put it down,' Bruce said.

Greg lunged forward with the blade. Bruce stepped backwards. Greg lunged again, Bruce sidestepped. Bruce reached into his pocket and pulled out a coin. The next time Greg moved, Bruce threw the coin in Greg's face. Greg didn't know what was coming towards him and blocked the coin with his free hand. Bruce used the distraction to grab Greg's wrist, twist his thumb into a lock and slide out the knife. Now they were back facing each other, only Bruce was holding the knife.

'I'll stick this knife in you if you don't start running,' Bruce said.

Greg was too proud to run, but he walked off fast. Lauren ran over to Bruce.

'That was like something out of Jackie Chan,' she said. 'You're the best fighter ever.'

'I like to think so,' Bruce said casually, tucking his coin back in his pocket. 'At least for my age.'

James was amazed. First Kyle had set the whole day up for him. Now Bruce had saved him from a beating.

'You guys are great,' James said. 'I owe both of you.'

'I'll settle for cash,' Kyle said, looking at the dirt on his trousers. 'These are Billabong trousers. Sixty quid they cost and they're filthy.'

'You know what I really want?' Bruce said. 'Some business

cards with *Bruce Norris Kicked Your Arse* printed on them. I can stick them in people's mouths when I knock them unconscious, just in case they don't remember me when they come round.'

'Bruce, what you *need*,' Kyle said, 'is some serious time with a psychiatrist.'

*

The kids were gathered in a quiet corner of the car park outside Edgware station. Dennis King passed out copies of the mission briefing.

'You all know the deal,' he said. 'Read the mission and sign your name at the bottom if you want to come along.'

'Don't sign it, James,' Kyle whispered. 'Remember you're not supposed to be here.'

CLASSIFIED MISSION BRIEFING
TARGET:

Bishops Avenue, London. Home of Solomon Gold, owner of Armaments Exchange plc. Gold is suspected of illegally selling American-made tank-buster missiles to terrorist groups in Palestine and Angola.

OBJECTIVES:

Solomon Gold has gone away for the weekend. His home is protected by a two man security post. Gas will be released inside the post. The gas will make the guards sleep for about three hours. This task will be undertaken by an M15 agent, posing as the security guard's supervisor.

Mr Gold is highly suspicious. The area around his house is monitored by thirty-six video cameras. Adult intruders will be suspected of being M15 agents or undercover police. A decision has been taken to use CHERUB operatives, who must behave like vandals to minimise suspicion.

CHERUB operatives will enter the house through the main gate. Three operatives will search the office on the first floor for documents and make copies using handheld photocopiers. Six operatives will be issued with spray paint, bats and hammers. Their objective is to damage fixtures and fittings, creating the impression that the only intention was mindless vandalism.

Afterwards all CHERUB operatives should leave the scene and meet at an agreed point two kilometres from the break-in.

Local police have no knowledge of this operation. If an operative is arrested, they should give false identification details and await release.

Bishops Avenue was locally known as Millionaires Row, though billionaires was more like it. The houses were all massive. Most were set back behind six-metre-high walls. Video cameras stared in every direction.

A bus dropped the ten kids a few streets away. Solomon Gold's house was fifteen minutes' walk. James, Bruce and Kyle were at the back of the group, walking fast. It was dark and raining hard.

'You excited?' Kyle asked.

'Nervous,' James said. 'It said in the briefing about getting arrested. If I get arrested they'll know I'm on the mission.'

'Try not to get arrested, then,' Kyle said. 'Bruce will look after you.'

'What about you?' James asked.

'I'm upstairs photocopying documents.'

'Boring,' Bruce said. 'We get to smash stuff up. It's gonna rock.'

Ever since the fight Bruce had been in the best mood.

'I thought missions would be all sneaking around and stuff,' James said. 'Not bursting in the front door and trashing the joint.'

'What?' Kyle said. 'A bunch of twelve-year-olds creeping around in balaclavas and gloves, disabling burglar alarms and cutting holes in windows? Can you think of anything more likely to attract attention? The first thing you'll learn in basic training is that a CHERUB always has to act like a normal kid.'

Bruce laughed. 'CHERUB has a fifty-year tradition of mayhem and destruction.'

'I never realised,' James said. 'Cool.'

The girl leading them stopped by an open metal gate. She was called Jennie. Fifteen years old, she was mission leader.

'Everyone inside,' Jennie said.

James stepped through the gate last. He noticed the security guards asleep in their glass booth. A couple of kids were already in there grabbing the house keys.

'We've got twenty minutes,' Jennie whispered. 'Keep the noise down and pull the curtains or blinds before you turn any lights on. The only exit is back the way we came, so if the police turn up we're all spending the night in a cell.'

It was a hundred metres along a path lined with sculpted hedges to the house. The hallway was huge. Kyle took a mini photocopier out of his backpack and ran upstairs to find the office. James and Bruce found the kitchen. Bruce opened the fridge, which was empty except for a packet of cream cakes and some milk.

'Thank you,' Bruce said, stuffing a whole cake in his gob and glugging the milk. 'I'm starving.'

James had popped the top off his aerosol paint and started spraying ARSENAL in metre-high letters on the kitchen units. Bruce found the crockery cupboard and tipped it all on to the floor. James stomped the few plates and cups that weren't already broken. A girl came in.

'Bruce, James, come and help us out.'

They ran after the girl to the swimming pool. A few plastic chairs had already been thrown in. Two kids were trying to move a grand piano.

'Come on, help us.'

Five kids, including Bruce and James, lined up behind the piano and pushed it into the pool. A great wave of water sprayed up. The piano hit the bottom of the pool, making a crack in the tiles, before floating back to the surface. Bruce leapt on to the floating piano, pulled down the front of his tracksuit bottoms and started pissing in the pool. Before he finished, a huge air bubble burst out from under the piano lid and capsized it. Bruce fell in and swam to the side. James and the others were cracking up.

They all ran to the living room. James tucked some DVDs in his jacket, then picked up a little coffee table and used it to destroy the plasma TV hanging on the wall. The room stank from all the aerosol paint that was being sprayed. James was smashing ornaments and really getting into the swing of mindless destruction when a deafening alarm sounded and the room started filling with purple smoke.

Jennie was shouting from the hallway, 'Everybody get the hell out of here.'

'Stay with me, James,' Bruce shouted.

They ran through the hallway. Jennie counted them out of the main gate. 'Run away,' she shouted. 'Split up.'

James and Bruce sprinted up Bishops Avenue. Two police vans were heading towards them.

'Walk,' Bruce said. 'It looks less suspicious.'

The vans sped past. James' skin and clothes were stained purple from the smoke.

'What's this stuff?' James asked.

'Never seen it before. Probably harmless. Food dye or something,' Bruce said. 'Whoever did the security survey on that house messed up big time.'

'There's none on you,' James said.

'I suppose it didn't stick to me because I'm still wet from the pool.'

'What about Kyle? Did you see him?'

'He was upstairs. He wouldn't have got out before us. Probably been nabbed. Better start running again. Those cops saw us, it won't take them long to work out what's going on and come back for us.'

16. PENALTY

'This is beyond stupid . . . This is beyond a shambles. And you three . . . I'm lost for words . . . You're the biggest idiots of the lot, aren't you?'

Mac was pacing up and down his office. Not happy. Kyle, Bruce and James kept sinking lower in their chairs.

Kyle had a black eye and his arm in a sling. He'd punched a policewoman trying to escape. Her three colleagues got revenge when he was handcuffed in the back of the police van.

'We never messed up the security survey,' Kyle blurted. 'That was MI5's fault.'

'The security survey was fine,' Mac said. 'The alarm was deactivated. Unfortunately some idiots cracked the bottom of the swimming pool with a grand piano and the leaking water caused the security system to short circuit. That's what set off the alarm and smoke.'

James and Bruce sank lower still.

'So, your punishments. What's it to be? Kyle, you messed up in the Caribbean. You messed up at Nebraska House, now you mess up here,' Mac said.

'You told me I did a good job when I got back from Nebraska House,' Kyle whined.

'When you first got back, Kyle. Then two days later I hear from Jennifer Mitchum that the social workers want you punished. Something about filling someone's room up with sand and spraying Coke everywhere?'

'Oh, that,' Kyle said. 'The guy was a dick.'

'You and James were supposed to disappear *quietly*. No questions asked. I don't like answering questions about where you've gone. I'm sending you on another recruitment mission, Kyle.'

'No,' Kyle said.

'A delightful children's home in a run-down area of Glasgow. I understand kids with English accents are particularly unpopular there.'

'I won't do it,' Kyle said.

'Do it, or I'll put you in a foster home.'

Kyle looked shocked.

'You can't kick me out,' he said.

'I can and I will, Kyle. Pack your stuff and get on the train to Glasgow tomorrow morning or you're out of CHERUB for good. So, Bruce.'

Bruce sat up in his chair.

'Why did you go along with Kyle's idea to take James on the mission?'

'Because I'm a total idiot,' Bruce said.

Mac laughed. 'Good answer. You spend a lot of time in the dojo, don't you?'

'Yeah,' Bruce said.

'For the next three months you're suspended from

missions. I want you in the dojo at the end of every day. Wash the floors, polish the mirrors, tidy the changing rooms and load all the towels and stinking kit into the washing machines. Then in the morning, unload all the kit, put it in the driers and fold it ready for use. Should take three hours a day if you work fast.'

'Fine,' Bruce said.

But he didn't look fine.

'Now, James.'

James was nervous. He didn't know where to look.

'You're new here. Keen to make friends. Two qualified agents put you up to something. Basic training starts in a few days and should straighten you out. You get away with this one. But next time I'll come down like a hammer. Understood?'

'Yes, Mac.'

'I'm Mac on a good day, James. Today you call me Doctor McAfferty or Doctor. Got that?'

'Yes, Doctor.'

James couldn't stop a little smile. Then he saw how upset Kyle and Bruce looked and straightened his face.

'Bruce, Kyle, you can go,' Mac said.

They walked out.

'I understand you went to London to see your sister,' Mac said.

'Yes,' James said. 'I know I shouldn't have. But I wanted to see her before Christmas.'

'I wasn't aware you had difficulty getting access. I'll try and sort something out.'

'My stepdad doesn't want me near her.'

'I can be very persuasive,' Mac said. 'I can't make any promises, but I'll do my best.'

'Thanks,' James said. 'I know it's not my place, but I think you're being too hard on Kyle. He only wanted to help me see Lauren.'

'He's nearly fourteen. Kyle should be in a navy shirt doing the most difficult missions; instead he keeps making silly errors of judgement. If you'd come and asked me, I would have let you go and see your sister. You could have waited at the station while the others went on the mission. Have you swum your fifty metres yet?'

'No,' James said.

'Only five days to go, James. I won't be happy if you fail.'

17. WATER

Amy and James walked towards another swimming lesson.

'I spoke to the head swimming instructor,' Amy said. 'He suggested we try something different. It's a bit drastic, but there are only two days left. Your stroke is good enough to swim fifty metres. What's holding you back is your fear of the water.'

They reached the learners' pool. James stopped.

'We're not going in there this morning.' Amy led James to another set of doors. There was a red warning notice: *Danger. Diving Pool: No Admittance Without A Qualified Diving Instructor.*

James stepped through the doors. The pool was fifty metres long. At one end diving suits and oxygen tanks hung from hooks. The water was clear, cleaned with salt instead of chlorine. James read the depth markings: six metres at the shallow end, fifteen metres at the deep end.

'No way am I swimming in that,' James said, scared out of his mind.

'I'm sorry, James,' Amy said. 'There's no more time for the gentle approach.'

Paul and Arif were walking towards James wearing

swimming shorts and bright red T-shirts with *Dive Instructor* printed on them. James had seen Paul and Arif around, but hadn't spoken to them since they'd helped him through the obstacle course.

'Come here, James,' Paul shouted. 'Now.'

James started walking. He looked back at Amy. She looked worried. Paul and Arif walked James to the deep end of the pool.

'These are the rules,' Arif explained. 'You either dive in or we throw you in. If you swim fifty metres that's the end. If you climb out before you swim fifty metres, you get a one-minute rest before you jump back in or we throw you back in. After thirty minutes you get a ten-minute rest, then we go for another thirty minutes. If you still don't swim fifty metres we'll do more lessons with the same rules. Don't try to run off, don't fight, don't cry. We're bigger and stronger than you. It won't get you anywhere and it will make you tired. Do you understand?'

'I can't do this,' James said.

'You haven't got a choice.'

They were at the end of the pool.

'Dive in,' Arif ordered.

James stood at the edge and hesitated. Arif and Paul each took an arm and a leg and flung him into the water. It was freezing. Salt burned James' eyes. James tipped his body forward to start swimming. His head went under and he breathed a mouthful of salty water. He started panicking. The side of the pool was only a few metres away. He struggled to the side, pulled himself up and took a long gasp of air.

'One minute,' Arif said, looking at his diver's watch.

James could hardly see.

'Please don't make me.'

'Thirty seconds,' Arif said.

'Please, I can't do this,' James begged.

Paul took James by the arm and marched him to the end of the pool.

'If you dive in you get an easier start than if we throw you,' Paul said.

'Time,' Arif said.

James tried not to think about the fifteen metres of freezing water below him. If he could just get his stroke going and not drink any water it wouldn't be so bad. James managed to swim ten metres, but the salt was blinding him and he had to give up.

By the fourth attempt James was used to the salt and cold. He made it nearly halfway along the pool, as far as he'd ever gone without stopping.

'Brilliant,' Amy shouted. 'You can do this, James.'

James was tired but Arif and Paul showed no mercy, giving him one minute and making him dive back in. James only got a few metres before his aching arms got the better of him.

'Not good enough,' Arif said. 'You don't deserve a rest.'

James could hardly hear above his pounding heart and gasps for air. They marched him up the pool and James jumped rather than suffer the humiliation of being thrown. He was so tired he'd forgotten to be scared. He swam a few metres, but his stroke was weak and he swallowed some water. Paul had to lift him out of the pool. James started coughing up water and snot on the poolside. Arif found a cloth and threw it at James.

'Wipe it up, fast.'

James meekly bent over and wiped the tiles. He was in a state, but he didn't want Paul and Arif to see. Paul grabbed him to march him back to the top of the pool. He broke free and swung a wild punch.

'Leave me alone,' James shouted.

Paul grabbed his arm and twisted it tight behind his back. James sobbed in pain.

'You think you can beat us up, James?' Paul asked. 'I'm twenty kilos heavier than you and I've got black belts in judo and karate. The only way you can beat us is to swim that pool.'

Paul let go of James' arm and shoved him into the water.

'Twenty metres this time, James,' Paul shouted. 'You want to punch me? Twenty metres or you're eating my fist.'

James started to swim. He was shattered, but he was scared of what Paul would do when he got out of the pool. James managed twenty metres and a couple more. He swam back to the side. Paul reached to lift James out of the water. James grasped his hand nervously.

'Not bad,' Paul said. 'That's thirty minutes. You've got a ten-minute rest.'

James slumped at the side of the pool. Amy rushed up and handed him a carton of orange juice. Arif and Paul sat down a few metres away.

'You OK?' Amy asked.

'Never better,' James muttered, gulping back a sob.

'Don't cry, James,' Amy said. 'This is tough, but so are you.'

'I'm not crying,' James lied. 'It's the salt in the water.'

James sucked his juice and worked something out. If he was able to swim fifty metres, his best chance would be when he was refreshed after the break. If he couldn't do it straight away, he was in for another half hour of humiliation. The prospect of being dragged about and forced back in the water seemed worse than drowning. If he passed out, so what? Anything was better than more of this.

'Time,' Arif said.

James walked to the end of the pool. It sounded fine in his head, but the pool still looked terrifying when his toes were curled over the edge. He started swimming strongly. He got some water in his mouth and spat it out. For the first time ever it didn't freak him out. Twenty-five metres. It didn't feel too bad. It was a personal best anyway.

James managed another ten metres. His pace was slowing. It was hard to keep his head up long enough to breathe. By forty metres his shoulders were agony. Amy was screaming her head off, James couldn't understand a word. The more effort he put in, the slower he seemed to get.

'Nearly there, James,' Amy screamed. 'Come on.'

The last few metres was just mad thrashing about. He'd lost his breathing pattern, swallowed gallons and was holding his breath. But he made it. James lifted his face out of the water and took in the most beautiful air of his life.

Amy lifted him out and gave him a hug. She was crying, which made James start crying again. He walked over to Paul and Arif.

'I can't believe I'm saying this,' James said, 'but thank you.'

'Your fear of us has to be greater than your fear of the water,' Paul said. 'It's not fun, but it works.'

18. BASIC

James was due at the basic training compound at 5 a.m. He set an alarm and left it on his bedside table. Worrying about training kept him awake for ages. When he woke it was light. It's never light at 5 a.m. in November. This was bad.

The alarm clock was gone. Not set wrong. Not tipped on the floor and the battery dropped out. Someone had crept in while he was asleep and taken it. Kyle warned him they'd play tricks, but James hadn't expected them to start before he'd even arrived.

Clothes and a backpack had been dumped on the floor. There were two differences from standard CHERUB kit. The T-shirt and trousers had white number sevens on them. Second, instead of being fabric-conditioned and pressed, everything was wrecked. Big stains, rips in the trousers. The underwear was disgusting and the boots had done hard time on somebody else's feet. James moved the backpack. There was tons of equipment in it. He probably should have got up early and looked at everything.

James had to wear the wrecked T-shirt and trousers because they had numbers. But he had his own pristine underwear, and boots that were broken in and only smelled of his own feet. Would he get punished for not wearing the clothes on the floor? Or would he get laughed at for being the only one dumb enough to put on second-hand underwear? The state of the boxer shorts made his mind up. He was wearing his own stuff.

There was no time for teeth, comb, or shower. He ran out with the backpack. The lift took ages, like it always does when you're in a rush. There were two older kids in the lift. They knew where James was going from the numbers on his uniform.

One of the kids looked at his watch.

'You starting basic training this morning?' the kid asked.

'Yeah,' James said.

'It's half past seven,' the kid said.

'I know,' James said. 'I'm late.'

The kids burst out laughing.

'You're not late. You're dead.'

'*So* dead,' the other kid said, shaking his head.

*

The training building was a concrete box in the middle of a huge muddy enclosure, with no windows and no heating. Five-metre-high fences separated it from the rest of campus. Just the look of the place scared James.

He ran inside, puffed from running. The room had ten rusty beds with wretched looking mattresses. Three girls and four boys were in front of the beds, crouching on the balls of their feet with hands on heads. After about ten minutes in that position the bottom of your legs goes dead. Six of the seven had been that way for two and a half hours, waiting for James. The odd one out had done an hour.

The head instructor, Mr Large, and his two assistants stood up and walked towards James. Large's white CHERUB T-shirt was the biggest size you could get, but it still looked like all the muscles inside wanted to burst out. He had buzz cut hair and a bushy moustache.

James flinched when Large reached out and delicately shook his hand.

'Good morning, James,' Large said in a soft voice. 'Smashing of you to pop in. Nice breakfast, was it? Put your feet up, did you? Good read of the papers? No need to worry, James. I didn't want to start without you, so I made all your new friends wait in a highly uncomfortable position until you arrived. Should I let them stand up now?'

'Yes,' James said weakly.

'OK, kiddies,' Large said. 'Up you get. James, why don't you shake all of their hands as a little thank you for waiting.'

The kids stood up, groaning in agony and trying to wriggle cramp out of the backs of their legs. James went along the line, shaking everyone's hand and getting killer looks.

'Stand at bed seven, James,' Large said. 'Nice clean boots, I see.'

Large lifted up the leg of James' trousers and peered at his sock. Large's wrist was bigger than James' neck.

'Clean socks too,' Large noted. 'Anyone else wearing their own boots and clean socks?'

James was relieved that a few hands went up.

'Very sensible,' Large said. 'Sorry about putting those filthy rags and boots out. Must have been some kind of terrible mix-up. Still, you've only got to wear them for a hundred days.'

James smiled and got daggers from the red-headed girl standing on his right in filthy boots.

'Now, before I make my welcome speech,' Large continued, 'let me introduce my two wonderful friends who'll be helping to look after the eight of you. Mr Speaks and Miss Smoke.'

If you wanted two people to make your life a misery, Speaks and Smoke looked ideal. They were both in their twenties and almost as muscular as Mr Large. Speaks was black, shaved bald, sunglasses. Total hard case. Smoke had blue eyes, long blonde hair and was about as feminine as a dustcart.

'Miss Smoke,' Large said, 'would you kindly fetch me a bucket. And James, would you be sweet enough to stand on one leg.'

James stood on one leg, trying to keep his balance. Smoke handed Large a metal bucket.

'Hopefully this will teach you to be more punctual from now on.'

Large stuck the bucket over James' head. James' world turned black and the smell of disinfectant blasted his nose. He could hear the other kids laughing. Large pulled a baton out of his belt and rapped it over the top of the bucket. Inside the noise was deafening.

'Can you hear me speak, number seven?' Large asked.

'Yes sir,' James said.

'Good. I wouldn't want you to miss my speech. The rule is, every time your foot touches the floor you get another crack with the baton, like this.'

The baton whacked the bucket again. James was learning that standing on one leg is harder when you're blind.

'So kiddies, you're mine for the next hundred days,' Large said. 'Every day will be equally joyous. There are no holidays. No weekends. You will rise at 0545. Cold shower, get dressed, run the assault course. 0700 breakfast, followed by physical training until school starts at 0900. Lessons include Espionage, Language, Weaponry and Survival Skills. At 1400 you run the assault course again. Lunch at 1500. At 1600 two more hours of physical training. At 1800 you return here.'

James' foot touched the floor. Large smashed the baton into the bucket. The noise inside was incredible.

'Keep that foot up. Where was I? At 1800 you return here. Another shower, warm water if I'm feeling kind. Wash your clothes in the sinks and hang them up so they're dry for morning. Then clean and polish your boots. At 1900 you get your evening meal. 1930 to 2030 homework. Brush your teeth, lights out at 2045. There will also be trips off campus for survival training, the last of which will take us to sunny Malaysia.

'If anyone is accusing me of cruelty, I remind you that the fences that surround us are not to keep you in, but to keep your little chums from slipping in and giving you a helping hand or a tasty snack. You are free to leave the training facility at any time, but if you wish to be a CHERUB agent you will have to resume basic training from day one. If you get an injury that stops you training for more than three days, you start again from day one. James, put your foot down and take off the bucket.'

James lifted the bucket off his head. It took his eyes a few seconds to readjust to the light.

'You were very late this morning, James, weren't you,' Large said.

'Yes sir,' James said.

'Well everyone, because James is still so full after his lie-in and his cooked breakfast, I think you can all skip lunch. Not to worry though. It's only eleven and a half hours until dinner.'

*

The eight kids in training were split into pairs. The first pair, numbers one and two, was Shakeel and Mo. Shakeel was as big as James but only ten years old. Born in Egypt, he'd been at CHERUB for three years and in that time he'd learned a lot that would help in basic training. James realised he was going to be at a big disadvantage to trainees who had spent years in a red shirt.

Mo was another veteran, three days past his tenth birthday. A policeman had found him abandoned at Heathrow Airport when he was four. Mo's parents were never found. Mo always jiggled his bony arms like he was trying to swat flies off himself.

Three and four were Connor and Callum, the twins James had met on the running track a few days earlier. James had had a few conversations with them and they seemed OK.

Five and six were Gabrielle and Nicole. Gabrielle was from the Caribbean; her parents had died a few months earlier in a car wreck. Eleven years old, she looked tough as boots. Nicole was smaller. Twelve, red-haired and overweight.

Number eight, James' partner, was Kerry. She was eleven

years old, small and boyish with a flat face and dark eyes. Her black hair was shaved down to a number one. James had seen her in a red shirt with shoulder length hair a few days earlier. Now she looked totally different. She didn't look as nervous as the others.

*

Large led them out to the assault course at a jog.

'Do exactly what I do,' Kerry said as their feet squished in the mud.

'Who made you boss?' James asked.

'I've been at CHERUB since I was six,' Kerry said. 'I did sixty-four days of this course last year before I broke my kneecap and got chucked off. You've been here what? Two weeks?'

'About three,' James said. 'Why did you cut off your hair?'

'Quicker to wash, quicker to dry, doesn't get in your face all day. If you do things quickly and get a few minutes' extra rest, it makes a difference. I'll do everything I can to make life easy for you, James, if you do one thing for me.'

'What?' James asked.

'Protect my knee,' Kerry said. 'There are titanium pins holding the bits together. When we do karate, please don't kick me on that part of my leg. If we have to run with heavy packs, take some of my weight for me. Will you help me, James, if I help you?'

'Whatever I can do,' James said. 'We're partners anyway. How come they're letting you take this course if your knee isn't better?'

'I lied. I said the pain was gone. All the kids I grew up

with are living in the main building and going on missions. I spend my evenings watching six-year-olds cut up sticky paper. I'm getting through basic this time or I'll die trying.'

*

Kerry knew all the cheats on the assault course. One side of the muddy tunnel was drier than the other. There was a knack to how you caught the rope to swing across the lake. She pointed out one of the hidden video cameras. The instructors dragged you out of bed at 3 a.m. and made you re-run the whole course if they caught you cheating on video-tape. Best of all, Kerry knew there was a raised bar under the water, which cut ten metres out of the swim across the lake.

'You swim like a five-year-old,' Kerry said.

After fifty minutes, James was muddy and freezing cold, but they'd finished tons ahead of anyone else. Kerry found a standpipe, turned on the water and pulled off her T-shirt. She started washing out the mud.

'James, always wash out your T-shirt. Use it to wipe yourself off, then wash it again. It will be freezing when you put it back on, but we do the assault course first thing every morning and have to wear the same clothes for the rest of the day. If you leave the mud on it dries out and itches like crazy.'

'What about the trousers?' James asked.

'Won't get time to wash them. But first chance you get, pull off your boots and wring the water out of your socks. You hungry?' Kerry asked.

'I never had breakfast despite what Large said. I'll be starving by this evening.'

Kerry unzipped a pocket on her trousers and pulled out a king-size Mars bar.

'Cool,' James said. 'I'm sorry it's my fault we're not getting any food till this evening.'

Kerry laughed. 'It's not you, James. There's always some excuse why you don't get lunch. Or why everyone has to do an extra run of the assault course. Or why everyone has to drag their beds outside and sleep in the open air with no covers on. They try and find ways to make you hate everyone else. Don't let it get to you, everyone will get their turn.'

Kerry bent the Mars bar in half.

'You want this, James? Make the promise first,' Kerry said.

'I promise I'll help protect your knee,' James said.

'Open wide.'

Kerry crammed half a Mars bar into James' mouth.

Shakeel and Mo were heading across the last obstacle, with Callum and Connor a few metres behind. James could hear Large shouting at Nicole in the distance:

'Move that bum before I stick my boot up it.'

James felt a bit sorry for her; but on the other hand, as long as they were shouting at Nicole, they weren't shouting at him.

*

Everyone had to do physical training in the mud. Crunches, squats, push-ups, star jumps. After an hour James was numb all over from cold and muscle pain. His uniform was a heavy sheet of mud.

Nicole was on the ground, too tired to move. Miss Smoke put her boot on Nicole's head, dunking her face in the mud.

'Get up, tubby,' Smoke screamed.

Nicole got up and stormed towards the gate.

'You can't come back,' Smoke shouted. 'One step outside and that's it.'

Nicole didn't care. She went out the gate. Fifteen minutes later she was back. Bawling her eyes out and begging for another chance.

'Come back in three months, sweetheart,' Large shouted. 'Get rid of that wobbly arse or you'll never make it.'

*

It was a bit of a sensation being down to seven kids on day one. All the trainees talked about it. Nicole seemed soft giving up so early. On the other hand they were all envious, imagining her back in her room watching TV after soaking in the bath.

James had warmed up as much as he could in the shower and now sat at the table with the other six trainees, waiting for dinner. Having Kerry for a partner was great. Especially watching the other kids make all the mistakes Kerry warned him about.

The dinners got wheeled up from the main building in a heated trolley. Smoke handed out the dishes. James ripped off the metal lid. The stir fry rice was a bit dry from being kept warm, but it tasted OK and everyone was starving. Kerry got her plate last. James could tell something was wrong from the noise when it hit the table.

Kerry lifted up the lid. She had no food, just an empty Mars bar wrapper in the middle of her plate. She looked gutted. Large rested his massive hands on Kerry's shoulders.

'Kerry poppet,' Large said, 'you're not the first kid to come back here. You may think you know all the tricks, but so do we.'

Large walked away. Kerry stared at her empty plate. James couldn't let her starve after all the help she'd given him. He made a line down the middle of his plate and gave half to Kerry.

'Thanks, partner,' Kerry said.

19. MERRY

Imagine you are on an early level of a video game. It seems hard. Everything happens too fast, but you eventually make it through. You progress through the game to much higher levels. One day you try the early level again. What was once fast and difficult now appears easy.

This is the principle behind basic training. You will be asked to perform difficult tasks while under physical and mental strain. You will achieve things far beyond what you dreamed possible. When basic training is over, your mind and body will be able to perform at a higher level.

(From the introductory page of the CHERUB Basic Training Manual)

Callum dropped out on day twenty-six. He fractured a wrist on the assault course. The course wasn't that hard, but it was easy to have an accident when you'd already done three hours' physical training and hadn't slept the night before because Large blasted everyone in their beds with a fire hose.

Connor got partnered up with Gabrielle, but he'd never spent more than a few hours without his identical twin before. He was thinking about giving up and restarting with his brother in a few months' time.

The physical training was the hardest thing James had ever done. The first time he threw up from exhaustion he froze in shock. Kerry told him to keep running but James didn't listen. Speaks shoved James in the back, then crushed James' hand under his boot.

'If you stop training, you'd better be dead or unconscious,' Speaks shouted.

That was the closest James had come to quitting.

James was getting used to life in hell. He counted twelve scabs and twenty-six bruises on his body. That didn't include places he couldn't see. He showered twice a day, but he never had time to scrub the filth from difficult spots like nails or ears. His hair felt like straw, and grit sprayed out if he ran his hand through it, even if he'd just washed. If he got a chance for a haircut he was having the lot chopped off.

The worst part about training wasn't exhaustion, it was always being cold. James slept under a wafer-thin blanket in an unheated room. In the morning the floor was like ice on your soles. The instructors forced everyone under a freezing shower. Breakfast was always cereal and cold juice. Clothes never dried, they were damp and stiff as soon as you put them on. Not that it mattered for long. After five minutes on the assault course you were drenched in icy water and mud that crept down your trousers and kept you soggy for the rest of the day.

The trainees only felt tiny hints of warmth and each was bliss. Hot drinks at lunchtime, the warm evening shower and meal. If you were lucky you got an injury serious enough for a visit to the medical centre but not so bad you were thrown off the course. Then you got to wait for the nurse in a room kept at 22°C with a coffee machine and chocolate digestives, which you could dunk in your coffee and eat soggy and warm. Shakeel and Connor got these golden injuries; James could only dream.

The five hours of lessons sandwiched between physical training were the easiest part of the day. Weaponry was coolest. Shooting was only part of it. James now knew how to strip and clean a gun, how to defuse a bullet so it doesn't go off, how to put a gun back together wrong so it jams. Even how to take a bullet apart so that it explodes inside the chamber and blows away the finger on the trigger. They were starting knives in the next lesson.

Espionage was all about gadgets. Electronic listening devices, computer hacking, lock picking, cameras, photocopiers. Nothing as fancy as you see in the movies. Mrs Flagg, the ex-KGB espionage teacher, always stood in the unheated classroom wearing fur-lined boots, a fur coat, hat and scarf while the trainees shivered in damp T-shirts. Occasionally she would bang her gloved hands together and moan about the cold not doing her varicose veins any good.

The best espionage lessons were about explosives. They were taught by Mr Large. He dropped his usual psycho persona and took childlike pleasure in showing off the finer details of dynamite sticks and plastic explosive putty. He blew stuff up at every opportunity, even sticking a directional charge on James' head. The charge leapt up and blew a golf ball sized hole in the ceiling.

'Of course, little James would have been killed if I had

placed the charge upside down. Or if the charge had misfired.'

James hoped he was joking, but judging by the size of the hole in the ceiling, he wasn't.

Survival Skills was taught by the three instructors and took place outdoors. It was interesting, building shelters, learning what parts of animals and plants were safe to eat. The best lessons were on fire-building and cooking because you got a chance to get warm and eat extra food, even if it was squirrel or pigeon.

There were two lessons James hated. The first was Language. Kids like Kerry who had been at CHERUB for a few years already had good language skills. Kerry was fluent in Spanish and decent at French and Arabic. For basic training everyone started a new language from scratch and had to master a thousand word vocabulary by the end of the course. CHERUB picked a language from a country that matched your ethnicity. Mo and Shakeel got Arabic, Kerry got Japanese, Gabrielle got Swahili, James and Connor got Russian. The languages were extra hard because none of them use a Latin alphabet, so you had to learn to read and pronounce weird-looking letters before you could try saying the words.

For two hours each day James and Connor sat next to each other while the Russian teacher barked orders and insults. He smacked pens out of their hands, whacked them with his wooden ruler and showered them in spit as he spoke. By the end of a lesson Mr Grwgoski left the two boys with sore hands and blurred minds. James wasn't sure he was learning anything except that learning Russian made his head hurt. On his exit, Grwgoski often shouted to one of the instructors that James and Connor were bad pupils and deserved to be punished. This usually cost the pair an hour of precious sleep while they were made to stand in the cold wearing shorts. If Large was bored he might give them a good blast with the fire hose too.

The other lesson James hated was Karate.

*

'Day twenty-nine,' Large said.

Large had a green baseball cap on his head. His two sidekicks weren't beside him, for the first time ever. It was 0550. The six remaining trainees stood rigid at the foot of their beds.

'Can anybody tell me what is special about day twenty-nine?'

They all knew the answer. They wondered if it was the answer Large wanted. Your answer to Large's questions could have nasty consequences. Best to cross your fingers and hope somebody else took the bullet.

'Number seven, can you tell me why today is special?'

James cursed his luck.

'It's Christmas Day,' he said.

'That's right, my little pumpkins. Christmas Day. Two thousand and three years since the birth of our Lord, Jesus Christ. What should we do to celebrate, James?'

This was the trickiest kind of question because it didn't have an obvious answer.

'Get the day off,' James said optimistically.

'Well that would be nice,' Large said. 'Miss Smoke and Mr Speaks have the day off. All your teachers have the day off. It's just you six little muffins and my good self. I think we'll have a little celebration of Christmas. Then we'll devote the rest of the day to karate and physical training without any of those pesky lessons that usually get in the way.'

Large pushed a button on his baseball cap. Red lights illuminated in the shape of a Christmas tree and it played a tinny rendition of Jingle Bells.

'That was so beautiful it brought a tear to my eye,' Large said, throwing away the cap. 'Now that celebrations are behind us, shall we get on with the training?'

*

The trainees didn't get to use the springy floors of the dojo. They learned Karate in the fields surrounding the training building, freezing mud smothering bare feet. All the lessons were the same. You learned a move or two, then drilled until it was perfect. Then you drilled on other moves you'd learned before. Each lesson ended with full contact sparring.

James liked the idea he was learning Karate. He'd always wanted to do it but had been too lazy to stick at it. He was doing five lessons a week now which meant he was learning fast, but he couldn't stand being partners with Kerry. She was already a black belt. While James was falling over and getting out of breath, Kerry did every move effortlessly. She helped James and saved him from getting punished by the instructors at least once every lesson, but James hated the smug look on her face when she pointed out his mistakes and she always killed him in the sparring at the end.

You were supposed to anticipate attacks and dodge or block most of them. But Kerry was fast and knew moves James hadn't even tried. He always ended up on the ground in pain, while Kerry hardly took a hit. James was too proud to admit he was getting hurt. Kerry was smaller, younger and a girl. How could he whimper that she was beating him up?

*

Without the usual lessons, Christmas morning turned into six hours of merciless physical training. The trainees could barely walk. Large didn't let them have breakfast. James' vision was blurry from the water running into his eyes, but his hands were so numb from the cold he couldn't do anything to wipe it away. On top of all his usual aches and pains, Kerry gave him a painful kick in the side during sparring.

At 1300 Large walked the six trainees out of the training compound. They buzzed with excitement. They hadn't been out since day one. Maybe they were getting a Christmas treat. But they'd all played enough of Large's mind games not to get their hopes up.

Large told the trainees to stop walking when they were close enough to see through the windows of the dining hall in the main building. The room had a four-metre tree in the centre, decorated with thousands of twinkling lights. The tables had been put together to make four long bars, covered with gold tablecloths. Each place was set with fancy cutlery and crackers. All James could think about was how warm it must be.

'If you quit right now,' Large said, 'you could run up to your room, have a shower and be down in time for Christmas dinner.'

James knew Connor was thinking about quitting and was sure this would push him over the edge. Large made them run on the spot and do squats and star jumps. Inside kids were taking up places at the dinner table. Some waved to the trainees outside. James looked for Kyle, Bruce and Amy, but couldn't see any of them.

'You might as well all give up now,' Large shouted. 'None of you will make it. Go inside. Have a nice dinner. Chat to all your friends. You know you want to . . . No? Are you sure, cupcakes? How about thinking the idea over while you do twenty push-ups?'

When they stood up after the push-ups Callum and Bruce were by the windows inside. Callum had a cast over his hand. He opened a window.

'Don't give up, Connor,' Callum shouted. 'The next time I see you, you'd better be wearing a grey T-shirt.'

Connor nodded to his brother, 'I'll do what I can. Happy Christmas.' Bruce shoved Callum away from the window.

'Don't worry about Mr Large,' Bruce shouted. 'He's just a sad old creep who likes pushing little kids around.'

James smiled a bit, but not enough that Large might see it. Large ran up to the window.

'Shut that window, now,' Large shouted.

'OK, saddo,' Bruce said.

Bruce shut the window. When Large turned around his face was burning. 'Right, all of you, run back to the assault course.'

*

Kerry and James led on the assault course. They still managed it a bit faster than the others. Large had gone. Kerry and James reckoned he was sitting in his heated office stuffing

Christmas lunch while watching their suffering on a TV screen.

Near the end of the assault course was a two-hundred-metre stretch where you ran over jagged rocks. As long as you didn't trip it was nothing, but when you were exhausted you made mistakes. Kerry lost her footing. James saw her hand on the rock in front of him and thought about all the times she'd hurt him in Karate class. He felt a surge of anger and crunched his boot over her hand. Kerry screamed out.

'What did you do that for, arse-wipe?'

'It was an accident,' James said.

'I saw you look at my hand. You practically had to turn round to step on it.'

'You're nuts, Kerry.'

Kerry shoved James backwards.

'We're supposed to be a team, James. Why did you hurt me?'

'You always hurt *me* in Karate class,' James screamed back.

'You only get hurt because you suck.'

'You could go easy on me, Kerry. You don't have to batter me every single time.'

'I *do* go easy on you.'

James lifted up his T-shirt to show Kerry a massive bruise across his ribs.

'You call that going easy?'

Kerry launched a kick at James. She always hit him in the ribs, but this was a few centimetres lower, slamming his kidneys. James doubled up in the most unbelievable pain.

'*That's* how I can kick you if I want to,' Kerry shouted. 'If

I go too easy the instructors will know I'm not trying and punish both of us.'

James could see Kerry was right. He'd been a total idiot, but he was past logic. James lunged at Kerry. She stumbled back on the rocks. James started throwing crazy punches. Kerry got him back with a powerful fist on the nose. James felt himself being pulled up.

'Break it up,' Gabrielle shouted.

Connor and Gabrielle struggled to pull James off Kerry.

'Care to tell me what's going on here?' Large said, running towards the scene.

Nobody knew what to say.

'Connor, Gabrielle, scram. Kerry, show me your hand.'

Large looked at the cut.

'Go to the medical centre.'

Large crouched in front of James and looked at his nose.

'You'd better go with her. When you get back you're *both* in a lot of trouble.'

*

James sat in the warm room waiting for the nurse. Hot coffee wrapped in his hand, downing one mushy chocolate digestive after another. Kerry sat opposite doing the same. They wouldn't even look at each other.

20. COLD

'Welcome back, my two little bunny rabbits,' Large said. 'Nice warm afternoon, was it? Lovely choccy biscuits? Nursey made you all better? Well I have another special treat for you two love birds. Take off your boots and everything but your underwear, then go outside and, in the unlikely event you make it through the night, I'll let you come back in the morning. Remember, it's nice and warm in the main building if you want to quit.'

James and Kerry stripped off and stepped into the dark.

'Merry Christmas,' Large shouted after them.

The door shut, closing off the last tiny arc of light. The wind was bitter. Frost burned their feet. Kerry was only a few metres from James, but he could barely see her. James heard her sob.

'I'm sorry, Kerry,' James said. 'This is all my fault.'

Kerry didn't answer.

'Please talk to me, Kerry. I know I was stupid. Seeing everyone sitting in the warm and it being Christmas made me crazy. You know?'

Kerry started crying quite noisily. James touched her shoulder. She backed off.

'Don't touch me, James.'

This was the first thing Kerry had said to James since the fight.

'We can get through this together,' James said. 'I'm so sorry. You want me to beg? I'll go down on the ground and kiss your feet if you just start talking to me.'

'James,' Kerry sobbed, 'we're done for. You can say you're sorry a thousand times, but you've still got us both thrown out.'

'We can get through this, Kerry. Find somewhere warm and go to sleep.'

Kerry laughed a little.

'Find somewhere warm! James, there is *nowhere* warm. There's a big muddy field and an assault course. Nothing else. It's already close to freezing. An hour out here and we'll start getting frostbite in our toes and fingers. It's fourteen hours until morning. If we fall asleep we'll die of cold.'

'You don't deserve this, Kerry. I'll bang on the door and ask to speak to Large. I'll say it's all my fault and that I'll quit if he lets you back inside.'

'He won't bargain with you, James. He'll laugh in your face.'

'We could start a fire,' James said.

'It's raining. It's pitch dark. We'd need something dry to start the fire and somewhere out of the wind to start it. Any suggestions?'

'The bridge over the lake on the assault course,' James said. 'There's a gap under there before the water starts. We could put branches and stuff along the sides to keep out the wind.'

'I suppose,' Kerry said. 'We've got to try. There might be stuff in the rubbish.'

'What?'

'There are two rubbish bins at the back of the building,' Kerry said. 'We could go through them. There might be stuff inside we could use.'

Kerry led James to the back of the training building. They each pulled the lid off a bin. Both were full of rubbish tied up in bags.

'Reeks,' James said.

'I don't care *what* it smells like,' Kerry said. 'Here's what I'm thinking. We take the bins with all the stuff in to the bridge. Then we go through all the bags. Hopefully there's something to start a fire with. The bags will help us keep warm if we wear them.'

It was hard finding the bridge in the moonlight. It was too dark to make out any more than the outline of the ground. There was a risk of hitting something sharp with every step. James and Kerry took a bin each. They weighed a ton. James tried rolling his instead of carrying it, but the bin kept jamming in the mud. Kerry was having an even tougher time because her hand was bandaged. They walked the path at the side of the assault course. James' feet were numb already. He thought about the gruesome photos of black frostbitten toes in the training manual and shuddered.

The wooden bridge spanned twenty metres over the river in the middle of the assault course, and was about two metres wide. When they reached it, Kerry started untying and rummaging around inside the stinking rubbish bags. James clambered into the low space under the bridge.

'It's pretty dry under here,' James said. 'It's concrete, no mud.'

'OK,' Kerry said. 'I'm trying to get stuff to start a fire.'

James ran back and forth, stripping off branches and wedging them against the side of the bridge. Kerry dunked her hand in a bag and hit a mix of food slops and muddy rags used for boot cleaning. She sniffed her hand and couldn't believe she was touching all this nasty stuff. She threw anything that was dry and would burn into an empty bin.

Kerry tore the bags up, covered her feet in the boot-cleaning rags and then wrapped them with plastic. She tore holes in bin bags to make a plastic smock and skirt for herself and James. They looked like muddy scarecrows, but the important thing was it kept out the cold. James finished turning the bridge into a shelter and they clambered under, rubbing their hands together.

'Here,' Kerry said.

She handed James two small boxes. It was too dark to see what they were. James felt the familiar shape of a straw on the side of a carton.

'Breakfast,' James said. 'This was in the rubbish?'

'God must be on our side,' Kerry said. 'Six cartons of orange juice, six mini packets of cereal, all unopened. Large must have thrown them out this morning when he didn't give us breakfast.'

James punched the straw into the orange juice carton and sucked the contents in two long gulps. Then he ripped open the cereal and scoffed dry flakes.

'We've got clothes, food and shelter,' James said. 'We should last until morning.'

'Maybe,' Kerry said. 'I'd be happier if I could get the fire going.'

'There's tons of stuff there that will burn,' James said.

'But the only way I know to start a fire is with two dry pieces of timber. We've got zero.'

They sat there for a few minutes, huddled close, jiggling arms and legs to keep warm.

'I think I know a way to start a fire,' James said. 'You know the security cameras all over the assault course?'

'What about them?' Kerry asked.

'They must be powered by electricity.'

'So what?'

'So if we find one and pull the power cord out the back then we can use it to make a spark.'

'It's pitch dark,' Kerry said.

'I know roughly where a few of the cameras are.'

'James, you're talking about messing with electricity. You could end up getting killed.'

James stood up.

'Where are you going?'

'Have faith, Kerry. I'm going to start a fire.'

'You're a total idiot, James. You'll get zapped.'

James clambered out of the shelter. The foot coverings Kerry made kept his feet warm but slid everywhere. He found the bin Kerry had filled with flammable stuff. He tucked bits of tissue and cardboard inside his plastic suit, then grabbed a dustbin lid and started his search. James found a camera only a few metres from the shelter. The tiny red lamp below the lens made it easier to spot the cameras in the dark than in daylight.

James felt behind the camera and tugged the wires out of the back. One looked like the picture output, so he threw it away. The other wire had a two-pronged rubber plug on the end. James figured this was the power supply. He twisted the plug until it snapped off, leaving two bare wires at the end of the lead.

It had seemed a good idea in theory. But now he was on the spot, with his little store of fuel standing on the dustbin lid, water all around and a live electric cable in his hand, James' confidence plummeted.

He crouched over the bin lid. He split the cable, pulling the two bare ends of wire further apart, then lined them up over a piece of tissue. He slowly moved the two ends closer together. A blue spark lit up James' face. The corner of the tissue ignited. A couple of embers flew off and the fire snuffed out. James' heart stopped. He doubted he'd get another chance because the spark had probably fused the circuit. Then a second burst of flame rose from the centre of the tissue. James dipped a scrap of cardboard in the flame. The fire caught hold.

He had to move back to the bridge before the fuel burned out. His feet slid everywhere and the wind was doing its best to kill the flames.

'Kerry,' James shouted. 'Get some of the fuel.'

Kerry dashed out and put more bits of card on the fire. The metal lid was getting hot in James' hands and the last part of the journey was trickiest, down the muddy river bank and into the shelter. Kerry helped keep the lid steady. James pushed the lid into the shelter, careful not to set light to the branches lining the sides. Kerry got the rest of the fuel and they cuddled up to each other as the shelter filled with flickering orange light. The smoke made their eyes sting, but all they cared about was being warm. Kerry rested her head on James' arm.

'I still can't believe you stomped my hand,' Kerry said, looking at her bandage. 'I thought we were a good team.'

'I know sorry doesn't make it all better, but I really am. If there's anything I can do to make it up, I will. Just name it.'

'You know what,' Kerry said. 'I'll forgive you now. But after training finishes I'll fight you in the dojo. I'll beat you until you scream for mercy. Then I'll beat you some more.'

'Deal,' James said, hoping she was joking. 'It's what I deserve for getting us into this mess.'

*

Mr Speaks stuck his head inside the shelter. It was starting to get light. The fire was burned out. James and Kerry were asleep with their arms around each other.

'Wake up,' Speaks said.

James and Kerry rustled to life in their plastic suits. Kerry had said it was best not to go to sleep; better to stay alert and not get frostbite. But the shelter was warm and they'd both drifted off.

'I love you two with all my heart,' Speaks said.

Speaks reached into his trouser pocket and pulled out a couple of bars of Fruit and Nut. James couldn't understand why Speaks was being nice to them.

'I am so impressed with the way you two got through this. Mr Large was convinced you would quit. He couldn't find you. All the video cameras have stopped working for some reason.'

'What time is it?' Kerry asked, cheeks stuffed with chocolate.

'Six-thirty. You two better run back to the main building and get dressed. Mr Large is going to be furious when he sees you.'

'Doesn't he like us?' James asked. 'I mean, I know he hates everyone, but why is he so keen to get rid of us?'

'You don't understand,' Speaks said. 'We had a bet. Fifty pounds that Mr Large could make a trainee quit on Christmas Day. He thought making Connor watch his brother eat Christmas dinner would work, but Callum told him to stick it out. Then you two started fighting, which gave him the excuse to punish you. He was sure he'd broken you. I can't wait to see the look on his face.'

'After this he's gonna make our lives even more miserable,' Kerry sighed.

21. AIR

The six trainees and three instructors were heading to Malaysia for the final days of basic training. James' only previous flight was an eight-hour holiday trip to Orlando, crammed with hundreds of wriggling kids and bawling parents. This time it was business class.

James' toes couldn't reach the seat in front. The puffy leather chairs had pull-up screens for Nintendo and movies and a button that tipped the seat back so it was like a bed. Before take-off the stewardess came round serving sandwiches and fruit juice. It would have been good any time. After thirteen hard weeks, he was in heaven.

The jumbo finished its climb out of Heathrow and the seatbelt sign beeped out. James slouched with his headphones on, flipping through the different music channels until he came across Elton John's song 'Rocket Man'. His mum had loved Elton. James felt guilty that he'd hardly thought about her since he got to CHERUB.

Kerry's sock flew over the screen between the seats and landed in James' lap. He sat up as Kerry lowered the screen and yanked off his headphones.

'What was that for?' James asked.

'You wanted to know how long the flight was. Turn your TV to channel fifty.'

James flicked his remote. The screen changed to a blue map with London on the left and Kuala Lumpur on the right. Every few seconds the screen switched to a bank of figures, which included distance travelled, air speed, external temperature and time to destination.

'Thirteen hours eight minutes,' James said. 'Cool. I think I could sleep about that long.'

Kerry looked disappointed.

'Don't you want to play Mario Kart?' she asked.

'A couple of games, I guess. I'll sleep after they serve dinner.'

*

The sign over the automatic door of the airport terminal said, *Enjoy Your Stay In Malaysia*. The doors split apart. James slung his backpack over his shoulder and took his first outdoor breath. The screen on the plane said it was 40°C when they landed. James knew that was hot, but the baking air was beyond anything he'd imagined.

'Imagine running in this heat,' Kerry said.

Connor and Gabrielle walked behind.

'I bet we won't need to imagine for long,' Gabrielle said.

Large, wearing shorts and a Hawaiian shirt, wound the group through lanes of jammed traffic to a shuttle van. Speaks peeled notes out of a bundle of currency and handed them to the driver while everyone else climbed in with their luggage.

They pulled into the flow and drove for half an hour

along wide empty roads, heading against the evening rush hour. The trainees watched out of the windows. It could have been a modern city anywhere. Only the wide storm drains and the odd palm tree amongst the concrete told them they were in the tropics.

*

The other trainees had been James' only human contact for three months. They hadn't spoken much. If you got a spare half hour you didn't waste it talking, you used it to sleep. The few conversations they'd had were mostly bitching about training over the dinner table.

The instructors punished everyone for an individual mistake, so the trainees developed a sixth sense for covering each other's weaknesses. James knew before a long swim that Kerry and Shakeel would stick close and grab him if he lost his nerve. Everyone took Kerry's stuff when her knee was painful. Mo was weedy and needed help climbing and lifting. They all needed each other for something.

James wasn't worried about the four-day tropical survival course. He knew it would be tough, but everything had been tough since day one. Training had succeeded: exhaustion and danger didn't scare James any more. He'd been pushed to the limit so often it felt routine. It was something you didn't enjoy but always got through, like a trip to the dentist or a science lesson.

*

The hotel was plush. James and Kerry shared a room with two queen beds and a balcony that overlooked the pool. It was nine at night, but they'd all slept on the plane and felt lively. The instructors were going to the hotel bar and didn't want to be bothered. The trainees were given the run of the hotel and told to order whatever they wanted from room service, but not to stay up late because there was an early start in the morning.

The six kids met by the outdoor pool, the first chance they'd had to relax as a group. It was dark now. There was a breeze but the temperature was still in the thirties. Millions of insects chirped and smacked into the mosquito nets that wrapped the pool area. An attendant in a bow tie handed out robes and cotton slippers.

It was the first time in weeks that James had felt well-fed and relaxed. He also felt awkward. All the others were dive-bombing the pool and swimming confidently. James was ashamed that all he could manage was a clumsy front crawl and sat with his ankles in the water sucking Coke through a straw.

'Come on, James,' Kerry shouted. 'Chill out.'

'I think I'll go back to the room,' James said.

'Misery,' Kerry said.

James walked up to his room. He took a leak, then caught himself in a mirror for the first time since training started. It was weird seeing his own body but not quite recognising it. The belly that rolled over the elastic of his shorts was gone. His chest muscles and biceps were bigger and he thought the razor cut hair and all the scabs and bruises made him look hard. James couldn't help smiling. He was totally in love with himself.

He lay on his bed and watched TV. Only a few channels were in English. He found BBC World and realised half the planet could have been rubbed out in a war for all he knew.

He hadn't seen a newspaper or TV for the three months he'd been isolated in the training compound. It didn't look like much had changed. People still killed each other for no good reason, politicians wore dull suits and gave five-minute answers that had nothing to do with the question. At least they showed Arsenal winning in the sports round-up. After the sports, James flipped through channels and wished he'd stayed downstairs with the others.

Suddenly, the door of the hotel room opened and the light went out.

'Shut your eyes,' Kerry shouted.

'Why?' James asked.

'We've got a surprise.'

James could hear the other trainees outside in the corridor.

'No way, what are you gonna do?'

'If you don't shut your eyes you'll never know.'

It was unlikely to be anything good if they were asking him to shut his eyes, but James didn't want to seem boring.

'OK, they're shut.'

James heard them all file in. Kerry emptied an ice bucket over his chest. The cubes slid inside his robe and down his back. Connor, Mo, Gabrielle and Shakeel followed with more ice buckets. James jumped off his bed and trod on an ice cube.

'Scumbags,' James yelped, shaking the cubes out of his robe and laughing.

The others were cracking up. Kerry put the light back on.

'Thought we'd all order room service in here,' Kerry said. 'If you're not still sulking.'

'Whatever, cool,' James said.

They sat on the balcony talking about training and picking bits of each other's food. Afterwards the four boys decided to impress the girls by standing in line and pissing on to the plants two floors down. Kerry and Gabrielle slipped inside and locked the French windows.

'Let us in,' Connor shouted.

'Tell us how beautiful we are,' Kerry said.

'Ugly pigs,' Shakeel shouted. 'Let us in.'

'Sounds like you're staying out there for a long time,' Kerry said.

James looked down. They were too high to jump. He walked to the glass and spoke.

'I think you're both beautiful.'

'Arse kisser,' Connor said.

James looked at Connor. 'You want to stay out here all night?'

'Very beautiful,' Connor agreed.

'Supermodels,' Mo added.

The girls looked at Shakeel.

'Well?'

Shakeel shrugged, 'You're two radiant beams of golden sunshine. Come on, let us in.'

'Shall we?' Kerry asked Gabrielle, enjoying her sense of power.

Gabrielle put a finger on her mouth and acted puzzled.

'If they kiss the glass to show how much they love us,' she decided.

Kerry laughed. 'You heard her, boys. Nice big smooch on the glass.'

The four boys looked at each other.

'Oh, for god's sake,' Connor muttered.

Connor kissed the glass first. The other three did the same.

Someone knocked at the door. Kerry answered. It was Large and Smoke. Gabrielle unlocked the French doors. The boys rushed inside, hoping they hadn't been spotted peeing on the plants.

Large sounded drunk. 'It's gone eleven. I want you all in bed in five minutes.'

The others filed out. James and Kerry got into bed.

22. BEACH

A military helicopter picked them up from the hotel roof before dawn. The trainees sat on their packs in the dusty cargo area behind the pilots. Their tropical uniform had lightweight trousers, long-sleeved blue tops without numbers or CHERUB logos, and hats with pull-down flaps to protect their necks and ears from the sun.

Large crawled around fitting each trainee with an electronic wristband. The plastic strap locked on so it could only be cut off with a knife.

'Don't remove the bracelet under any circumstances,' Large shouted over the noise of the rotor. 'In an emergency, unscrew the button on the side and press it down firmly. The helicopter is on standby and will reach you within fifteen minutes. If you get bitten by a snake press it right away.

'We'll be at the first drop point soon. Everything you could possibly need is in the backpacks. It's now 1000 hours. Each team has four checkpoints to reach within the next seventy-two hours. If you don't reach all the checkpoints before the target time, you have failed training and you'll have to start again at day one. Remember, this is not a training area. Mistakes down there will not get you punished, but they might get you killed. There are about a thousand things in the jungle that will kill you or make you so sick you'll wish you were dead.'

The helicopter stopped moving about ten metres off the ground. The side door slid open, filling the cargo area with sunlight.

'One and two, get out there,' Large shouted.

Mo and Shakeel dangled their feet over the side of the helicopter. Large threw out their backpacks. James saw the boys disappear, but couldn't see if they'd landed OK because of the dust blown up by the rotor. Large gave the pilot a thumbs-up and the helicopter moved on to the next drop. Kerry looked unhappy. Jumps put a strain on her weak knee. Gabrielle and Connor dropped, then they moved to the final position.

James looked down. There was wet sand covered with a few centimetres of seawater beneath him. He watched his pack splash down, summoned his courage and slid off the platform. They'd been trained how to jump safely. The trick was to collapse on to your side so the impact was absorbed by the whole body. If you landed too straight you risked smashing your hips or ankles. Too flat and your whole body smacked down hard, often breaking an arm or shoulder. James got the landing spot on. He scrambled up, splattered in wet sand but unhurt.

Kerry screamed as she hit the ground. James rushed over.

'You OK?' he asked.

Kerry got up slowly and took a few nervous steps on her weak knee.

'No worse than usual,' she said.

The helicopter flew off. James shielded his eyes from the swirls of sand. They dragged their backpacks out of the wash and up the beach. The sun made the white sand dazzle.

'Let's get into the shade,' James said.

They settled under a palm. James rubbed wet sand off his hands on to his trousers. Kerry found the mission briefing in her pack.

'Oh crap,' Kerry said.

'What?'

Kerry showed James a page of her briefing. It was in Japanese. James quickly found his own copy. His heart sank.

'Great, all in Russian,' James said. 'If I'd known my life would depend on it I probably would have paid more attention in class.'

They realised the two briefings were identical. James could understand half the Russian, Kerry was a bit better with the Japanese. By comparing the two versions and making a few assumptions they worked out almost everything.

There were a couple of sketchy maps, marked with the position of the first checkpoint, but no indication of where they had been dropped, or where they had to go after that. They had to reach the first checkpoint by 1800 and sleep there overnight.

'I suppose there'll be another briefing when we get there,' Kerry said.

James went through his backpack. There was tons more than they could carry. What was worth taking? Some stuff was obvious: machete, compass, plastic pool for collecting rainwater, emergency rations, empty water canteen, first-aid kit and medicine, water purification tablets, sunscreen, mosquito nets, matches, Swiss army knife. A roll of plastic bin-liners weighed next to nothing and had a dozen potential uses. There was also a tent with metal poles.

'Leave it,' Kerry said. 'It weighs a ton and we can make a shelter out of palms.'

They threw out a lot of heavy items: spare boots, umbrellas, cutlery, thick jackets. Some items were bizarre. They couldn't think of any use for a rugby ball or a table tennis bat. The paperback edition of *The Complete Works of Shakespeare* might have helped start a fire, but they decided it was too bulky. The packs were manageable once they were stripped out. James kicked through the stuff in the sand, hoping they hadn't left anything that would turn out useful.

'What now?' James asked.

Kerry held out the map and pointed to a mountain in the distance.

'The checkpoint is on the bank of the river,' Kerry said. 'That mountain over there is marked on the far side of the river so we walk towards it.'

'How far?'

'Impossible to tell. There's no scale on the map. We'd better move fast though, we'll never find the checkpoint once it gets dark.'

The plan was to follow the coastline until they hit the river mouth, then walk upstream to the checkpoint. Walking inland was more direct, but there would be no way to tell which direction to turn when they reached the river.

Walking on the beach was impossible because of the bright sun and heat. Instead they stuck to the jungle a hundred metres or so inland. The trees here formed a shady canopy filled with screeching birds. The only plants beneath the canopy were a few mosses and fungi. Apart from giant tree roots and the odd detour around a fallen trunk, the terrain was level and they made a steady pace.

It was a battle keeping insects off. Kerry had a screaming fit when a ten-centimetre-long millipede tickled up her leg. Its bite swelled into a red lump. Kerry reckoned it hurt worse than a wasp sting. After that they tucked their trousers into their socks.

Once an hour James and Kerry moved on to the beach. Trees nearer the beach were smaller and more spread out. They knocked down coconuts and, once they got the knack of opening them, gorged on the sweet milk. There were fruit trees everywhere, but they only ate fruits they recognised in case any were poisonous. After drinking they would put down their packs, kick off their boots and run fully clothed into the sea.

The biggest risk in the jungle doesn't come from predators but mosquitoes. The tiny flying insects stick their proboscis under the skin to drink your blood. The bite only leaves an itchy red mark, but the microscopic malaria parasites they spread from one victim to the next can make you sick or even kill you. The kids hadn't been given malaria tablets, so all they could do was cover up their skin, try to keep dry and wear insect repellent.

Mosquitoes are attracted to the smell of sweat, so after each dip James and Kerry put on dry clothes. They wrung out the sea-drenched clothes and draped them over their backpacks, knowing the heat would dry them before the next stop. After changing they smeared on mosquito repellent and sunscreen before heading back into the shade under the dense trees.

The coconuts and fruit juice were too rich to keep drinking in large quantities. The fruit acid gave James a sickly burn in the back of his dry mouth. By early afternoon thirst was slowing them down.

Sea water is too salty to drink and all they could find in the jungle were stagnant pools, swarming with mosquitoes and probably contaminated by animal urine. There was no chance of finding a spring unless they diverted towards higher ground inland. They wouldn't get fresh water until it rained. A storm was a certainty. The tropical heat evaporated so much water that by afternoon the skies were bursting with clouds. James and Kerry watched the sky gradually darken. When the first lightning cracked they ran to the nearest stretch of beach, inflated a plastic paddling pool and waited.

The rain was like nothing they'd ever seen. The first spots were the size of ping-pong balls. James tipped his head back to drink. When the sky opened properly it was like being under Large's fire hose. The water blasted holes in the smooth sand. James wrapped one arm over his face and struggled to hold the pool as it filled up.

Kerry sheltered their packs under a tree. They stuck their faces in the pool and gulped. When the shower finished there was enough in the pool to fill both canteens. Rather than risk going thirsty again they tipped the rest into a plastic sack and took it with them.

Once they reached the river mouth the going was easier.

The river was bordered by an unmade path, chewed up with tyre tracks. Kerry counted the bends in the river to find the checkpoint. They arrived an hour inside the deadline, feet killing them after walking for nearly seven hours.

The checkpoint was marked by a flag. A three-metre-long wooden boat with an outboard motor stood at the edge of the river under a tarpaulin. James lifted back the cover and was pleased to discover junk food, cooking pots and cans of fuel inside the hull. Then something moved. At first James thought it was just a trick of the light, but it moved again and hissed. James dropped the tarp and scrambled backwards.

'Snake,' he screamed.

Kerry rushed across from the riverbank.

'What?'

'There's a bloody enormous snake in that boat.'

'Are you sure?' Kerry asked. 'The manual says snakes are very rare out here.'

'The instructors must have put it there,' James said. 'I suppose if we pull off the cover it will slide away.'

'How big did you say it was?' Kerry asked.

'Huge,' James said, making a twenty-centimetre circle with his hands.

'There's no snake in Malaysia that big,' Kerry said, puzzled.

'You're welcome to stick your head in there if you don't believe me.'

'I believe you, James. But I don't think we should let it go, I think it was put there for our dinner.'

'What? That thing could be poisonous. How are we going to kill it?'

'James, were you listening during survival training? The only snakes that size are constrictors: snakes that crush you by wrapping themselves around you. It's not poisonous, but if we let it go what's to stop it coming into our shelter and squishing us in the night?'

'OK,' James said. 'You want snake for dinner. How do you plan to kill it?'

'Pull back the cover, poke it till sticks its head out then hack it off with the machete.'

'Sounds like fun,' James said. 'This is your idea, so I'm poking it and you're doing the hacking.'

'Fine,' Kerry said. 'But if I kill it, *you're* cutting all the guts out and cooking it.'

*

There was loads to do before dark. Kerry made a clearing near the river. James built a fire and butchered the snake, throwing the remains into the river to keep scavengers away.

Kerry put the finishing touches to a shelter made with giant palms as the sky blacked out. She protected the floor with the tarpaulin and lined the inside with mosquito nets.

They ate the snake meat with coconut and instant noodles. James made wire traps baited with leftover meat and pressed them into the river bed by torchlight, hoping they would have fish in them by morning. Well-fed but exhausted, they climbed into the shelter. They tried to translate the briefing while pricking the blisters on their feet with a sterile needle.

Reaching the second checkpoint involved a twenty-five kilometre cruise upstream, navigating a complicated network of channels and tributaries, until they reached a giant lake. The checkpoint was located aboard an abandoned fishing trawler on a mud bank near the far side of the lake. They had to get there by 1400. It would be an early start.

*

The temperature hardly dropped in the night. It was boiling in the shelter, hard to sleep. The wailing birds were harmless, but served as an eerie reminder that civilisation was a long way off. They kept a small fire burning to deter animals and insects.

James was awake to see dawn. Sun burst over the river and in minutes the dry ground was too hot to touch. James checked inside his boots for nasties before slipping them on his painful feet and walking to the river to check the traps. Two of the four traps had caught fish, but one fish had been ripped apart by a predator. James grabbed his catch and held it in the air until it stopped struggling. It was enough to make breakfast for the two of them.

Kerry built up the fire and began purifying river water. She boiled it for ten minutes, then dropped in chlorine tablets. James cooked the fish and picked a heap of mangoes. He saved one each for breakfast and loaded the rest into the boat.

The fish cooked quickly. He sliced one of the mangoes in half and called Kerry. 'Breakfast's ready.'

James couldn't see Kerry either near the camp or at the riverside.

'Kerry?' he called, slightly worried.

He pulled the steaming fish off its skewer and split it on to two plastic plates. Kerry emerged from behind some trees.

'I had to crap,' Kerry said. 'All that fruit I ate yesterday cleaned me right out.'

'Thanks for the detail, Kerry. I'm just about to eat.'

'Something occurred to me,' she said.

'What?'

'Remember we left *The Complete Works of Shakespeare* on the beach?'

'Yeah.'

'I think we were supposed to use it as toilet paper.'

23. CRUISE

James and Kerry stood on either side of the outboard motor with their palms pressed against the back of the boat. It had taken a succession of almighty shoves to nudge the bow over the edge of the riverbank.

'We should have emptied everything out first,' Kerry said, wiping a gallon of sweat off her face.

'Not worth it now,' James puffed. 'I think the next one will do the trick. Ready?'

They pushed the hull past its centre of gravity. It tipped forward and began sliding. A backwash ran up the shallow embankment, the muddy water swirling over the toes of their boots.

Water surged over the bow as the boat punched the water. For a second, they both thought it was going under. When the craft stopped rocking, the rim of the hull was only a couple of centimetres above the waterline. Each swell in the river splashed a drop more water over the side. The river wasn't deep enough to put the boat beyond rescue if it sunk, but the engine and half their equipment would be wrecked, along with any chance they had of making the next checkpoint.

Kerry waded in up to her waist and grabbed a can of fuel out of the boat, being careful not to lean on the hull. James positioned himself nearer to shore, took the can off Kerry and hurled it towards dry ground.

Once they'd pulled out their sodden packs, fresh water and fuel cans, the boat sat higher in the water.

'Phew,' James gasped. 'That was too close.'

'Brilliant time-saving idea,' Kerry said furiously. 'I told you we should have taken the stuff out.'

'You didn't,' James said.

James was nearly right. Leaving the stuff in the boat was his idea, but Kerry's objection had been on the basis that they wouldn't have the strength to push it, not that the extra weight might make the boat sink when it hit the water.

James grabbed a couple of cooking pots from the shore and they bailed out all the water. When the bottom of the boat was dry, they turned to the fuel and equipment scattered along the embankment.

'I suppose it's the same as yesterday,' Kerry said. 'What do we need? What can we leave behind?'

*

It made James queasy when he thought about how close they'd come to failing on the ninety-eighth day out of a hundred. Failing this close to the end of training would completely do your head in. The boat was now trundling upstream, against the current. Their sodden packs and equipment were spread over the deck, drying in the morning sun.

The river varied in size. Some places, shallow water stretched over thirty metres wide. They had to go slowly, with James leaning over the bow, shouting directions so that Kerry didn't ground the hull. When things got desperate, James used a wooden oar to nudge them away from disaster. In the narrow sections, the river was deeper and the currents stronger. Trees and bushes loomed over the water and they had to duck under low branches.

When it was plain sailing, Kerry would open up the throttle and the gentle put-put of the engine turned into a whine, accompanied by thick blue exhaust fumes. She stayed on the wooden bench near the outboard motor, making gentle adjustments to their course and marking off progress on her chart. James' job was more physically demanding; but even though the sun was fierce and working with the oar strained his shoulders, he preferred it to taking responsibility for navigating them safely through the dead ends and tributaries leading towards the lake.

*

It was the hottest part of the day when they broke on to open water. The lake ran further than you could see through the glaring sun. James abandoned his oar and sat on a fuel can in the middle of the boat, occasionally bailing out the water sloshing around the hull.

'Can you see the trawler anywhere?' Kerry asked. 'If I've read the Japanese in my briefing right, it's on a mud bank at the north end of the lake, marked by three red warning buoys.'

James stood up, squinting in a vain attempt to cut out the glare off the water. It was a pity they didn't have sunglasses.

'I can't see squat,' James said. 'We'll just have to keep cruising around the edge until we spot it.'

Kerry looked at her watch.

'We've got two hours until the deadline, but the sooner we get to this checkpoint, the longer we have to reach the next one.'

There was no other traffic on the lake. The fishing wharves, shacks and warehouses along the shoreline were desolate. There were well maintained roads and even a couple of telephone boxes, but no people anywhere. Red warning posts were hammered into the mud every few hundred metres. The writing was in Sarawak, so James couldn't read the words, but the yellow and black stripes and the bolts of lightning sent out a message that was clear in any language: stay the hell out of here.

'This is freaky,' James said. 'What's going on?'

'According to this map, they're building a giant dam upriver,' Kerry said. 'I guess this whole area is going to be flooded. Everyone's had to leave, which makes this the ideal spot for us to train without any locals sticking their noses in.'

James toppled backwards as Kerry put on full rudder and opened up the throttle. For a couple of nervous seconds he thought he was going over the side.

'For god's sake,' James shouted furiously. 'Tell me before you do that next time.'

The boat bounced over tiny waves towards the silhouette Kerry had spotted in the distance. The rusting trawler was about fifteen metres long, leaning on its side in the mud. Another boat, identical to their own, was tied to the metal deck rail.

Kerry bumped the boat into the mud bank. James hopped over the bow and tied it off.

'Anybody in there?' James shouted.

Connor stuck his head through a window.

'What took you two so long?' Connor asked.

The exterior of the boat was crusted in bird crap. They tried not to touch it as they crawled through a lopsided doorway into the bridge. There were masses of holes and hanging wires. Everything of value had been stripped for salvage, including the navigational equipment, the glass in the windows and even the seat cushion off the captain's chair. Connor and Gabrielle looked muddy and tired. They had maps and briefing papers spread out over the floor.

'How long have you been here?' Kerry asked.

'Twenty minutes or so,' Gabrielle said

'Any sign of Shakeel and Mo?'

'They'd been and gone before us,' Gabrielle said. 'They left the envelope from their dossier on the floor. Yours is over there as well.'

Kerry grabbed the padded envelope, tore it open and handed James the half written in Russian.

'So we're running last,' James said.

'We've already worked out most of ours,' Connor said. 'Maybe we can help you two catch up.'

James thought it was a kind offer, but Kerry took it the wrong way.

'We're quite capable of working it out for ourselves,' she said indignantly. 'We've all come from different camps and we're all going to different places. Maybe we had a longer first stint and a shorter second stint. I don't see how anyone could have done the journey much faster than we did.'

'We wasted a good half hour when we nearly sank the boat,' James said.

Connor laughed, 'How did you manage that?'

'It was loaded up when we pushed it off the embankment.'

'God,' Gabrielle gasped. 'You never would have got up the river if you'd flooded the engine.'

'I know you guys are on a different route to the final checkpoint,' Connor said. 'But if your briefing is the same as ours, it tells you to take a different route back towards the sea and get to the third checkpoint, less than fifteen kilometres away, by 2200.'

Kerry had done a quick skim through her briefing and nodded. 'Different route . . . Fifteen kilometres by 2200 . . . That's more or less what it says here.'

James broke into a grin. 'Fifteen kilometres in nine hours. That's easy.'

Connor, Gabrielle and Kerry all stared at him like he was a total idiot.

'Oh,' James said, when it clicked into place how dumb he was being. 'There's going to be some kind of catch, isn't there?'

24. FLASH

'We could play I spy,' James grinned, trying to break the tension as they headed downstream.

Kerry didn't appreciate his stab at humour.

'Shut your face, and keep your eyes open.'

'It'd better not be rapids,' James said anxiously. 'I couldn't handle that.'

'For the hundredth time, James, they won't send us down rapids. This is the wrong type of boat, we'd disintegrate in two seconds.'

James could cope with swimming in a pool, or a fairly still section of river, but the idea of a getting thrown into raging water without a life-jacket scared him like mad.

Things were easier for Kerry. She had the map spread over her lap and the boat to steer. All James had was twitchy fingers and a brain packed with unpleasant thoughts about whatever awaited them.

'Maybe nothing will happen,' James said. 'Maybe the trick is to make us think something horrible is going to happen when nothing really is.'

'A few seconds' warning could make all the difference,'

Kerry said sharply. 'Be quiet and concentrate.'

When the skies darkened for the afternoon rains, James stretched the tarp over their stuff and lashed the paddling pool on top, to capture a fresh supply of drinking water. The violent rain made it impossible to navigate safely. As soon as it started, Kerry pulled into the embankment. James tied the boat to a branch and they snuggled under the tarp until it stopped.

Before setting off again, they quickly changed into dry clothes and put on more insect repellent. James' body was a mass of angry red bites.

'This is getting out of hand,' James said. 'Even my bites have got bites on them. Do you think we could get malaria?'

'Maybe,' Kerry shrugged. 'But there's nothing we can do, so what's the point dwelling on it?'

*

An hour after the rain, they spotted a light pulsing in the trees up ahead.

'Did someone just take our photo?' James asked.

Before Kerry could answer, an electronic squeal broke out under the top of the outboard motor. She cut the throttle and reached into her pocket for her utility knife.

'Is that some kind of warning buzzer?' James asked.

Kerry shrugged. 'I'll have a look under the engine cover, but I'm no mechanic.'

She undid two plastic catches with the blade of her knife and lifted off the plastic faring.

'Jesus,' Kerry gasped. 'I think we've got a bomb on board.'

Not quite believing his ears, James scrambled down the boat and looked at the metal cylinder duct-taped to the engine block. James recognised the timing switch from Mr Large's weapons and explosives class. Unlike the ones you see in the movies, it didn't have a clock saying how long you had until the bomb exploded.

A wire ran from the timer and out of the engine, alongside the rubber hose linking the outboard motor to the auxiliary fuel tank. James had noticed the wire before, but he'd never given it a thought.

'Did the flashing light set off the timer?' James asked.

'It must have a photo trigger,' Kerry said. 'Remember when Mr Large showed us how you could set up a motion detector and a photographic flashgun to set off a bomb? It's ideal if you want something to explode when it reaches a certain position.'

'We could die,' James said.

'Don't be dopey,' Kerry said. 'They're not gonna kill us. It's probably just a tiny bit of explosive that will blow a hole somewhere in the . . .'

The centre of the boat suddenly ruptured upwards. James got the first whiff of burning as the shockwave threw him into the water.

He blacked out for a few seconds. The next thing he knew, he was floating in the river, surrounded by smoke and chunks of wood. His ears were ringing and petrol in the water was stinging his eyes so badly that he couldn't open them.

'Kerry,' James shouted desperately as he thrashed about. 'Please . . . Kerry.'

The petrol was burning his throat and he felt like he was choking.

'Kerry, I can't see.'

'Stand up,' she shouted.

James could barely hear her voice over the ringing in his ears. Her hands slid under his armpits.

'Put your feet down.'

James felt a surge of relief as his boot touched the sandy river bottom, just over a metre below the surface.

'I thought I was gonna drown,' James gasped, as Kerry steadied him. 'I thought it was deep.'

Kerry led James by the hand towards a boulder sticking out of the water. His eyes felt like they were on fire. All he could see were blurs of light.

'Sit there a minute,' Kerry said. 'Keep blinking as much as you can.'

'Are your eyes OK?' James asked.

'Fine,' Kerry said. 'I jumped off the back of the boat and swam away from the debris.'

Kerry had spotted her backpack tangled in a bush on the riverbank and waded to its rescue. By the time she got back, the stinging had died down enough for James to keep his eyes open for a couple of seconds at a time.

'Give us some drinking water,' James said.

Kerry looked inside her sodden pack.

'There isn't any,' Kerry said. 'My canteen was out on the deck.'

'How far do you reckon it is to camp?'

'Three kilometres,' Kerry said. 'We'll have to swim it.'

'I've never gone more than a hundred metres,' James said warily.

'I'll make you a float out of the backpack.'

'It's a long way,' James said. 'Couldn't we could walk along the bank?'

Kerry pointed at the tangle of branches and leaves hanging over the edge of the river.

'You'll never crawl three kilometres through that lot in a million years.'

'I suppose,' James said.

'You'll swim better without boots. Give them to us and I'll tie them around my waist.'

'Seriously, Kerry, I don't think I'm up to this.'

As James pulled off his soggy boots, Kerry found the roll of plastic bin liners in her pack. She stripped out everything but absolute essentials: knife, map, insect repellent and compass. Then she got one of the bin liners and blew it up until it was big enough to fill the backpack.

'We'll both hold on to the straps and float downstream,' Kerry said. 'Just kick gently, the current will do most of the work for us.'

*

Training was supposed to push you to the limit. They could starve you, humiliate you and work you until you were begging to quit; but at the end of the day, they didn't want to kill you. The route downriver had been carefully selected by the instructors, so that the danger to anyone who could swim was minimal. The water was never more than a few metres deep, the currents were moderate and the banks were rarely more than twenty metres apart.

That still left water snakes and sharks to worry about. The sharks were only little, but they looked perfectly capable of nipping off fingers and toes, and it wasn't a nice feeling when one swam up close, showing off rows of teeth. James panicked a couple of times when he lost sight of Kerry and grazed his thigh on a jagged rock, but they reached the checkpoint as it was turning dark, with three spare hours before the 2200 deadline.

They were desperate for water and James had a couple of leeches stuck on his back, but apart from that, they felt OK as they staggered out of the water. The checkpoint was on an open stretch of land that had been cleared out by a logging company. There was a tin shed that had once served as sleeping quarters to half a dozen loggers. Ever wary of traps, James nervously poked his head inside the metal door and was surprised to find Mr Speaks sitting in a hammock doing a crossword.

'Good trip?' he asked, pushing his ever-present sunglasses down his nose and giving them the once-over.

'Not bad,' Kerry gasped.

Their eyes fixed on a giant bottle of mineral water, glinting on the window ledge.

'Help yourself,' Mr Speaks said. 'There are fresh packs and equipment for both of you, plenty of food in the ice box and there's a tank of rainwater on the roof that links up to the shower head if you want to use that. After that, I suggest you read your briefings and try to grab some sleep before the helicopter picks you up. It's the only rest you'll get in the next thirty-eight hours.'

'Aren't we sleeping here tonight?' James asked.

'If you want to reach the fourth checkpoint, you're not sleeping anywhere, either tonight or tomorrow night. The chopper picks you up here at 2200 and drops you on a footpath 188 kilometres from your final checkpoint. That's the exact distance from London to Birmingham and you've got until 1000 hours on the final day to get there. If you fall asleep, you'll never make it.'

25. JELLY

Going 188 kilometres in thirty-six hours works out at slightly over five kilometres an hour. That's about normal walking pace, but you had to stop to eat and drink, to check you weren't veering off an overgrown footpath in the middle of the night, and when the pain got so bad that you couldn't take another step. It wasn't just James' and Kerry's legs that hurt from the walking, their whole bodies ached with tiredness.

Precautions went out of the window. Sweaty and covered in insect bites, there wasn't time to put on dry clothes or insect repellent. Their canteens were empty. They didn't have time to stop and collect rainwater, so they had to drink water trapped on giant palms and leaves. James and Kerry dumped most stuff and carried one light pack between them, with nothing in it but a torch, compass and maps.

They reached the final checkpoint less than half an hour before the deadline. As they staggered towards a wooden building, Gabrielle and Shakeel ran out and gave them fresh water.

'We were getting worried about you two,' Shakeel said. 'You cut it pretty close.'

The building was locked, but there was a tap on the outside. Kerry filled a rusty bucket, threw half at James and poured the rest over her head.

The trainees were too tired to do anything but crash out on the shady side of the building, waiting for the instructors to turn up.

'I hope we don't get malaria,' James said, scratching the bites on his neck.

'It's not a malaria zone,' Gabrielle said, matter-of-factly.

'What makes you say that?' Kerry asked.

'I knew we were going to the jungle and they didn't give us malaria tablets before we left,' Gabrielle said. 'That made me think. The night we were in the hotel I sweet-talked the guy behind the front desk and he let me use the Internet. No malaria in this part of Malaysia.'

'Smart thinking,' Kerry said. 'You could have told us.'

'I told James in the helicopter before the drop,' Gabrielle said. 'Same time I told Shakeel.'

'You didn't,' James said defensively.

'She told both of us. I saw you nod,' Shakeel said.

'Oh,' James said. 'It was noisy. I thought you were saying good luck, so I nodded.'

Kerry punched James on the arm.

'Dumbo,' Kerry said. 'You know how much time we could have saved not changing clothes so often? And I was worried to death we were going to get sick.'

'I'm *sorry*,' James said. 'There's no need to start hitting me.'

'Idiot,' Kerry laughed. 'I can't wait to get you in that dojo.'

'What?' James asked.

'Remember our deal after you stomped on my hand? The day after training stops I get to fight you in the dojo.'

'I thought you were joking,' James said.

Kerry shook her head. The others were all laughing.

'She'll mash you,' Connor said. 'Can we watch?'

'Who says you're both gonna make it through training?' Mo asked. 'It's a four-day course and it's only the morning of the fourth day. I bet the instructors will have something else up their sleeves.'

*

The instructors led them inside. The trainees each had a chair with two buckets in front of it. Speaks covered their eyes with a mask. Smoke tied their ankles to the frame of the chair.

'Welcome to the ultimate test,' Large said. 'Before we can make you six tired little bunnies into operatives, we need to be sure you can cope with the worst thing that could ever happen to you. Number eight, what do you think is the worst thing that can happen on a mission?'

'We could be killed,' Kerry said.

'Death would be easy by comparison,' Large said. 'I was thinking about torture. What happens if you're captured on a mission? You know something, and some people will do anything to get that information from you. Don't expect mercy because you're children. They'll still slice your toes off. Rip out your fingernails or teeth. Wire you up and blast those sweet little bodies with a thousand volts of electricity. We hope it never happens to any of you, but we have to know you can take the pain if it does.

'This test will show us if you've got guts. It will last one hour. You each have two buckets in front of you. Miss Smoke is placing a jellyfish in the buckets to your left. Its tentacles have hundreds of microscopic spikes; each one packs a dose of poison. A few minutes after contact your skin will start to burn. Within ten minutes the pain is extreme. A few years ago an operative jumped a fence, misjudged the jump and ended up with a metal railing stuck in her back. Afterwards she said it was less painful than this test.

'The bucket on your right contains an antidote to the poison. Within a few seconds of touching the antidote the pain will begin to decrease. After two minutes the pain will be almost gone.'

James felt his head being grabbed.

'Open wide,' Smoke said.

Smoke shoved a rubber plug into James' mouth. It was held in with an elastic strap that wrapped around the back of his head.

'You are being given mouth guards,' Large continued, 'because it is not unknown for people in extreme pain to bite off their own tongues. You will each place your hands in the bucket, knuckles touching the bottom, for thirty seconds. The jellyfish will grab you. You will feel nothing at first. You will have to tolerate the pain for one hour. Anyone placing their hands in the antidote before one hour has elapsed has failed the entire course. Due to the toxicity of the poison you may not retake the test. Any questions?'

None of the trainees could talk with the plugs in their mouths.

'OK then. Put your hands in the bucket.'

James leant forward, feeling blindly for the bucket. He'd

thought he had the measure of training but this was scary. What if the pain was so bad he couldn't help sticking his hands in the antidote? Ninety-nine days of training for nothing.

The water was tepid. He felt something light and rubbery wrap itself around his wrists.

'Take them out,' Large said. 'If the jellyfish sticks, slide it off gently.'

James lifted his hands and pushed off the gripping tentacles. He sat up straight and waited for the pain to start.

'Two minutes,' Large said. 'It should start hurting soon.'

James' hands started feeling hot. Sweat was running down his forehead, building up along the rim of the eye mask. He didn't wipe it off in case it spread the poison to his face.

'Five minutes,' Large said.

The heat in James' hands was gone. He wondered if he'd imagined it. Kerry sounded like she was struggling with her mouth guard. It looked like the pain had got to her sooner.

'Ten minutes. You all seem to be holding up quite well. But I can see some twisted faces,' Large said.

Kerry shouted out:

'What would be the point of an animal stinging you if it didn't hurt straight away?

Large ran over to Kerry.

'Get that guard back in now.'

James could hear Kerry squealing as they shoved the plug back in her mouth.

'The next person who spits out their guard has to go two hours without touching the antidote,' Large shouted.

Kerry had made James think. There still wasn't any pain

from the jellyfish and what Kerry said made sense. What good would an animal sting do if it only hurt its enemy *after* it had been eaten or attacked?

'Fifteen minutes,' Large said.

'Two hours without the antidote?' Gabrielle shouted. 'Why not make it ten? Tell you what, I'll stick my head in the bucket.'

James couldn't see the commotion, but heard water running and a plastic bucket rolling across the floor.

'This is totally bogus,' Kerry said calmly.

James was sure it was a trick now. He pulled down his eye mask. Kerry had plucked a harmless white squid out of her bucket and was holding it up for inspection. James took off his mouth guard.

'OK people,' Large said. 'Glad you all enjoyed my little joke. Don't forget to untie your ankles before you stand up.'

Kerry was looking at James with a massive grin.

'Were you scared?' James asked.

'I thought it was a trick,' Kerry said. 'Why put the eye masks on us unless it was fake?'

'That never occurred to me,' James said. 'I was too scared to think straight.'

'Look under your seat,' Kerry said.

Something had been put under everyone's chair while they were blindfolded. James undid his ankles and picked up the present. It was grey. He unfurled it and looked at the winged baby sitting on the globe and the letters: CHERUB.

'Beauty,' James shouted.

Kerry was already putting her T-shirt on. James pulled off his blue shirt for the last time. When his smiling head popped through the neck hole, Large was standing in front of him holding out his hand. James shook it.

'Congratulations, James,' Mr Large said. 'You two worked well together.'

It was the first nice thing James had heard him say.

26. BACK

You weren't supposed to wear CHERUB uniform off campus for security reasons, but James wore his grey shirt all the way home hidden under his tracksuit. He woke up on the plane and peeked down his chest to make sure it wasn't a dream. Kerry was asleep in the next seat. James could see the grey tail of her CHERUB shirt hanging out the back of her jeans.

Everyone was in a good mood. Even the instructors, who got a three-week holiday before the next batch started training. Kerry stopped acting tough and surprised James by turning into a normal eleven-year-old girl. She told James she couldn't wait until her nails and hair grew back. She even bought a pen and card in the airport gift shop and got everyone to sign it for the instructors. James told her he thought it was dumb. He remembered that Large had been happy to get them thrown off the course to win a bet. It might be Large's job to make trainees suffer, but he seemed to enjoy it as well.

*

The van from the airport left them at the training building. The new operatives picked a few things up from their lockers and changed out of their casual travel clothes into uniform. James kept one of the filthy blue shirts with the number seven on as a memento. Kerry was holding out a key.

'Help me move my stuff?' Kerry asked.

'Where to?' James asked.

'The main building. Red shirts live in the junior block.'

The instructors wanted them all out of the training area fast so they could get home.

Callum was waiting for his twin outside the training compound. His arm was out of the sling. James felt sorry for Callum having to start training again. James gave him a friendly shove.

'You'll get there,' James said. 'No worries.'

Connor put his arm round his brother.

Kerry was running ahead, excited, 'Come on, James.'

James went after her to the junior block. He hadn't been there before. It was the middle of the morning so everyone was in class. Kerry's room had kiddies' furniture: a plastic desk, bunk beds and a big wooden trunk with My Toys painted on the side. The wardrobe had a green teddy on the doors.

'What a divine room,' James said, trying not to laugh.

'Shut your pie hole,' Kerry said, 'and carry.'

She had packed everything before training started.

'You must have been confident,' James said.

'If I failed this time, I was going to leave CHERUB. You don't have to become an agent if you don't want to.'

'Where do you go if you leave?' James asked.

'They send you to a boarding school. In the holidays you stay with a foster family.'

'You really would have left?'

'I promised myself,' Kerry said. 'That's why I got so upset on Christmas Day when you got us in trouble.'

James stayed quiet. He didn't want the conversation straying towards their agreement to fight in the dojo. They packed Kerry's stuff on to one of the electric buggies that staff used around campus.

'Where's your new room?' James asked.

Kerry showed him the number on her key ring.

'Sixth floor,' James said. 'Same as me, we're practically neighbours.'

They walked back to Kerry's old room and did a final check to make sure nothing was left behind. Kerry had tears streaking down her face.

'What?' James asked.

'This has been my room since I was seven,' Kerry sobbed. 'I'll miss it.'

James didn't know where to look.

'Kerry, the rooms in the main building are about fifty times cooler. You've got your own bathroom and computer and everything.'

'I know, but still . . .' Kerry sobbed.

'Give over,' James said. 'Can I drive the buggy, I've never done it before?'

*

The buggy was overloaded with Kerry's stuff and felt like it might tip over on a bump. The bell had gone for a lesson change. Kids were going between the buildings. A few of Kerry's friends stopped the buggy and congratulated them on passing basic.

Amy burst out of a door.

'Hey,' she shouted.

James hit the brake.

'Congratulations,' Amy said, leaning into the buggy and hugging both of them.

'You taught James to swim, didn't you, Amy?' Kerry asked.

'Yes,' Amy said.

'What's with all this?' Kerry asked, flapping her arms about in a wobbly front crawl.

'I don't swim like that,' James said peevishly.

Amy and Kerry both laughed.

'I only had three weeks to teach him,' Amy said. 'He's getting more lessons.'

Amy copied Kerry's impression of James' swimming and they both laughed even harder. James would happily have thumped them, only they could both easily batter him.

'Anyway, James,' Amy said. 'I've been looking for you everywhere. I've got something to show you.'

'What?' James sulked.

'James, I'm sorry,' Amy said. 'I'm your teacher so I shouldn't laugh at you. I promise I'll cheer you up if you come with me.'

James climbed out of the buggy.

'Where to?'

'You look really fit, James,' Amy said.

James wasn't sure if she was saying it to make him feel better.

'Are you OK to move that stuff on your own?' Amy asked Kerry.

Kerry nodded. 'Someone will help.'

Amy led James back towards the junior building.

'What is this?' James asked.

'I wasn't sure you'd make it through training first time,' Amy said. 'I'm impressed.'

James smiled. 'Another three or four compliments and I'll forgive you for what you said about my swimming.'

They walked into the education block in the Junior building. It looked like any ordinary primary school, with little kids' paintings on the walls and plasticine models on the window ledges. Amy stopped by a classroom door.

'There,' Amy said.

'What is this?' James said. 'Can't you just tell me?'

Amy pointed at the door. 'Have a look.'

James stuck his face up to the glass. Inside, ten kids sat on the floor chanting phrases in Spanish. The red shirts wore the same uniform as everyone else, only with trainers instead of boots.

'See it?' Amy asked.

'No,' he said impatiently. 'I don't even know what I'm looking for.'

Then it hit James like a bomb.

'Shit,' he said, grinning.

He knocked on the classroom door and walked in.

'Shit,' James said again, loudly, in front of the teacher and all the kids.

The Spanish teacher looked furious.

'My sister,' James said.

He couldn't think of anything else to say and stood with his mouth open.

'Excuse our interruption, Miss,' Amy said calmly. 'This is

Lauren's brother, James. He's just finished basic training and was wondering if you could excuse her.'

The teacher flicked her hand at Lauren. 'Go on, just this once.'

Lauren scrambled up from the carpet and jumped into James' arms. She was heavy. James stumbled back a couple of paces before he got his balance.

'Hola hermano grande,' Lauren said, grinning.

'What?' James asked.

'It's Spanish,' Lauren said. 'It means hello, big brother.'

*

Amy had a lesson to go to. Lauren walked James to her room.

'I can't believe this,' James said, grinning uncontrollably.

The best he'd hoped for was being able to see Lauren a couple of times a month. Having her walking along in front of him in a CHERUB uniform was too much to take in.

Lauren's room was like Kerry's old one, except everything was newer.

'Can't believe this,' James said again, slumping on to a beanbag. 'I just cannot believe this.'

Lauren laughed. 'So you're pleased to see me?'

She got Cokes out of her fridge and threw one at James.

'I mean how . . . I mean . . .' James giggled. 'Why are you here?'

'Because Ron punched me in the face,' Lauren said.

'He did *what?*' James said, shocked.

'Punched me. I had massive black eyes.'

'That arsehole,' James shouted, kicking out at the wall.

'They never should have let him look after you. I knew something like that would happen.'

Lauren squeezed up next to James on the beanbag.

'I hate Ron's guts,' Lauren said. 'Mrs Reed asked what happened to my eyes when I went to school the next day.'

'You told her the truth?' James asked.

'Yeah. She got the police. They saw all the smuggled cigarettes when they went round to arrest him; so they busted him for that as well.'

James laughed. 'Serves him right.'

'I got taken to Nebraska House,' Lauren said. 'Nobody could find where you'd gone. I got really upset. I thought I was never gonna see you again.'

'So how long did it take them to find me?' James asked.

'I was at Nebraska House three days. Fourth day I woke up here.'

James laughed. 'Freaks you out, doesn't it?'

'They wouldn't let me speak to you. Mac took me to see you though. I watched you and that Chinese girl doing Karate. She was killing you. It was so funny.'

'Did you have to do the tests to get in?'

'No,' Lauren said. 'They're only if you're older and you're going straight into training.'

'That's so jammy,' James said. 'The tests half killed me.'

Lauren whacked him across the arm. 'Leave my hair alone.'

James was winding it around his fingertips. She hated him doing that.

'Sorry,' he said. 'Never even realised I was doing it.'

'I'm on a special programme,' Lauren said. 'Loads of

running, swimming, Karate and stuff, so I'm really fit when I start basic training.'

'You're ten this year, aren't you?' James said.

Lauren nodded. 'September. I'm trying not to think about basic training.'

'But you think it's cool here, don't you?' James asked. 'You're happy?'

'It's superb,' Lauren said. 'There's always loads to do. Did I tell you, they took us skiing? I got this bruise on my arse the size of a CD.'

James laughed. 'I can't imagine you on skis.'

'And you want the best news?'

'What?'

'They found drugs and tons of stolen stuff in Ron's flat. Guess how long they put him in prison for?'

James shrugged. 'Five years?'

Lauren pointed a finger at the ceiling.

James grinned. 'Seven years?'

'Nine,' Lauren said.

James punched the air.

27. ROUTINE

They had a week off after training finished. James went to check out Kerry's room now she'd unpacked. He wasn't happy.

'My new timetable is mental,' James said. 'Six hours of lessons every day. Two hours' homework a night and two hours of lessons on *Saturday* morning. That's forty-four hours a week of schoolwork.'

'So?' Kerry said. What did you do at your old school?'

'Twenty-five hours at school and a few hours' homework, which I never did. There's no way I'm doing all that homework.'

'Better get used to scrubbing floors then,' Kerry said.

'For not doing homework?'

'Yep. Or cleaning out the kitchen, mowing lawns, wiping windows. Repeat offenders get toilets and changing rooms. The reason you do all those lessons is you miss loads when you're on missions and you have to catch up. They're not all lessons anyway, some of them are sport and teaching and stuff.'

'That's the other thing,' James said. 'I've got to teach maths to little kids.'

'All grey and dark shirt kids have to teach. It gives you a sense of responsibility. Amy teaches swimming. Bruce teaches martial arts. I've got to do Spanish with the five- and six-year-olds. I'm really looking forward to it.'

James slumped on Kerry's bed.

'You sound exactly like Meryl Spencer, my handler. I can't believe you're happy about all this work.'

'It's not much more than I had as a red shirt.'

'I wish I'd never come here.'

'Stop being a drama queen,' Kerry said. 'CHERUB gives you a great education and a cool place to live. When you leave here you'll speak two or three languages, have qualifications coming out of your ears, and be set for life. Think where you'd be now if you hadn't come here.'

'OK,' James said. 'My life was down the toilet. But I hate school. It's so boring I want to smash my head up against the wall half the time.'

'You're lazy, James. You want to sit in your room with your stupid Playstation going blip, blip, all day. You said yourself you were gonna end up in prison the way you were carrying on. If you get bored in a classroom, how would you like eighteen hours a day in a cell? And take those filthy boots off my bed before I bust your head open.'

James put his feet down.

'Playstation is not a waste of time,' he said.

'You want the best reason why you should work hard?'

'What?'

'Lauren. She loves you. If you do good, she'll do good. If you muck up and get thrown out, she'll have to make a choice between staying with you and staying at CHERUB.'

'Stop being right,' James said. 'Everyone in this place is clever, level-headed, and I'm always wrong. I hate all of you.'

Kerry started laughing.

'It's not funny,' James said, starting to smile.

Kerry sat beside him on the bed.

'You'll get used to it here, James.'

'You're right about Lauren,' James said. 'I have to think about her.'

Kerry moved a bit closer and rested her head on James' shoulder.

'Beneath that dumb exterior you're a good person,' Kerry said.

'Thanks,' James said. 'So are you.'

James put his arm round Kerry's shoulders. It felt like the natural thing to do, but two seconds after he did it his brain was spinning. What did this mean? Did he want Kerry to be his girlfriend, or was it just that they'd been through so much together in training? He'd showered with her and slept next to her, but until training ended James had barely noticed that Kerry was a girl. Not a dream girl like Amy, but not bad either. He thought about kissing her cheek, but chickened out.

'The room looks nice,' James said, scratching for something to say. 'All your pictures and stuff. I'll have to get some. My walls are white.'

'I was thinking,' Kerry said. 'We should renegotiate our deal.'

James had avoided Kerry for two days, hoping she'd forget.

'How?' he asked.

'Friday night,' Kerry said. 'Take me to the cinema. I pick

the movie. You pay the bus fare, the cinema tickets, hot dogs, popcorn, Pepsi and whatever else I want.'

'That's gonna be easily twenty quid for the two of us,' James said.

'That kid you're friendly with, Bruce.'

'What about him?'

'He broke his leg once,' Kerry said. 'When we were eight.'

'He said it broke in nine places.'

'He exaggerates. I only broke it in seven places.'

'You?' James said.

'Snapped it like a twig. Kicked him in the head for luck.'

'OK,' James said. 'Cinema, my treat.'

*

Kyle arrived back from a mission Friday morning with sunburn and a sack-load of fake designer gear. James followed Kyle into his room. It was freakishly neat. Even inside the wardrobe Kyle's clothes were all in dry cleaner's bags, above a row of boots and trainers with shoe trees in them.

'Philippines,' Kyle said. 'I'm back in Mac's good books.'

'What happened?' James asked.

'Confidential. Here, these were supposed to make you feel better when you got kicked out of training.'

Kyle tossed over a pair of fake Ray Ban sunglasses. James slipped them on and posed in the mirror.

'These are cool, cheers,' James said. 'Everyone thought I'd fail.'

'You would have,' Kyle said. 'If you hadn't got Kerry as a partner, Large would have chewed you up in a week.'

'You know Kerry?' James asked.

'Bruce does. He said you had a chance once he found out Kerry was your partner. She cost me ten quid.'

'You bet against me getting through training?'

'No offence, James, but you're a spoiled brat and a total whiner. I thought I'd make an easy tenner.'

'Thanks,' James said. 'Good to know who your friends are.'

'You want to buy a fake Rolex watch?' Kyle asked. 'Same as the real thing, four quid each.'

*

The whole crowd went to the cinema Friday night. Bruce, Kyle, Kerry, Callum, Connor, James, Lauren and a few other kids. James was happy being part of a big group, all messing about and slagging each other off. The film was a twelve. The rest of them could pass for twelve, but they had to smuggle Lauren through the emergency exit.

James worried about what would happen with him and Kerry, especially with everyone else watching. He sat down. Kerry sat with one of her girlfriends a few seats away. James was relieved, but disappointed as well. The more he thought about it, the more he realised how much he liked her.

*

Four days into his timetable James realised he could live with it. In his old life he'd always got up late, sat in class mucking about all day then come home and either played Playstation, watched TV, or hung out on the estate with his friends. Most of the time he was bored. The routine at CHERUB was hard but it never got dull.

You weren't allowed to slack off in lessons. Every class had ten kids or fewer, which meant as soon as you stopped working the teacher was on your back asking what the problem was. Pupils were picked by ability not age. Some classes, like James' advanced maths group, had kids who were fifteen and sixteen. His Spanish, Russian and self-defence classes were with six- to nine-year-olds.

Punishments were psycho if you got out of line. James swore in history and got a ten-hour shift repainting the lines in the staff car park. Next day his palms and knees were blistered from crawling around on tarmac.

Most days had a PE session. After training, James was really fit. Two hours' running around felt like a warm-up. They started with circuit training inside the gym. The second half was always a game of football or rugby. James liked it best when they played Girls versus Boys, which usually went a bit mad, with insane tackles and punch-ups breaking out everywhere. What the girls lacked in strength they made up for with cunning and gang tactics. Boys always scored most goals, the girls edged the carnage.

After lessons James got an hour's rest before dinner, then it was a scramble to do homework, before rushing off to extra martial arts training. James volunteered because he was ashamed that half the nine-year-olds at CHERUB could beat him in a fight. On the nights he didn't have martial arts he'd go to the junior building and hang out with Lauren.

At the end of each day James was worn out. He'd sit in his bath and watch whatever was on TV through the doorway before drying off and collapsing into bed.

28. DETAIL

It was two months since training. Kerry had done a mission, come back, and gone on another. She was so superior about it, James could have thumped her. Gabrielle was in Jamaica. Connor had disappeared with Shakeel. Bruce was away for days at a time. Kyle went off one morning promising that this mission was going to earn him his navy shirt. James was still at CHERUB and felt like a lemon.

Amy was the only one who hadn't been away. She spent hours on the eighth floor in one of the Mission Preparation rooms. James still got to swim with her four times a week. He was good now. Four hundred metres front crawl, keeping his body under the water and tipping his face to the side to breathe without lifting his head out of the water. He never got scared and Amy said his stroke was almost perfect.

*

James and Amy were putting their uniforms back on. All they'd done was swim lengths together, then sit on the poolside and talk for a bit.

'That was our last lesson,' Amy said.

James had known it was coming for ages, but that didn't

stop him feeling bad. He liked hanging around with Amy. She was funny and always gave good advice on stuff.

'Is your mission starting?' James asked, sitting down to lace up his boots.

'In a couple of weeks,' Amy said. 'I need to devote all my time to it.'

'I'll miss having lessons with you. You're a brilliant teacher.'

'Thanks, James, you're sweet. You should go swimming with Kerry when she gets back. You swim as well as she does now, probably better.'

'She'll be too busy rubbing my nose in it about her mission experience. I saw Meryl Spencer again yesterday, she still says there's no mission for me.'

'I can confess now,' Amy said. 'I had you suspended from mission activity.'

'Because of swimming?' James asked.

Amy went in her swimming bag and got out a plastic card. James had seen people swipe them in the lift to get up to the secure part of the main building where missions were planned.

'This is yours,' Amy said, handing it across.

James broke out smiling. 'I've got a mission with you?'

'Yes,' Amy said. 'I put in some work on this job before you even came here. When you arrived I realised we looked alike. Same colour hair, similar build. I knew you could pass as my little brother. We set you up with Kerry so you had the best chance of passing training. I wasn't happy when I heard you started a fight with her and nearly got thrown out.'

'Don't remind me,' James said. 'I was so dumb.'

'You're lucky Kerry didn't retaliate. All she had to do was flip you up and break your arm and you would have been out of training. Nobody would have blamed her either.'

'I was on top of her,' James said. 'She couldn't get up.'

Amy laughed, 'If you got on top of Kerry it's because she let you. She could squash you like an egg under her boot if she wanted.'

'Is she that good?' James asked.

Amy nodded. 'She must like you a lot to let you off like that.'

*

The eighth floor was exactly like the accommodation floors below: a long corridor with rooms off either side. Entering the Mission Preparation room meant swiping your security card and staring into a red light while the blood vessels in your retina were scanned for identification.

After the hi-tech entry, James expected something flash inside: a map of the world with a bank of computer screens above it or something. It was actually a bit of a dump. Old computers, chairs with sponge bursting out of cushions and metal cabinets covered with stacks of files and papers. The only good feature was the view over campus.

Ewart Asker stuck his hand out for James to shake and introduced himself as the Mission Controller. He was in his twenties, CHERUB uniform, bleached hair with black roots and a stud through his tongue.

'First mission, James,' Ewart said. 'Worried?'

James shrugged. 'Should I be?'

Ewart laughed. 'I'm nervous, James. This baby is complicated. You wouldn't normally get something like this until you'd done a few easy missions, but we needed a twelve-year-old boy who could pass for Amy's brother, and you're the best we've got.

'There's a ton of stuff to learn. I've cut your school schedule back. Amy has written a mission dossier for you. Don't be afraid to ask questions. The mission starts in about ten days.'

James pulled up a chair and opened the briefing:

CLASSIFIED

MISSION BRIEFING FOR JAMES ADAMS
DO NOT REMOVE FROM ROOM 812
DO NOT COPY OR MAKE NOTES

(1) Fort Harmony
In 1612 King James made a fifty square kilometre area near the Welsh village of Craddogh into common land. The charter allowed people to graze animals and build a small shelter on the land. By the 1870s everyone who lived on Craddogh Common had moved to the village to work in the coal mine. Nobody lived on the land for the next ninety-seven years.

In 1950 Craddogh Common was made part of West Monmouthshire National Park. In 1967 a small group of hippies led by a woman called Gladys Dunn settled on Craddogh Common. Gladys named the settlement Fort Harmony. They kept chickens and built wooden shelters, claiming they could do so under the 1612 charter.

At first the National Park tolerated the settlers, but numbers grew, and within three years about 270 hippies lived in a hundred or so ramshackle buildings. The National Park Authority began legal action to evict the hippies. After two years the High Court decided that the king's charter ended when Craddogh Common was made part of the National Park. The court gave the hippies one week to pack up and leave.

The hippies would not go. Police began destroying huts and arresting the hippies in the winter of 1972. The size of the community soon dropped to less than fifty, but this hard core was determined to stay.

(2) The Battle
The Fort Harmony residents fled every day, allowing police to demolish the shelters. They returned and made new shelters every night. The hippies dug underground tunnels. They also dug traps for the police to fall into.

In one incident a series of nets were hidden under leaves. When police moved in to demolish huts, the trap was sprung. Three policemen were left swinging in nets twenty metres above ground. The hippies tied off the nets and ran away. A fire engine came to the rescue, but got bogged down in thick mud. It was seven hours before firemen found a way to cut down the nets without their cargo crashing to earth. Pictures of the policemen in the nets made most newspapers the following day.

Newspaper coverage of the battle attracted dozens of new residents to Fort Harmony.

On 26 August 1973, police launched an all-out effort to destroy Fort Harmony. Three hundred police were drafted from across Britain. Television and newspaper journalists watched. Roads were blocked to stop supporters reaching Fort Harmony. Police destroyed the camp and arrested anyone who resisted. By late morning only twenty hippies remained, all barricaded in underground tunnels. Police decided entering the tunnels was too dangerous and waited for the hippies to come out for food and water.

At 5 p.m. a section of tunnel collapsed under a passing police car. Police rushed to grab a pair of legs sticking out of the earth. Joshua Dunn, aged nine, son of the founder of Fort Harmony, was pulled out of the mud. While two officers held the wriggling boy by his ankles, a third officer hit him over the head with a truncheon. A photographer captured the brutality. Pictures of the boy being stretchered into an ambulance made the television news. This incident caused a surge of public support for the hippies.

The crowd tying to break through blockades and reach Fort Harmony grew to more than a thousand. By midnight the police were exhausted. There were no reinforcements. By 3 a.m. the following morning police lines were broken. At sunrise on 27 August, over 700 supporters were camping in the mud around Fort Harmony. A stream of cars and vans brought wood and supplies to build new shelters. The hippies left the tunnels and began rebuilding their homes.

Next morning the photograph of police beating nine-year-old Joshua Dunn made the front page of every newspaper in Britain. The police announced they would withdraw and destroy the camp at a later date. The police made a plan. A thousand officers would be needed to remove all trace of Fort Harmony while successfully blockading the surrounding countryside. The police and National Park Authority didn't have enough money to pay for such a massive operation, so nothing further was done.

(3) Fort Harmony Today

Thirty years later Fort Harmony still exists. The residents live a harsh life, without running water or electricity in their homes. Camp founder, Gladys Dunn, is now seventy-six. She wrote a bestselling autobiography in 1979. Her three sons – including Joshua, who suffered brain damage from the police assault – still live on site, as do many of her ten grandchildren and twenty-eight great-grandchildren. The camp has about sixty permanent residents. In warmer months Fort Harmony swells to as many as two hundred, mostly students and backpackers who think Gladys Dunn is a hero.

(4) Green Brooke

By 1996 the nearby village of Craddogh was in crisis. The coal mine was closed. Over half the population was unemployed and the village population had fallen from 2,000 residents in 1970 to less than 300. Run-down houses and mountains of black coal waste meant tourists didn't stop at Craddogh on their way to Fort Harmony or the National Parks.

Because of the high local unemployment, the National Park allowed Green Brooke Conference Centre to be built on part of Craddogh Common. Green Brooke opened in 2002. It is enclosed by a five-metre-high fence with video cameras and electrified razor-wire along the top. The Centre hosts conferences and training courses. Facilities include a 765 room hotel, 1200 seat auditorium, gym, spa, and two golf courses. There is parking for 1000 cars and thirty helicopters.

Many residents of Craddogh and Fort Harmony work in Green Brooke as receptionists, cooks and cleaners.

(5) Petrocon 2004

In late 2003 Green Brooke announced the most prestigious event in its brief history. Petrocon takes place in May 2004. It is a secretive three-day meeting of two hundred oil executives and politicians. The media is kept out. Among the guests will be oil ministers from Nigeria and Saudi Arabia and the chief executives of every major oil company. The two most important guests will be the United States Secretary of Energy and the Deputy Prime Minister of Great Britain.

Security will be handled by the Diplomatic Protection Branch of the police, with MI5 and a small unit from CHERUB.

(6) Help Earth

At the end of 2003 a series of bombs were posted to United States Congressmen and members of the British Parliament who support the oil industry. Four workers in the US Congress building suffered injuries. Help Earth claimed responsibility. A month later a French oil company executive working in Venezuela was killed by a car bomb. Help Earth again claimed responsibility.

Shortly before its first attacks, Help Earth sent letters to the editors of several international newspapers, stating its aim to 'Bring an end to the environmental carnage wreaked on our planet by the international oil companies and the politicians who support them.' It then added, 'Help Earth! is the desperate cry of our dying planet. Time is running out. We are prepared to use violent means in the battle to save our environment.'

Peaceful environmental groups are at pains to distance themselves from Help Earth and have helped investigators compile a list of likely terrorist suspects. Despite this, nobody involved with Help Earth has been identified, although several environmental campaigners with a violent history are under suspicion. Four of these suspects are current residents of Fort Harmony.

The limited information on Help Earth suggests an attack on Petrocon 2004 is likely. The size and nature of the attack is unknown. It could range from a small bomb destroying a car or helicopter, to a device capable of killing hundreds.

Any Help Earth members planning terrorist action at Petrocon 2004 will probably attempt to make links with Fort Harmony residents for the following reasons:

a) Many Fort Harmony residents are veteran environmental campaigners.

b) All Fort Harmony residents have a good knowledge of the local area.

c) Many Fort Harmony residents have worked inside Green Brooke and can provide terrorists with information on operations and security.

(7) The Role of CHERUB

MI5 already has informers and undercover agents within the environmental movement. However M15 wants extra agents at Fort Harmony in the build-up to Petrocon 2004.

Any new adult residents arriving at Fort Harmony before Petrocon will be suspected of being undercover police or MI5 operatives. The chances of them getting useful information are small. Therefore it has been decided that two CHERUB operatives posing as relatives of Cathy Dunn, a long-standing member of the Fort Harmony community, will have the best chance of a successful undercover mission. Children will not be suspected of being intelligence agents, and they should mix easily with other members of the community.

29. AUNTIE

James reckoned he now knew more about Fort Harmony than anyone, including the people who lived there. He'd read Gladys Dunn's autobiography and three other books, as well as seeing tons of press cuttings, videos and police files. He'd memorised the names and faces of every current Fort Harmony resident and loads of regular visitors. James also read the criminal records and MI5 files on anyone likely to be involved in the terrorist group Help Earth.

James' undercover name was Ross Leigh. His job was to hang out with kids at Fort Harmony, picking up gossip, sticking his nose where it didn't belong and reporting anything suspicious to CHERUB.

James had a mobile to call Ewart Asker. Ewart was staying at Green Brooke for the duration of the mission. James' other equipment included a digital camera, his lock gun and a can of pepper spray that was only for an emergency.

Amy was his sister, Courtney Leigh. Her job was to befriend Scargill Dunn, the seventeen-year-old grandson of Fort Harmony founder Gladys Dunn. Scargill was a loner who had dropped out of school and washed dishes in the kitchen at Green Brooke.

Scargill's twenty-two-year-old twin brothers, Fire and World, had both served short prison sentences for attacking the chairman of a fast food chain. MI5 believed Fire, World and a couple called Bungle and Eleanor Evans were the residents of Fort Harmony most likely to be part of Help Earth.

*

Cathy Dunn had briefly been married to Fire, World and Scargill's dad, some years before they were born. Since then, Cathy had lived alone at Fort Harmony. Like most residents she grew food and kept a few chickens, but it wasn't enough to survive. She did odd jobs when they cropped up: cleaning, fruit picking. Sometimes Cathy sold information to the police.

There were always a few dodgy people at Fort Harmony. If a drug dealer or a runaway kid turned up, Cathy would walk to Craddogh and call from the village phone box. Half the time the police weren't interested in what Cathy had to tell them. If they were, they only paid ten or twenty quid. Maybe fifty if it was a drug dealer and they caught him with a lot of stuff.

Cathy wasn't comfortable being a snitch, but sometimes it made the difference between having enough to buy a bottle of gas for the heater and freezing in her hut.

After Petrocon was announced the police got more interested in what Cathy had to say. The value of information went up. Cathy got at least thirty pounds every time, and they wanted to know everything that was going on at Fort

Harmony. Who came, who went, if anyone did anything suspicious, if there was an argument. Cathy got a taste for the money. She soon had a roll of notes stashed in a baked bean tin.

MI5 made Cathy an offer: £2,000 to let a couple of undercover agents stay with her at Fort Harmony in the weeks before Petrocon. Cathy didn't like the idea much; she'd lived alone for thirty years. MI5 offered more money until Cathy gave in.

*

James, Amy and Ewart walked into the Bristol Travelhouse. It was a basic hotel attached to a motorway service station. Cathy Dunn was waiting in her room in a cloud of cigarette smoke.

'My name is Ewart, these two are Ross and Courtney.'

Cathy sat up on her bed. She looked half drunk and tons older than in all the pictures James had seen of her.

'Who the hell are you?' Cathy asked.

'We spoke on the phone,' Ewart said. 'You're going to be looking after Ross and Courtney until the conference.'

'You've had me stuck in this hole for three days,' Cathy said. 'Now you turn up with two kids. If this is your idea of a joke, I'm not laughing.'

'You made a deal with us,' Ewart said. 'This is the deal.'

'I agreed to let two undercover agents stay with me. Not look after two kids.'

'Ross and Courtney are agents. Make their breakfast and send them to school for a few weeks, it's not brain surgery.'

'The government uses *children* to do its dirty work?' Cathy asked.

'Yes,' Ewart said.

Cathy laughed. 'That's absolutely appalling. I won't do it.'

'You already took our money,' Ewart said. 'Can you afford to pay us back?'

'I went to Greece, and I spent some money tidying up my hut.'

'Looks like you're stuck with us then.'

'What if I refuse to take them?' Cathy asked 'What if I went to the press and told everyone you're using kids to spy on people?'

'If you go to the press, they'll just think you're some flaky old hippy,' Ewart said. 'Nobody will believe a word out of your hole. Even if you get someone to believe you, you signed the Official Secrets Act before you took the money. You'd be looking at ten years in prison for releasing classified information.'

Cathy looked upset. 'I've always helped the police, now you treat me like dirt.'

Ewart grabbed Cathy's jumper. He lifted her up and knocked her against the wall.

'You don't break deals with us,' Ewart shouted. 'There's six months' work gone into this operation. You're getting eight grand to look after these kids for a few weeks. If that's being treated like dirt, you can treat me like dirt whenever you like.'

James was shocked seeing Ewart flip out. Until now the mission had felt like part of a competition to do better than Kyle, Bruce and Kerry. Now it felt real. People could get blown apart by bombs or end up in prison for the rest of their lives. James suddenly didn't feel up to the job. He was a twelve-year-old kid who should be going to school and messing around with his mates.

Amy noticed the scared look on James' face. She put a hand on his shoulder.

'Stand outside if you want to,' Amy whispered.

'I'm fine,' James lied.

Amy gave Ewart a shove.

'Calm down. Leave her alone,' Amy said.

Ewart backed off, giving Amy a filthy look. Cathy sat on the bed. Amy passed Cathy a cigarette. Amy had to light it because Cathy's hands were shaking.

'Sorry about Ewart,' Amy said. 'Bit of a short fuse. You OK?'

Cathy nodded.

'Listen Cathy,' Amy said gently. 'We get up, go to school, hang out at Fort Harmony. Then we go away again. It's the easiest money you'll ever make.'

Cathy shook her head, 'It's all a bit of a shock, that's all.'

Amy smiled, 'It always is. Nobody gets told we're kids until the last minute.'

'How can I explain that I've got you two living with me?' Cathy asked, taking a deep puff on her cigarette.

'Niece and nephew,' Amy said. 'Remember your sister?'

'I haven't seen her in twenty years,' Cathy said. 'She wrote a few times.'

'Remember what your sister called her kids?' Ewart asked, voice back to normal.

Cathy worked it out.

'Ross and Courtney,' she said.

We tracked down your sister,' Ewart said. 'She lives in Scotland. Still married. The real Ross and Courtney are fine. But here's your story:

'A week ago, you got a letter. Your sister is going through a nasty divorce. You rushed to London to meet her. She couldn't cope with her kids, especially Ross who's been expelled from school. You got on well with the kids, so you offered to look after them at Fort Harmony until your sister gets her life back on track.'

Ewart handed Cathy a set of car keys.

'Land Cruiser,' Ewart said. 'Big four wheel drive. It's a couple of years old. Worth about ten grand. Tell everyone it's your sister's car. If you look after the kids and the mission works out, we won't be asking for it back.'

*

The four of them made their way down to the hotel lobby.

'You better go in the toilet with me,' Ewart said. 'It's a long drive down to Wales.'

'I just went,' James said.

Ewart gave James a look. James realised Ewart wanted to speak to him. The toilet was deserted.

'You OK, James?' Ewart said, unzipping his jeans. 'You looked a bit off-colour when I grabbed Cathy.'

'Why'd you go psycho with her?'

Ewart smiled. 'Ever heard of good cop bad cop?'

'They do it on TV,' James said. 'Is that what you and Amy just did?'

'If Cathy's not sure whose side she's on, you and Amy wouldn't be safe. Once I realised Cathy was getting stroppy, I had to be the bad cop and scare her. Amy's job was to be the good cop. Amy defended Cathy when I threatened her, then calmed her down.'

James smiled. 'So Cathy's afraid of what might happen if she doesn't do what we want her to do, but at the same time she thinks Amy is her friend.'

'Exactly, James.'

'You could have told me when you arranged to do it.'

'We didn't arrange it. Amy knew what to do when I started getting rough with Cathy. Amy's brilliant at picking up stuff like that.'

'What if Cathy caused any more problems? Would you really hurt her?'

'Only if the mission depended on it and I had no other choice. Sometimes we have to do bad things to make missions work. Remember when you sneaked to London before training?'

'Sure,' James said. 'Smashing up that big house.'

'The security guards on the gate got gassed by MI5. What do you think happened to them after they woke up?'

'How should I know?'

'They got sacked for sleeping at work. They won't get another security job with that on their records.'

'So what happened to them?'

'We ruined their lives,' Ewart said. 'Hopefully they got jobs doing something different.'

'We didn't help them or nothing?'

'No. We couldn't without risking the secrecy of the mission.'

'That's terrible,' James said. 'How can we do that to people?'

'We were trying to get info about a man selling weapons

to terrorists. The weapons could kill hundreds of people, so we decided it was OK if two people lost their jobs.'

'And it's the same with scaring Cathy,' James said. 'People could get killed.'

'Like they say, James: you can't make an omelette without breaking eggs.'

*

Cathy enjoyed driving James and Amy in the Land Cruiser; blasting down the M4, testing all the buttons and gadgets. Amy was up front. James laid flat across the back seat. Cathy and Amy chatted like old pals.

When they stopped for petrol Cathy bought a Jefferson Airplane CD with some housekeeping money Ewart had given her. She put it on full blast. Amy and Cathy puffed one cigarette after another. James stuck his coat over his head to escape the noise and smoke.

James sat up when they got off the motorway. He was impressed with the green fields and hills with sheep dotted over them. They stopped in Craddogh for cigarettes and groceries and reached Fort Harmony soon after 3 p.m. Half a dozen grimy kids ran towards the four wheel drive as it climbed uphill to Cathy's hut. James knew the name and age of every kid.

Cathy's ex-husband, Michael Dunn, and his brother, Joshua, walked towards the car. Michael thumped the bonnet.

'Nice wheels, Cathy,' Michael said. 'You win the lottery or something?'

James got out. His trainer was swallowed by mud. The camp looked a mess, flaking paint and windows stuck up with tape. James decided he was going to hate living here.

Amy squelched to the back of the car and grabbed two pairs of wellies.

'My niece and nephew,' Cathy said.

James sat in the car and pulled on his wellies. Joshua Dunn held out a gloved hand. James shook it.

'Come soup,' Joshua stuttered.

Amy and Cathy were heading towards a big hut. James and Joshua followed. About fifteen people were inside. Chickens and a huge pot of vegetable soup cooked over an open fire.

'Vegetarian?' Joshua asked.

James shook his head.

Joshua fetched James a bowl of soup and some chicken. There were cushions and beanbags along the walls, but the kids all sat cross-legged near the fire. James sat with them. He ate a couple of spoonfuls of soup. It tasted pretty good. Then he looked at his hands. They were filthy, but the other kids, who were all ten times dirtier, scoffed the chicken with bare fingers.

A hand rested on James' shoulder. It was Gladys Dunn.

'A bit of dirt won't harm you, boy,' she laughed.

Gladys looked her seventy-six years, but the outdoor lifestyle kept her lean and she moved well for her age.

A five-year-old girl sitting beside James ran her tongue up her filthy palm and held it out for James to see. James grabbed a bit of chicken and stuffed it in his mouth. The girl smiled.

*

A group led by Michael Dunn built an extension on Cathy's hut for James and Amy to sleep in. It was impressive watching the community work as a team.

First they laid out paving slabs to raise the floor off the ground. The floor was chipboard wrapped in plastic. The framework was timber. Michael Dunn had obviously built loads of huts. He sawed each piece without measuring and never made a mistake. Others took the wood as soon as it was cut and knew where each piece fitted.

Thick corner posts were bashed into the ground. Trusses were nailed between them. Hardboard was nailed to either side of the frame, with shredded paper packed in the cavity as insulation. A hole was made in one side and a recycled window was fixed in. When it got dark Cathy turned on the Land Cruiser headlamps. Once the roof was on two boys were lifted up. They crawled around nailing down a layer of waterproof felt. Inside James helped seal the gap between the floor and the walls with grey putty.

After it was finished Amy got a rug from the Land Cruiser and set out sleeping bags and pillows. Cathy found a small paraffin heater. Michael Dunn said he would paint the outside in the morning. Finally, James and Amy were left alone.

30. CAMP

The new shelter was quite cosy once you got used to the wind blasting the outside. James' sleeping bag rested on a foam camping mattress. He couldn't get comfortable. Amy snored. James shouted at her twice. The third time, Amy said she'd punch him if he woke her up again. James stuck a pillow over his head.

*

James woke at 3 a.m., busting for a pee. He was used to walking two steps to his bathroom at CHERUB. It was tougher here. He couldn't find his torch, so he had to put on jeans in the dark, then make his way blindly through the main part of the hut, stepping around Cathy who was sprawled over a futon. James felt for the door, where all the wellies were lined up. He wasn't sure which pair was his, so he stuck on the first pair he found and stepped into the blackness.

There were portable toilets on site, but James couldn't find them in the dark so he wandered into the nearest group of trees. He wiped mud off his hands on to his trousers, undid his jeans, and started to piss. Something shrieked and brushed against his leg. James jolted. He was peeing on one of the chickens that roamed around camp.

He turned away, but that was into the wind, so his urine got blown all over his jeans. James stumbled back, tripped over the hysterical chicken and hit the mud. There was no way to get clean. He wondered why this type of thing never happened to spies in films.

*

Amy was up, and she'd slept fine. She stuck her foot over James' face to wake him up.

'Shower day, Ross,' Amy said.

James burst into life.

'Get that stink off my face,' James said, pushing Amy's foot away. 'Who's Ross?'

'You are, stupid,' Amy whispered.

'Sorry,' James gasped, realising where he was. 'I *must* remember that.'

'There's a rota for hot water,' Amy said. 'You get one shower a week. Friday is boys.'

'One shower a week?' James said. 'With all this mud.'

'How do you think I feel? I've got to wait four days and I don't exactly smell great now.'

Cathy showed him where the wash hut was. It was narrow, with a reservoir of rainwater on the roof. Every morning a gas boiler heated enough water to run the showers for ten minutes. If you missed out, you stank for another week. James dashed to the shower hut and stripped. There were eight boys under the water, sharing bars of soggy white soap and messing about. Mums stood outside, telling the little ones to get a move on. The water was barely warm. James rubbed soap in his hair as the hot ran out. The others knew better and scrambled off. James had to rinse with a bucket of freezing rainwater. He sprinted back to Cathy's hut wearing wellies and a big towel.

Cathy was cooking bacon and eggs on a portable gas stove. It smelled good and there was plenty of it.

'Do you kids drink coffee?' Cathy asked. 'It's all I've got.'

James didn't care what it was as long as it was warm. He drank two cups and stuffed down four rashers of bacon and two runny fried eggs, mopping the yolk off his plate with white bread.

'I've got to go enrol Ross in school,' Cathy said. 'Then I'll go to Tesco. Anything you two want?'

'Mars bars,' James said. 'What about enrolling Courtney?'

'After you went to bed I met this guy Scargill,' Amy said. 'He said he'd try and fix me a job at Green Brooke.'

James was impressed Amy had made such a fast attachment to Scargill. He was also miffed that she'd got out of school.

'I guess you'll start school on Monday, Ross,' Cathy said. 'Friday night here is usually a laugh. Everyone turns up after dark. We build a bonfire and play music and stuff.'

*

Amy stayed in the hut making phone calls to Ewart Asker, telling him the change in her plans and getting him to sort out the paperwork she needed to get a job. James spent the morning exploring.

There were about fifty buildings at Fort Harmony. They varied – from the main hut, with space for thirty and its own supply of electricity, down to rat holes fit only for storing junk. Between huts were chicken coops, vegetable patches, strings of washing and a range of battered cars. There were rusty vans everywhere, though most had no wheels and rested on bricks.

Everyone James met had grubby clothes and long tangled hair. The older men had beards, most of the younger ones had daft goatees and piercings everywhere. They all acted friendly and everyone asked James the same questions about how he ended up here and how long he was staying. By the time he'd met five people James was sick of repeating himself.

Before long James realised he had a tail: three-year-old Gregory Evans. He was the son of Brian 'Bungle' Evans and his partner Eleanor. MI5 thought they might have links to Help Earth.

Gregory followed James at a distance. When James looked around Gregory would crouch down and cover his face with his hands. It turned into a game. James stopped walking and looked around every few steps. Gregory was giggling. After a bit Gregory got up his courage and start walking beside James. James remembered he had a couple of Maltesers in his pocket and gave them to the toddler. After stuffing them, Gregory ran off. He stopped, turned, and shouted at James.

'Come to my house.'

James felt odd being bossed around by a three-year-old. They ran about a hundred metres, Gregory leading James by the hand.

Gregory sat down on the doorstep of a smartly painted hut and pulled off his wellies.

'Come in,' Gregory said.

James put his head in the door. The hut had room for six to sleep. The floor was painted bright orange, with shocking green walls and a purple ceiling. Plastic dolls hung everywhere. James noticed they were mutants, with blood painted on their faces and freaky punk hairstyles.

'Who's that?' Bungle asked, with an American twang.

James was embarrassed, standing in a strange doorway on the orders of a three-year-old.

'Sorry, Gregory brought me here,' James explained.

'What you sorry for, boy?' Bungle said. 'We're a community. Come in, get your boots off. Gregory's always dragging kids in here. You want hot milk?'

James pulled his wellies off and stepped inside. It was wonderfully warm, but smelled like farts and sweat. Eleanor lay on a mattress. She had nothing on but knickers and a Nirvana T-shirt stretched over a pregnant belly.

Gregory gave his mum a cuddle. Bungle made introductions, asked James the same questions as everyone else, then handed him a mug of hot milk.

'Unzip your tracksuit top, Ross,' Bungle said.

James was mystified but did what he was asked.

'Reebok,' Bungle said triumphantly.

'What?' James asked, confused.

'He hates people who wear clothes with trademarks on,' Eleanor explained.

'What's wrong with what I'm wearing?' James asked.

'I don't hate the people,' Bungle said. 'I hate the clothes. Look at yourself, Ross. Puma jacket, Nike tracksuit, Reebok T-shirt, even his socks have got a logo on them.'

'Just ignore Bungle,' Eleanor said. 'He thinks people wearing labels on their clothes is a sign that they can't think for themselves.'

Bungle rushed over to a bookshelf and passed James a book called *No Logo*.

'Give your brain a bit of exercise,' Bungle said. 'Read it. If you want we can discuss it when you bring it back.'

James took the book.

'I'll look at it,' James said. 'All my stuff is Nike and that. At my old school you got your head stuck down the toilet if you wore unfashionable clothes.'

'For god's sake, Bungle,' Eleanor said. 'He's a kid. He's not interested in that stuff.'

James didn't care what some hippy thought about his clothes, but the book gave James an excuse to come back and hang around a prime suspect, so he put it in his pocket and said thanks.

'Ross, ask him about the dolls before he bores you to death talking about the evils of world capitalism,' Eleanor said.

Bungle sounded annoyed. 'You handed out leaflets with us, Eleanor.'

Eleanor laughed. 'Ross, in principle, I support fair wages for people in poor countries. I want to help save the environment. I want Bungle and his pals to save the world. But I'm eight months pregnant. The baby presses on my insides, so every half hour I waddle through two hundred metres of filth to go sit on a stinking portable toilet. Gregory is driving me crazy. My ankles are swollen like beach balls and I'm half terrified the car we borrowed is going to break down on the way to the hospital when I go into labour. I'd happily surrender all my principles for a comfy bed in a private hospital.'

James sat on the floor and sipped his hot milk.

'The dolls are excellent,' he said. 'Did you make them?'

'That's my living,' Bungle said.

Bungle pulled one of the dolls off the ceiling and dropped it in James' lap. It was the torso and head of an Action Man. but it wore a tutu and had skinny ballerina legs glued on. The hair was spiky purple. One hand was cut off and the stump was painted with fake blood.

'Cool,' James said.

'I buy the dolls at jumble sales and boot fairs. Then I mix all the bits up and make weird costumes and stuff out of scraps.'

'How much?' James asked.

'Depends where,' Bungle said. 'Cardiff market, they're all poor, nobody will pay more than ten pounds. If I get a stall at Camden in London you can sell them for eighteen a throw. When it's packed out in the summer you can shift sixty dolls a day. One time I sold eighty-four.'

'One thousand, five hundred and twelve quid in a day,' James said. 'You must be loaded.'

'You some sort of human adding machine?' Bungle asked.

James laughed. 'Kind of.'

'Takes over an hour to make each one. Painting all the fiddly bits does your eyes in. You want a doll, Ross?'

'They're cool,' James said. 'I haven't got any money though.'

'Take one,' Bungle said. 'Maybe you can do us a favour. Look after Gregory for a couple of hours one day or something.'

*

It was an unwritten Fort Harmony rule that there was a free evening meal in the main hut for anyone who wanted it. Gladys Dunn bought vegetables from local farmers with the money she earned from her book. Joshua spent his afternoons preparing the vegetables and making either stew or a curry. Everyone eating together was what made Fort Harmony a community rather than a bunch of separate families.

James ate with the kids when they got out of school. Michael Dunn collected a vanload of scrap from a local dump. All the kids helped pile up old doors and bits of furniture to make a bonfire for the evening festivities. James tried to make friends with Sebastian and Clark Dunn. They were ten and eleven-year-old brothers; cousins of Fire, World and Scargill. The Dunns were a close family, and Sebastian and Clark were James' best chance to pick up all the gossip.

31. NIGHT

James found Amy and Scargill sitting on Amy's bed smoking. Scargill looked like a geek: spindly arms and legs, greasy black hair tied back in a pony-tail. He wore a kitchen uniform from his job at Green Brooke.

'It stinks in here,' James said, stepping in through the hole between the old and new parts of Cathy's hut.

'This is my little brother, Ross,' Amy said. 'He's a whiny little shit.'

'You're *harsh*, Courtney,' Scargill said, laughing.

James was hurt. They had to act like brother and sister, but he didn't see why she had to be nasty. He was also jealous: Scargill was getting to spend all his time with Amy.

'Why are you here, Ross?' Amy asked.

'This *is* my room as well,' James said.

'Scargill and me want privacy, so get what you came in for and sod off.'

'Did you get a job?' James asked.

'I'm an attendant at Green Brooke spa,' Amy said. 'Four days a week.'

James started rummaging through his stuff.

'What do you want, Ross?' Amy asked.

'My mobile,' James said. 'I was gonna see how Mum is.'

'Take mine, it's charging up in the car.'

'Thanks, Courtney,' James said.

*

James sat in the front seat of the Land Cruiser and made a call to Ewart Asker.

'Hey, James, how's it going?' Ewart asked.

'Not bad, Amy's pissing me off.'

'She with Scargill?'

'Permanently,' James said.

'That's her job, James. She's got to get as close to him as she can.'

'She told him I was a whiny shit.'

Ewart cracked up. 'That gives Scargill a sign that she prefers him to her kid brother. She doesn't mean it.'

'Scargill must be in heaven,' James said. 'Scrawny little nerd and he's got Amy all over him.'

'You've got a bit of a soft spot for Amy, don't you?' Ewart asked.

James' instinct was to deny it.

'A bit,' he admitted. 'If I was older I'd ask her out. How did you know?'

Ewart laughed. 'You get this glazed look in your eyes when she's in the room.'

James panicked. 'What? Is it that obvious?'

'I'm joking, James,' Ewart said. 'So how's Cathy?'

'Seems OK now,' James said.

'How did you get on with Sebastian and Clark Dunn?'

'Bad,' James said. 'They're weird kids. Tough-looking and

smelly. They talk to each other as if you're not even there. None of the other kids hang out with them much either.'

'Keep trying, but don't force it. Any other news?'

'I got one good break,' James said. 'I made friends with Gregory Evans, Bungle's son. I spent nearly an hour with them. Bungle gave me a book called *No Logo* to read.'

'Good book,' Ewart said. 'Read it. Go and see him, pretend you don't understand something and use it as an excuse to hang around.'

'There's not much about Bungle on file, is there?' James said.

'No. He's been seen with all the bad guys, but he's never been arrested. There are over a thousand people called Brian Evans in Britain; we don't know which one he is. We don't even know exactly how old he is or where he comes from.'

'He sounds American,' James said. 'He's got that twangy sound in his voice. I think they call them rubbernecks.'

'What's a rubberneck?'

'Like in the movies. Cowboy types, kind of stupid, he sounds like one of those.'

Ewart laughed. 'You mean a redneck?'

'That's it,' James said. 'He sounds like a redneck.'

'That's useful to know. I'll get the Yanks to see if they have anything on him. What we need is for you to get in Bungle's hut, take some pictures and have a rummage through any paperwork you can find. But don't take any risks to make it happen. If you're seen taking pictures for no good reason it will blow your cover.'

'Bungle said they might ask me to keep an eye on their little boy when they go out.'

'That would be an ideal opportunity, specially if the kid falls asleep. Are you sure they'd trust someone your age to look after him?'

'Bungle suggested it,' James said.

'Don't sound too eager, they might think it's odd. Anything else?'

'That's all I can think of,' James said.

'Keep in touch, James,' Ewart said. 'It sounds like you're doing a grand job.'

'Thanks, bye Ewart.'

*

It was past eleven and people were still arriving. They came in groups of four and five, pulling booze, food and firewood out of cars. Portable CD players competed with didgeridoos, tom-toms and guitars. The crowd was mostly teenagers and twenty-somethings: students from Cardiff and kids from the local villages, with a few old hippies who had turned up every Friday since the year dot.

James wandered. He felt awkward. Younger kids rushed around chasing and fighting, older ones drank beer and snogged. James didn't fit well with either group. He moved away from the party into the forest. He could hear bangs from a clearing in the distance. As James got closer he worked out it was the sound of an air pistol. The kids were Sebastian and Clark Dunn. They were freaks. If James wasn't on a mission he would have steered clear, but it was his job to make friends. He decided to have another go.

Sebastian and Clark vanished before James reached the clearing. There was a bird on the ground, cooing loudly and struggling in the mud. It was hard to see what was wrong in the dark, but the bird was in a bad way. James crouched down. He wondered if he should bash the bird with a rock to put it out of its misery.

Sebastian bolted out from the trees. He landed on top of James and tried to pin him, but James was too strong. James elbowed Sebastian in the stomach. Clark came out to help with the ambush. He was almost as tall as James and probably heavier. Clark bashed James over the head with a heavy torch. The brothers managed to get James under control.

Clark pressed the torch head into James' eye and clicked the bulb on. Squeezing his eyelid tight didn't stop the light from burning his eye. James was worried. Hopefully they would just rough him up, but who knew how crazy these kids were? If James yelled nobody would hear over all the noise from the party.

'Why are you following us, scum?' Clark asked.

'I wasn't,' James said. 'I just came this way.'

Clark grabbed a chunk of James' hair and tugged his head out of the mud. James felt Sebastian, who was sitting on his legs, shift his weight slightly. James kicked up both legs, hitting Sebastian in his back. Sebastian yelled out and tumbled off. Now his legs were free, James thrashed about and tried to release his arms, which were pinned to his sides by Clark's thighs.

'I'll knock you out,' Clark said.

Clark punched James in the head. James put all his strength into lifting his stomach off the ground, making space under himself to slide out his hands. He scrambled from under Clark and stood up. Clark ran at James. James realised that months of getting hammered by black belts at CHERUB was about to pay off. Without the element of surprise, Sebastian and Clark didn't have a chance.

James waited until Clark got close. He sidestepped, kicked Clark full force in the stomach, punched him in the mouth and finished off stamping him behind the knee so he smacked into the ground. Sebastian looked angry but didn't fancy joining in. Clark looked pleadingly at James from his knees, hoping his beating was finished.

'I don't want to hurt you,' James said. 'Just say you quit.'

Clark scrambled up, gasping for air. He was hurt, but a smile came on to his face.

'I've battered kids heaps bigger than you,' Clark said. 'Where'd you learn to fight?'

James found a tissue in his pocket. He gave it to Clark to wipe the blood off his split lip.

'Self defence classes,' James said. 'Back in London.'

Clark turned to his brother.

'They were serious punches, Sebastian.'

'You have to put your whole body into it,' James said. 'Starts at the hips. If you get the technique right it's eight times harder than a normal punch.'

'Let him hit you in the guts, Sebastian,' Clark said. 'I bet you double over.'

'I don't want to hit him,' James said.

'We hit each other to keep tough,' Clark said. 'If I hit him in the guts he doesn't even flinch.'

Sebastian stood with his hands behind his back ready to take a hit.

'I'll hit his shoulder,' James said.

'You can hit my guts,' Sebastian said. 'I can take it.'

'In the arm first,' James said. 'Then I'll do it in your guts if you still want me to.'

Sebastian turned so his side was facing James. James didn't want to have to hit him in the stomach, he knew it could do serious damage, so he gave Sebastian his hardest shot in the arm. Sebastian stumbled sideways and screamed out in pain, clenching his upper arm with his hand. Clark was wetting himself laughing.

'I told you it was hard,' Clark said.

Sebastian tried not to show the pain. James felt bad for hitting him so hard.

All this time the pigeon was still thrashing about in the mud. James looked at it.

'What happened to it?'

'Shot it with the air pistol,' Clark said.

'Wasn't dead,' Sebastian said. 'So I cut one of its wings off with my pen knife.'

'You guys are lunatics,' James said, grimacing.

'Better hope the shot kills you,' Clark grinned. 'If it doesn't it's torture time.'

'Can't you put the poor thing out of its misery?' James said.

'If you want me to,' Sebastian said.

Sebastian walked towards the bird. It didn't have much life in it. Sebastian pressed his heel into the bird. It let out a final desperate noise as its bones were crushed. Sebastian had a big smile on his face.

James realised he'd made friends with a couple of seriously twisted kids.

32. GIRL

Sebastian, Clark and James went to the main hut to feed. Guests had brought meat to barbecue, as well as the cold dishes laid out on a long table. Joshua Dunn was serving vegetable curry. James wasn't mad on curry, but it was good stuff after being out in the cold. They took the food outside to the bonfire. A few dozen people sat on waterproof sheets around the fire. Sebastian and Clark found Fire and World and sat beside them.

'Hey, little psychos,' Fire said.

'Hey, jailbirds,' Clark said, referring to his cousins' spell in prison.

Fire and World were non-identical twins, with plaited hair and pierced eyebrows.

World looked at James. He sounded drunk. 'Care to tell me what your sexy sister sees in our baby brother?'

James shrugged. 'She's not fussy. Snogs anything with a pulse.'

'What was that?' Amy said.

James hadn't noticed her sitting a few metres away. All the Dunns laughed. Amy faced James off with her hands on her hips. James couldn't decide if she was angry or just messing.

'Nothing,' James squirmed. 'I was just saying what a nice couple you and Scargill make.'

Amy crushed James with a hug that took his feet off the ground.

'That's really sweet of you, Ross,' Amy said. 'Because after what I thought you said, I was going to kick all your teeth out.'

*

James finished his curry and wandered off on his own. He noticed a girl leaning against a tree smoking. Long hair, baggy jeans. She was about James' age, nice looking. He didn't remember her from any of the intelligence files.

'Hey, can I have a drag?' James said, trying to sound cool.

'Sure,' the girl said.

She passed James the cigarette. James had never tried one before and hoped he wasn't about to make an idiot of himself. He gave it a little suck. It burned his throat, but he managed not to cough.

'Not seen you here before,' the girl said.

'I'm Ross,' James said. 'Staying here with my aunt for a bit.'

'Joanna,' the girl said. 'I live in Craddogh.'

'Haven't been there yet,' James said.

'It's a dump, two shops and a Post Office. Where you from?'

'London.'

'I wish I was,' Joanna said. 'You like it here?'

'I'm always covered in mud. I want to go to bed, but there's a guy playing a guitar three metres from where I sleep. I wish I could go home, have a warm shower, and see my mates.'

Joanna smiled.

'So why are you staying with your aunt?'

'Long story: parents getting divorced. Mum freaking out. Got expelled from school.'

'So you're good looking *and* you're a rebel,' Joanna said.

James was glad it was quite dark because he felt himself blush.

'You want the last puff, Ross?'

'No, I'm cool,' James said.

Joanna flicked the cigarette butt into the night.

'So, I paid you a compliment,' Joanna said.

'Yeah.'

Joanna laughed. 'So do I get one back?' she asked.

'Oh, sure,' James said. 'You're really like . . . nice.'

'Can't I get any better than nice?'

'Beautiful,' James said. 'You're beautiful.'

'That's more like it,' Joanna said. 'Want to kiss me?'

'Um, OK,' James said.

James was nervous. He'd never had the courage to ask a girl out. Now he was about to kiss someone he'd known for three minutes. He pecked her on the cheek. Joanna shoved James against the tree and started kissing his face and neck. Her hand went in the back pocket of James' jeans, then she jumped backwards.

'What did I do?' James asked. He'd just started enjoying himself.

'Police car,' Joanna said. 'Hide me somewhere.'

James saw a flashing blue light and a couple of cops getting out of a car a few hundred metres down the hill.

'Are you a runaway or something?' James asked.

'Hide me first, questions later.'

James led Joanna up the hill. The policemen were heading in the same direction. They seemed friendly and stopped to chat with a couple of people. James undid the padlock on Cathy's hut and clambered inside. Joanna slammed the door behind her.

'What's going on?' James asked.

'Peek outside,' Joanna said. 'Tell me what the police are doing.'

James stepped up to the window. 'I can only see one of them,' he said. 'He's talking to some guy.'

'What's he saying?'

'He's standing twenty metres away and it's dark. You expect me to read his lips? . . . Wait . . . The guy he's talking to is pointing at this hut.'

Joanna sounded hysterical. 'I'm in so much trouble.'

'Why?'

'I'm supposed to be sleeping over at my friend's house, but we came up here instead.'

'Where's your friend?' James asked.

'She met up with her boyfriend and abandoned me.'

'But why are the police out searching for *you*?'

The door of the hut came open and a policeman shone his torch in Joanna's face.

'Hello, Daddy,' Joanna said.

'You'd better get out here, young lady. I'm driving you home. And as for you . . .'

The policeman moved the beam of his torch so James' face lit up.

'. . . I don't know what you and my daughter have been up

to, but you'll stay away from her if you know what's good for you.'

James watched Joanna's dad take her to the police car. He didn't feel like going back outside. He lit the gas lamp, found his packet of Mars bars and poured a glass of unrefrigerated milk.

*

'I hear you tried to jump Sergeant Ribble's daughter,' Cathy said.

She looked smashed.

'I met her five minutes before her dad turned up,' James said. 'We had one little kiss.'

'So you claim, stud,' Cathy said.

She pinched James' cheek and laughed. Nobody had done that to James since he was about five.

'It's nice having you kids here,' Cathy said. 'Livens the place up.'

'I thought you didn't want us,' James said.

'It was a shock. But it gets dull here after thirty years.'

'Why don't you move on?'

'I might after you two go,' Cathy said. 'Cash in that monster car, travel for a bit. Don't know what after that. Maybe I'll try getting a flat and a job. I'm getting too old to keep scratching for a living round here.'

'What kind of job?' James asked.

Cathy laughed. 'God knows. I don't suppose there's anyone queuing up to employ fifty-year-old women who last had a job in 1971.'

'What doing?' James asked.

'I worked in the Student Union shop at my university.

Met Michael Dunn there. Married him a few years later. Came here. Had a little boy. Got divorced.'

'You have a son?' James asked.

'Had a son,' Cathy said. 'He died when he was three months old.'

'I'm sorry,' James said.

Cathy looked upset. She dragged out a wicker hamper and found a photo album. She flicked to a picture of a newborn in a white crochet hat.

'Harmony Dunn,' Cathy said. 'That's my only picture of him. Michael took it the day he was born.'

Seeing Cathy upset about her baby made James think about his mum. He felt a tear well up. He wanted to tell Cathy about his mum dying, but it would be breaking the rules of the mission. Cathy noticed James looked upset and put her arm around him.

'There's no need to get upset, Ross. It happened a long time ago.'

'Your whole life might have been different if he'd lived,' James said.

'Maybe,' Cathy said. 'You're a nice boy, Ross, or whatever your real name is.'

'Thanks,' James said.

'I don't think it's right the government using kids. You two could get hurt.'

'It's our choice,' James said. 'Nobody forces us to do it.'

'Courtney is using Scargill to get to Fire and World, isn't she?'

James was impressed Cathy had worked it out. It seemed pointless to deny it.

'Yeah,' he said.

'All the Dunn family have been good to me, even after I divorced Michael,' Cathy said. 'But those two have always been different. They're definitely up to something.'

'What makes you sure?' James asked.

'I've known Fire and World since they were born. There's something not right about them. A shiver goes up me when they walk into a room.'

33. FREAK

7 a.m. Monday, James' travel alarm went off to wake him for school. Amy threw a pillow at him when he didn't turn it off. He stumbled out of bed, rubbing his face, and unpinned a corner of the sheet over the window to let in some light.

'Can't you leave it dark?' Amy moaned from under her covers.

'I've got to go to school.'

James started putting on a sweatshirt and tracksuit bottoms.

'It's freezing,' James said.

'It's warm under here,' Amy said smugly. 'I don't have to get up for three hours.'

'I can't believe you got out of school, it's not bloody fair.'

Amy giggled under her covers. 'It's toasty at Green Brooke. The water in the Jacuzzi is beautiful, and I get a hot shower before and after my shift.'

'I'm filthy,' James said. 'I'm gonna get so much stick from the other kids going to school looking like this.'

'Put clean clothes on and use some of my deodorant.'

'I'm wearing clean stuff. I'll still be covered in mud three steps out the door. Where's your deodorant?'

'Down the end of my bed.'

Amy's deodorant was in a pink can with pictures of butterflies on it. James figured it was better smelling girly than stinking of BO so he gave himself a good blast.

'I'm glad I don't have to get up,' Amy giggled. 'This bed is really comfortable.'

James noticed Amy's leg poking out and tickled the sole of her foot. She pulled her leg in and squealed.

'Serves you right for teasing,' James said.

Amy flew out of bed, grabbed James around the waist and started tickling under his ribs.

'No, please,' James giggled.

James' legs buckled from laughing. His face was red and spit dribbled down his chin.

'Beg for mercy, weakling,' Amy said.

'No way,' James spluttered.

James couldn't wriggle free. Amy unleashed another wave of tickles.

'Oh no. Please. . . OK mercy. Stop. . . Mercy. I SAID MERCY.'

Amy stopped. Cathy's head poked in from her part of the hut. Her hair was all tangled.

'What's going on?' Cathy asked.

'Tickling,' James said, gasping for air.

'I thought you were dying or something. I was trying to sleep.'

'I've got to go to school,' James said.

'Do it quietly, Ross,' Cathy said. 'I'm laying in all morning.'

'Nice life for some,' James said. 'Is there anything for my breakfast?'

Cathy thought for a second.

'There's cold curry, or you could have the last one of your Mars bars.'

'Great,' James said.

Amy had snuggled back into bed and was laughing under her sheets.

*

It was a two-kilometre walk to the school bus stop in Craddogh. A few older Fort Harmony kids showed James the way. Joanna was at the stop with some friends. James said hello but she ignored him. The village kids wore smart casual clothes. Fort Harmony kids were tramps in comparison.

It was a half-hour ride to school, stopping a few times to pick up more kids. James rested his face against the window and watched the sun rise over the passing countryside.

*

Gwen Morgan school looked better than James' old school in London. The modern classrooms were in single storey clusters with covered walkways between them. The areas between buildings had flower beds and neatly trimmed grass with *Keep Off* signs. When the bell rang kids walked to registration. No shoving or fights breaking out. Even the boys' toilets were clean. James washed as much filth as he could off his face and hands before finding his class. He handed a note to his form teacher and found a desk.

'This is Ross,' the teacher announced. 'Please make him feel welcome here at Gwen Morgan and help him find his way around.'

The kids all looked polite and well behaved. Nobody spoke to James.

First lesson was science. James asked a kid if it was OK to sit next to him. The kid shrugged.

The lesson was dull. They were halfway through a topic, but James was bright enough to pick up what had gone on before and was soon bored. It felt really different to CHERUB where all the kids were clever and the teachers kept you on your toes. He wrote neatly in his new exercise book and homework diary, but it seemed like a waste of time. He would only be here a few weeks.

Between first and second lesson a couple of kids in James' class called Stuart and Gareth gave him a shove.

'Wait till break time, hippy boy,' one of them said.

James wasn't worried. He'd be able to fight them off if they tried anything.

He got another shove and a punch in the back from Gareth at the start of morning break. James knew he'd become a target if he looked soft, but he didn't want to end up rolling around the floor fighting on his first day, so he punched Gareth in the face and ran off. He spent the rest of morning break wandering on his own, paranoid that everyone was staring at him like a freak.

Gareth had a tissue plugged up his nose to stop it bleeding for the whole of third period. After lunch James wanted to join the kids playing football on the all weather pitches, but Gareth, Stuart and a couple of their pals were playing. James thought it best to steer clear. He found a quiet spot at the back of the school, sat against the outside wall of a classroom and started doing his homework.

James noticed a shadow over his science book and looked up. Gareth and Stuart were standing over him with six friends for back-up. James was furious with himself for letting them get so close without noticing.

'You killed my nose, Harmony boy,' Gareth said.

'I didn't ask for trouble,' James said. 'Leave me alone.'

Gareth laughed. 'In your dreams.'

'We hate all you Fort Harmony filth,' Stuart said. 'They should send the police up there and set dogs on you.'

James reckoned he could have beaten any two of them, managed to get a few hits in and escape against three or four, but eight against one . . . No chance.

'Stand up, hippy,' Gareth said.

If he stayed on the ground he could roll in a ball to protect himself. Standing would only mean getting knocked back down.

'Get your arse *up*,' Gareth repeated.

'Piss off,' James said. 'Haven't got the guts to fight me on your own, have you?'

Gareth kicked James in the knee. A few of the others moved closer so there were ten legs circling. James braced himself for pain. Kicks came fast, luckily there were so many legs flying they used a lot of energy hitting each other. James tried to tuck his knees into his chest, but a trainer clamped his stomach to the floor. He kept his legs together to protect his balls and wrapped his arms over his face.

The main beating lasted about a minute. A couple of the kids who weren't in the surrounding group gave some brutal kicks in the side to finish off.

'Better learn some respect, hippy,' Gareth said.

The gang walked off, mocking the way James was groaning in pain on the floor. James couldn't stop the tears forming, but he was determined not to cry out. His arms and legs were dead from the beating.

James got his books into his backpack and stumbled a couple of metres holding on to the wall before his knee gave out. He sat there until a teacher came to unlock his classroom. He tried to pretend he'd slipped and twisted his ankle, but the teacher could see James was hurting all over. The teacher put his arm around James and helped him hobble to the first-aid room.

*

Mr Crow, the Deputy Headmaster, came into the first-aid room. James was sitting on the edge of a bed in his boxers, holding a cup of orange squash. He had plasters on his legs and arms.

'Who did this to you, Ross?' Crow asked.

He was a small, friendly-sounding man with a Welsh accent.

'I don't know,' James said.

'Were any of them in your class?'

'No,' James said.

James thought it was best not to grass. The school wouldn't expel eight kids. They would only get suspended for a few days. Then all their mates and older brothers would be after James for grassing. His life would be hell. If he didn't grass and managed to make a few friends to back him up, things might be OK.

'Ross, I understand it's your instinct not to tell on your

classmates. But this is your first day here and you've been seriously assaulted. That is not acceptable. We want to help you.'

'I'll be OK,' James said. 'It's no big deal.'

*

By home time, James could walk again, sort of. He was let out of the first-aid room before the bell, giving him a chance to get on the bus without being caught up with everyone else. Joanna climbed on and sat next to him. It was the first good thing that had happened to him all day.

'What happened to you?' Joanna asked.

'What does it look like?' James said angrily. 'I got the crap beaten out of me.'

'Gareth Granger and Stuart Parkwood,' Joanna said.

'How did you know?' James asked.

'It's always them. They're not even tough; it's just they hang out in a big group and stick up for each other.'

'I just hope they don't make it a regular thing,' James said.

'You need a bath,' Joanna said.

'No chance of that at Fort Harmony.'

'Have one at my house if you want.'

'What about your dad?'

'Working till six. Then he usually goes for a drink.'

'Your mum?'

'Lives in Cardiff with my big brothers.'

'Are they divorced?' James asked.

'A few months ago.'

'What happened after your dad caught you on Friday?'

'Lost my pocket money, grounded for a fortnight.'

'Rough,' James said.

Joanna smiled. 'It's so stupid. My dad grounds me, but he's never home to stop me going out.'

*

Joanna's house was a little cottage on the edge of Craddogh with frilly net curtains and ornaments everywhere. Joanna flicked on MTV. They ate cheese on toast and drank tea while James' bath ran.

The soap made his cuts sting, but the hot water soothed his pains and it was nice feeling clean again. Joanna opened the bathroom door and tossed in a clean T-shirt and an old set of her brother's boxers. She cracked up when she saw James in the huge pair of shorts and a Puma T-shirt almost down to his knees.

Joanna took him into her room.

'Lie on my bed.'

She peeled off all James' soggy plasters, wiped his cuts with disinfectant and stuck on new ones. James stared at Joanna's long hair and the curve of her back as she leant over him. She looked beautiful.

James wanted to kiss her again, but Joanna was a year older and she'd mentioned a couple of previous boyfriends. He felt like he was in way over his head.

34. SICKIE

It was cold, spitting with rain. Every step back to Fort Harmony was agony for James' battered legs. He was facing an evening sitting around in a cold hut with no TV. Then he had to spend the night on a crappy mattress listening to Amy snore. Tomorrow he'd probably get beaten up at school.

But James was in the best mood: ninety minutes lying on Joanna's bed kissing and moaning about their lives. She put on a Red Hot Chilli Peppers CD and they sang all the words out loud. Every time James thought about Joanna he got such a rush nothing else mattered. When he got back to the hut Cathy and Amy were out. He was too excited to eat. James crashed on to his bed and daydreamed about Joanna.

*

'Are you deaf?' Sebastian shouted, a few centimetres from the end of James' bed. 'I knocked four times. Fire's got our radio-controlled cars running. Want to try them?'

James turned over. He didn't want to get up, but it was part of his mission.

James had had a radio-controlled car before his mum died. It was good fun, but it wasn't safe using it around his flats. Someone would have stolen or smashed it in five minutes. Sebastian and Clark's cars were superb. They were beach buggies with big rear tyres that sprayed up mud. Instead of batteries there were tiny petrol engines between the rear wheels. Clark stopped his car in front of James and handed him the radio control.

'Gently,' Clark said.

'I've driven a car before,' James said, as if Clark was stupid.

James put the car full on forward. The engine buzzed noisily and a blue plume shot out the exhaust. It didn't move a millimetre. The wheels dug into the mud.

'Gently, dingus,' Clark said.

Sebastian lifted the car. James lightly nudged the stick and the car blasted off at about fifty kilometres an hour.

James laughed out, 'Cool.'

He drove a big circle, nearly crashing into some trees, running under the Land Cruiser and almost rolling the car on its side as he did a sharp turn to bring the car back near to his feet.

'That was excellent,' James said. 'So fast. Where did you get them?'

'Fire and World made them when they were teenagers.' Clark said. 'Only thing is they're always going wrong and Fire never wants to fix them for us. He's got about six more cars in his workshop.'

'Can I see them?'

'Won't let us in there any more.'

The workshop sounded interesting, but James didn't want to seem pushy about finding more out.

'What do they do there?' he asked.

'Dunno,' Sebastian said. 'Trying to take over the universe knowing those two.'

'Anyway, I heard you got battered at school today,' Clark said.

'Yeah,' James said.

'Didn't grass, did you?'

'No way.'

'Me and Sebastian used to get beaten up all the time because we're from Fort Harmony. It's not so bad now, we're two of the biggest in our school.'

'We're the kings,' Sebastian said. 'There's a guy in my class so scared of us we click our fingers and he licks our trainers. Don't have to hit him or nothing.'

'You start at Gwen Morgan in September?' James asked.

'Both of us do,' Clark said. 'There's only a ten-month age gap between us.'

'At least you can back each other up.'

'We've been suspended for fighting three times,' Clark said. 'Next time we get expelled, but I'd rather be expelled than let people dump on us.'

'What do your mum and dad say?'

'Never met our dad. Our mum knows the score. All the boys who live at Fort Harmony get bullied by the normal kids.'

'What did you think of us at first?' Sebastian asked.

James laughed. 'Not much. You weren't exactly friendly.'

'If you got treated like you were today, every single day since you were five years old, you wouldn't be friendly either.'

'What should I do?' James asked.

'You were right not to grass,' Clark said 'If you're a snitch the whole school will be against you. Never give in. Never grovel or beg, it only encourages them. For a tough kid like you, Ross, best thing to do is get one of the leaders on his own and massacre him.'

'They'll kill me if I do that,' James said.

'There's a big choice of targets,' Clark said. 'A gang will think twice before picking on a kid who can get them back when they're on their own.'

'I don't want to get in trouble,' James said. 'I got expelled from my last school.'

Sebastian laughed. 'Better get used to having someone standing on your nuts then.'

*

After eating in the main hut James lay on his bed again. Amy was furious when she got out of work and saw the state he was in.

'I'll go down that school and kick their butts myself,' Amy screamed. 'Nobody does that to my baby brother.'

'I can handle it,' James said.

'You *can't* handle it. Why didn't you tell the school who did it?'

'I'm not a grass,' James said. 'Grasses are lower than kids who wet their pants.'

'I think you should go to a hospital, you might have concussion,' Amy said.

'I can't have concussion, I didn't get kicked in the head,' James lied. 'Can we talk about something more important?'

'What's more important than you coming home looking like a bus ran over you?'

'Have you seen Fire and World's workshop?' James asked.

'I've seen their hut. You certainly couldn't call it a workshop.'

'Sebastian said they've got a workshop. Him and Clark aren't allowed in it any more. Sounds like the sort of place we should be checking out.'

'Did you ask where it was?'

'No, I'll try and find out.'

'I'll see if I can wangle something out of Scargill,' Amy said. 'I bet it's one of those huts that looks like it's been abandoned.'

*

James sat in the Land Cruiser and phoned his daily report to Ewart. He left out how much of a crush he had on Joanna.

'Does it matter if I get in trouble at school?' James asked.

'Like how?' Ewart asked.

'If I get suspended. I figured it might even be good for the mission because I'd get to spend more time snooping around here.'

Ewart laughed. 'And by lucky coincidence you get out of school for a few days.'

'That hadn't even crossed my mind,' James said, but gave himself away by laughing.

'I suppose it wouldn't be much of a problem. But you're not above the law just because you're on a mission, so don't go burning down the school or anything.'

*

7 a.m. Tuesday, James' travel alarm went off for school. He turned it off and pulled the covers over his head.

'You'll miss the bus if you don't get a move on,' Amy said.

'Not going,' James said. 'My back's stiff. I can hardly move.'

'You were shooting stuff with Sebastian and Clark until nearly midnight. You seemed all right then.'

'Must have tightened up in the night,' James said.

Amy laughed. 'Pull the other one. It's got bells on.'

James lay in until ten, deliberately staying under the covers until after Amy got up for work. Cathy was in a good mood. She sent James out to collect eggs from the chicken coop and made omelettes with mushrooms and bacon.

James read the first few chapters of *No Logo*, in case Bungle asked him any questions about it, then went for a walk. Joshua Dunn was in the main hut preparing a mountain of vegetables. Gladys Dunn was there as well, reading the morning paper.

'Can I look at the sports?' James asked.

She handed him the paper.

'Rough time at school, I hear,' Gladys said.

'Yeah.'

'Not a good place for young boys here,' Gladys said. 'All my grandsons are a funny lot. Get bullied at school. Take it out on the local wildlife or hide inside books.'

James smiled. 'They're not so bad.'

'You've brought it home to me, Ross. One day and you're beaten up. You don't even look or dress like the other kids here. Boys are so cruel.'

'What can you do?' James asked.

'We had a school here once. Parents took it in turns to teach the kids. All turned into squabbling about who taught the lessons.'

'Everyone here has been really nice to me,' James said. 'But I don't understand why people want to live here.'

Gladys wagged her finger, 'You put your finger on a question I've been asking myself lately. At first Fort Harmony was about freedom and some young people having fun. When the police tried to destroy us, we sent out a signal that a bunch of nobodies could stand up against the government and win. But what are we now? A trendy campsite for backpackers. Half the people who live here clean and cook for rich businessmen in that bloody conference centre.'

James was a bit stunned. 'So why stay?'

'Can you keep a secret, Ross?' Gladys asked.

'I guess.'

'My second book comes out in September. It should earn me enough to buy a house somewhere warm. I'll take Joshua. The others can fight over Fort Harmony.'

'I read your first book,' James said. 'It was interesting.'

Gladys looked surprised. 'I didn't have you pegged for a bookworm, Ross.'

James kicked himself for revealing that he'd read the book. Twenty-year-old memoirs of life on a commune aren't exactly standard reading for twelve-year-old boys.

'Cathy had a copy,' James stuttered, wondering if she actually did. 'And there's no TV here.'

'Thank goodness,' Gladys smiled.

'I liked the bit where you were all hiding from police in the tunnels and you were trying to keep the kids quiet. Must have been scary.'

'I should never have taken my boys underground. Joshua

was the brightest one, now he's happy spending four hours a day peeling vegetables.'

'I suppose the tunnels are all gone,' James said.

'There's bits and pieces left. I wouldn't try playing in them, Ross, not very safe.'

'Don't worry, I wouldn't go into them. It's just that I've not seen any sign of them.'

'That's because the camp has moved. We started off at the bottom of the hill down by the road. The main hut was under a metre of water sometimes, so we moved up here where the water drains away.'

*

James stuck his head round the door of Bungle's hut. He was sitting around drinking coffee with Fire, World and Scargill. Gregory was racing Matchbox cars over his parents' bed.

'I just came to say hello,' James said. 'I'll go away if you're busy.'

Bungle laughed. 'You're too polite, Ross. Sit down, you want coffee or tea?'

'Tea,' James said.

James sat on the floor. He assumed Bungle and the Dunns would be having some deep political conversation, but they were debating who was sexier out of Julia Roberts and Jennifer Lopez. Gregory got a picture book and sat on James' leg.

'Trains,' Gregory said.

James opened the book on Gregory's lap. Gregory told him what colour all the trains in the book were and James pretended to be impressed. Bungle passed out jam rings and Gregory thought it was great dipping his biscuit in James' mug, especially when the end dropped off into the tea.

'I'm taking these guys into town and picking Eleanor up from the village,' Bungle said. 'Can you keep an eye on Gregory for an hour?'

'No worries,' James said.

'If you have any probs there's a mobile phone on the table, and there are plenty of adults around. I'm on the speed dial.'

James was well pleased. Now he could get photos of Bungle's hut and have a rummage around. It made his decision not to go to school look like a masterstroke.

35. PAST

James left Fort Harmony after lunch. He ran a couple of kilometres, checked nobody was around, and waited for Ewart. Ewart drove up in a BMW. He'd taken all his earrings out and was dressed like a businessman in a pinstriped suit and tie.

'Nice threads,' James laughed.

'Got to blend in at Green Brooke.'

Ewart drove a few kilometres and parked in a farm access road.

'So, what did you get?' Ewart asked.

James handed over the memory card from his digital camera and some screwed-up pieces of notepaper.

'Plenty of pictures there,' James said. 'Everything in Bungle's room, on the bookshelves, close-ups of stuff like his address book. I've written a list of all the numbers stored in his mobile, plus there's his bank account and passport details.'

'Good job, James. Look at this.'

Ewart handed James a folder with an FBI crest on the front. James opened it and saw a black and white picture of Bungle, looking about ten years younger with long hair.

'That's him,' James said.

James flipped to the next page. It was a standard FBI record. James had seen a few when he was preparing for the mission. Bungle's rap sheet only had three typed lines.

Student at Stamford, MA. Room-mate of known felon Jake Gladwell.
Questioned. Released. 6.18.1994
Traffic violation Austin TX 12.23.1998

'Not very exciting,' James said.

'That's what I thought,' Ewart said. 'Then I had a little look into Jake Gladwell. He's doing eighty years in San Antonio prison, Texas.'

'What for?'

'Trying to blow up the governor at a charity fundraiser. The bomb was found before the event and defused. Police caught Gladwell on the night of the fundraiser. He was outside the hotel with a radio control under his jacket. Know what the former governor of Texas is up to these days?'

'What?' James asked.

'George Walker Bush. President. And you know what else? There were eight big cheeses from the Texas oil industry sitting around Bushy when that bomb was supposed to go off.'

'Bungle was hanging around with Fire and World today,' James said.

'I found the connection between Fire, World and Bungle.

Fire and World did two years at York University before they went to prison. York has a teacher exchange program with Stamford University in America. Bungle was a guest professor at York. He taught Fire and World microbiology for two terms before he quit his job and moved to Fort Harmony.'

'So we're sure they're part of Help Earth?' James asked.

'We can't prove squat. We always thought Bungle, Fire and World were involved. Now we've found out Bungle's background I'd bet my life savings, but there's still no hard evidence. All we can do is keep working and hope you or Amy get a lead before a bomb goes off.'

Ewart reached around to the back seat and handed James a small box of fancy chocolates.

'Give them to Joanna, they're her favourites.'

James was freaked out.

'What are you on about? I only went round to her house for a bath.'

Ewart laughed. 'That's not what I heard. What about all the smoochies?'

'Are you having me watched?' James asked.

'No.'

'So how do you know we kissed?'

'M15 is monitoring all the Internet use around here. They send me a briefing if anything interesting crops up. About eight o'clock last night Joanna logged into a chatroom. Spoke about a new boyfriend called Ross. Says he's a total hunk. Got really cute blond hair. Can't wait to see him at the bus stop in the morning.'

'I wish I'd gone to school now,' James said. 'What about the chocolates?'

'I hacked her user profile on the website. She likes Thornton's handmade chocolates, rock music, blond-haired boys and her ambition is to ride a Harley Davidson across America.'

'Can you drop me near the village so I can give them to her when she gets off the bus?'

*

Joanna hugged him when he gave her the chocolates. They went back to the cottage, drank cocoa, slagged off all the bands on MTV Hits and chased around tickling and throwing sofa cushions at each other. James stayed until her dad got in from work, then sneaked out the back door and walked to Fort Harmony with an ear-to-ear grin.

James was starting to understand all those terrible romantic films his mum used to watch where the leading man ends up in a state over some woman. He lay awake half the night thinking about Joanna. He realised when the mission ended he'd have to go back to CHERUB and never see her again.

He got up extra early and waited for her at the bus stop.

*

Everyone looked at James when he got to class. Stuart and Gareth dropped snide comments all morning.

'After school it's round two,' Stuart said, as James stood in the line to get lunch.

The last thing James wanted was to miss the bus and lose time with Joanna.

'What about right here, right now?' James said. 'Without all your pals backing you up?'

'If you want to start it, hippy boy, we'll finish it.'

The kids standing around them in the queue were excited

about a punch-up. Normally James wouldn't start a fight where everyone could see, but he was trying to get suspended so it didn't matter. James waited while the queue shuffled forward.

'Chickened out, did you?' Gareth asked.

James flicked Gareth off. He was waiting until they were level with the baked beans. When they got there, he hit Gareth in the stomach, grabbed him behind the neck and dipped his face in the beans. Gareth screamed, hot orange sauce burning his face. Stuart whacked James over the head with his lunch tray. James doubled Stuart up with an elbow and followed with some punches that took him down. Gareth was blind, screaming, and wiping his face with his sweatshirt. James battered Stuart until he got dragged off by a couple of teachers. Two hundred sets of eyes were on James as the teachers dragged him off, kicking and shouting.

*

Joanna thought James getting suspended was superb. James was lying face down on her bed after a bath. Joanna rubbed his wet hair with a towel.

'You're so bad,' Joanna purred. 'And you don't even care.'

She threw the towel on the floor and kissed the back of James' neck.

'We'll run away to Scotland and get married when we're sixteen,' Joanna said. 'Then we'll go all over the country robbing banks. We'll live big with all the money we steal. Flash restaurants, big sports cars.'

'You've put a lot of thought into this,' James said, grinning. 'I've only known you for a week.'

'Then you'll get shot by the police in a robbery.'

'You're so full of shit.' James giggled.

'Don't worry, Ross. You'll recover, but you'll have to do five hard years in prison. You'll kiss my photo every day. I'll go to America and ride a Harley Davidson across the country. When you get out, you'll be all beefy from lifting weights, and have tattoos all over you. When the prison gates open I'll be waiting on my Harley. We'll kiss. You'll climb on the back and we'll ride off into the sunset.'

'I'm not so sure about getting shot and going to prison,' James said. 'Why can't *you* get shot and I'll ride the Harley across America?'

'You want me to be all muscled and covered with tattoos?' Joanna asked.

James rolled over and kissed Joanna on the cheek.

36. MESS

'Ring Ewart,' Amy said when James got back to the hut. 'He's pissed at you.'

James went out to the Land Cruiser and made the call.

'Hello James, nice time with your girlfriend?' Ewart asked bitterly.

'What did I do?' James asked.

'Your headmistress blew her stack over your antics in the canteen. She rang one of your supposed old schools; luckily she got the number from the fake file and the call went through to CHERUB, but if she'd got the school's real number and they told her they'd never heard of you it would have made a right mess.'

'Is the headmistress really mad?' James asked.

'I called her back pretending to be one of your old teachers and I think I smoothed things over. I said you were mischievous but basically harmless.'

'You said I was allowed to get suspended.'

'Yes,' Ewart said. 'But I didn't expect you to dunk a kid's head in a vat of baked beans. He's apparently got a nasty burn on his nose.'

'Sorry,' James said, trying not to laugh.

'Sorry solves nothing,' Ewart shouted. 'What time did you get back to Fort Harmony?'

'Just now. About half seven.'

'Have you seen Clark and Sebastian today?'

'No.'

'Why not?'

'You know why, I was with Joanna.'

'The mission is about Sebastian and Clark, not your little girlfriend. I've told Cathy to ground you for getting suspended from school. You can't leave Fort Harmony for a week.'

'But what about Joanna?' James asked.

'Tough,' Ewart said. 'Focus on your mission. You mess up like this again and I'll have you back at CHERUB scrubbing toilets on your hands and knees.'

'I've got to see Joanna, please,' James begged.

'Don't wind me up, James, I'm in no mood. There's two things for you to keep an eye out for. In your photos of Bungle's shack there's a white folder with a RKM logo on the side. It's on the bottom of the bookshelf under the window. Try and get a look at it. It looks like a computer manual, but Bungle doesn't have a computer. It might give us a clue what they're up to. Second, look out for a red van. Amy spotted Fire and World getting out of it, but couldn't get the whole number plate. Got all that?'

'Yes, Ewart,' James said miserably.

'Start using your brain, James.'

James heard the line go dead. He punched the dashboard, ran back to his bed and yelled into his pillow.

'What happened?' Amy asked.

'Leave me alone,' James said.

'It can't be so bad, Ross. You got out of school.'

'He said I can't go down to the village and see Joanna.'

'You know we'll only be here for a few weeks,' Amy said. 'I wouldn't get too fond of her.'

James got off his bed, put his boots on and walked out into the dark.

He lay in the long grass down the bottom of the hill and didn't care that his clothes got soaked. He thought about sneaking down to the village to see Joanna, but he wasn't brave enough to mess with Ewart. If Ewart sent him back to campus in disgrace he'd never get another decent mission.

James wanted to go back to the hut, but Amy would be there with a lecture waiting. He thought about finding Sebastian and Clark, but he didn't want to spend all night shooting the local wildlife. So he stayed where he was, sulking.

*

James heard an animal or something running through the grass around him. He looked up and saw it was two radio-controlled cars. Electric ones. The only noise was rustling as they brushed the grass. He spotted the chromed radio control aerials reflecting moonlight. World and Scargill had them. After a couple of quick circuits they picked the cars up, pulled up their sweatshirt hoods and jogged away.

James decided it was too risky to follow. He crawled through the mud towards where Scargill and World had been standing and almost fell into a hole. It was one of the old tunnels. James grabbed his mobile and called Amy.

'Where are you?' Amy asked.

'Down near the road, something weird is going on.'

James explained everything.

'The tunnel has a door with a padlock on it,' James said. 'I don't have my lock gun.'

'I'll be five minutes,' Amy said. 'Do nothing. If they come back, say you were just exploring.'

Amy ran down to James, keeping herself low to the ground. She shone a torch into the hole and quickly shut it off again.

'They could be back any minute,' Amy said. 'You any good with the lock gun?'

'OK,' James said.

'Got your camera?'

'Yes.'

'Go have a look,' Amy said. 'Take as many pictures as you can and get out fast.'

'Will you keep look-out?' James asked.

'No. If they catch you, say the lock was left off and you just walked inside. Me sitting out here looks suspicious. I'll keep back unless something starts getting heavy.'

James took Amy's torch and lock gun and dropped into the hole. There was a deep puddle in the bottom. The padlock was easy. Inside was three metres of wood-lined tunnel with a low room at the end. James crawled down and started taking pictures. There wasn't much to see. Shelves of radio-controlled cars and spares, and a workbench with an orange plastic tub underneath. James opened every drawer and took pictures inside.

James turned to leave, half-convinced someone would be

behind him. Nobody was. He scrambled back down the tunnel, shut the padlock and ran uphill to Amy.

'Sweet,' Amy said. 'See anything?'

'Toy cars and junk. Hard to see with the torch.'

'The flash on the camera will pick up more than you saw in the dark,' Amy said. 'Maybe something will turn up on the photos.'

'There must be stuff worth hiding in there,' James said. 'Otherwise they wouldn't bother keeping it secret.'

'I'm gonna stick around and see if they come back,' Amy said. 'You go up to the hut and ring Ewart. Arrange to meet him somewhere. He'll want to look at the pictures straight away.'

*

After he'd met Ewart, James went back to the hut and fell asleep. He got the best sleep he'd had in ages, without Amy there snoring.

Amy shook James awake at 2 a.m. She looked happy.

'It's all going down, James. Fire came to the workshop. You were nearly caught, only missed him by about three minutes. He took a big backpack of stuff out and walked off. I followed him up the hill to Green Brooke. You'll never guess what the radio-controlled cars are for.'

'What?' James asked.

'They have a storage tray. They load them up with stuff and push them through a tiny gap in the security fence around Green Brooke. They drive the cars inside the fence and drop the cargo at the back of the conference hall. The cars are too small and fast to get detected by the security cameras and alarms.'

'Couldn't they book a room and bring the stuff into the hotel?' James asked.

'Every guest brings luggage into Green Brooke hotel,' Amy said. 'But the conference hall is under police guard until Petrocon starts. Everyone gets searched on the way in. There's X-ray machines. All your bags get turned out, they pat you down and go in your pockets.'

'So,' James said. 'They're smuggling a bomb into the conference hall, bit by bit, on the back of radio-controlled cars. There must be someone working on the inside screwing all the pieces together.'

'Must be. I spoke to Ewart. They're sending people down to look at the stuff the cars dropped, but they won't take it away. They want to see who comes and picks it up.'

James laughed. 'They're gonna lock those guys up and throw away the key.'

'Poor Scargill,' Amy said.

'You don't actually *like* that freak, do you?' James asked.

Amy shrugged. 'I feel sorry for him. He's just a lonely kid trying to impress his big brothers. The tough guys in prison will eat him for breakfast.'

'You *do* like him,' James laughed. 'He's the world's biggest nerd.'

'You're such a twelve-year-old sometimes, James,' Amy said. 'You've never even had a conversation with Scargill. There's more to a guy than looking good and having big muscles.'

'Marry him and get it over with,' James said. 'So what happens next?'

'Nothing changes. We keep our ears to the ground and

see what comes up. Ewart wants you to concentrate on Bungle and Eleanor. We know they're involved, but there's still no proof.'

37. BUG

Amy shook James awake. It was still dark.

'Get dressed now,' Amy snapped. 'I just had Ewart on the phone. He's coming to get us.'

James rubbed his eyes. Amy was on one leg, stepping into a pair of ripped jeans.

'What's going on?'

'I have no idea,' Amy said. 'Ewart said our lives are in danger if we don't get out fast.'

James put on jeans and trainers. He grabbed his jacket and dashed after Amy. Cathy woke up and asked what was going on. She didn't get an answer. They ran to the bottom of the hill where the BMW was waiting.

'Both of you in the back,' Ewart said.

The tyres squealed. Ewart was in a major hurry about something. He threw some medical supplies at Amy.

'Give James four tablets and two shots in the arm. You OK with injections, Amy?'

'In theory,' Amy said.

Branches thrashed the side of the car as it sped down an unlit country lane.

'What's wrong with me?' James asked nervously.

'Get your coat off,' Amy said.

She squeezed four pills out of their blisters and handed them to James. James looked at the box. It was an antibiotic called Ciprofloxacin.

'I need water to swallow them,' James said.

'None here,' Ewart said. 'Forgot. Ball up some spit. The faster they're in your system the better.'

James' mouth was dry from running. It took a while to get the tablets down.

'I can't hold the needle still while the car's moving,' Amy said.

Ewart stamped the brakes and pulled into the side of the lane. Amy roughly stabbed James with the first needle. It hurt like hell.

'Have you ever done that before?' James asked.

Amy didn't answer and punched him with the second jab. Ewart hit the accelerator.

'Will you tell me what the hell is going on?' James shouted.

'It wasn't a bomb they were building,' Ewart said. 'It was a bio-weapon. The radio-controlled cars were carrying cylinders of bacteria.'

'Oh, god,' Amy said. 'It's obvious now you say it. Bungle was a microbiology professor. Fire and World studied biology at university. They'd know all about that stuff.'

'It all fell into place at once,' Ewart said. 'The best way to spread a disease through a large building is the air-conditioning. I checked out the van Amy saw. It belongs to a man who services the air-conditioning at Green Brooke. Then there was the folder with the RKM logo in Bungle's hut. I thought it was a computer manual, but RKM also make air conditioners.'

'What is it?' Amy asked.

'The police haven't analysed the cylinders,' Ewart said. 'But anthrax is most likely.'

'Jesus,' Amy said.

'I don't understand half what you two are on about,' James said. 'Can one of you speak to me in English?'

'Do you know what anthrax is, James?' Ewart asked.

'No idea, but I'm guessing it's not good and you think I've got it.'

'Anthrax is a unique disease. Most diseases can only survive outside your body for about eight minutes,' Ewart explained. 'Anthrax can survive in almost any temperature for up to sixty years. That makes it easy to store and use as a weapon. A cupful of anthrax spores in the air could kill hundreds of people.'

'How did I get it?' James asked.

'You might not have it,' Ewart said. 'The antibiotics are a precaution. Remember the bright orange box under the bench in the underground workshop?'

'Yeah,' James said.

'It's a sealed disposal unit for toxic waste. You're supposed to incinerate it in a two-thousand-degree furnace.'

'I pulled the lid off and stuck my hand inside,' James said.

'Unfortunately you did,' Ewart said. 'I've got a picture you took of the contents. Gave me a heart attack when I saw it. Looks like the gloves and face masks they used when they were handling the anthrax bacteria ended up in there.'

'Could I die?' James asked.

'I've got to be honest, James. If you breathed the bacteria you're in trouble. Even with the antibiotics we've given you there's a fifty per cent death rate.'

'Could I have given it to Amy or anyone?' James asked.

'It's possible some bacteria stuck on your fingers, but the disease is only serious if you breathe thousands of spores. They'll check out Amy at the hospital to be safe.'

'If I die,' James asked, 'how long will it take?'

'It starts off like the flu about a day after infection. Most people die within nine days.'

'What hospital are we driving to?' Amy asked.

'There's a military hospital near Bristol, about seventy kilometres away,' Ewart said. 'They've got a doctor flying in from Manchester. He knows as much about anthrax as anyone on the planet.'

*

Four nurses in army uniform grabbed James out of the car and stuck him on a trolley, even though he could walk. They burst through doors. Lights on the ceiling whizzed by. James spotted Meryl Spencer and Mac running behind the trolley. They had flown from CHERUB by helicopter.

The nurses wheeled James into a huge ward. There were thirty beds in three rows, all empty. A male nurse pulled James' trainers and socks off, then grabbed his jeans and boxers down in one. James was embarrassed because Amy, Ewart, Meryl and everyone were standing around watching. Once James was naked they lifted him on to a bed.

'Hello, James. I'm Doctor Coen.'

The doctor looked like he'd been dragged out of bed. He

wore Nikes, jogging bottoms and a shirt with the buttons done up in the wrong holes.

'Has the disease been explained to you?' the doctor asked.

'Mostly,' James said. 'Do I need thirty people standing around looking at me naked?'

Dr Coen smiled. 'You heard the patient.'

Everyone but three nurses and a couple of doctors headed out. Dr Coen continued:

'First we need to take blood samples and see if you've been infected with anthrax. However, if you have the disease your chances of survival decrease with every minute treatment is delayed, so we're going to assume the worst and begin treatment now. A nurse will fix a tube into your arm. We're going to pump you with a mixture of antibiotics and other drugs. Some of the drugs are toxic. Your body will react violently. You can expect vomiting and fever.'

*

Amy and Meryl stayed by James' bed. He started feeling weak and shaky a couple of hours after treatment started. His face went pale and he asked for something to throw up in.

Amy went outside looking upset. Meryl gripped his hand.

It got worse in the hours that followed. James' stomach and ribcage felt like they were tearing apart. The tiniest movement, even a deep breath or a cough, made his vision blur and a wave of nausea shoot up from his stomach. The two Army nurses wiped up every time he got sick. When he got really bad they injected him with anti-vomiting drugs.

The wait for test results was unbearable. James wanted to pass out or fall asleep. He watched the door, silently praying for Dr Coen to come back with good news. James wondered if this room might be the last thing he ever saw.

*

Doctor Coen didn't come back until 8 a.m. on Thursday.

'It's bad,' Dr Coen said. 'We just got the results from your tests. We'll keep giving you the drugs.'

38. DEATH

James woke up. He'd been in the hospital thirty hours. A drip ran up his nose and down into his stomach. Meryl had stayed the whole time.

'How do you feel?' Meryl asked.

'Weak,' James croaked; the tube down his throat made it hard to speak.

'The doctor says the level of bacteria in your system is going down. The antibiotics are working.'

'What are my chances?' James asked.

'Dr Coen said over eighty per cent because the treatment started so early.'

'I feel so rough I wish I was dead.'

'Lauren's here,' Meryl said.

'Is she OK?'

Meryl shrugged. 'Pretty shook up. She waited all day for you to come around. She's sleeping upstairs.'

'Me dying, after Mum and that,' James said. 'She'll be in a right state.'

Meryl stroked the back of James' hand.

'You won't die,' she said. 'Fort Harmony has been in all

the papers. Headline news.'

Meryl handed James a *Daily Mirror*. He could see the giant headline, but his vision was too blurry to read the text.

'Read it to me,' James said.

FORT TERROR

Britain's oldest hippy commune, Fort Harmony near Cardiff, was rocked in a stunning raid by anti-terrorist police yesterday.

Three grandsons of the cult writer Gladys Dunn were arrested after anthrax bacteria was found at the nearby Green Brooke Conference Centre.

Twins, Fire and World Dunn, 22, and their brother, Scargill Dunn, 17, were arrested early yesterday morning.

Also in custody are Kieran Pym, an air conditioning engineer, and Eleanor Evans.

Police are seeking a sixth suspect, Brian 'Bungle' Evans. Police believe he is the ringleader and a founder member of the terrorist group Help Earth.

Police also discovered an underground bunker where the deadly cargo was stored before being smuggled into a secure area at Green Brooke. The bunker was not equipped to manufacture the bacteria.

A nationwide search has been launched for the hi-tech laboratory where the killer bug was bred.

It is believed the terrorists were targeting the upcoming Petrocon conference at Green Brooke. If anthrax had been successfully used during the conference, most of the 200 oil industry delegates would have been killed, alongside more than fifty Green Brooke staff and bodyguards.

MORE ON PAGES 2,3,4 & 11
LOTTERY PAGE 6

'It's the main story on TV,' Meryl said. 'Bungle's picture was on the cover of every paper. There's all kinds of rumours about where he's gone.'

'I feel sorry for their little boy,' James said, 'He's only three.'

*

Mac came into the ward an hour later. Lauren was with him, dressed in pyjamas. She jumped on the bed and gave James a hug. She looked like she'd just heard the funniest joke ever.

'There's nothing wrong with you,' Lauren squealed. 'Thanks for scaring me.'

'What are you on about?' James asked.

'James,' Mac said. 'Have you spoken to Doctor Coen yet?'

James shook his head. 'No.'

'We just found out that the bacteria in your system is harmless,' Mac said. 'Scargill Dunn claimed they were using a weak strain of anthrax. They were only going to use the bad stuff on the day of the conference. A laboratory in London rechecked your blood sample and the anthrax inside you couldn't kill a flea.'

James let out a big smile.

'I don't understand,' he said. 'What's the point of harmless anthrax?'

'Bungle only wanted to kill the Petrocon delegates,' Mac said. 'He made the first batch of anthrax with what's called an *attenuated strain*. It's used in the anthrax vaccine. It makes you immune to the nasty variety. It's been in the air-conditioning at Green Brooke conference hall for weeks.

'Security guards, cleaners, catering staff and anyone else who works regularly in the conference hall would be vaccinated by the time Petrocon started. On the first day of the conference a lethal strain of anthrax was going to be put in the air-conditioning, but only the conference guests would get the disease.'

*

Dr Coen stopped James' antibiotics. By Friday evening he felt much better. The drip was taken out and James managed to eat without feeling sick. By Saturday morning he was almost back to normal. Ewart drove up from Wales.

'Is Amy with you?' James asked.

'No, she's back at Fort Harmony, keeping her ear to the ground to see if any information comes through about Bungle. It's not very likely with all that's going on: there are about fifty cops camped out at the bottom of the hill and loads of huts have got police on the doorstep guarding evidence.'

'How did Amy explain me disappearing?'

'You got into a fight with Amy in the night. Ran off. Stormed down the road and got run over by some lunatic driving a BMW. Amy lifted you into the car and the driver rushed you to hospital. You lost some blood and you've got a broken arm, but otherwise you're OK. They're keeping you in for observation.'

'Good story,' James said. 'I should be allowed out of here today.'

'After all you've been through this week I'll understand if you want to go back to CHERUB and rest,' Ewart said. 'But I'd appreciate it if you could show your face at Fort Harmony for a few days. A week at most.'

'Will I be allowed to see Joanna?' James asked.

'Why not?' Ewart grinned. 'Keep hanging out with Sebastian and Clark. Some little titbit of information might pop out, but mostly it's to cover Cathy. It would look suspicious if you disappeared on the morning before the arrests never to be seen again.'

*

A nurse fitted James with a plaster cast on his fake broken arm. On the drive back to Wales James read all the latest stuff in the papers about the anthrax terrorists and the continuing hunt for the laboratory and Bungle. It was odd seeing the newspapers filled with stuff he knew about.

The stories made Bungle sound like a supervillain, but James could only remember a big friendly American who cared about workers' rights and the environment.

*

Cathy was waiting in the Land Cruiser fifteen kilometres outside Craddogh. James ran between the two cars and waved to Ewart as he drove off.

'Hello, Ross,' Cathy said. 'Fake broken arm?'

James nodded. 'It itches exactly like a real broken arm.'

As they got near the camp a policewoman pulled the Land Cruiser over and asked Cathy where she was going. Cathy got waved on. She had to drive across country because the bottom of the hill near the underground workshop was sealed off by police.

The main hut was packed when James and Cathy arrived. The residents seemed edgy about all the police and media people hanging around. A few journalists and photographers were scrounging free stew. Amy hugged James when she saw him. James wanted to go down the village and see Joanna, but it was already late and he didn't know if her dad was home.

Sebastian tapped James on the back.

'Hey, cripple,' Clark said. 'Feeling OK?'

'Not bad, a bit weak.'

'You're lucky that driver didn't splatter you,' Clark said.

'Would have been wicked getting up and seeing you mashed into the road,' Sebastian laughed. 'Got any scars?'

James pulled up the sleeve of his T-shirt and showed the mass of bruises and cuts where the antibiotics had been injected.

'Is that where the car hit you?' Clark asked.

James nodded.

'We were gonna ask you something the night you got run over,' Clark said. 'But we couldn't find you.'

'Ask what?'

'If you wanted to sleep over in our hut.'

'Cool,' James said.

39. FUNERAL

James couldn't decide if he liked Sebastian and Clark. They had a dark side, but that made them interesting to be around. They slept in a rusty panel van next to their mum's hut.

James thumped the metal. Clark slid the side door open.

'Get your butt in here,' Clark yelled.

James bent over to slip off his boots. It had become habit after a few days at Fort Harmony.

'Leave them on,' Clark said. 'The filth is what gives our van character.'

James stepped inside. Two gas lamps pushed out gloomy orange light. His hair brushed the roof. Clark's mattress was below the cracked windscreen where the seats used to be. Sebastian lay at the other end, toying with a big hunting knife. The metal floor was wet and had grass poking up through rust holes. Everything was thrown about: dirty clothes, air guns, knives, shredded school books.

'Duck,' Sebastian shouted.

Sebastian flung his boot across the van. It skimmed past Clark and clanged into the side, leaving a muddy splat on the wall. The second boot hit James in the back.

James looked at the muck on his sweatshirt and smiled.

'You're so dead,' he said.

He hurled the boot back, then dived on to Sebastian and squashed him under the cast on his arm.

'Bundle,' Clark shouted and jumped on the pair of them.

The three boys rumbled until they were all red-faced and out of breath. James was almost as dirty as Sebastian and Clark by the time they'd finished. Clark passed a bottle of water. James took a few gulps and tipped some over his head to cool off.

'Want to go out and do something?' Clark asked.

James shrugged. 'Long as it doesn't involve killing stuff.'

You're such a girl,' Clark said. 'I want to go down the hill and shoot one of the cops up the arse with my air pistol.'

Sebastian laughed. 'That would be so cool. You haven't got the guts.'

Clark picked his air pistol off the floor, pumped it and loaded a pellet.

'Want a bet?'

'Five quid,' Sebastian said, holding out his hand for Clark to shake.

Clark thought about taking the bet, then started laughing.

'I knew you wouldn't,' Sebastian said.

'I hate the cops,' Clark said. 'Fire and World were the best guys around here.'

'I hope Mum lets us see them in prison this time,' Sebastian said.

'It would have been superb if they'd pulled it off,' Clark said. 'We would have been related to two of the biggest murderers in British history, and by the time people started getting sick Fire and World would have been gone. Nobody could have touched them.'

'Two hundred dead though,' James said. 'They all would have had families and stuff.'

'They were rich scum,' Clark said. 'With fat, ugly wives and spoilt kids. The world would have done fine without them.'

'Ross, you should have heard some of the stuff Fire told us about all the evil shit the big oil companies do,' Sebastian said. 'This farmer in South America had an oil pipe burst over his land. His whole farm was trashed. So he goes to the oil company and asks them to clean up the mess. They beat him up. He complained to the police, but the police were getting bribes from the oil company. They stuck the farmer in a cell and didn't give him anything to drink until he signed a confession saying he blew up the pipe himself. Once he'd signed the confession he got fifty years in prison. They only let him out when loads of environmentalists complained.'

'That sounds fake,' James said.

'Next time you go on the Internet look it up for yourself,' Clark said. 'There are tons of stories like that on there.'

'Fire told us loads of babies in poor countries die because their drinking water gets poisoned by spilled oil,' Sebastian said.

'Still, you can't go round killing people,' James said.

'You say we're sick,' Clark said. 'So how sick are those guys going to Petrocon? They've all got millions, but they won't spend any of it to stop babies getting poisoned.'

*

They decided it wasn't worth going out; you couldn't do

much with all the police and journalists around. Clark rigged up a target box at one end of the van and they had a shooting competition with air guns. James had shot real guns in basic training and wasn't bad, even though he could only hold the gun with one hand. Sebastian and Clark were brilliant. Every pellet passed through the centre of their paper targets. Afterwards the brothers showed off tricks. Clark managed to shoot between the eyes of the grinning kids on the cover of his maths textbook while holding the gun behind his back.

At midnight Clark and Sebastian's mum stuck her head in and told them to go to sleep. They rearranged the mess so there was room for James to lay out his sleeping bag and turned out the gas lamps. The boys talked in the dark, mostly about Fire and World. Sebastian and Clark knew tons of funny stories about things Fire and World did at school and in prison. They sounded cool. James almost felt bad about being one of the people who'd got them caught.

*

Somehow they ended up fighting again. Battering each other with pillows and throwing stuff around. The darkness made it more exciting because everyone could launch sneak attacks. James' sleeping bag got ripped open in a tug of war and the stuffing flew everywhere.

Clark fired his air pistol. Sebastian and James dived for cover. They couldn't tell if they were being shot at, or if Clark was only trying to scare them. Sebastian and Clark's mum came back. All three boys dived under their covers, giggling.

'It's one in the morning,' she shouted. 'If I hear any more noise I'm coming in there and you'll be sorry.'

Their mum must have been tough because after she threatened them Sebastian and Clark straightened up their beds and said goodnight. James was sweaty, filthy, and his burst sleeping bag was on a metal floor, but he was so knackered after the last few days that he closed his eyes and was instantly asleep.

*

James first thought the banging was some prank by Sebastian and Clark. Clark lit his torch.

'What is that?' James asked.

Someone was thumping on the outside of the van.

'Open up in there. Police.'

Clark shone the torch on the back of Sebastian's head.

Clark laughed. 'Nothing wakes him up. I set a firework off next to his ear once and he didn't even budge.'

Clark got out of bed wearing shorts and a T-shirt and unlocked the door. Two powerful torches pointed in his face. A policeman grabbed Clark out of the van and turned his torch on James.

'Boy,' the policeman shouted to James, 'get out of there now.'

James put his bottoms and boots on with his free arm and stepped out. Fort Harmony was ablaze with flashing blue lights and torch beams. Police in riot gear were dragging everyone out of their huts. Kids were crying. Residents and police shouted at each other.

The policemen knocked James against the van beside Clark.

'Anyone else in there?' one policeman shouted.

'My little brother,' Clark said. 'I'll go and wake him up.'

'No you don't, I'll do it,' the policeman said.

One policeman stepped into the van. James spoke to the other one.

'What's going on?'

'Court order,' the policeman said. He pulled a piece of paper out of his pocket and read from it. 'By order of the High Court all residents of the community known as Fort Harmony shall leave within seven days. Dated 16th September 1972.'

'That's over thirty years ago,' James said.

The policeman shrugged. 'It took us a bit longer than expected.'

The policeman inside the van screamed. He staggered out, holding his thigh. James spotted the glint of Sebastian's hunting knife sticking out of his leg. The other policeman shouted into his radio.

'Code one. Code one. Officer down. Serious injury.'

About ten cops came swarming over. Two grabbed the cop with the knife in his leg and carried him off. Two slammed James and Clark hard into the side of the van and started searching them for weapons.

'Not those two, there's a kid in the van,' a policeman said.

Clark shouted out, 'I said I'd wake him up for you. He's scared of the dark so he sleeps with the knife beside him.'

'Shut your hole before I shut it for you,' a policeman said.

Six policemen surrounded the door of the van. Three of them had guns drawn.

'Get out here, now,' a sergeant shouted.

Sebastian shouted from inside, 'Don't shoot me. Put the guns away.'

'Put them down, he's only a kid,' the sergeant said. 'What's your name, son?'

'Sebastian.'

'Sebastian, I want you to come slowly out of the van with your hands in the air. We know it was an accident. We won't hurt you.'

Sebastian stepped into the torchlight. When he got near the door the police grabbed him and slammed him into the mud. One cop put his boot on Sebastian's back and locked on handcuffs. He looked tiny compared to the policemen all bulked out by riot gear. They dragged Sebastian off to a police car.

'Let me go with him,' Clark said.

A policeman slammed Clark against the van again.

'You don't learn, do you?' the policeman said.

Sebastian's mum was dragged out of her hut and put in the police car with her son.

'What about us?' James asked.

'We're taking everyone to the church hall in the village. There's a coach at the bottom of the hill,' the sergeant said.

'I need to get my tracksuit and boots,' Clark said.

'You can't go in there, it's a crime scene.'

'I'm barefoot,' Clark said. 'It's freezing.'

'I don't care if you've got to walk across broken glass,' the policeman shouted. 'Get down to that coach or you'll have more than cold feet to worry about.'

James and Clark walked off.

'I've got to find my sister and Auntie Cathy,' James said.

Police were everywhere, over a hundred. A chain of residents was heading down the hill. Anyone who put up a fight found the riot cops weren't shy about pulling batons. James and Clark dodged into some trees and re-emerged beside Cathy's hut. There was no sign of Amy, Cathy or the Land Cruiser. They went in the hut. Amy and Cathy had taken most stuff with them.

'What you looking for?' Clark asked.

'My mobile,' James said. 'Looks like my sister took it with her. What shoe size are you?'

'Two.'

James kicked a pair of his Nikes into the middle of the floor.

'Those are a three, you'll grow into them. Take whatever clothes you want.'

'Cheers,' Clark said.

Clark put on tracksuit bottoms and trainers. James found him a warm top with a hood.

'My sister's probably down at the village,' James said. 'Might as well get on the coach.'

*

James and Clark sat next to each other on the coach. It gradually filled up with residents, all of them carrying what they could. Clark was trying to hide how upset he was from James, but couldn't hold himself together.

'He's only ten, they'll realise it was an accident,' James said.

'Don't bet on it, Ross. The cops will switch their stories around so he gets done. Whose story are they going to believe? A couple of kids who are always in trouble, or the police?'

'I'll be a witness,' James said.

'If Sebastian gets sent away I'll stab a cop myself so I can stay with him.'

40. HALL

Craddogh Church Hall was a madhouse. Eighty people with no air to breathe. Kids ran around screaming. Journalists kept asking Gladys Dunn for quotes and pictures, but the old lady needed rest. Michael Dunn threw a punch and got dragged away by police in a blaze of camera flashes.

The residents wanted to go back to Fort Harmony to get their stuff, but police cars blocked the road and nobody got through. The police said everything was being collected and would arrive in a few hours.

Clark had turned into a basket case. Sobbing for his brother and mum and screaming to any nearby cop that he was going to kill him first chance he got. James tried to calm him down, without much success.

'You're the first kid who's ever been nice to us,' Clark said to James.

James felt bad. Clark wasn't his real friend. He'd used him to help with the mission.

*

On TV you knew who the baddies were and they got what they deserved at the end of the show. Now James realised baddies were ordinary people. They told jokes, made you cups of coffee, went to the toilet and had families who loved them.

James totted everyone up: Fire, World and Bungle were obviously bad guys for trying to kill everyone with anthrax. The oil company people were also bad for trashing the environment and abusing people in poor countries. The police were bad guys; they had a tricky job to do, but they seemed to enjoy throwing their weight around more than they should. The only good guys were the Fort Harmony residents and they'd all got chucked out of their homes.

James couldn't figure what he was himself. As far as he could tell, he'd stopped one small bunch of bad guys killing a big bunch of bad guys and as a result the good guys got chucked out of their homes by another bunch of bad guys. Did that make him good or bad? James only knew that thinking about it gave him a headache.

*

James left Clark with his family and went outside. There was no sign of Amy or Cathy. James didn't have his mobile and the village phone box had about twenty people queuing up, trying to find somewhere to stay now Fort Harmony was shut off. James realised he might be able to phone Amy or Ewart from Joanna's house. He was sure Joanna's dad would be on duty with all that was going on.

Joanna and her dad stood by their garden gate in night clothes, watching the arguments and blue lights in the centre of the village.

'Hey,' James said.

Joanna gave James a smile that made him feel better. James was still wary of Sergeant Ribble after he'd caught them in Cathy's hut, but he sounded OK.

'What's going on up there?' Sergeant Ribble asked.

'Everyone's been chucked out of Fort Harmony,' James said. 'How come you're not involved? You're a policeman.'

'That lot don't give me the time of day. I'm just the local bobby,' Sergeant Ribble said. 'As soon as they found the anthrax, the terrorist squad turned up and took everything off my hands.'

'Can I use your phone?' James asked. 'I've lost my aunt and my sister.'

'Of course you can, son. Jojo will show you where the phone is.'

James took off his boots and stepped into the house with Joanna. She was wearing slippers and a Daffy Duck nightie.

'Hi Jojo,' James said, laughing.

'Shut up, Ross. Only my dad and big brothers call me that.'

'I'll probably have to go back to London now,' James said.

'Oh,' Joanna said.

James was glad she sounded upset. It meant Joanna liked him as much as he liked Joanna. She showed him the phone. It took a minute to remember Amy's mobile number.

'Courtney,' James said. 'Where are you?'

'Cathy went nuts,' Amy said. 'She thinks what happened tonight is her fault for letting us into Fort Harmony. She dumped me a few kilometres outside Craddogh with most of our stuff. Ewart's coming to fetch me. He should be here any minute.'

'I'm at Joanna's house in the village,' James said. 'What should I do?'

'Stay where you are,' Amy said. 'I'll get Ewart to pick you up after me. If anyone asks questions, say Ewart's a mini-cab driver and Cathy has arranged for us to get the first train to London from Cardiff in the morning. We should be with you in about half an hour.'

'Are we going home?' James asked.

'Mission's over, James. With no Fort Harmony, there's no reason to stay.'

James put the phone down and looked at Joanna.

'Mini-cab is on its way. I'm going back to my mum in London.'

'Let's go to my room,' Joanna said. 'Goodbye kiss.'

Joanna's dad was too busy watching outside to notice his daughter sneaking James into her bedroom. She didn't care that James was all muddy. She leant against her bedroom door to stop her dad bursting in and they started kissing. Joanna was soft and hot to touch, her hair smelled like shampoo and her breath like toothpaste. It felt great, but James ached knowing they only had a few minutes and then he'd never see her again.

The door hit Joanna in the back.

'What are you two doing in there?' Sergeant Ribble said.

James and Joanna moved away from the door. Her dad came in. They probably could have made some excuse, if Joanna's nightdress hadn't been covered in James' muddy handprints.

'Joanna, you're thirteen years old,' her dad yelled.

'But Daddy we were just . . .'

'Put something clean on and go to bed. And you . . .'

Joanna's dad grabbed James by the back of his neck.

'Did you make your phone call?'

'Yes,' James said. 'There's a mini-cab coming for me.'

'You can wait for it outside.'

Joanna's dad shoved James out of the house and made him sit on the garden wall facing the road. James felt totally miserable. He was worried what would happen to Sebastian, he felt guilty that he and Amy finding out about the anthrax had led to Fort Harmony being destroyed, and worst of all the best girl he'd ever met was trapped in a house a few metres away and he'd never see her again.

James heard a window open behind him. He watched Joanna throw out a paper aeroplane. Her dad charged back into the house.

'I ordered you to bed, young lady.'

James jumped into the garden and picked up the aeroplane. He realised there was something written on the paper and unravelled it.

> *Ross,*
> *Please phone me. You're so cute.*
> *Joanna.*
> *XXX*

James folded up the paper, put it in his pocket and felt even sadder.

*

Ewart drove Amy and James back to Fort Harmony in the BMW.

'Why are they smashing it up?' James asked.

'I spoke to someone at the anti-terrorist squad,' Ewart said. 'They say Fort Harmony is a security risk. They wanted it wiped before Petrocon started, and the law was on their side.'

'I wish I'd never come here,' James said. 'It's our fault this has happened.'

'I thought you hated Fort Harmony,' Amy said,

'I didn't say I wanted to live there,' James said. 'Just, it's not fair kicking everyone out.'

'Fort Harmony was doomed either way,' Ewart said. 'If Fire, World and Bungle had killed all those people, they would have wiped the camp out after the conference instead of before. All you would have done is delayed the end by a month.'

'Did you know it was going to happen, Ewart?' James asked.

'I wouldn't have sent you back for one night if I had.'

'Where's Cathy gone?' James asked.

'She was upset,' Amy said. 'She said something about staying with friends in London.'

'Cathy broke the deal,' Ewart said. 'She wasn't supposed to abandon Amy in the middle of nowhere. I want that money back when I catch up with her.'

'Leave her alone,' Amy said. 'She's lived at Fort Harmony for thirty years and got in a bit of a state when all those cops showed up. She did a perfect job looking after us until tonight.'

'A sixteen-year-old girl dumped in the middle of the countryside at night, with four bags of luggage,' Ewart said.

'Lucky your mobile had reception. You could have been picked up by some nutter and murdered.'

'But I *wasn't*,' Amy said sharply. 'So leave Cathy alone. We got everything we wanted from her.'

Ewart banged the steering wheel. 'OK Amy, if you say so. Cathy's come out of this with eight thousand quid and a car. It's better than she deserves after treating you like that.'

Ewart slowed down at a police checkpoint. He showed an ID and they waved him through. The sun was coming up. Riot police were working their way across Fort Harmony. One crew emptied out the shelters, bagging up the contents and loading them into a truck. A follow-up team worked with chainsaws and sledgehammers, knocking the huts down and smashing the timber into small pieces so there was no way anything could be rebuilt.

Ewart, James and Amy got out of the BMW. Ewart was wearing scruffy jeans and looked too young to be anyone important. A couple of policemen walked towards them.

'Get back in the car and drive on,' a policeman shouted.

Ewart ignored him and headed for Cathy's hut. James and Amy followed.

'You're asking for a day in the cells,' the policeman said cockily.

The cop made a grab for Ewart. Ewart dodged him and pulled out his ID. The policeman looked a bit stunned.

'Um, what are you here for?'

'Sir,' Ewart said.

'What?' the policeman said.

'Don't you call a senior officer sir?'

'What can I do for you, *sir*?'

'Get me some plastic bags,' Ewart said.

They walked across to Cathy's hut and started packing up. A chief inspector rushed over. She sounded apologetic.

'Sorry about the mix-up. We got a message not to touch this hut. Can I double-check your ID?'

Ewart handed it to her.

'I've never seen one of these before,' she gushed. 'Level one clearance. The Commissioner of the anti-terrorist unit only has level two. What are you doing here?'

Ewart snatched it back out of her hand.

'You should know better than to ask questions,' Ewart said. 'Take this down to my car.'

Ewart dumped a bin-liner stuffed with clothes in the chief inspector's arms. James thought it was funny watching a senior policewoman carrying a bag of his dirty clothes down a muddy hill.

'I thought only Mac had level one security clearance,' Amy said.

Ewart shrugged. 'That's right.'

'So what did you show her?' Amy asked.

'A very good fake.'

James laughed. 'That's so cool.'

They loaded all their stuff in the back of the car. James turned back for a last glance at Fort Harmony and took a couple of pictures of a tree with his digital camera.

'What's with the tree?' Amy asked, after they'd driven off.

'Not telling,' James said. 'You'll take the piss.'

Amy wriggled her fingers in the air. 'I'll tickle it out of you.'

'OK,' James said. 'But promise not to laugh.'

314

'I promise,' Amy said.

'It's where I first kissed Joanna.'

Amy smiled. 'That is *so* sweet.'

Ewart put his fingers in his mouth and pretended he was being sick.

'You promised,' James said.

Ewart laughed. 'Amy promised. I never said a word.'

'I can't wait to tell Kerry all about your smooching with Joanna,' Amy said.

'Oh god, don't . . . Please,' James said.

'Why would you care what I told Kerry about you, unless you like her more than you're willing to admit?' Amy teased.

James wanted to storm off, but that was difficult in a car doing eighty kilometres an hour. He folded his arms and stared out the window, trying to hide how upset he was about not being able to see Joanna again.

41. DARK

When they got back to CHERUB Amy took James to the woodwork shop. She found an electric drill and fixed on a circular cutter. James gave the silver teeth a grim look.

'You're not cutting it off with that,' James said. 'You'll kill me.'

'Stop being such a pansy. Put these on.'

Amy threw James a set of protective goggles and fixed a pair on herself.

'Put your arm on the bench,' Amy said.

'Have you ever done this before?'

Amy smiled. 'No.'

James rested his cast on the workbench. Amy gave the drill a couple of test spins then set to work. Plaster shards pelted James' face and the white dust dried his mouth. James thought he felt the blade tickling the hairs on his arm, but hoped he was just imagining it.

Amy stopped the drill and cracked off most of the cast, leaving the part around the elbow.

'OK, last bit,' Amy said.

Amy cut in at a different angle. When she was done James pulled the last bit of plaster down his arm and went into a scratching frenzy.

'That feels so much better,' James said. 'OHHHHHH.'

'Leave it alone, you'll tear all your skin off,' Amy said.

'Don't care.'

James took off the goggles and flicked white dust out of his hair.

'Go have a shower and take your clothes to the laundry,' Amy said. 'Mac will want to see you in his office when you're ready.'

'Just me?' James asked.

'It's a standard thing,' Amy said. 'He does it with everyone after their first mission.'

*

Mac was dressed in shorts and a T-shirt when James got to his office.

'Come in, James. How you feeling?'

'Fine now,' James said. 'Bit tired.'

'Ewart seemed to think you had some doubts about the value of your mission.'

'It's confusing,' James said.

'He said you didn't seem sure that we'd done the right thing,' Mac said.

'I heard some stuff about the people going to Petrocon,' James said. 'They poison people and beat people up and stuff. I'm not even sure it's true.'

'It's mostly true,' Mac said. 'Oil companies have a terrible environmental and human rights record. Without oil and gas the world stops working. No aeroplanes, no ships, no

317

cars, very little electricity. Because oil is so important, companies and governments bend rules to get it. Help Earth and a lot of other people, including me, think they go too far.'

'So you support Help Earth?' James said.

'I want to stop people getting exploited and poisoned by oil companies. I don't agree that terrorism is the way to do it.'

'I understand,' James said. 'Killing people never solves anything.'

'Think about what would have happened if all those people got killed at Petrocon,' Mac said. 'Would Help Earth have attacked somewhere else? What if the anthrax got into the hands of another terrorist group? You'll never know for certain what would have happened if Fire and World Dunn weren't caught. The next attack could have been in the middle of a city. Stick some anthrax in a London Underground station and you'd be looking at five thousand dead people. That's how many lives you and Amy might have saved.'

'Bungle's still on the loose though,' James said.

'Can I trust you with some information?' Mac asked.

'What?' James said.

'You're the only person who knows besides Ewart and myself, so if this gets out I'll know you leaked it.'

'I swear,' James said.

'MI5 knows where Bungle is,' Mac said.

'So why don't you get him?'

'They're tracking him,' Mac said. 'Bungle won't tell us anything if we arrest him, but by letting him wander he might lead us to other members of Help Earth.'

'What if you lose him?' James asked.

Mac laughed, 'You always ask me the question I don't want to answer.'

'Have they lost anyone before?' James asked.

'Yes,' Mac said. 'It won't happen this time. Bungle can't stick a finger up his nose without ten people knowing about it.'

'It makes more sense now you've explained it,' James said. 'I still feel sorry for all the people who got chucked out of Fort Harmony. They're a weird lot, but basically they're OK.'

'It's a shame,' Mac said. 'But a few families losing their homes is better than thousands of people getting killed.

'So I want to thank you for doing a brilliant job, James. You made friends with the right people, didn't break your cover and polished off the mission in half the time we expected.'

'Thanks,' James said.

'I also owe you a massive apology,' Mac said. 'You nearly died. We had no idea Help Earth was planning an anthrax attack. If we'd known, we never would have sent someone as inexperienced as you on this mission.'

'It's not your fault.'

'You must have been frightened, but you handled yourself tremendously. You kept a level head and even agreed to return to the mission. I've decided to classify your overall performance as outstanding.'

Mac pulled a navy CHERUB T-shirt out of his desk and threw it to James.

'Wow,' James said, grinning. 'When Kerry sees this she's gonna be so pissed off.'

'I'll pretend I didn't hear that,' Mac said. 'But if you use that sort of language in my office again I'll make you a very unhappy boy.'

'Sorry,' James said. 'Can I put it on?'

'Don't be modest on my account,' Mac said.

James ripped off his Arsenal shirt and pulled the navy CHERUB T-shirt over his head.

*

The kids at CHERUB were allowed to sleep late and wear normal clothes on Sundays. It was still early and nobody was around. James ate breakfast alone in the dining room, with one eye on the television. There was a story about Fort Harmony being destroyed on News 24. They cut to a clip of Michael Dunn waving his fists in the air and vowing he would spend the rest of his life rebuilding Fort Harmony if that was what it took.

Kerry came down in shorts and a denim jacket. She gave James a hug.

'I was so happy you *finally* got a mission,' Kerry said. 'I got back from my third mission on Thursday.'

James loved the way she couldn't resist mentioning it was her third mission. He wondered how long it would be before she noticed his navy shirt. Bruce came down and joined Kerry at the breakfast buffet.

'Good mission?' Bruce asked, as he put his tray on the table next to James.

James acted casual. 'Mac seemed to think I did OK.'

Kerry sat opposite James. She only had a bran muffin and a couple of bits of fruit.

'On a diet?' James asked.

'I'm trying to eat less greasy stuff,' Kerry said.

'Good,' James said. 'You're starting to look a bit fat.'

Bruce burst out laughing and spat half his bacon across the table. Kerry kicked James in the shin.

'Pig,' Kerry said.

'That kick hurt,' James said. 'I was only joking.'

'Did you see me laughing?' Kerry asked.

James got a punch in the back. 'Stop being rude to Kerry,' Lauren said. 'You should ask her out now you're back. It's *so* obvious you two fancy each other.'

James and Kerry blushed. Lauren got her breakfast and sat next to Kerry.

Callum and Connor sat at the next table a few minutes later. James hadn't seen them together since Callum restarted basic training.

'Which one of you is Callum?' James asked.

Callum raised a finger.

'You passed basic training now?' James asked.

'Got back from Malaysia on Tuesday,' Callum said. 'Slept for twenty hours solid.'

'Bet you're glad that's out the way,' James said.

'You know that navy T-shirt you're wearing is a CHERUB shirt?' Callum said.

James was pleased someone had finally noticed.

'Yes,' he said casually.

'You'd better take it off, James,' Bruce said. 'Kids work really hard to earn them. They'll kill you if they catch you wearing it.'

'It's my shirt,' James said. 'I did earn it.'

Kerry laughed. 'Yeah, James, and I'm the Queen of China.'

'Don't believe me then,' James said.

Bruce sounded a bit desperate. 'I'm serious, James. People get angry when you wear a shirt without earning it. Take it off. They'll stuff your head down the toilet or something.'

'I'd pay money to see him bog-washed,' Lauren giggled. 'Leave it on.'

'I'm not taking it off,' James said. 'It's mine.'

'You're such an idiot,' Kerry said. 'Don't say we didn't warn you when we're scraping you off the floor.'

Amy came in. She had Arif and Paul with her. The three of them rushed over to James.

'Too late now,' Bruce said. 'You're dead.'

James was worried. He wasn't sure if Amy knew Mac had awarded him the navy shirt. He stood up from the table and turned to face Amy. Paul and Arif looked intimidating, muscles everywhere.

Amy wrapped James in her arms.

'Congratulations,' Amy said. 'You really deserve that shirt. You were brilliant.'

Amy let go. Paul and Arif shook James' hand.

'I can't believe you're that wimp we had to keep throwing in the diving pool,' Arif said.

James looked back at his friends sitting around the table. They all looked amazed. Lauren jumped up and hugged her brother. Kerry's mouth was open so wide you could have shoved a tennis ball in it without touching a tooth. James couldn't help smiling.

It was beautiful.

EPILOGUE

RONALD ONIONS (UNCLE RON) has had difficulty adjusting to life behind bars. He received two broken arms during a fight with a fellow inmate. He is scheduled to be released in 2012.

GLADYS DUNN used the money from her second book to buy a farm in Spain. She lives on the land with her son JOSHUA DUNN, who makes curry, stew or paella every day for the thirty former Fort Harmony residents who joined them. Gladys jokingly refers to her farm as '*Fort Harmony 2, but warmer and without the mud.*'

CATHY DUNN sold the Land Cruiser, purchased a round-the-world air ticket and went backpacking in Australia.

SEBASTIAN DUNN was released from police custody without charge. The stabbing of the policeman was classified as an accident. The policeman returned to duty a few months later.

Sebastian now lives in a cottage in Craddogh with his

mother and brother CLARK DUNN. Sebastian and Clark have denied links to a number of cats that have disappeared since their arrival in the village.

FIRE & WORLD DUNN were tried and convicted at the Old Bailey in London. They were each sentenced to life in prison. The Judge recommended they serve a minimum of twenty-five years.

As SCARGILL DUNN was only seventeen and had no previous criminal convictions, he was sentenced to only four years in a young offenders' prison. With early release for good behaviour he could be out within two years. He has begun studying for A-level exams and hopes to go to university after he is released.

Police suspect ELEANOR EVANS is a member of Help Earth who helped to plan the anthrax attacks on Petrocon 2004. No evidence was found and she was released from custody without charge. She now lives in Brighton with her mother, her son GREGORY EVANS and her newly born daughter Tiffany.

BRIAN 'BUNGLE' EVANS slipped M15 surveillance after a few weeks. He is now one of the world's most wanted men. Police in Britain, the United States, France and Venezuela all wish to question him about terrorist activity.

JOANNA RIBBLE was disappointed that Ross Leigh didn't write or call. She now has a new boyfriend. James kept her paper aeroplane and the photograph of the tree where they first kissed.

KYLE BLUEMAN returned from his eighteenth mission and finally got his navy CHERUB shirt. He was reportedly '*upset*' that James got his navy shirt before him. Kyle reckons James only got the navy shirt because Mac felt sorry for him when he got anthrax.

BRUCE NORRIS & KERRY CHANG frequently remind James that although he earned a navy shirt, they have both done more missions than him and can easily kick his butt any time he starts to get cocky.

AMY COLLINS hopes to complete a couple more missions before she leaves CHERUB and goes to university.

LAUREN ADAMS (formerly LAUREN ONIONS) is enjoying life at CHERUB. She starts basic training shortly after her tenth birthday in September 2004.

JAMES ADAMS (formerly JAMES CHOKE) got his Karate black belt shortly after returning from his mission. His exuberant celebrations ended badly and his punishment was one month cleaning up in the CHERUB kitchen every night after dinner.

He is currently preparing for his second mission.

CLASS A
Robert Muchamore

Copyright © 2004 Robert Muchamore
First published in Great Britain in 2004
by Hodder Children's Books
This edition published in 2008

WHAT IS CHERUB?

CHERUB is a branch of British Intelligence. Its agents are aged between ten and seventeen years. Cherubs are all orphans who have been taken out of care homes and trained to work undercover. They live on CHERUB campus, a secret facility hidden in the English countryside.

WHAT USE ARE KIDS?

Quite a lot. Nobody realises kids do undercover missions, which means they can get away with all kinds of stuff that adults can't.

WHO ARE THEY?

About three hundred children live on CHERUB campus. JAMES ADAMS is our twelve-year-old hero. He's basically a good kid, but he has a habit of getting himself in trouble. There's also his younger sister, LAUREN. KERRY CHANG is a Hong Kong born Karate champion. GABRIELLE O'BRIEN is Kerry's best friend. BRUCE NORRIS, another

Karate champion, likes to think of himself as a hard-man but still sleeps with a blue teddy under his chin. KYLE BLUEMAN is a more experienced CHERUB agent. He's two years older than James, but still a good mate.

AND THE T-SHIRTS?

Cherubs are ranked according to the colour of the T-shirts they wear on campus. ORANGE is for visitors. RED is for kids who live at CHERUB campus, but are too young to qualify as agents. BLUE is for kids undergoing CHERUB's tough 100-day basic training regime. A GREY T-shirt means you're qualified for missions. NAVY is a reward for outstanding performance on a mission. If you do well, you'll end your CHERUB career wearing a BLACK T-shirt, the ultimate recognition for outstanding achievement. When you retire, you get the WHITE T-shirt, which is also worn by staff.

1. HEAT

Billions of insects fizzed about in the sunset. James and Bruce had given up trying to swat them off. The boys had jogged ten kilometres along a twisted gravel path. It was uphill, heading towards a villa where two eight-year-olds were being held hostage.

'Better give us a minute,' James huffed, leaning forward and resting his palms against his knees. 'I'm wiped.'

If James had wrung out his T-shirt, he could have filled a mug with the sweat.

'I'm a year younger than you,' Bruce said impatiently. 'You should be the one pushing me. It's that gut you're carrying.'

James looked down at himself. 'Give over, I'm hardly fat.'

'Not exactly thin either. You're gonna get crucified at your next medical. They'll put you on a diet and make you run all that off.'

James straightened up and drank some water from his canteen.

'It's not my fault, Bruce. It's genetic. You should have seen the size of my mum before she died.'

Bruce laughed. 'There were three Toffee Crisp and one

Snickers wrapper in our bin last night. That's not genetic, that's you being a pig.'

'We can't all have little stick-insect bodies like you,' James said, bitterly. 'Are you ready?'

'We might as well check the map now we've stopped,' Bruce said. 'See how far it is to the villa.'

James got a map out of his pack. Bruce had a GPS clipped on his shorts. The tiny unit told you your exact position anywhere on the planet to within a couple of metres. Bruce transposed the coordinates on to the map and used his finger to trace the winding gravel path towards the villa.

'Time to go off road,' Bruce said. 'It's less than half a kilometre away.'

'It's really steep,' James said, 'and the ground crumbles around here. It's gonna be a nightmare.'

'Well,' Bruce said, 'unless your plan is to walk up to the front gate of the villa, ring the doorbell and say, *Excuse me love, can we have our hostages back?* I think we'd better cut into the bushes.'

Bruce had a point. James gave up trying to fold the map properly and stuffed it in his pack. Bruce led the way into the scrub, the tinder-dry plants crunching under his trainers. It hadn't rained on the island for two months. There'd been bush fires in the east. When the sky was clear, you could see the plumes of smoke.

James' damp skin soon had a coating of grit. He grabbed on to plants, using them to pull his way up the steep slope. You had to be careful: some plants had barbs, others erupted from the dry ground as soon as you pulled on them, leaving you holding a clump of roots, clutching desperately for something sturdier before you tumbled backwards.

When they reached the wire fence around the villa, they backed up a few metres and lay flat on the ground, collecting their thoughts. Bruce was moaning something about his hand.

'What are you whinging about?' James asked.

Bruce showed James his palm. Even in the half-light, James could see the blood trickling down Bruce's arm.

'How'd you do that?'

Bruce shrugged. 'Somewhere coming up the hill. I didn't realise until we stopped.'

'I'd better clean it up for you.'

James tipped some water out of his canteen, washing away most of the blood. He got the first aid kit out of his pack; then lit a small torch and clamped it between his teeth, so he could see what he was doing while keeping both hands free. A thorn bulged under the webbing between Bruce's middle fingers.

'Nasty,' James said. 'Does it hurt?'

'What kind of stupid question is that?' Bruce snapped. 'Of course it does.'

'Am I supposed to pull it out?' James asked.

'Yes,' Bruce said wearily. 'Do you ever listen in class? Always remove splinters, unless there is severe and profuse bleeding, or you suspect you've punctured a vein or artery. Then apply disinfectant and a clean dressing or sticking plaster.'

'You sound like you swallowed the textbook,' James said.

'I was on the same first aid course as you, James. Only I

didn't spend the entire three days trying to get off with Susan Kaplan.'

'It's a pity she had a boyfriend.'

'Susan doesn't have a boyfriend,' Bruce said. 'She was just trying to get rid of you.'

'Oh,' James said, crushed. 'I thought she liked me.'

Bruce didn't answer. He was biting down on the strap of his backpack. He didn't want anyone in the villa to hear if the pain made him scream out.

James lined up his tweezers. 'Ready?'

Bruce nodded.

The thorn slid out easily enough. Bruce moaned as a fresh dribble of blood trickled down his hand. James mopped it up, rubbed on antiseptic cream and wound a bandage tightly between Bruce's fingers.

'All done,' James said. 'Are you right to carry on?'

'We can't turn back after going this far.'

'You rest for a minute,' James said. 'I'll sneak up to the fence and check out the security.'

'Watch out for video cameras,' Bruce said. 'They'll be expecting us.'

When James switched off the torch, there was only moonlight left. He shuffled to the fence on his belly. The villa looked impressive: two storeys, four-car garage and a kidney-shaped pool out front. The lawn sprinklers chugged gently, the spouts of water illuminated by the porch lights. There was no sign of any cameras or hi-tech security stuff; just the yellow siren box from a cheapo burglar alarm, which would be switched off while anyone was in the house. James turned back towards Bruce.

'Get up here. It doesn't look too serious.'

James got out his wire cutters and snipped links in the fence, until there was a slot big enough to squeeze through. He followed Bruce over the lawn, crawling swiftly towards the house. James felt something squish against his leg.

'Oh . . . man,' James said, sounding totally revolted. 'Jesus.'

Bruce hushed him up. 'Quiet, for god's sake. What's the matter?'

'I just dragged my knee through a colossal pile of dog crap.'

Bruce couldn't help smiling. James looked set to puke.

'This is bad,' Bruce said.

'Tell me about it. I've had it on my shoe before, but this is on my bare skin.'

'You know what a massive pile of dog mess means?'

'Yeah,' James said. 'It means I'm extremely pissed off.'

'It also means there's a massive dog around here.'

The thought focused James' mind and got him crawling again. They stopped when they got to the wall of the villa, adjacent to a row of French windows. Bruce sat against the wall and checked out the room inside. The light was on. There were leather sofas and a snooker table inside. They tried sliding the French doors, but every one was locked. The keyholes were on the inside, so there was nothing to use their lock guns on.

WOOF.

The boys snapped their necks around. The mother of all rottweilers stood five metres away. The huge beast had muscles swelling through its shiny black coat and strings of drool hanging off its jaw.

'Nice doggy,' Bruce said, trying to keep calm.

The growling dog moved closer, its black eyes staring them down.

'Who's a nice doggy-woggy?' Bruce asked.

'Bruce, I don't think it's gonna roll over and let you tickle its tummy.'

'Well, what's *your* plan?'

'Don't show it any fear,' James quaked. 'We'll stare it down. It's probably as scared of us as we are of it.'

'Yeah,' Bruce said. 'You can tell. The poor thing's cacking itself.'

James began creeping backwards. The dog let out more volcanic barks. A metal hose reel clattered as James backed into it. He considered the reel for a second, before leaning over and unrolling a few metres of the plastic hose. The dog was only a couple of steps away.

'Bruce, you run off and try to open a door,' James gasped. 'I'll try fending it off with this pipe.'

James half hoped the dog would go after Bruce, but it kept its eyes fixed, pacing closer to James until he could feel its damp breath on his legs.

'Nice doggy,' James said.

The rottweiler reared up on its back legs, trying to knock James over. James spun away and the paws squealed down the glass door. James lashed out with the hosepipe. It cracked against the dog's ribcage. The beast made a high-pitched yelp and backed up slightly. James cracked the pipe against the patio tiles, hoping the noise would scare the dog away, but if anything the whipping seemed to have made it crazier.

James felt like his guts were going to drop out, imagining how easily the huge animal could rip into his flesh. James had nearly drowned once. He'd thought nothing could ever be scarier, but this had the edge.

A bolt clicked behind James' head and the French door glided open.

'Would Sir care to step inside?' Bruce asked.

James threw down the hose and leapt through the opening. Bruce rammed the door shut before the rottweiler made a move.

'What took you so long?' James said anxiously, trying to stop his hands from shaking. 'Where is everyone?'

'No sign,' Bruce said. 'Which is definitely weird. They'd have to be deaf not to hear that psycho mutt barking at us.'

James grabbed one of the curtains and used it to wipe the dog crap off his leg.

'That's so gross,' Bruce said. 'At least it's not on your clothes.'

'Have you checked all the rooms out?'

Bruce shook his head. 'I thought I'd make sure you weren't being eaten first, even if it meant we got caught.'

'Fair play,' James said.

They worked their way across the ground floor, creeping up to each door and checking out the rooms. The villa looked lived-in. There were cigarette butts in ashtrays and dirty mugs. There was a Mercedes in the garage. Bruce pocketed the keys.

'There's our getaway vehicle,' he said.

There was no sign of life on the ground floor, which made the staircase likely to be some sort of trap. They stepped up gingerly, expecting someone to burst on to the landing pointing a gun at them.

There were three bedrooms and a bathroom on the second floor. The two hostages were in the master bedroom. The eight-year-olds, Jake and Laura, were tied to a bedpost, with gags over their mouths. They wore grubby T-shirts and shorts.

James and Bruce pulled the hunting knives off their belts and cut the kids loose. There was no time for greetings.

'Laura,' James barked. 'When did you last see the bad guys? Have you got any idea where they might be?'

Laura was red-faced and seemed listless.

'I dunno,' she shrugged. 'But I'm busting to pee.'

Laura and Jake knew nothing about anything. Bruce and James had been expecting a battle to get at them. This was far too easy.

'We're taking you to the car,' James said.

Laura started limping towards the bathroom. Her ankle was strapped up.

'We don't have time for toilet breaks,' James gasped. 'They've got guns and we haven't.'

'I'm gonna wet my knickers in a minute,' Laura said, bolting herself inside the en-suite bathroom.

James was furious. 'Well, make it snappy.'

'I need to go too,' Jake said.

Bruce shook his head. 'I don't want you disappearing. You can pee in the corner of the garage while I start the car.'

He led Jake downstairs. James waited half a minute before thumping on the bathroom door.

'Laura, come on. What the hell is taking you so long?'

'I'm washing my hands,' Laura said. 'I couldn't find any soap.'

James couldn't believe it.

'For the love of god,' he shouted, hammering his fist on the bolted door. 'We've *got* to get out of here.'

Laura eventually hobbled out of the bathroom. James scooped her over his shoulder and sprinted downstairs to the garage. Bruce sat at the steering wheel inside the car. Laura slid on to the back seat next to Jake.

'It's kaput,' Bruce shouted, getting out of the car and kicking the front wing. 'The key goes in but it won't turn. It's showing a full tank of petrol. I don't know what's wrong with it.'

'It's been sabotaged,' James yelled back. 'I bet you any money this is a trap.'

Bruce looked awkward as the realisation dawned.

'You're right. Let's get out of here.'

James leaned inside the Mercedes.

'Sorry you two,' he said, looking at Jake and Laura. 'Looks like we've got to make a run for it.'

But it was too late. James heard the noise, but only turned around in time to see the gun pointing at him. Bruce screamed out, as James felt two rounds smash into his chest. The pain knocked the air out of his lungs. He stumbled backwards, watching bright red streaks dribbling down his T-shirt.

2. STINGING

Fired from close range, the next paintball knocked James backwards on to the concrete floor. Kerry Chang kept the gun on him as she closed in. James had his hands in the air.

'I surrender.'

'Pardon?' Kerry said, blasting a fourth paintball into James' thigh.

It wasn't going to do permanent damage but, fired from close range, the paintballs had left him in a heap on the ground.

'Kerry, please, not again,' James gasped. 'That *really* hurts.'

'Pardon?' Kerry said. 'Can't hear what you're saying.'

She stood astride James, pointing the muzzle of the paintball gun at him. On the other side of the car, Bruce screamed as Gabrielle shot him a couple more times.

Kerry fired into James' stomach from less than a metre away, doubling him over.

'You mad *cow*,' James howled. 'You could have my eye out doing that. You're supposed to stop shooting as soon as I surrender.'

'Did you surrender?' Kerry grinned. 'I misheard. I thought you said, *Please shoot me again.*'

The girls rested their guns on the roof of the car.

'Did we whip your little pink butts?' Gabrielle whooped in her thick Jamaican accent. 'Or did we whip your little pink butts?'

James struggled to sit up, clasping his hands over his stomach. The pain was bad, but losing to the girls on a stupid training exercise hurt a hundred times more.

The powered garage door started rolling upwards. A huge man stood silhouetted against the moonlight. It was Norman Large, CHERUB's head training instructor. He had the rottweiler on a leash at his side.

'Well done, ladies,' Mr Large shouted. 'You've distinguished those pretty little heads on this one.'

Kerry and Gabrielle smiled. Mr Large stopped walking when his size fifteen boots were almost touching James' leg. James put his hand over his face, shielding his nose from the growling dog's rank breath.

'That thing's not gonna bite me, is it?' James asked.

Mr Large laughed. 'Luckily for you and Bruce, Thatcher has been trained to pin a man to the ground and never bite. Her brother, Saddam, now that's a different question. He's trained to sink his teeth in. We'd have been picking chunks of flesh off the lawn if you'd been up against Saddam. Unfortunately, the chairman banned me from using him . . . Anyway, James, get on your feet. Gabrielle, help that other little idiot to stand up.'

Bruce limped around the car, using the bonnet for support. The yellow paint from Gabrielle's gun trickled down his legs. Both boys stood with their backs against the car. Mr Large hollered right in their faces:

'Tell me everything you did wrong.'

'I'm . . . not sure really,' James shrugged.

Bruce looked down at the floor.

'Let's start at the beginning,' Mr Large bawled. 'Why did it take you so long to reach the villa?'

'We jogged all the way,' James said.

'Jogged?' Mr Large shouted. 'If I'm being held hostage at gunpoint, I at least expect my rescuers to have the decency to *run* to my rescue.'

'It's boiling hot out there,' James said.

'I could have run,' Bruce said, 'but James was knackered after ten minutes.'

James gave Bruce a fierce look. Teams were supposed to stick together, not drop one another in it at the first opportunity.

'Can't manage a little ten-kilometre run, eh, James?' Mr Large said, breaking into an evil grin. 'Looks like you've let yourself get out of shape holidaying out here in the sunshine.'

'I'm fit,' James said. 'It's just the heat.'

'So, because you took so long to arrive, it was dark when you got to the villa, making it much more difficult to survey. Not that it matters, because you didn't do a proper survey anyway.'

'I had a good look through the fence,' James said, defensively.

Large banged his fist on the roof of the car.

'That's a survey, is it? What have you two been taught?'

'Before entering hostile premises, always do a thorough survey, investigating the building from all sides,' Bruce said mechanically. 'If possible, climb a tree or go to higher ground and get a look at the layout of the building from above.'

'If you remember what it says in the training manual, Bruce, why did you decide that a glance through the fence was sufficient?'

Bruce and James both looked sheepish. Kerry and Gabrielle loved watching the boys squirm.

'If you'd done a proper survey, maybe you would have seen the dog kennel. Maybe you could have planned a proper entry and exit strategy, instead of crawling up to the house and hoping for the best. Then, once you'd recovered the hostages, you decided to escape using the car. Didn't it occur to you that the car was the most obvious way to escape and was almost certainly booby-trapped? Or were you blinded by the prospect of lighting up the tyres and taking it for a spin?'

'It did occur that it was obvious,' James said.

'So why did you try to escape that way?' Large screamed.

'I mean . . . But . . . I only realised right before I got shot.'

'This has got to be the worst performance on a training exercise I have *ever* seen,' Mr Large shouted. 'You two have ignored every piece of training you've been given. If this was a real operation, you would have been killed ten times over. You're both getting grade F and James, I'm putting you on an emergency fitness plan. Ten kilometres running a day and, as you're so worried about the heat, I'll let you start when it's nice and cool. How does five in the morning sound?'

James knew better than to answer back, it only earned you push-ups. Mr Large stepped back and took deep breaths. His head looked like a redcurrant after all the shouting.

'What grade did me and Gabrielle get?' Kerry asked, using her crawliest voice.

'B, I suppose,' Mr Large said. 'You did a bang-up job, but I can't give you an A because you were up against such feeble opposition.'

Gabrielle and Kerry smiled at each other. James wanted to knock their stupid smug heads together.

'Right, time to head back to the hostel,' Large said. 'Bruce, I need the car key.'

Bruce chucked it over.

'That won't work,' Gabrielle said. 'That's for the front door of the villa. I put it on a Mercedes key ring so it looked like the car key. You want this one.'

Mr Large caught the real car key and loaded Thatcher the dog on to the front seat. Gabrielle and Kerry got in the back, squashed up with the two eight-year-olds.

'Oh no,' Mr Large grinned, as his massive body sank into the driver's seat. 'Not enough room in the car. It looks like James and Bruce will have to find their own way home.'

'But we drove in the van for ages before they dropped us off,' James gasped. 'I've got no idea how to get back to the hostel from here.'

'How *awfully* sad,' Mr Large said, sarcastically. 'I tell you what, if you manage to make it home before midnight, I'll put your grade up to a D and you won't have to repeat the exercise.'

Mr Large turned the key in the ignition and the car started rolling forward. Thatcher poked her head out of the window and barked as the car crunched down the gravel driveway. James and Bruce looked despondently at each other.

'I don't think it's that hard,' Bruce said. 'It's three hours until midnight and it's all downhill.'

James looked totally miserable. 'My legs feel like blocks of wood.'

'Well,' Bruce said, 'I'm gonna start walking. You can go through this again if you want, but I'm not going to.'

'What I can't believe,' James said, 'is that everyone told me to get my act together and I never listened.'

3. SUN

Unless they're away on a mission, every kid at CHERUB spends five weeks in the summer on the Mediterranean island of C—. It's mostly a holiday: a chance to muck about on the beach, play sport, ride quad bikes over the sand dunes and have a shot at being normal kids. But cherubs aren't normal kids: they could be sent on an undercover mission at any time. Even on holiday, they are expected to stay fit and do the odd training exercise.

Like loads of cherubs before him, James found it easy to slack off when there was a beach on the doorstep and tons of other kids to muck around with. For the last four weeks, he'd skipped fitness training. He'd spent his days messing about on the beach and his nights watching DVD marathons while stuffing his face with popcorn and chocolate. When James got his training assignment, he ignored Kerry's advice to study it thoroughly and went out on a jet ski instead.

James considered his folly as he sauntered through the sticky night air towards the CHERUB hostel. The physical training instructors were going to make his life a misery. Once you gave them a reason, they didn't let off until you were back in top shape. James couldn't make any excuses: Amy, Kyle and loads of teachers had warned him to exercise and take the training seriously, but he'd lost all sense of responsibility the second he hit the beach.

Even after getting lost a couple of times, James and Bruce beat the midnight deadline for getting back. James had a grazed elbow where he'd tripped in a pothole in the dark and they were both gasping for a drink.

A bunch of older kids were having a moonlit barbecue in the gardens at the front of the hostel. Amy Collins came running over the lawn when she noticed James. She was beautiful, sixteen years old, with long blonde hair. She wore denim shorts and a flowery top that stopped above the gold ring through her navel.

'Nice paint job, boys,' she giggled. 'Gabrielle and Kerry said they scrubbed the floor with the pair of you.'

'You're drunk,' James said.

Drinking alcohol wasn't allowed, but CHERUB staff turned a blind eye with the older kids, as long as they didn't go mad.

'Just a teensy drop,' Amy said. 'We went out on a boat and caught fish.'

Amy spread her arms out to the size of a big fish, almost lost her balance and doubled over in drunken hysterics.

'You want barbecued fish?' she spluttered. 'And there's fresh bread from the village.'

'It's late,' James said, shaking his head. 'We'd better clean up.'

'We emptied the whole ocean,' Amy giggled. 'Anyway, I'm busting to pee. I'll see you two scumbags in the morning.'

As Amy staggered away, she thought of something and turned back.

'Oh, James.'

'What?'

'I told you so.'

James gave her the finger and wandered towards the main entrance of the hostel with Bruce in tow. The less contact they had with other kids, the less they would get flamed for mucking up the training exercise. They ducked down as they passed the recreation room, where about thirty kids were watching a horror movie on a projector screen. A couple of little red-shirt kids snickered at their paint-spattered clothes as the boys walked upstairs to the second-floor bedroom they shared with Gabrielle and Kerry.

The room was an L shape, with the girls' beds at one end and the boys' around the corner at the other. It was basic compared to their individual rooms back at campus: ceiling fans, tile floor, wicker chairs and a tiny TV. It hardly mattered because the kids were always busy and only used the rooms to wash and crash out.

Kerry and Gabrielle had been back a couple of hours. The TV was showing an episode of *The Simpsons* in Spanish, which both girls could understand. They kept quiet, not even commenting on the stench of sweat.

'Well?' James said.

Kerry gave an innocent smile. 'Well, what?'

'I know you're gonna start on us,' James said, sitting on his bed and pulling off his trainers. 'So go on, get it over with. Rub our noses in it.'

'We'd never do that,' Gabrielle said. 'We're nice girls.'

'My arse,' Bruce said.

Kerry sat up on her bed. She was pink and shrivelled, like she'd just finished a long bath. James dumped his filthy polo shirt on the floor.

'You better take that stuff down to the laundry when you've had your showers,' Kerry said. 'It'll stink the whole room out.'

'If *you* don't like my stink,' Bruce said, kicking off his trainers, '*you* take it down there.'

He balled up his crusty sock and lobbed it on to Kerry's duvet. She flicked it away with the end of a biro.

'So, how come it took you so long to get back here?' Kerry asked, trying not to grin.

As soon as she said that, Gabrielle started cracking up.

'What are you laughing for?' James asked. 'It's fourteen kilometres between here and the villa. I'd like to see you two do it any quicker.'

'They're *so* thick,' Gabrielle howled. 'I can't believe it.'

'What?' James asked. 'What's thick?'

'Didn't you bother checking out the house?' Kerry grinned.

'We couldn't hang around,' Bruce explained. 'We had to be back here by midnight.'

'There was money all over the kitchen cabinet,' Kerry said.

'What good could that do us?' Bruce asked.

'And there was a working telephone,' Kerry continued. 'And a telephone directory.'

James was getting impatient. 'So what?'

'This isn't Outer Mongolia,' Gabrielle said, making a telephone receiver out of her hand and putting it to her ear. 'Why didn't you pick up the phone and call a taxi?'

'Eh?' James gasped, turning around and giving Bruce a blank stare.

'Taxi,' Kerry snorted, hardly able to get the words out over her giggles. 'T – A – X – I, they're like a normal car, with a man to drive you and a little orange lamp on the roof.'

'Oh . . .' James said bitterly, looking at Bruce. 'Why didn't we get a cab?'

'Don't have a go at *me*,' Bruce said. 'You never thought of it either.'

Gabrielle was rolled up in a ball, laughing so hard the frame of her bed was shaking.

'You two dickheads walked fourteen kilometres when you could have called a taxi and been home in an hour,' Kerry said, pedalling her feet in the air with delight.

James' socks were bloody where they'd chafed on the long walk. His back and shoulders hurt from carrying the pack, his elbow was agony and his leg still stank of dog mess, even though he'd washed it. One day, he would be able to laugh about this, but right now he was ready to explode.

'This is *bull*,' James screamed, hurling his trainers against the wall.

He kicked out at his wardrobe, but he was tired and lost his balance. He ended up in a heap on the floor, making the girls laugh even harder. Bruce looked just as mad, but he concentrated his energy into ripping off his clothes and heading towards the shower.

'Give us two minutes before you go in there,' Kerry said, wiping tears of joy from her eyes. 'I want to go to bed in a minute. Can I quickly brush my teeth?'

Bruce tutted. 'Go on then, but don't take all night.'

Kerry padded barefoot into the bathroom and squeezed out a ball of toothpaste. Bruce and James waited by the open doorway in their boxers while she brushed. Kerry tried to control her laughing, but she couldn't resist having another dig.

'Fourteen kilometres,' she shrieked, spluttering white toothpaste foam all over the bathroom mirror.

Bruce couldn't take any more abuse.

'Let's see how you like being laughed at,' he shouted.

As Kerry bent over the tap to rinse her mouth, Bruce dunked her head. He only meant to nudge her so she got water over her face, but he did it too hard. Kerry's front tooth hit the tap and she sprung up furiously.

'You idiot,' Kerry stormed, nervously feeling inside her mouth. 'I think you've chipped my tooth.'

Bruce realised he'd overdone it, but he wasn't about to go apologising to someone who'd spent the last ten minutes taking the mickey out of him.

'Good,' he snapped. 'Serves you right.'

Kerry grabbed a glass off the sink and threw it at Bruce's head. He ducked and the glass shattered against the wall.

'Cool it,' James said. 'This isn't worth fighting over.'

'Do you think I'm gonna grow a new tooth?' Kerry screamed.

She stepped forward and gave Bruce an almighty shove. Bruce adopted a fighting stance.

'You want a piece of me?' he shouted.

Kerry looked ferocious as she wiped her lips on to the sleeve of her nightshirt.

'If you want to get your arse kicked by a girl for the second time today,' she snarled, 'that's fine by me.'

James wedged himself between Kerry and Bruce. He was taller and stockier than the two kids he was trying to keep apart.

'Get out the way, James,' Bruce said.

'I'm going for Bruce whether you like it or not,' Kerry said, drilling James with her eyes. 'If you're in my way, you'll get damaged.'

James could beat either Kerry or Bruce for strength, say in an arm-wrestle, but fighting was more about skill. Kerry and Bruce had done combat training at CHERUB for five years, whereas James had come to CHERUB less than a year earlier. He'd be out of his depth in a stand-up fight against either of them.

'You're not fighting,' James said unconvincingly, hoping Kerry was bluffing. 'I'm staying right here.'

Kerry stepped forward, swept James' ankle away and jammed two fingers into his ribs. It was an elementary technique for knocking someone over without seriously hurting them. James crawled towards his bed as violence exploded over his head.

Kerry was off balance after knocking James out of the way. Bruce used this to his advantage, putting Kerry out of action with one blow. Kerry staggered forward, gasping for breath as the end music for *The Simpsons* came on the TV.

Bruce thought the fight was as good as won. He moved to put Kerry in a headlock, but she'd played Bruce for a sucker. She quickly regained her balance, spun out of the way, hooked a foot around Bruce's ankles and swept his legs away.

James clambered on to his mattress; half horrified, half curious to see who would win. There was no way for him or Gabrielle to get help: the fight was blocking the doorway.

Within seconds of hitting the floor, years of self-defence training collapsed to the level of two drunks grappling on a pavement. Bruce had a clump of Kerry's hair wound around his wrist and Kerry was dragging her nails down Bruce's cheek. They thrashed about, cursing one another and eventually rolling into the TV table. The first couple of knocks rocked the TV close to the edge. The third made the TV topple, face first, into the floor. The glass screen cracked and orange sparks spewed across the floor. Some of them hit Bruce and Kerry's bare legs, then the lights went out and the ceiling fans went silent.

James looked out of the window. All the lights outside had gone too. The exploding TV had fused the electricity for the whole hostel. The fight kept going, but all James could discern were shadows and grunts.

Now Bruce and Kerry were over by the TV, James had an opportunity to get help. He sprang off his bed and grabbed the door handle. Gabrielle thought the same thing at the same moment and they nearly collided in the dark.

The corridor was tinged with green emergency escape lighting. Kids had their heads sticking out of their rooms, all asking each other why the electricity had gone off. James could hear Arif, a seventeen-year-old kid who was over six feet tall. He was exactly what was needed to break up the fight.

'Help us,' James shouted. 'Bruce and Kerry are killing each other.'

That exact moment, someone reset the fuse and the lights came back on. Arif ran towards James' room, along with twenty other kids who wanted to get a look at the action. Arif was first into the room, followed by James and Gabrielle.

Bruce was nowhere. Kerry was in the middle of the floor. Her face was twisted with pain and she had her hands wrapped over her knee.

'Oh god,' she sobbed. 'Help me.'

Kerry had shattered her kneecap in training a couple of years earlier. It had been repaired with titanium pins, but it was still weak. Arif scooped her off the floor and sprinted downstairs to the first aid room.

'Where the hell is Bruce?' Gabrielle asked angrily.

James shooed the onlookers out and slammed the door. He leaned into the bathroom.

'God knows. He's not in there.'

Then he heard a sob under Bruce's duvet. Bruce was a skinny thing, so when he pulled the covers up over his head it was easy to assume he wasn't there at all.

'Bruce?' James asked.

'I didn't mean to hurt her knee,' Bruce sobbed. 'I'm sorry.'

'If you start a fight, people get hurt,' Gabrielle said severely. 'That's how it works.'

James had more sympathy. He sat on the edge of Bruce's bed.

'Leave me alone, James. I'm not coming out.'

'Bruce, come downstairs with me,' James said. 'Everyone loses their temper sometimes. I'm sure the staff will understand and – speaking from personal experience – it's always best if you get your own side of the story in first.'

'No,' Bruce sobbed. 'Go away.'

Meryl Spencer, a retired Olympic sprinter who was James' handler, burst into the room. She'd been in bed and was wearing a nightshirt and unlaced trainers.

'What's happened here?' Meryl shouted.

'They got in a fight,' James explained. 'Bruce is under his duvet and won't come out.'

Meryl smiled. 'Won't he now?'

She leaned over the bed.

'Bruce,' she shouted. 'You're gonna have to face the music for hurting Kerry. Stop acting like a baby and get out of there.'

'Go away,' Bruce said, tightening the duvet around his head. 'You can't make me come out.'

'You've got three seconds,' Meryl shouted. 'Or I'm gonna seriously lose my temper.'

Bruce didn't move a muscle.

'One,' Meryl said. 'Two . . . Three.'

On three, Meryl grabbed the tubular frame of Bruce's bed and tipped it on to its side. Bruce thumped on to the floor and Meryl whipped the duvet off him.

'Stand up,' she shouted. 'You're eleven years of age, not five.'

Bruce jumped to his feet. His face was a teary mess. Meryl grabbed his shoulder and shoved him up against the wall.

'I want all three of you in my office. You're in serious trouble. This kind of behaviour is not acceptable.'

'Me and Gabrielle didn't do anything,' James pleaded. 'We tried to break it up.'

'We'll discuss it in my office,' Meryl said. She took a breath and realised that James and Bruce still stank.

'You two have ten minutes to shower, put clean clothes on and get downstairs. And if anyone starts up this hiding under the duvet nonsense again, I'll have them running laps until they puke, every day for the rest of their miserable lives.'

4. GRASS

'What did you do this time?' Lauren asked. 'When did you get back to campus? How come they sent you home early?'

James was half asleep in bed and he wasn't in the mood for his nine-year-old sister. Lauren had knocked on his bedroom door three times. When James ignored her, she picked the lock. The most irritating thing about living at CHERUB was that every kid knew how to pick locks. James was planning to buy a bolt next time he went into town. There's no way to pick a bolt.

'Come *on*,' Lauren said, sitting herself on the swivel chair at James' desk. 'Spill the beans. Everyone saw the ambulance take Kerry to the medical unit.'

Lauren was James' only family since their mum had died the year before. James loved his sister, but he still spent a lot of his life wishing she'd go some place and stick her head in a bucket. She could be a total pain.

'Tell us,' Lauren said sharply. 'You know I'll just sit here bugging you until you do.'

James threw back his duvet and sat up, picking at a gluey eye.

'Why are you up so early?' he asked. 'It's pitch black outside.'

'It's half past ten,' Lauren said, turning slowly around on the chair. 'But it's raining.'

James swung out of bed and peered through the blind. Rain trickled down his window. The sky was grey and the outdoor tennis courts were under water.

'Great,' James said. 'There's nothing like British summer to cheer you up.'

'You've got a good tan,' Lauren said. 'Mine's almost gone and I've only been back from the hostel three weeks.'

'Best holiday I've ever had.' James grinned. 'We'll have to try and fix it so we go at the same time next year. Me, Kerry and about six other kids had this massive race on the quad bikes.'

'Racing's not allowed,' Lauren said.

'Isn't it?' James smiled, guiltily. 'Anyway, there was a humungous crash. Me and Shakeel. You should have seen the state the bikes were in. Front tyres ripped off, petrol gushing everywhere. It was mad.'

'Did you get hurt?'

'Shakeel twisted his ankle, that's all. I can't wait for next year.'

Lauren smiled. 'We dared Bethany's brother to drive one of the quad bikes through the dining room. It was so funny when he got busted . . . Anyway, are you gonna tell us why they kicked your butts home early, or not?'

James slumped miserably back on his bed, realising he was now about as far as you get from racing over sand dunes.

'I got totally stitched up,' he said.

'Give over, James, you always say that.'

'Yeah, but this time it's true. Bruce and Kerry had a punch-up. They trashed our room and Kerry busted her knee, but Meryl sent me and Gabrielle home early as well. We've got to go and see the Chairman this afternoon.'

'You must have done *something*,' Lauren said.

'Lauren, all me and Gabrielle did was try to break the fight up. It was a total miscarriage of justice. Meryl wouldn't let me get one word in.'

'Makes up for all the things you haven't been caught for,' Lauren grinned. 'How's Kerry?'

'She's in loads of pain. They had to do a medivac: flew her home on a special plane because she can't bend her leg.'

'Poor Kerry,' Lauren said.

'I'll go and see how she is when I've got my uniform on. You coming?'

'I've got Karate class in a minute,' Lauren said, shaking her head. 'I want to be in top form when my basic training starts.'

'Oh yeah,' James grinned. 'Only a month to go now. I'm gonna have such a laugh hearing about all the ways the instructors make you suffer.'

Lauren folded her arms and scowled at her brother. 'You're not scaring me, you know.'

*

The medical unit was a ten-minute walk from the main building. When James got to Kerry's room, Gabrielle was already there.

'Look what *your* friend did to her,' Gabrielle said, as if it was somehow James' fault.

Kerry was propped up on pillows beneath a *Nil By Mouth* sign. MTV blared from the portable TV hanging over her bed. She was on painkillers, but still had wet eyes and looked like she hadn't slept.

James put Kerry's MP3 player on her bedside table.

'Thought some tunes might help take your mind off it,' he said. 'Hope you don't mind me going in your room.'

'No problem,' Kerry said. 'Cheers.'

'Has the doctor seen you?' James asked.

Kerry nodded, pointing to a light box on the wall.

'Show James the thingy,' she said.

There was already an X-ray mounted on the light box. Gabrielle walked up and switched on the lamp.

'That's Kerry's kneecap,' Gabrielle explained, pointing to a round grey area on the X-ray. 'See the four black bars?'

James nodded.

'Those are the metal pins put in when Kerry broke her kneecap two years ago. When Bruce twisted Kerry's leg, that pin there shifted. So now Kerry's got a piece of metal sticking out the back of her kneecap. Every time she moves, the metal cuts into the tendons underneath.'

'Yuk,' James winced. 'What can they do about that?'

'They're taking her to hospital,' Gabrielle said. 'They're operating this afternoon. Kerry can't eat or drink before the anaesthetic. They're going under her kneecap and cutting out the bent metal. The broken bone has grown back together, so the metal isn't doing anything now anyway.'

James felt queasy imagining surgical instruments poking around inside his leg.

'OOOOOOOOHHH god!' Kerry screamed.

'What?' James asked, rushing over to the bed. 'Are you OK?'

'It's nothing,' Kerry said. 'I just moved my foot. This is actually more painful than when I broke my knee.'

She let out a low groan. James sat beside the bed and stroked her hand.

'Has Bruce been to see you?' he asked.

'No,' Gabrielle huffed. 'Like that little jerk would have enough class to come and apologise.'

'James,' Kerry said, 'will you do us a favour?'

'Course,' James said. 'Name it.'

'Go and see Bruce. Tell him I'm not making a big deal out of this.'

'You call this no big deal?' James laughed. 'You're joking.'

'I'm not,' Kerry said. 'I don't want this turning into some massive feud. Remember I told you I broke Bruce's leg when we were red shirts?'

'Sure,' James said.

'It was in Karate practice. Bruce fell awkwardly. I came down on him full force and crunched his leg. I never should have done something like that in a practice. Bruce was cool about it. He shrugged it off like it was nothing. Everyone does stupid stuff sometimes. Remember that one, James?'

Kerry held out the palm of her right hand. It had a long scar where James had stomped it during training. 'You can't hold grudges against people for every mistake they make,' she said.

'Point taken,' James said. 'I'll speak to him.'

*

James hated the row of plastic seats outside the Chairman's office. If you had to see him for something good, Dr McAfferty – usually known as Mac – let you straight in. When you were in trouble, he kept you hanging outside in suspense. James sat between Gabrielle and Bruce. He was combed and deodorised, in his neatest set of CHERUB uniform: polished boots, army-green trousers and a navy T-shirt with the CHERUB logo embroidered on the front. The other two wore the same, except they were only entitled to wear grey T-shirts. Bruce had four red lines down his face where Kerry had clawed him.

Kerry might have forgiven Bruce, but Gabrielle wasn't talking to him. James felt like he was on a tightrope. Every time he said something to one of them, the other one huffed as if he was siding against them. James realised it was easiest if he kept quiet.

They waited a good half hour before Mac finally leaned out of his doorway. He was in his sixties, with a neat grey beard and a Scottish accent.

'Come on then,' Mac said wearily. 'Let's sort you three out.'

James led the way towards Mac's mahogany desk.

'No, no, come and look at this,' Mac said, heading towards an architectural model standing on a table by the window.

The kids stepped up to the model of a crescent-shaped building. It was a metre long, made entirely out of white plastic, with polystyrene trees and tiny white figures walking along paths outside.

'What is it?' James asked.

'It's our new mission preparation building,' Mac said enthusiastically. 'We're turning those shabby offices on the eighth floor into extra living space and building this beauty to replace them. Over five thousand square metres of office space. Every big mission will have its own office, with new computers and equipment. We'll have encrypted satellite links to our mission controllers all over the world, as well as to British Intelligence headquarters and the CIA and DOHS in America. This model just arrived from the architect's office. Isn't it fantastic?'

The kids nodded. Even if they'd hated it, they wouldn't have wanted to get on Mac's bad side by saying so. Mac treated CHERUB campus like his own personal Lego set. He was always having something built or knocked down.

'It's an eco-building,' Mac enthused, lifting the plastic roof off so the kids could see the offices filled with miniature furniture inside. 'Special glass retains the heat, so it stays warm in the winter. Solar panels on the roof power fans and heat the water.'

'When's it being built?' Bruce asked.

'It's already being made in prefabricated sections in a factory in Austria,' Mac said. 'That way we can minimise the number of construction workers we have to let loose on campus. Once the concrete base is poured, the whole lot is bolted together in a few weeks. Fitting out the interior should be completed early in the New Year. You wouldn't believe the amount of arm twisting I've had to do to secure the funding.'

'It's really cool,' James said, hoping his enthusiasm would translate into a lighter punishment.

'Anyway, I suppose I have to sort you three hooligans out,' Mac said. He clearly would have preferred to go on about his new building for the rest of the afternoon. 'Plant your bums at my desk.'

The three kids sat in the leather chairs opposite Mac. Mac leaned over his desk, interlocked his fingers and stared at them.

'I've already spoken to Kerry,' he said. 'So what have you lot got to say for yourselves?'

'It's well unfair that me and Gabrielle got sent home,' James said. 'We were the ones who tried to break the fight up.'

He noticed Lauren and her best friend, Bethany, with their noses squished against the outside of the window behind Mac's desk.

'As I understand from Meryl Spencer,' Mac said, 'the four of you came back from a training exercise, went into your room and began taunting one another and bickering. Is that true?'

The kids gave a mix of shrugs and nods. Outside, Lauren and Bethany were sticking their tongues out and mouthing rude words.

'As far as I'm concerned, that makes all four of you responsible for what happened,' Mac said. 'Gentle ribbing leads to teasing, which leads to nastiness and, as in this instance, it sometimes leads to violence and an eight-thousand-pound bill for an air ambulance. While each of you is serving your punishment, I want you to reflect that you'd all be enjoying another two weeks of holiday if you'd had the sense to behave decently towards one another instead of winding each other up. Is that understood?'

The three kids nodded. James hated how Mac's way of twisting the facts around made him feel partly responsible for Kerry getting hurt. What made him even more annoyed was Lauren sticking a sheet of paper up to the window that said *JAMES SUCKS* in giant black letters. Gabrielle couldn't stop herself smirking.

'By way of punishments, I want the three of you to report to the head gardener after you finish lessons every afternoon. We don't have enough staff to give the lawns the attention they deserve in the summer, but you guys putting in two hours' mowing a day for the next month will certainly help.'

James groaned to himself. With extra fitness training in the mornings and mowing in the evenings, the next month was turning into a nightmare.

'Any questions?' Mac asked.

The kids shook their heads and stood up to leave.

'And James,' Mac said.

James turned back. 'What?'

Mac raised a picture frame off his desk and turned it towards James. It showed Mac, standing with his wife, his six grown-up children and an ocean of little grandkids.

'James, would you kindly inform your sister that the glass in this picture frame gives me a very good reflection of everything that's going on outside my window. I want to see Lauren and Bethany in this office and you can tell them that they'll be joining you on gardening duty for the rest of the week.'

5. SLEEP

TWO WEEKS LATER
James got up at 5.30 a.m., despite his whole body begging him to stay under the duvet. He put on his running kit and headed to the athletics track as the sun rose over campus. It took him an hour to run twenty-five laps: a distance of ten kilometres. He showered, then traded some homework with Shakeel over breakfast. Lessons went from 8.30 until 2.00, with half an hour for lunch. After lessons, there was Karate practice topped off with forty-five minutes' circuit training. Boiling hot, James downed half a litre of orange juice and collected one of the ride-on mowers from the gardeners' storeroom. It wasn't hard driving the mower, but the sun was on him the whole time and the grass pollen made his eyes itch.

It was 6.15 p.m. by the time James got his first chance to relax. Dinner was a social event, with everyone mucking about and catching up on gossip. Most cherubs had done their homework before dinner and had the evening to themselves, but the mowing meant James hadn't even got started. Homework was supposed to be two hours a day.

Some teachers were decent. Others piled on so much work it took heaps longer.

When James got back to his room it was gone 7.00. He sat at his desk, spread out his textbooks and opened his homework diary. In the two weeks he'd been back on campus, James had acquired a backlog of homework that sucked up every second of his free time.

It was a warm evening, so James left his window open. A breeze clattered into the plastic slats of his blind. James' eyes were gluey and the words in his textbook drifted out of shape. His head slumped on the desk and he dozed off before he'd written a word.

*

Kyle lived across the hall. He was nearly fifteen, but he wasn't much bigger than James.

'Wakey wakey,' Kyle said, flicking James' ear.

James' head shot up from his desk. He opened his eyes, inhaled deeply and looked at his watch. It was gone ten o'clock.

'OHHHHHH crap,' James said, startled. 'If I don't get this history report done by tomorrow, I'm dead meat. It's a two-thousand-word essay and I haven't even read the chapters in the textbook.'

'Get a deferral,' Kyle said.

'I've had a deferral, Kyle. And I've had a deferral of the deferral. I've got extra laps to run before school and mowing after. There aren't enough hours in the day. I spent all day Sunday doing homework and I still keep getting further behind.'

'You should speak to your handler.'

'I tried,' James said. 'You know what Meryl said?'

'What?'

'She said, if I was so snowed under with work, how come I had time to spend sitting in her office whinging.'

Kyle laughed.

'I swear, they're trying to kill me,' James moaned.

'No,' Kyle said. 'They're trying to instil a sense of discipline in you. After a month of being worked like a dog, maybe you'll think twice about ignoring the rules next time. It's your own stupid fault. All you had to do on holiday was keep in half reasonable shape and study the briefing for the hostage training. Everybody warned you. Me, Kerry, Meryl, Amy. But you always reckon you know better.'

James angrily swept his arm across his desk, shooting his books and pens on to the floor.

'Good idea,' Kyle grinned. 'That'll solve your problems.'

'Spare me another lecture,' James shouted. 'I'm so knackered I can hardly keep my eyes open and I'm sick of everyone saying I told you so.'

'What's that report you're doing?' Kyle asked.

'Two thousand words on the foundation of the British Intelligence Service and its role in the First World War.'

'Interesting stuff,' Kyle said.

'I'd rather eat a bowl of snot,' James said.

'I might just be able to help you out, kiddo. I did that course two years ago. I've got my old notes and an essay in my room.'

'Cheers, Kyle,' James grinned. 'You're a lifesaver.'

'Ten quid,' Kyle said.

'*What?*' James gasped. 'Some friend you are, trying to make money out of me when I'm at my lowest ebb.'

'This essay is a beauty, James. Grade A material. The girl I nicked it off is now studying history at Harvard University in the States.'

'Fiver,' James said. He reckoned the essay was easily worth a fiver. He'd have to swap bits around and rewrite in his own handwriting, but that would take about an hour, whereas doing the essay from scratch was a whole night's work.

'You're bleeding me dry,' Kyle said, twisting his mouth as if he couldn't make up his mind. 'But I'm a little low on funds. You can have it for a fiver, if you give us the money right now.'

James went in his desk and got a fiver out of his cash box. Kyle stuffed it in his pocket.

'This better be a good essay,' James said.

'Anyway,' Kyle said, 'I didn't come here to help with your homework. I'm the senior agent on a big mission that's coming up. We need three other kids. Me and Ewart Asker discussed it and you're on the team if you want the gig.'

James wasn't that enthusiastic.

'I don't want to work with Ewart as my mission controller again. He's a psychopath.'

'Ewart raves about you,' Kyle said. 'He thinks you did a great job on that anti-terrorist mission. Plus, this is a big team. Ewart's wife will be there as well. She keeps him under her thumb.'

'Who else is going?' James asked.

'Me, of course,' Kyle said. 'And Kerry. She's walking with a stick, but they reckon she'll be healed up before blast-off.

There's a vacancy for another girl. It was going to be Gabrielle, but she's being held back for something in South Africa.'

'Nicole Eddison,' James said.

'Who?' Kyle asked.

'You know her,' James said. 'She was on my basic training and quit after one day. She got her grey shirt at the second attempt. I think she's done a couple of missions, but nothing major.'

'I think I know who you mean,' Kyle said. 'Is it that girl with the huge chest you're always going on about?'

'She is *so* stacked,' James grinned.

'James,' Kyle said, indignantly, 'you can't pick a girl for a mission because she has big breasts.'

'Why not?'

'Well, for starters, it's unbelievably sexist.'

'Come on, Kyle. Nicole's a really good laugh. She's in my Russian class and she's always getting chucked out for messing around. And as long as Kerry doesn't find out and kick my butt, who cares if it's sexist or not?'

'I'll ask Ewart to put her name on the list of candidates,' Kyle said, reluctantly. 'But he'll only pick her based on merit. The first mission briefing is tomorrow. There's tons of background studying to do.'

'Oh, great,' James said. 'When am I gonna get time to do that?'

'Didn't I mention?' Kyle said innocently. 'It's been arranged with Meryl. You still have to do morning laps, but we've cut out some of your lessons and Mac has agreed to knock the mowing on the head.'

'Cool,' James grinned. 'Another two weeks of that

workload was gonna send me under. What lessons have I been dropped from?'

'Art, Russian, religion and history,' Kyle said.

'Superb,' James said, deliriously drumming his hands on his desktop. Then the penny dropped. 'Did you say *history*?'

'Uh-huh,' Kyle nodded.

'I just paid you five quid for a history essay.'

'A good price for a good essay.'

James leapt furiously out of his chair. 'I don't care if it's written on gold parchment by that bloke who does the history shows on Channel Four,' he spluttered. 'I don't need the essay if I don't have to go back to history class.'

'It goes to prove the old saying,' Kyle giggled.

'What saying?'

'Cheats never prosper.'

'I tell you who'll never prosper,' James stormed, grabbing one of the pens off his carpet. 'You. And you know why? Because you're gonna have an extremely hard time prospering after I've rammed this biro up your nose. Give us my fiver back.'

'What fiver?' Kyle asked. 'I don't recall any fiver. Did you get a receipt?'

James gave Kyle a shove.

'You're a bandit, Kyle. Normal people don't go around conning their mates.'

Kyle backed up, with a giant grin and his hands out in front of himself.

'I tell you what,' he said, 'I'm seriously short of cash. So, even though it goes against my sacred ethical code, I'll do you a deal.'

'What deal?'

'If you let me keep the fiver, I'll get Nicole on to the mission.'

'That's worth five quid,' James smiled. 'What's this mission about anyway?'

'Drugs,' Kyle said.

6. BRIEF

MISSION BRIEFING:
FOR JAMES ADAMS, KYLE BLUEMAN,
KERRY CHANG AND NICOLE EDDISON
DO NOT REMOVE FROM ROOM 812
DO NOT COPY OR MAKE NOTES

CHILDREN IN THE DRUG BUSINESS
Children are used by drug dealers throughout the world, to sell,
smuggle and deliver illegal drugs. There are a number of reasons
why children are used:

(1) Kids selling or using drugs are usually viewed as victims rather
than criminals. In most countries, children are punished lightly for
drug offences, whereas an adult caught with a large quantity of a
drug like heroin or cocaine faces five to ten years in prison.

(2) Children have access to schools and young people. Drug
dealers encourage children to give free samples of drugs to their

friends. Someone who starts dealing drugs at twelve or thirteen can have hundreds of customers by the time they reach adulthood.

(3) Children have few sources of income and plenty of spare time. Many will do a drug dealer a favour, such as making a delivery for just a few pounds, or even for nothing because they think it makes them look cool.

What is Cocaine?

Cocaine is an illegal drug extracted from the leaves of the coca plant (not to be confused with the cocoa plant, which is used to make chocolate). Coca grows at high altitude in the mountainous regions of South America. The leaves are refined into a crystalline white powder. Before reaching users, the powder is diluted with cheaper substances, such as lactose or borax, or it is mixed with other drugs such as methamphetamine (commonly called speed).

The powder is snorted up the nose. It can also be injected, or mixed with other chemicals to form a smokable version of the drug called crack. Users of cocaine feel a sense of confidence and well being that lasts fifteen to thirty minutes. Cocaine also causes numbness and was once used as an anaesthetic by surgeons and dentists. More effective anaesthetics are now available.

While cocaine doesn't create a physical craving of the kind you get with heroin or cigarettes, many users enjoy the drug's effects so much that they use it to excess and do enormous damage to their bodies. Whereas a heroin or cigarette addict needs a regular fix, cocaine users often go days without using before going on a binge. Serious side effects of cocaine include heart attacks, liver failure, brain seizures, strokes and damage to the lining of the nose and mouth.

Cocaine in Britain

Cocaine was once the champagne of the drug world: a luxury only the rich could afford. A moderate user might get through a gram of powdered cocaine in an evening. In 1984, a gram of cocaine cost £200–£250. Twenty years later, the street price of cocaine has dropped to less than £50 a gram. In some areas of Britain, a gram of low quality cocaine can cost as little as £25.

The United States pays South American governments to hunt and destroy coca plants in the highlands where they grow. Despite this, the street price of cocaine has continued to drop, suggesting that supplies are still plentiful.

Most cocaine brought into Britain arrives via the Caribbean. There are thousands of smugglers in British prisons. Tough sentences have done little to stop the trade. Cocaine dealers continue to find people willing to act as drug couriers, often in return for less than a thousand pounds and an airline ticket.

It is impossible to catch every smuggler entering Britain. The police must aim higher and capture the people in control of the drug gangs. Close to one third of the cocaine entering Britain passes through an organisation commonly referred to as KMG. The initials stand for Keith Moore's Gang.

Keith Moore and KMG: Biography

1964   Keith Moore was born on the newly built Thornton estate on the outskirts of Luton in Bedfordshire.

1977   After being caught selling cannabis in his school library, Keith was arrested by police and excluded from school. He became a chronic truant, suspected of many car thefts and burglaries.

1978   Keith began training as a boxer at the JT Martin Youth

Centre. JT Martin was a retired boxer and armed robber who controlled the underworld in Bedfordshire from the early 1960s until 1985. JT used his boxing club as a recruiting ground for young criminals.

1980   Keith was spotted in police surveillance photographs of JT Martin. In the pictures, Keith is a slightly built sixteen-year-old who looks out of place amongst JT's crew of boxers and nightclub bouncers.

1981   Keith became JT Martin's chauffeur when a previous driver was banned for speeding. Moving around with JT gave the seventeen-year-old an insight into all aspects of the drug business.

1983   After eleven amateur fights, with a record of one win, two draws and eight defeats, Keith retired from boxing. Shortly afterwards, he married Julie Robertson, a girl he had known since infant school.

1985   Police captured JT Martin and a number of associates selling drugs. JT was sentenced to twelve years in prison. Keith Moore had been JT's driver for four years, but the rest of JT's crew regarded him as a wimpish hanger-on.

1986   With JT in prison, a power struggle erupted amongst his former employees. Keith kept away from the violent struggles and developed an interest in JT's cocaine business. Cocaine was a tiny proportion of the criminal empire, which made most of its money selling heroin and cannabis. JT also owned nightclubs, pubs and casinos, as well as dozens of small businesses such as laundrettes and hairdressing salons.

1987   The price of cocaine kept falling and supply was growing. Keith Moore was one of the first people in Britain to realise that the cocaine business was about to explode.

While his colleagues battled over heroin and nightclub profits, Keith travelled to South America and met with members of a powerful Peruvian drug cartel known as Lambayeke. He agreed to buy regular bulk shipments of cocaine at a discounted price. To sell this increased supply of cocaine, Keith launched a telephone delivery service, based on similar services that were thriving in the United States. It took advantage of two new technologies: mobile telephones and message pagers. Instead of having to go searching for a drug dealer, rich clients dialled a number and Keith had someone deliver drugs to their doorstep, usually within an hour.

1988   The cocaine business was earning Keith over £10,000 per week. This cash enabled him – at just 23 years of age – to take effective control of JT Martin's criminal empire. Keith avoided violence whenever possible. He manipulated jealous rivals, setting them against one another. When manipulation failed, he bought rivals off by handing them parts of the business that did not interest him.

Keith's next ambition was to build his profitable cocaine business into the biggest in the country. The only part of JT's empire Keith held on to was the youth centre/boxing club in the neighbourhood where he grew up.

1989   Keith's first son, Ringo, was born (now aged 15).

1990   Keith's business grew tenfold in three years. Cocaine delivery expanded into Hertfordshire and London. He also began selling wholesale quantities of cocaine to other dealers all over Britain and mainland Europe.

1992   *Julie Moore gave birth to twins, April and Keith Jr (now aged 12).*

1993   *Keith's youngest child, Erin, was born (now aged 11).*

1998   *Drug dealing is often a short career. Anyone who is successful attracts attention from police and customs. They usually end up behind bars.*

After investigations failed to gather enough evidence, police tried to get undercover officers into Keith's inner circle. Dozens of people working for KMG have been prosecuted. Even when they have agreed to cooperate, police have never been able to produce clear evidence linking Keith Moore with his drug business. At the core of KMG, an expensive legal team and fiercely loyal deputies have so far succeeded in keeping Keith Moore out of prison.

2000   *As the cocaine business continued to thrive, Keith Moore's personal fortune was estimated at £25 million. After being arrested for non-payment of tax, he pleaded guilty to a minor charge and paid a £50,000 fine.*

2001   *Julie Moore left Keith after eighteen years of marriage. Keith kept custody of the children and the family home. Julie moved into a house across the street and remains on good terms with her ex-husband.*

2003   *Police launched Operation Snort, the largest taskforce of drugs officers ever assembled in Britain. The official aim was to stop the cocaine business. Unofficially, everyone knew Operation Snort was gunning for Keith Moore and KMG.*

The operation descended into chaos when it uncovered corruption within police forces all over the country. Forty officers were found to have taken bribes from KMG. Eight of these were working on Operation Snort and included the Chief Superintendent who was in command of the whole operation.

Although Operation Snort is still running, its effectiveness has been blunted by infighting over the bribery allegations.

One national newspaper reporting on Operation Snort said, 'If all the corruption allegations are true, it would appear that Keith Moore has more police officers protecting him than the Queen and the Prime Minister combined.'

2004   (Present Day) Despite a personal fortune now estimated at between £35 and £50 million, Keith Moore has shunned the trappings of the super rich. He lives with his four children in a large detached house less than twenty minutes' drive from the housing estate where he was born. His four children attend the local comprehensive school. He works from an office at home and socialises with family members and friends he has known since boyhood. His only extravagances are a collection of Porsche sports cars and a beachfront house in Miami, Florida.

MISSION REQUEST

In early 2004, frustrated by the lack of success in bringing down KMG and outraged by police corruption, the government asked the intelligence service to find a way of infiltrating KMG at the highest level. MI5, the adult branch of British Intelligence, could see no reason why it would have any more success at this than the police. CHERUB was suggested as a method of last resort.

Keith Moore is close to his four children. Appropriately placed CHERUB agents may be able to befriend them and gather vital information.

MISSION PLAN
Husband and wife mission controllers, Ewart and Zara Asker, will move into a house on the Thornton housing estate with their baby son and four CHERUB agents. For the purposes of the mission, the agents will be adopted children of Zara and Ewart. The family surname will be Beckett. To minimise confusion, everyone will use their normal first names.

PRIMARY OBJECTIVE:
Each agent has been selected to befriend one of Keith's children, as follows:

James Adams   – Junior Moore (Keith Junior)
Kyle Blueman   – Ringo Moore
Kerry Chang   – Erin Moore
Nicole Eddison – April Moore

If the cherubs succeed in making friends, they must attempt to socialise out of school and try to get inside Keith's home, gathering information wherever possible. Each cherub will be placed in the same tutor group as the child they are supposed to befriend.

Many children on the Thornton estate run errands and deliver drugs for KMG associates. Each cherub should identify children who are working for KMG and try to get involved themselves. Children usually work for small-time dealers, delivering drugs to individual clients using mobile phones and pushbikes.

Evidence suggests that children who attend Keith Moore's boxing club and make reliable couriers are promoted rapidly and given responsibility for moving wholesale quantities of drugs. If these children can be identified and befriended, they may provide information that will enable police to prosecute senior figures inside KMG.

NOTE: ON THE 13TH DAY OF AUGUST 2004 THIS MISSION PLAN WAS PASSED BY THE CHERUB ETHICS COMMITTEE BY A 2:1 VOTE, ON CONDITION THAT ALL AGENTS UNDERSTAND THE FOLLOWING:

This mission has been classified HIGH RISK. All agents are reminded of their right to refuse to undertake this mission and to withdraw from it at any time. Agents will be at risk of violence and exposure to illegal drugs. Agents are reminded that they will be excluded from CHERUB immediately if they willingly use cocaine or any other class A drug.

*

It was breaking all sorts of rules, but Zara Asker let them take the mission briefings outside and read them in the sun. She'd made a picnic, spreading a tablecloth over the grass and covering it with sandwiches and snacks. It was a chance for baby Joshua to get used to Kyle, Kerry, Nicole and James. The eight-month-old sat under a sunshade, wearing nothing but a nappy. Kerry and Nicole leaned over him with giant grins.

'Look at his tiny fingers, James,' Kerry beamed. 'He's so cute you could gobble him up.'

James lay back in the grass with sunglasses on, thinking he looked cool and wondering how Kyle had managed to get Nicole on the mission.

'It's a baby, Kerry,' he said, 'I've seen one before, they all look exactly the same.'

Kerry tickled Joshua's belly.

'That's James,' she said. 'Isn't he Mr Grumpy today?'

'Ooogy woogy woo,' Nicole added.

Ewart was striding across the grass towards them, carrying an icebox and some bottles of soft drinks. He was a big muscular guy, with bleached hair and half a dozen earrings. He wore a Carhartt T-shirt and old jeans with the legs ripped off.

Zara was older than her husband. She looked like a typical harassed mum, with scraggy hair and puked-up milk on her T-shirt. Like most CHERUB staff, she was a former pupil. She'd gone to university and worked for the United Nations before returning to CHERUB as a mission controller. Kyle had worked with Zara a couple of times before. He said she was one of the best mission controllers to get. Everyone agreed Ewart was the toughest.

'Hey, Nicole,' Kyle said, swatting a fly away from his paper plate. 'You should have seen how happy James was when he found out you got on this mission.'

James sat up, surprised by Kyle's outburst. Nicole turned away from the baby.

'Was he?' she said, breaking into a smile. 'Is that right, James?'

James was flustered. Kerry would kill him if she found out he'd paid Kyle to get Nicole on the mission.

'That's right,' James spluttered. 'I've never got a chance to know you, but the few times I've spoken to you, you've always seemed . . . nice.'

'Thank you, James,' Nicole smiled. 'I was worried I'd be the odd one out because you three are already close.'

Kyle grinned. 'And James fancies you.'

'Piss off, Kyle,' James said.

Kyle was one of James' best mates, but he was always trying to con you or wind you up. Sometimes it got annoying. Zara cuffed Kyle around the back of the head.

'I'm only telling the truth,' Kyle said.

'Kyle, *behave*,' Zara said sharply. 'And James, you watch your language in front of the baby.'

James could feel his face burning with a mix of anger and embarrassment.

'I know James doesn't fancy me,' Nicole said. 'Everyone knows James and Kerry have a thing going.'

'Says who?' Kerry gasped.

'Yeah,' James said defensively. 'Me and Kerry did basic training together and we're good mates. It doesn't mean we fancy each other.'

Kyle laughed. 'If you say so, lovebirds.'

'At least I've *had* a girlfriend,' James said, looking at Kyle. 'You're nearly fifteen and I've never seen you anywhere near a girl.'

Kyle looked offended. 'I've had girlfriends.'

James grinned, sensing he'd put Kyle on the back foot.

'Girls in dreams don't count, dickhead.'

A second later, James found himself dangling in the air with Ewart eyeballing him.

'Fifty laps,' Ewart barked.

'What?' James gasped.

'You shut that filthy mouth in front of my son.'

'He's a baby,' James said. 'He can't understand a word.'

'But he'll learn,' Ewart snarled. 'Get over to the running track, now.'

Fifty laps of the track took two hours and left you for dead when you stiffened up the next morning. Zara intervened before James boiled over and told Ewart where to shove his laps.

'Ewart, darling,' Zara said gently. 'James needs to be here while we discuss the mission. I'm sure an apology will be sufficient.'

James, still suspended in mid-air, didn't think anyone deserved an apology, but it was better than running the laps.

'OK,' James said. 'I'm sorry.'

'For what?' Zara asked.

'I shouldn't have sworn in front of the baby.'

'Apology accepted, James,' Zara said. 'And Kyle, quit being smart. You're the senior agent on this mission. I expect you to help the less experienced agents, not keep stirring up trouble.'

After Ewart had put him down, James straightened his clothes, sat on the grass and started piling chicken drumsticks and sandwiches on to a paper plate. Nicole shuffled up beside him and pinched a couple of his crisps.

Zara began reading notes from a long list.

'OK, as you all know, we're leaving first thing the day after tomorrow. Pack light. There are seven of us and it's a small house. State schools start Tuesday, giving us a nearly a week to settle in before term starts. I've prepared a hundred and sixty page dossier on Keith Moore, his associates and his family, I want all of you to read it and memorise as much as you can . . .'

7. MOVING

It was pandemonium. They had a big moving van and a people carrier. The van was already stuffed, mostly with baby stuff like pushchairs and walkers. Kerry had five bags of clothes and junk, which James had to hump downstairs because her knee was still weak. Kyle, who was always ridiculously neat, wanted to take his clothes rail, eight pairs of shoes and his own ironing board. Ewart was going berserk, using language that would have earned James thousands of laps.

'I'm only making one trip,' Ewart shouted. 'So you lot better sort yourselves out.'

James was the only one who'd followed instructions to pack light. He had a backpack, with toiletries, spare trainers, a jacket and a few changes of clothes. His Playstation and TV had gone ahead the day before with the furniture.

Lauren came tearing around the corner towards them. She was in uniform and she was crying. It was the last thing James expected.

'What's the matter?' he asked, bundling his sister into his arms.

Her T-shirt was sweaty and the sobs made her whole body shudder.

'Just . . .' Lauren sniffed.

James pulled her tighter and rubbed her back.

'Is someone bullying you, or something?'

'I'm ten in two weeks,' she explained. 'It's doing my head in thinking about basic training.'

Lauren acted tough most of the time, but she couldn't always keep the nine-year-old girl inside herself under control. Whenever there was a chink in her armour, she came to James for comfort.

'Lauren, *I* passed training,' James said, feeling a bit emotional himself. 'I'd never done Karate and I could barely swim. With all the fitness and combat exercises you've done, you're a million times better prepared than I was.'

Lauren dragged her wrist over her eyes. Kerry got Lauren a tissue.

'Come on, kids,' Zara shouted, as she climbed into the people carrier. 'I want most of this drive out of the way before Joshua wakes up and starts screaming.'

'I wish you weren't going away,' Lauren said.

'Bethany's going into training with you,' James said. 'She'll probably be your partner. You two will do great.'

Lauren stepped back from James. Kerry gave her a quick squeeze.

'Just think, Lauren,' Kerry said. 'In four months, basic training will be a memory and you'll be able to go on missions. I'll bet you, any money you like.'

Lauren smiled a bit. 'Yeah. I hope so.'

'If you want,' James said, 'I can probably arrange for you to visit us in Luton on your birthday. We can have a laugh.'

Lauren looked surprised. 'Will they let me?'

'They won't mind. It'll be good experience for you: getting a taste of what it's like being out on a mission and stuff.'

'You better go then,' Lauren sniffled, dabbing her eyes with the tissue. 'I don't know what made me start crying. It just . . . Sorry . . . I feel really dumb now.'

James pecked his sister on the cheek, before saying goodbye and climbing in the back of the people carrier.

Kyle leaned out of the side window. 'You'll make it through training, Lauren,' he shouted. 'Don't go losing any sleep.'

James pulled up the door and buckled his seatbelt.

'Sorry I shouted, James,' Zara said, from the driver's seat. 'I didn't realise Lauren was upset. Is she OK?'

'I think so,' James nodded.

Lauren waved as they drove away. James' eyes were a bit damp, but he wasn't worried. Lauren had a good brain and she was fit. A serious injury was the only thing likely to stop her getting through basic training.

*

Ewart and Nicole travelled in the moving van with the luggage. Zara drove the people carrier, with Kyle next to her in the front. James and Kerry sandwiched Joshua's baby seat in the back. The baby woke up an hour before they arrived. Kerry had a go at feeding him, but he screamed his head off. She passed him over to James while she hunted round her feet for a bottle Joshua had batted on to the floor.

Joshua stopped screaming as soon as James took him. When Kerry tried to take Joshua back, he went nuts again.

Kerry gave James the bottle and Joshua began drinking calmly.

'Looks like we've found James' job for this mission,' Zara said, grinning. 'He likes you for some reason.'

Kyle laughed. 'Kerry probably traumatised him with the funny faces she was pulling the other afternoon.'

James wasn't used to babies. He was terrified he might do something wrong and either hurt Joshua or get puked over. It turned out OK, apart from a few dribbles of milk. After feeding, Joshua lay quietly in James' lap playing with the laces on his shorts. Once James got used to it, he thought having the warm little body wriggling on his lap was quite cool.

*

A third of the houses on the Thornton estate were boarded up. The detached homes looked decent enough, but nobody wanted to live in them because of the airport a kilometre south. Every few minutes, a couple of hundred people thundered overhead, shaking the ground and filling the air with the sickly smell of jet fuel.

You only ended up living on Thornton if you didn't have a choice. The residents were a mix of refugees, students, ex-convicts and families who'd been chucked out of better places for not paying the rent.

A gang of lads had to stop their football match to let Zara drive through. Ewart and Nicole had arrived minutes earlier. Nicole had unpacked the mugs and started making tea.

The windows in the house were triple glazed to keep out the aircraft noise, but that didn't stop everything vibrating. Besides, it was too warm to leave every window closed.

There were three bedrooms between seven people. Kyle and James got a box room with bunk beds, a chest of drawers and a tiny wardrobe.

'Just like old times,' James said, remembering when he and Kyle shared a room in a council home before he joined CHERUB.

'There's nowhere to hang my clothes,' Kyle said miserably. 'They'll get creased.'

'You can have the whole wardrobe,' James said. 'I'll just dump my stuff in the bag or under the bed.'

'If there's anything that stinks in this room, I'm chucking it out,' Kyle said. 'I don't care if it's a sock or a seventy-quid pair of trainers – if it smells like you, it's going in the bin.'

James laughed. 'I'd forgotten what a complete tart you are.'

*

Zara made dinner for everyone: fish fingers and oven chips, with frozen peas.

'Sorry,' she said, handing plates to the line of kids in front of the TV. 'You better get used to my cooking. It's not exactly gourmet.'

Something crashed outside the living-room window. All the kids downed cutlery and bundled towards the window. There was rubbish all over the front lawn and a metal dustbin rolling towards the gutter. A couple of boys were sprinting off down the pavement. Ewart burst out of the front door, but they'd disappeared up an alleyway.

As James mopped his last chip through his ketchup, Ewart strode in and switched off the TV.

'I always watch *Neighbours*,' Kerry gasped.

'Not today you don't,' Ewart said. 'You kids have a job to do.'

'Go outside and start making friends,' Zara said. 'There's bound to be some dodgy characters in an area like this, so stick together. I want you back here as soon as it gets dark.'

'And James,' Ewart said, 'you better pick all that rubbish off the front lawn before you go.'

'Why's it my job?' James said bitterly.

Ewart broke into a smile. 'Because I said so.'

James thought about starting a row, but you never win against someone like Ewart.

*

It was easy starting conversations. The summer holidays had dragged on for weeks and the local kids were bored. James and Kyle played street football until they got knackered. Kerry and Nicole stood by the kerb, nattering with a bunch of girls. When it started getting late, the four of them got invited to a kiddies' playground.

There was nothing special about it: a burned-out park keeper's shed sprayed with graffiti, a busted roundabout, a climbing frame and a slide. But once the sun started to go down, it came alive. Kids aged between ten and sixteen gathered in fours and fives; smoking, arguing and being loud. There was a tense atmosphere. Flash kids dressed like Nike commercials ripped into refugees dressed out of the charity box. Boys were trying to get off with girls and there was a rumour going around about a gang from another estate turning up and starting a fight.

Apparently, a kid had been stabbed in the playground a couple of months earlier. He'd ended up with between eight and two hundred stitches, depending on what version of the story you believed.

'This is boring,' Kerry said, after half an hour of standing around without anything happening except a lot of talk. 'We better go home.'

'You go if you want,' James said. 'I'm staying to see if a fight breaks out. It might be good.'

'It might also be dangerous,' Kerry said. 'I've seen a couple of kids with knives and Zara told us to be home before . . .'

James interrupted, mocking Kerry's voice. 'Zara told us da-de-da-da . . . Chill out, Kerry, what's the point having a curfew unless you're gonna break it?'

Kerry looked at Nicole for moral support. 'Are you coming?'

'No way,' Nicole said. 'I want to see some action.'

They all waited another twenty minutes. A guy aged about fifteen came over and started chatting up Nicole. Then someone's mobile rang and a rumour shot around. There was a car coming.

'So what?' Kerry asked.

'Stolen car,' one of the local kids explained. 'Joyriders. They usually put on a good show.'

Fifty-odd kids piled out of the playground and hurried to a deserted car park a few hundred metres down the road. A cheer went up when everyone spotted the headlights. It was a Subaru Impreza turbo, metallic silver with a giant wing on the back. The driver did a couple of handbrake turns, spinning the car and stinking up the air with tyre smoke. Then he overdid it and smacked into a bollard, leaving a massive graze down one side of the car. The audience whooped and cheered, even though he'd nearly splattered a couple of girls standing astride their bikes.

'These guys are nutters,' James giggled. 'I'd love to have a go at that.'

Kerry gave him a filthy look. 'It's so stupid. They could kill themselves, or an innocent bystander.'

'Loosen up, Kerry,' James said. 'You sound like an old fart.'

The Subaru squealed to a halt a few metres away. As the cloud of tyre smoke cleared, the driver and his mate opened the doors and ran around the car to switch seats. They both looked about fifteen.

'Where are our babes?' the new driver shouted.

A couple of tarty-looking girls jogged to the car and clambered in the back. When they were inside, the driver lit up the rear tyres and started driving circuits around the estate. He skidded on every corner, nearly losing the back end a couple of times on sharp turns. When the car was out of sight, you could still hear the engine and squealing tyres. The joyriders kept coming back to the car park for more adulation from their audience.

The excitement level went into overload when a police siren went off. James was hoping to see a chase, but the joyriders didn't fancy their chances. They slammed on the brakes, jumped out and merged into the crowd of kids as three police cars turned into the car park.

Everyone started running. One of the guys they'd been playing football with tugged James by his T-shirt.

'Don't stand there gawping,' he said urgently. 'The pigs will bust you if they get hold of you.'

Kerry, Kyle and Nicole were already gone. James sprinted off, but the whole of Thornton estate looked identical in the dark and he couldn't remember the way home. He ended up in the centre of the estate, in a large paved square with lanes of identical houses branching off in six different directions.

'You know which way?' a voice asked breathlessly.

James spun around. It was a massive relief to see Kyle. Kerry and Nicole were with him.

'We can ask one of the policemen,' Kerry said.

'Are you totally brain-dead?' James asked, tapping his head. 'The police are looking for two boys and two girls. They'll nick us.'

Kerry looked perplexed. 'But we didn't steal the car.'

'Kerry,' Kyle said, laughing, 'how naive are you? In an area like this, cops and kids are like oil and water: they don't mix.'

'Well,' Kerry said indignantly, 'none of this would have happened if we'd gone home when I said.'

'Oh, shut your smug hole,' James said.

'So, which way?' Nicole asked.

*

They were all out of breath when they burst through the front door. It was pure luck finding the right street at the second attempt, without bumping into any cops. Zara leaned out of the kitchen into the hallway.

'Ahh . . . Here they are. My little monsters,' Zara grinned. 'Late as usual.'

The kids were expecting a roasting, but they got off because there was an old couple sitting at the table in the kitchen, drinking tea with Zara and Ewart.

'This is the adopted family,' Ewart explained. 'Kids, meet Ron and Georgina. They live next door and they brought us home-made biscuits to welcome us to the neighbourhood.'

'You kids dip in,' the old girl said. 'My biscuits have won prizes.'

They stuck their hands in the tin and grabbed one. They tasted like they'd been baked in 1937, but they could hardly start gobbing them out in front of the old lady.

'Delicious,' James said, gagging for some water to get the stale taste out of his mouth.

'Would you like another one?' the old dear asked.

Zara clamped the lid on the biscuit tin.

'They're off to their rooms now,' Zara said. 'They're not really allowed sweet stuff this late. It's bad for their teeth.'

They were all thankful that Zara had saved them from another biscuit. James led the scramble upstairs to the bathroom.

'SHUSSSHH, you lot,' Zara whispered after them. 'Joshua's asleep.'

The four of them queued at the bathroom tap to get a drink; then they slugged mouthwash to get the taste out of their mouths.

'It's like a single bite sucks every bit of saliva out of your mouth,' Kerry said.

'I bet she knows how disgusting they are,' Kyle said. 'Probably gets a kick out of watching everyone suffer.'

'Hope the old bag dies,' Nicole said.

James started laughing. 'I think that's a *tiny* bit extreme, Nicole.'

'I can't stand old people,' Nicole said. 'Wait till they're sixty, then give all of 'em both barrels of a shotgun.'

'My nan was great,' James said. 'I got a Kit Kat or Wagon Wheel every time I saw her ... I was her favourite. She never liked Lauren much.'

Kerry grunted. 'No accounting for taste, I suppose. When did she die?'

'When I was ten.'

'Is Lauren OK now?' Kyle asked.

'I haven't spoken to her since this morning,' James said. 'Suppose I'd better ring her before I go to bed.'

After he'd undressed, James climbed into his bunk and gave Lauren a call on his mobile. She was embarrassed about crying earlier and didn't want to talk about it.

8. CONTACT

It was the first day of a new school year. The lines of miserable kids had short haircuts and new uniforms to grow into. Kyle offered to run the iron over James' stuff to *make it nice and crisp*, as he put it. James had forgotten how annoying it was to wear a tie and blazer all day. The only good thing was, Nicole looked fit in her white blouse, with her tie loose around the collar. She'd altered her skirt so it was half the length of Kerry's.

James had been to a few different schools since his mum died. Grey Park looked like it was at the bottom of the pile. The smell was a mixture of toilets and floor polish. The curtains and walls in the entrance hall were stuck up with thousands of bits of chewing gum, half the kids weren't in uniform and there was an aquarium full of dead fish with a chair floating in it.

James broke off from the others and found his classroom. He recognised Junior Moore straight away, sitting at the back with a mate. You could tell, by the state of their uniforms and the way they were sitting with their trainers on the desk, that they wanted everyone to think they were bad guys.

James had to work his way in with them gradually. If you went straight up and introduced yourself to kids like that, they'd treat you like a joke. James' plan was to act cool and win them over with bad behaviour.

The teacher came in. He was a titchy little donut in a beige suit called Mr Shawn. He seemed full of himself; the kind of teacher who gave you an urge to muck about, just so you got the pleasure of seeing him flip out.

'O-KAYYYYYYY,' Mr Shawn shouted, slamming a book on his desk to get everyone's attention. 'Summer is over, welcome to Year Eight . . . Find your seats and settle down.'

James sat at an empty desk in the middle. This seriously weird kid sat next to him. He was tall, but stick thin. His uniform was too small and his walk was bizarre, like he was trying to move in twenty directions at once.

'You're new,' the weirdo said. 'I'm Charles.'

James didn't want to be nasty, but a geeky pal was the last thing he needed if he was going to make friends with Junior.

'I can show you around if you want,' Charles said.

'It's OK,' James replied awkwardly. 'I'll manage, but cheers for the offer.'

Charles didn't carry a backpack like the other kids; he had a brown leather briefcase. Judging by the noise when he put it down, he kept a couple of bricks inside. Charles stooped over the desk and began frantically scratching at the back of his hand. A snowstorm of skin flakes drifted on to the table in front of him.

'I've got eczema,' Charles explained noisily. 'It gets worse in the summer when I sweat.'

Mr Shawn started handing out timetables and burbling about the fabulous opportunities presented by the after-school chess and drama clubs. Ten minutes into school, James already wanted to burst out of the front gate and run for the hills. He'd always found school boring, but after being at CHERUB, where the classes were small and the teachers pushed you, normal school made him feel like his life was running in slow motion.

Charles was bored as well. He got an apple out of his briefcase and crunched into it. Mr Shawn stopped talking and glowered at him.

'Charles, what on earth are you doing?'

'Eating an apple,' Charles said, as if he'd been asked the world's stupidest question.

'We don't eat in class, do we?' Mr Shawn said.

Everyone started laughing. If a cool kid had bitten the apple, they would have laughed at how funny it was. But they all had Charles down as class loser, so everyone was shaking their heads and there were a few murmurs of *spastic* and *retard*.

'Put it in the bin, Charles.'

Charles took a final bite of the apple, before hurling it at the metal bin behind Mr Shawn's desk. He missed, so he lumbered over and picked it off the floor. The back of his trousers looked set to rip open when he bent down and you could see his bright green Y-fronts.

'Nice knickers, Charles,' one of the girls shouted.

'Yeah,' someone else shouted. 'But they were white when he put them on.'

The kids went into another round of laughs.

Charles missed the bin a second time, even though he was dropping the apple from less than a metre. He lost his temper and kicked out. The bin smashed against the wall and the metal got bent out of shape.

'Charles, calm *down*,' Mr Shawn shouted.

'I hate bins,' Charles steamed, booting it again.

'Into your seat now, Charles, unless you want a detention tonight.'

Charles stumbled back to his seat.

*

Their maths teacher was a fruitcake. She had the key for the wrong classroom. Everyone stood around in the corridor while she went looking for the caretaker. Junior and his pal wandered up to Charles. James was standing next to him.

'Did you miss us this summer?' Junior asked.

Charles kept quiet. Junior grabbed his wrist and bent back his thumb.

'Did you bring us any presents from your holidays?' Junior asked, tightening his grip until Charles' face twisted up in pain.

'No,' Charles gasped.

'That's not nice. I think you deserve a slap.'

Junior let Charles' thumb go and clocked him around the face. It wasn't hard. It was mainly done for humiliation.

'And who's your new friend?' Junior asked.

'James,' Charles stuttered.

Junior faced James off. He was a fair bit shorter than James, but he had beefy arms and shoulders, as well as a mate to back him up. He gave James a little shove.

James felt edgy. CHERUB training had taught him that

your first encounter with someone sets the tone for everything that follows. If James appeared weak, Junior would never consider him an equal and they'd be unlikely to make friends. But if James lashed out, they might become enemies and that would be even worse. He had to get the right balance between the two.

'Try pushing me around if you want to,' James said casually. 'But I wouldn't recommend it.'

Junior turned to his mate and smiled.

'What's this, Del?' he laughed. 'Looks like the new boy thinks he's a hard man.'

Junior tried to grab James' wrist. James dodged out the way and jabbed two fingers into Junior's belly, sending him into a spasm.

'Too slow,' James said, shaking his head in contempt.

Junior lunged again. His fist hit James in the guts, knocking the wind out of him. The force behind it surprised James. In a flash of anger, he hooked his foot around Junior's ankle and shoved him over. All the other kids backed up, expecting a fight.

James stood over Junior with his fists bunched, defying him to get up. Junior didn't look too confident. After a couple of tense moments, James smiled and reached out his hand.

'If you want a row, there's plenty of easier targets around than me,' he said.

Junior looked pissed off, but grudgingly let James help him up.

'Where'd you learn to do that?' Junior asked, brushing off his uniform.

'From Zara, my stepmum,' James said. 'She's a Karate instructor.'

'Cool,' Junior said. 'What belt are you?'

'Black, of course,' James said. 'What about you? Who taught you to throw a punch?'

'Boxing club,' Junior said. 'I'm undefeated. Eight fights, eight victories.'

By the time the teacher got the classroom door open, the lesson was half finished. There was a spare seat next to Junior.

'Mind if I sit here?' James asked.

'Free country,' Junior shrugged. 'This is Del and I'm Keith; but that's my dad's name, so everyone calls me Junior.'

'I'm James. Thanks for rescuing us from sitting with freak-boy over there.'

James was pleased with himself. It had only taken an hour to break the ice. He sealed the deal by blowing a massive raspberry when the teacher asked him to be quiet. Junior and Del cracked up laughing.

Junior slapped James on the back as they walked out to morning break.

'You've got bottle, James,' he said. 'What lesson's next?'

Del got a timetable out of his pocket.

'History,' he said.

'Balls to that,' Junior said. 'What about this afternoon?'

'Maths and French.'

'Don't fancy that,' Junior said. 'You coming, Del?'

Del looked anxious. 'I dunno. I don't think we should bunk off first day. My dad's gonna kill me if we get suspended again.'

'Well,' Junior said, 'it's sunny outside. There's no way I'm sitting cooped up in some classroom. You wanna tag along, James?'

'Where you going?'

'God knows. We can get burgers or something, hang around the shopping centre.'

'Whatever,' James said. 'Anything beats lessons.'

One of the coolest things about missions was being able to break all the rules without getting into trouble.

*

The two boys crawled under the back gate and ran a couple of hundred metres away from the school. Junior did a strip. He had a Puma T-shirt and shorts under his uniform.

'If you're gonna bunk off,' Junior explained, 'it's best to get rid of the uniform. Otherwise you get some old bat spotting the badge on your blazer and ringing up your school to complain.'

'Smart,' James nodded. 'But all I've got under here is bare skin, so unless you want me to walk round in my boxers, I'm stuck with it.'

'You want to go to the Reeve Centre?' Junior asked.

'What's that?'

'Big shopping place. You're seriously telling me you've never been there?'

'We only moved here a week ago,' James explained.

'Why's that?'

'We were in London,' James lied, repeating the cover story they'd all had to memorise. 'My stepdad got a job at the airport, so we moved up here.'

'If you've never been to the Reeve Centre, we should

definitely go. It's half an hour on the bus. There's sports shops, games shops and a big food court.'

'Sounds cool,' James said. 'But I've only got the three quid Zara gave me to buy lunch.'

'I can lend you a fiver, James. But I'll send my geezers round to smash your legs if you don't pay me back.'

James laughed. 'Cheers.'

9. THEFT

They wandered round the Reeve Centre for an hour, looking at trainers and computer games that they didn't have any money to buy. It wasn't as boring as school, but it wasn't exactly exciting either. When they got hungry, they got stuff off a Mexican stand in the food court.

'My dad's loaded,' Junior said, taking a chunk out of his burrito. 'But he's so tight. He says he doesn't want me turning into a spoiled brat. I'm telling you, half the poor scum living down on the Thornton estate get more cool stuff than I do.'

'That's where I live,' James said.

'Sorry,' Junior smiled. 'No offence.'

'None taken.'

'Actually, it's quite a laugh hanging out on Thornton. I was down there in the holidays and some kids started chucking bricks at the police.'

James laughed. 'Excellent.'

'It was brilliant. One cop car got the windscreen smashed and everything. I go to boxing club down there as well. Have you been round there?'

'No.'

'My dad sponsors it, actually. You should come along, everyone who goes boxing is a nutter. It's a good crowd.'

'Maybe I'll try it,' James said. 'Does boxing hurt?'

'Only when you get punched,' Junior said, grinning. 'So that's something you should definitely try to avoid.'

'So how come your dad's loaded?' James asked. 'What does he do?'

James knew what Keith Moore did, of course, but he wondered what Junior would say.

'Oh, he's a businessman. Import and export. He's a millionaire actually.'

James acted impressed. 'Seriously?'

'No kidding. That's why I get so pissed off he won't give me decent pocket money. There are six Playstation games I want really bad. I'll get a couple of them for my birthday, but that's not till November.'

'Steal 'em,' James said.

Junior laughed. 'Yeah, but knowing my luck I'd get busted.'

'I know a few things about shoplifting,' James said. 'My mum was into it, before she died.'

'Did she get nicked much?'

'Never,' James said. 'Shoplifting is a snip, as long as you use forward planning and kitchen foil.'[1]

---

[1] The author of this book would like to point out that the shoplifting technique described here only works with certain outdated security systems. I've got no intention of telling you which ones they are because I don't want angry Dads turning up on my doorstep and kicking my head in because their little darling just got busted trying to nick something from a shop.

'How many times have you done it?' Junior asked.

'Hundreds,' James lied.

In fact, the only time James had tried shoplifting was when he was in care shortly after his mum died. He'd ended up in a police cell.

'So what's the tin foil for?' Junior asked.

'I'll show you, if you want to go for it.'

'I'm in if you reckon it's safe.'

James gurgled up the last of his Coke. 'There's no guarantee, but I've never been caught before.'

He reckoned shoplifting was a good way to cement his friendship with Junior. If they got away with it, he'd be a hero and he could invite himself round to Keith Moore's house to play the games. It would be trickier if they got caught, but the experience of getting in trouble together would probably bring them closer.

James wouldn't get in real trouble with the police, because they would arrest and charge James Beckett, a boy who didn't really exist. As soon as the mission ended, CHERUB would pull James Beckett's criminal file and have it destroyed, so no fingerprint or DNA evidence would ever be linked back to James' real identity.

James bought a roll of tin foil in one of those everything for a pound shops. They locked themselves in a disabled toilet. James gave Junior the stuff out of his backpack and lined it with a double layer of the shiny aluminium.

'What does it do?' Junior asked.

'You know those alarms that go off when you take something out of a shop?'

Junior nodded.

'They're metal detectors,' James explained. 'They put those sticky metal tag thingies on everything, and the alarm goes off when it detects them.'

'So, won't the metal foil make it go off?'

'It only goes off when it detects the right-sized piece of metal. Otherwise, it would ring for every umbrella and belt buckle. So, as long as you wrap the security tags inside something made of metal, the alarm thinks it's something different and doesn't go off.'

'Genius,' Junior said, breaking into a grin.

'All we need is a shop where they keep the Playstation discs in the boxes, not behind the counter.'

'Gameworld does,' Junior said.

'We'll have to go in separately. I'll go up and stick the games in my pack. Your job is to distract the security guard, or any staff that come near me.'

'How?'

'Anything to take their attention off me. Just walk up and ask where something is.'

'You're sure this isn't going to go wrong?' Junior asked excitedly. 'If we get caught, my dad will crucify me.'

'Trust me,' James said. 'Besides, you're only a lookout. I'm the one taking the big risk.'

James felt confident as Junior led him through the shopping centre towards Gameworld.

The security guard stood in the entrance. James went straight up the back to the Playstation games. His foil-lined backpack was already unzipped. He found four of the games Junior wanted, then realised he might as well grab a few for himself while he was taking the risk. It was dead easy: the security guard was picking his nose and the guy at the checkout was texting on his mobile.

James zipped the pack up and slung it over his back. Junior stood in the doorway, with the security guard pointing out the DVDs to him. James headed towards the exit as nonchalantly as he could, but his heart was thumping. As he passed through the detector, an alarm went berserk and a mechanical voice boomed out:

'We're sorry, an inventory tag has been left on your item. Please return to the store. We're sorry, an inventory . . .'

The guard took hold of James and tried to drag him into the shop. Junior could have kept his head down and nobody would have been able to prove he was involved, so James was impressed when he charged towards the security guard and punched him in the side of the head. James kneed the guard in the stomach and started running, with Junior a few paces behind.

The security guard in the store opposite had seen the whole show and came after them. When James glanced back over his shoulder, the guard was shouting into his walkie-talkie, requesting back-up.

'You tit,' Junior shouted, as shoppers dived out of their way. 'What a great plan.'

James couldn't work out what he'd done wrong. Two security guards came out of a department store up ahead, blocking their path and forcing them to cut into a women's clothing store. A woman with a buggy went flying into a display of leggings as James crashed into her. The store was crammed with rails of clothing that brushed against James as he ran. Junior stumbled. One of the security guards got a hand on him, but he spun away and recovered his balance.

James burst out of the fire exit at the back of the shop, setting off another alarm. He'd hoped the door would lead out on to the street, but he'd emerged into the central concourse of the shopping centre. There was a big fountain and a stand where they did temporary exhibitions. The yellow banner hanging over the exhibition stand sent James into shock:

BEDFORDSHIRE POLICE THEFT PREVENTION SQUAD.
FIND OUT HOW TO PROTECT YOUR
HOME AND CAR FROM CRIME.

There was a long fold-out table, with three policemen behind it handing out crime prevention leaflets.

'Holy shit,' Junior gasped, stopping in his tracks.

With the police up ahead and security guards behind, their chances looked about nil. James considered surrendering, but Junior noticed a door with a toilet sign a few metres away and barged it open. He led James down a narrow corridor, with six pairs of men's shoes clattering after them. They passed the entrance to the ladies' toilet and crashed through a fire door, into the dim confines of a multistorey car park.

They sped towards the lift, but there was no time to wait for it. Instead, they scrambled on to the staircase and ran down, leaping three steps at a time, fuelled by adrenalin. James twisted his ankle, but he didn't have time to think about the pain, or the fact that if he tumbled he'd smash his head open on bare concrete.

The policemen were more cautious on the stairs and the boys had gained ground by the time they booted open a set of doors that led into a sunlit alleyway. There were massive steel bins and boxes of rubbish piled around them. They clambered over everything, reaching the front of the shopping centre as the police emerged through the doors at the bottom of the stairs. The security guards had given up.

There was a pedestrian crossing, with two lanes of waiting traffic. James saw the green man flashing and they made a dash for it. They ran into the outdoor car park, crouching low and jogging between the bumpers of two lines of parked cars.

The police got stranded on the other side of the road, waiting for the lights to change. One cop tried to stop the traffic with a hand signal and nearly got splattered by a motorbike. By the time the cops had halted the traffic and made it across, James and Junior were crouching behind a car a hundred metres away.

The three cops stood on the pavement by the car park, staring hopelessly at row after row of parked cars. The boys kept low until they came to the far side of the car park. They pushed themselves through shrubs, emerging on to the narrow pavement beside a fast-moving dual carriageway. Junior started to run.

'WHOAH,' James said. 'Keep cool.'

Junior turned around. 'What?'

'Walk,' James said. 'It looks less dodgy if we're spotted.'

They walked nervously for twenty minutes, looking back over their shoulders and having miniature heart attacks every time they spotted a white car. When they noticed a bus coming, they sprinted to the stop and hopped on. They went upstairs and sat at the back, well away from the other passengers. James finally felt safe.

'Sorry about that,' he said breathlessly. 'You're not pissed off with me, are you?'

Junior burst out laughing. 'That was *mental*. The look on those cops' faces when we lost 'em. Oh man . . .'

'I'm an idiot,' James said. 'You know what I did? When I put the games in, I must have pushed the foil down the bag so it wasn't covering them over.'

'Who cares now?' Junior grinned. 'Gimme, gimme, gimme.'

James unzipped his pack and pulled out nine Playstation games. Junior read out the price stickers.

'Forty, forty, twenty-five, thirty-five. How much is that?'

'A hundred and forty.'

'Thirty-eight, twenty-four and three at thirty-five.'

'Three hundred and seven quid,' James said.

'You add fast,' Junior said. 'Over three hundred quid's worth of games. That's so cool, we've got to do it again some time.'

'I dunno,' James said. 'I'm not sure if my underwear can take the strain.'

*

'You're late, James,' Zara said. 'Dinner's nearly ready.'

Kerry and Kyle were sitting at the kitchen table while Zara did frozen lasagne in the oven.

'Sorry,' James said.

'You could have rung us,' Zara said. 'We were all worried.'

Kerry looked up. 'Where were you? I didn't see you at lunchtime.'

'I was around,' James said, defensively.

'So how was school?' Zara asked.

'Oh, you know,' James shrugged. 'Same old, same old. Boring as hell.'

Zara wouldn't have minded that he'd bunked off with Junior, but James didn't want her finding out about the shoplifting and the chase. If cherubs steal something, or make money while they're on a mission, they're supposed either to return the goods or donate them to charity. James had no plans to give away five top Playstation games after going through so much exertion stealing them.

'How did you get along with Junior?' Zara asked.

'Really good,' James said. 'He's my sort of person. I reckon we would have ended up mates even if I hadn't tried. Where's Nicole?'

'Doing homework with April Moore and a bunch of other girls,' Kyle said.

'Wow,' James smiled. 'She's a fast worker. How did you two get on with your targets?'

'Erin Moore and her weird friends chucked paper at me and started calling me *peg-leg* because of my limp,' Kerry said miserably.

'Ringo's a swot,' Kyle said. 'Nice kid, taking his GCSEs very seriously. The thing is, I reckon he's too straight to be involved in his dad's drug business.'

'James,' Kerry said, 'why's there tin foil sticking out of your backpack?'

'What?' James gasped.

Kerry leaned towards the pack. James whipped it away before she got a chance to see inside.

'You've been up to something,' Kerry grinned. 'What's in there?'

'Nothing,' James said, jumping up from the table. 'I better go and um . . . I'll give Lauren a call before dinner's ready.'

Kyle and Kerry exchanged looks as James thumped upstairs to his room.

'Tin foil?' Kerry whispered, not wanting Zara to hear.

'Don't ask me,' Kyle shrugged. 'But he's been up to something, that's for sure.'

10. PUNCH

It was Friday, after school. James, Kyle, Kerry and Nicole sat on the living-room couches in their school uniforms, drinking cans of Coke. The TV was on but nobody was watching.

James looked at Kyle. 'I'm going boxing tonight, with Junior. You wanna come?'

'You in a boxing ring,' Kerry giggled. 'That's something I'd pay money to see.'

James clucked. 'It's training, stupid. They don't make you fight on the first night.'

'I'll pass on getting punched in the head,' Kyle said. 'I got invited to a party.'

'Oh,' James said. 'Thanks for inviting me.'

'It's Ringo Moore and his mates,' Kyle said. 'Year Ten and Eleven kids. They won't want the likes of you biting their ankles.'

'I'm meeting April at the youth club,' Nicole said. 'The boxing gym is upstairs.'

'So, Kerry,' James said, breaking into a grin. 'I'm going out with Junior Moore tonight. Kyle's partying with Ringo

Moore and Nicole's at the youth club with April Moore. What are you and Erin Moore doing?'

'Ha ha, very funny,' Kerry said miserably. 'Erin is the biggest geek. There's this student Spanish teacher.'

'Miss Perez,' James said. 'I've got her as well.'

'That's her,' Kerry said. 'Erin and her little friends wound her up so much, they made her run out of the classroom in tears. I felt really sorry for her.'

'Yeah,' James giggled. 'Perez is always crying. My class had her bawling three times in one lesson. It was *soooo* funny.'

Kerry looked mad. 'James, that's horrible. How must that poor woman feel?'

James shrugged. 'Who cares? She's only a teacher.'

'You know what, James?' Kerry snapped. 'Teachers have feelings the same as anyone else.'

'Whatever,' James said. 'I know you're only angry because you can't get on with Erin and you'll probably get your botty kicked off this mission.'

'Oh, shut up, James,' Kerry shouted, putting her palm in front of her face. 'I spend all day stuck in a class with a bunch of stupid, noisy morons. I don't want to come home and deal with another one.'

'Touchy touchy,' James giggled.

Kyle gave James a nudge. 'Leave it out, eh?'

James realised he'd overdone it. He was getting a filthy look off Nicole as well.

'Sorry, Kerry,' James said. 'But you were taking the mickey out of me going boxing just a second ago.'

Kerry didn't answer. She just scowled into the bottom of her empty Coke can.

'You don't have to sit here all night watching telly, Kerry,' Nicole said. 'You can come to the youth centre with me if you want.'

'I don't want your pity, Nicole,' Kerry said tersely. 'Our mission briefing says if you can't get on with your target, you should try and get involved in KMG through another kid. So, for your information, I won't be sitting in front of the TV. I'll be at the youth centre with someone tonight, the same as Nicole and Mohammed Ali over there.'

Kerry got off the sofa and stomped up to her room. Kyle reached over and punched James' shoulder.

'What the hell was that for?' James asked, furiously.

'Being an insensitive pig,' Kyle said. 'You know what a big deal Kerry makes about being the best at everything.'

'Jesus,' James said, rubbing his arm. 'I was only having a laugh. It's not my fault she's so touchy.'

'Go up and apologise,' Kyle said.

'I better not,' James said. 'She probably wants to be on her own.'

James noticed the look he was getting off Nicole.

'OK then,' James huffed, standing up. 'I'll go and say sorry.'

James went upstairs. Kerry and Nicole's room was at the end of the corridor. As James got closer, he started to bottle it. Kerry had a violent temper and he didn't want to get on the wrong end of it. For the first time ever, James was happy to hear Joshua crying. He leaned into Ewart and Zara's room, making sure they weren't in there, then walked over to the cot and picked the baby up. Joshua rested his head on James' shoulder and changed his bawling to a gentler sucking kind of noise.

'Come on,' James said, rocking Joshua gently. 'Let's find Mummy.'

He went down to the kitchen. Ewart was at the table.

'Cheers for picking him up, James,' Ewart said. 'Zara's just gone down the shop for some bread.'

'Get his bottle warmed up,' James said. 'I'll take him into the living-room. He likes watching the telly.'

Ewart smiled at James. 'Joshua still won't let Kyle or the girls go near him. You know why I think he likes you?'

James shrugged. 'Why?'

'You've got blond hair, the same as me and Zara.'

'Maybe,' James said.

He carried Joshua through and sat next to Nicole on the sofa.

'Look who's here,' Nicole said, grinning and wiggling Joshua's big toe.

Since he'd been on the mission, James had learned something about girls: if you want them to like you, don't worry about buying gifts, or saying the right thing, or where to take them. What you need to do is grab the nearest brat and stick it on your lap. Nicole, who'd been furious at James a few minutes earlier, shuffled up close to him on the couch.

'You know, James,' Nicole beamed, 'some day you're gonna make a really good dad.'

*

The stairs leading up to the boxing club had signed photos and newspaper cuttings of boxers James had never heard of on the walls. The door at the top of the stairs creaked and James got a nose full of thirty-degree heat and old sweat. About twenty guys were working out. Dark patches on their clothes, lifting weights, punching bags. James felt awkward, imagining they were all sizing him up, estimating how many milliseconds it would take to punch him out.

A massive guy stopped a set of crunches and started mopping his bald head with a towel.

'New fish?' he asked, looking at James.

James nodded. 'I um . . .'

The guy pointed his thumb. 'You want the back room, with the other kids. Try not to tread on anyone.'

James had to step over gym mats and bar-bells to get through. The back room was bigger, with twenty-odd boys aged between nine and fourteen working out. Two young coaches stood in a ring up the back, mucking about and taking punches off some little kids. James recognised Junior, Del and a couple of guys he'd seen around Thornton estate and at school.

'You Junior's new pal?' a voice asked from behind.

James turned. The guy sat in a plastic chair. He wore tracksuit bottoms and a stained vest. His shoulders were a mat of wiry grey hair. Even though the guy was thirty years past his prime, he still didn't look like a man you wanted to mess with.

'I'm Ken,' the guy growled. 'If you're here for the night, it's fifty pence.'

'Junior said it's cheaper if I get a monthly ticket,' James said.

'Fifty pence for tonight,' Ken said. 'I don't want to rob you. This is too much like hard work for most kids. They don't come through that door more than once or twice. If you're one of the ones who sticks it, I'll take what you've already paid off the monthly pass.'

James nodded and dug some coins out of his shorts.

'Go see your friend Junior and try to follow what he does,' Ken said. 'You're here to train. That means you don't stand around talking. You don't mess around and you don't make jokes. Any kid starts a fight without my say-so and I'll give the nod to someone who'll make them sorry. You got that?'

James nodded. 'Don't I get coaching or something?'

Ken laughed. 'I sit here with my eyes open. Give it a week or so. Follow what the others do. When I think you're ready, I'll get one of the trainees to start you off with a little sparring.'

James wandered over to Junior.

'Enjoy the lecture?' Junior asked, grinning.

Junior, Del and a couple of other guys trained in a group. Everything was a competition: how many push-ups or crunches, how fast you could skip, how many times you could punch the hanging ball in thirty seconds. CHERUB training had made James fit. He could hold his own at everything except skipping, which he'd only ever tried in PE lessons years earlier. Everyone except James got a turn in the ring, either sparring with each other or getting coached by Kelvin and Marcus, the two brutal-looking seventeen-year-olds the club employed as apprentice coaches.

When they were all half-dead, the group piled into the locker room, showered off the sweat and put on fresh clothes. On their way out, Ken blocked James' way with his leg.

'You coming back?' Ken asked.

'I'd like to,' James nodded, still out of breath. 'If that's OK.'

'You've done some kind of martial arts training, haven't you?'

'Yeah, Karate and judo. How could you tell?'

'You're in good shape and you can punch,' Ken said, 'but a boxer needs fast feet as well. You want to be able to skip a hundred and fifty times a minute. Take this home and practise half an hour a day.'

James took hold of a frayed skipping rope. He stuck it in his carrier bag, on top of his damp kit.

Junior slapped him on the back as they went down the staircase.

'He must think you've got talent, James. I kept coming here for three weeks before he said a word and my dad practically owns the joint.'

James couldn't help smiling, though it was hardly surprising he showed promise after all the combat training he'd done at CHERUB.

'You coming down the youth club with me and Del?' Junior asked. 'It's packed out with girls, Friday night.'

The youth club was on the ground floor, under the gym. It was supposed to be a disco, but the music wasn't very loud and nobody was dancing. James sat with Junior and Del on some slashed-up seats in a dark corner. There were plenty of boys and plenty of girls, but everyone sat in single-sex groups.

'So,' Junior said, 'which babes are us three studs gonna snap up tonight?'

Del looked at his watch. 'Not me. I'm off to work once I've drunk this.'

Del always had money and James thought it probably came from delivering drugs. He straightened up in his seat, sensing an opportunity to get information, but trying not to make it obvious he was prying.

'Work?' he asked. 'At this time of night?'

Junior burst out laughing. 'Ah . . . The voice of innocence.'

'I work for KMG,' Del said.

'KM what?' James said.

'Keith Moore's Gang,' Del explained. 'I deliver coke for Junior's daddy.'

'Who wants Coke at this time on a Friday?'

'Not Coca-Cola, you wazzock,' Junior said. 'Cocaine.'

James acted like he was surprised. 'Cocaine? Isn't that seriously illegal? You told me your dad was in import export.'

'He is,' Junior said. 'Imports drugs, exports cash.'

'Hell,' James grinned. 'No wonder he's loaded.'

Del went into his backpack. He pulled out a small polythene bag filled with white powder.

'Cocaine,' he explained.

James grinned as he took the packet and inspected it.

'Don't let everyone see it, you moron,' Del gasped, knocking James' hand out of the air.

'Sorry,' James said. 'So how much is this?'

'One gram in every bag. They give me ten grams at a time, then they ring me on my mobile and tell me where and when to deliver it.'

'How much do you make?'

'Fifteen per cent,' Del said. 'This is sixty a gram, so I get nine quid. If I work Friday and Saturday evenings, I can easily make a hundred quid. Sometimes though, like at

Christmas, you get people loading up for office parties and stuff. I had this one guy who lived two streets away from me. He was buying ten grams at a time. Ninety quid for a ten-minute bike ride. It was beautiful.'

'Do you blow all the money?'

Del shook his head. 'I used to, but you end up wasting it all on junk. Now I only spend twenty pounds a week. I stick the rest in my savings account and when I'm eighteen, I'm gonna buy a ticket and go off backpacking.'

James looked at Junior. 'So how come you're always broke?'

Del burst out laughing. 'This baby's not allowed to go anywhere near drugs.'

Junior explained miserably. 'My dad's paranoid that he'll get arrested. If I get caught with drugs, it gives the police an excuse to question Dad and search our house.'

'That's a shame,' James said.

'Tell me about it,' Junior said bitterly. 'My dad's a millionaire and half my mates are making a packet selling coke. What have I got? Holes in my jeans and supermarket-brand football boots.'

'Can't you do it on the sly?' James asked.

'Won't happen,' Junior said. 'The word is out. Anyone who gets me or Ringo involved in the drug business will be in serious trouble if my dad cops them.'

'So you're stuffed,' James laughed. 'You reckon there's any chance I can get in on this delivery lark?'

Del shrugged. 'I'll go upstairs and have a word with Kelvin if you like. I don't know if he needs anyone right now, but I can try and get him to set you up with a few bags of coke and your own phone.'

'I've already got a mobile,' James said.

Del shook his head. 'You have to use the phone they give you, so the police can't trace it.'

'But there's definitely a chance?'

'I haven't got a clue,' Del said. 'All I can do is put a word in.'

'Thanks,' James said.

Del stood up. 'Anyway, I've got a nine o'clock delivery, so I better dive home and pick up my bike. I'll see you two hard-up losers at school on Monday.'

James smiled. 'Yeah, see you.'

'I'll be thinking about you sweating away on your bike in a couple of hours,' Junior said. 'When I've got my hand up some girl's shirt.'

'In your dreams, Junior,' Del shouted as he walked towards the exit.

James shook his head, grinning in false disbelief. 'I can't believe your dad is a drug dealer.'

'Who cares?' Junior said. 'Do you want to try and get off with someone?'

They both glanced around.

'Look at that bird sitting by the Coke machine,' Junior gasped. 'I've not seen her here before.'

James turned around. He'd guessed it was Nicole before he even saw her.

'She's reserved for me,' he said. 'That's my stepsister.'

'You can't get off with your sister, you pervert.'

'*Step*sister,' James said. 'We're not blood relatives. Why don't you go for the one sitting next to her? She looks like a right dog.'

'That's my twin, you cheeky git,' Junior said. 'And you better not call April a dog again, unless you want a slap.'

April had her hair done differently from the surveillance photos. James hadn't recognised her.

'I tell you who else is good looking,' Junior said. 'Pity she's already with someone.'

'Who?' James asked.

'At the table behind our sisters. That Chinese-looking girl, with long black hair. She's well tasty.'

James peered over. All he could see was the back of the girl's head. Then she turned and he saw her in profile.

'That's my other stepsister,' James gasped. 'That's Kerry. Who's that she's with?'

'Dinesh Singh. He lives up my road. His dad runs a firm that makes those microwave meals for supermarkets. So, you want to go over?' Junior asked. 'I'll go for Nicole and you can have a run at April. She's not too picky, to be honest with you, so even you might stand a chance.'

'Jesus,' James said, feeling like his head was going to burst with jealousy. 'Dinesh just put his arm around her.'

'What's the problem? Do you fancy all your sisters, or something?'

'It's just, Kerry's really young.'

'How old is she?' Junior asked.

'Twelve.'

Junior burst out laughing. 'We're twelve.'

'Yeah,' James said. 'But we're in Year Eight, she's only a Year Seven.'

'If you ask me,' Junior said, 'it's none of your business

what your stepsister is up to. But if it makes you feel better, Dinesh is a weed. Just go over there and slap him one.'

'I've a good mind to,' James said.

This was a total lie. Kerry would break him into fifty million pieces if he even thought about it.

'Anyway,' Junior said, 'I'm not sitting here all night. Are you gonna ask April out or not?'

'You go,' James shrugged. 'I'm not in the mood.'

April Moore was OK-looking and being friendly with her would be good for the mission, but James couldn't get Kerry out of his head.

Junior pulled up a chair next to Nicole and started chatting her up. James sat by himself and kept glancing over to see what Kerry was up to with Dinesh. He realised he couldn't sit on his own all night being jealous of Dinesh and decided to go across to April, but company arrived before he got a chance.

It was Kelvin and Marcus, the two coaches he'd seen at boxing club. They were both over six feet tall and solid muscle. They sat either side of James, squashing him even though there was plenty of room.

'I'm Kelvin,' the black one said. He pulled a mobile phone out of his pocket and stuck it on the table. 'Del tells me you're interested in doing deliveries.'

James nodded. 'I could do with the cash.'

'Del said you're a solid kid,' Kelvin continued. 'What you gonna say if the cops pick you up holding drugs?'

'Nothing, of course.'

Kelvin nodded. 'That's right. You don't know us, you ain't never seen us. Tell 'em you found the drugs in a bush and stick to that story no matter how they try to mess with you. You know what happens if you grass us up?'

'I get beaten up?'

'Cut up, more likely,' Kelvin said. 'And that's just for starters. They'll send people round your house and start on your family. Smash the furniture, batter your mum and dad. Del said you had two sisters, they won't look so pretty after we finish with them. So you better understand, James, even if there's some massive cop threatening to lock you up and throw away the key, you better keep your trap shut.'

'Don't worry,' James said. 'I'm no grass.'

'You got a good bike?'

'It's pretty crap actually.'

'Good,' Kelvin said. 'You don't want nothing fancy or you'll get mugged. How cool are your parents about you being out late?'

'It's OK until about half-ten.'

'Marcus, set the kid up with three bags. I think we'll give him a trial run.'

Marcus got three bags of cocaine out of his tracksuit.

'I want you on call school nights,' Kelvin said. 'Monday through Thursday. That means you keep your phone switched on and you're always ready to go. We don't want to hear that you're grounded, or you're busy doing something. Whenever they call, you jump to it.'

'Can't I do weekends?' James asked. 'Del reckons that's when you make the real money.'

'Everyone starts at the bottom with weekday deliveries and no regular customers. The powers that be will see how you do. If you're reliable and you deliver fast, you get moved on to better paid work. Questions?'

'I've only got three bags of coke, how do I get more?' James asked.

'There's people at your school. We'll arrange for you to meet up with them when you need to.'

'What if someone tries to rob me or something?' James asked.

'If you lose the stuff or get mugged, that's your problem and you owe us for what you lost. If the customer tries any funny business, don't sweat it. Give the customer whatever they want and some of our muscle will show them the error of their ways.'

Kelvin and his silent pal got up from the table.

'One last thing,' Kelvin said. 'If you're out late, you'll get hassled sooner or later. Never carry more coke than you need to. A lot of kids carry knives, but if you ask me, you're safer throwing the stuff on the ground and legging it.'

11. KITCHEN

James ended up walking home from the youth club with Nicole. He didn't feel too good: a mix of nerves about his delivery job and seeing Kerry with Dinesh. They ended up in the kitchen, drinking glasses of milk. Zara and Ewart were already in bed.

'Did Kerry say anything to you about this Indian guy?' James asked.

Nicole grinned. 'Jealous, are we, James?'

'No. It's just we're good friends and I like to look out for her.'

'Can you smell something?' Nicole asked.

'No,' James said, looking at the bottom of his trainers.

'I can,' Nicole sniffed. 'You know what it is?'

'What?'

'Bullshit.'

'Very funny, Nicole.'

'James, you *totally* fancy Kerry,' Nicole said. 'Why don't you just admit it and ask her out?'

'Give us a break, we're just friends. How did you get on with Junior?'

'He's not bad-looking,' Nicole said. 'But the kid could seriously use some mouthwash.'

James laughed.

'So,' Nicole said, 'if you're not as keen on Kerry as everyone says, what do you think of me?'

James looked uneasy. 'You're a nice person, Nicole.'

'That wasn't what I asked.'

'Well . . .' James squirmed. 'Actually, yeah . . . You've got a nice body and that.'

'You're not so bad yourself,' Nicole said, leaning against the kitchen cabinet. 'Come over here.'

'Why?' James asked.

'Kiss us.'

James laughed. He leaned in and pecked Nicole on the cheek.

'Is that all you've got?' Nicole asked.

The second time James moved in, Nicole wrapped her arms around his back and they started snogging.

The door clicked open and they burst apart. James crashed into the kitchen table as Kerry stepped into the room.

'Hello, hello,' Kerry grinned. 'Did I break something up?'

'No,' James gasped. 'It's nothing. We're just drinking milk before we go up to bed. You want some?'

'Cheers,' Kerry said.

James got a glass off the draining board and poured out some milk.

'Anyway,' he said, stretching into a yawn. 'It's gone eleven. I might as well go up to bed.'

Kerry called him back.

'What?' he asked.

'You better wash the lipstick off your face,' she said. 'Unless you want it all over your pillowcase.'

James walked up the stairs in a confused state. He fancied Nicole, but he didn't like Kerry knowing about it.

Kyle was in the top bunk when James got to their room.

'Some party animal you are,' James said. 'Home before eleven.'

'Put the light on if you want,' Kyle said, sitting up in bed. 'I'm not tired. It was a decent party, but one of the neighbours complained and the cops came and broke it up. How was boxing?'

James explained about everything that had happened. He tried to make it sound matter of fact, but the Kerry and Dinesh thing was getting to him and he blurted out something he'd never admitted to anyone.

'Kerry kind of . . . Sometimes I lie awake at night thinking about her. She's really, I mean . . . She's not stunning . . . Not the sexiest girl in the world or anything, but there's something about her that goes through me like a big warm whoosh.'

'You've *got* to ask her out,' Kyle said.

'But I want her to carry on being my mate. What if we end up rowing and hating each other?'

'You've got to risk it,' Kyle said.

'What if she doesn't even want to go out with me?'

'Look,' Kyle said firmly. 'You just got off with Nicole, so you should be excited about that; but all you're talking about is Kerry, Kerry, Kerry.'

'What do I say to her?'

'Try the truth,' Kyle said. 'Tell Kerry how much you like her and then it's up to her.'

'Maybe you're right,' James said. 'I'll say something to her first chance I get. I mean, you never know, it might even work out between us.'

'That's right,' Kyle said.

James clicked out the light and climbed under his duvet.

'Kyle, what I don't get is: how come I'm taking all this advice off you when I've never seen you with a girl?'

'I've never had a girlfriend,' Kyle said.

James was surprised by the honesty. He'd expected Kyle to be defensive.

'Seriously?' James asked.

'Yep,' Kyle said.

'But there's loads of girls at campus. I'm sure I could fix you up with one.'

'I don't want a girlfriend,' Kyle said.

'What?' James asked. 'Did a girl hurt you really badly or something? Is it like one of those romantic films my mum used to watch?'

'No, James. I don't like girls.'

'What, you mean you only like old birds? Like, in their twenties or something?'

Kyle laughed. 'No. I like boys.'

James shot up off his mattress. 'Piss off you do.'

'James, I'm gay.'

'No bloody way,' James said. 'This is another Kyle wind-up.'

'I'd appreciate it if you don't go shouting it off to the whole world, but you were honest to me about Kerry, so there you go. It's the truth, whether you want to believe it or not.'

'Wow,' James said. 'Do you swear that you're gay, on your life?'

'Yes,' Kyle said.

'Wow,' James said.

He felt like his head was going to explode. He already had too much going on in there, with Kerry and Nicole and the drug dealing.

'Who else knows?'

'I've told a few people,' Kyle said.

'I can't believe it,' James gasped. 'You don't seem anything like a poof.'

'Actually, I'd prefer it if you didn't call me that.'

'Oh, right . . . Sorry.'

*

James lay awake the whole night, listening to the aeroplanes rumbling over the house. He got up with the sun, had a shower, got a bowl of Shreddies and made himself tea. When the newspaper dropped through the letterbox, he read the sports page at the kitchen table, but it was like the words were going through his eyes and bouncing straight off his brain. All he could think about was Kerry with Dinesh and Kyle being gay.

Kerry and Nicole came downstairs. James didn't like that they were together; it made his paranoid side imagine that the two of them were working together and scheming against him.

'I'm making bacon sarnies,' Nicole said. 'You want one, James?'

'Mmm,' James said. 'Cheers.'

Kerry sat on the opposite side of the table and poured orange juice. Kyle had asked him not to tell people he was gay, but James was practically bursting. He had to tell someone. It felt too big to keep locked up.

'I spoke to Kyle last night,' James said.

Kerry looked up from the colour supplement. 'And?'

'He told me something. It's totally mind-blowing, but you can't spread it around.'

'Whatever,' Kerry said. 'Spill the beans.'

'Kyle told me he's gay.'

Kerry smiled a bit. 'Well duh. Of course Kyle's gay.'

Nicole looked away from the spattering bacon. 'It took you *this* long to work out Kyle's gay,' she said.

'He said he'd only ever told a couple of people.'

Kerry smiled. 'You must at least have suspected.'

'No. Why would anyone suspect that Kyle's gay?'

'Well, dingus,' Kerry said. 'He's always clean and neatly dressed. Unlike most of you guys, his room isn't covered in disgusting pictures of half-naked women and nobody has ever seen him within five kilometres of a girl. I mean, short of walking around with a plaque on his forehead saying *Gay Boy*, how obvious do you want it to be?'

'But I share a room with him,' James gasped. 'He sees me naked.'

'So what?' Kerry said. 'I've seen you naked.'

'Well, he's gay.'

'You think he fancies you?' Kerry giggled. 'I wouldn't flatter yourself.'

Nicole turned away from the frying pan with a big smile on her face. 'Come to think of it, I've seen him eyeing you up, James.'

'Shut up,' James said. 'It's not funny. It's disgusting.'

'You think being gay is disgusting?' Kerry tutted. 'I thought Kyle was your friend.'

'He is,' James said. 'But . . . I'm not comfortable with the whole gay thing.'

'Do us some bread, Kerry,' Nicole said. 'Bacon doesn't take long.'

Kerry got the loaf off the cabinet and started buttering.

'You know, James,' she said, 'it must have been hard for Kyle to admit something like that to you. Especially when you're always calling people faggots and queers.'

Nicole moved the pan off the heat and helped Kerry make up the sandwiches.

'I heard that one person in ten is gay,' Nicole said. 'So it's not that unusual. If you think about it, every football team probably has one gay player on it.'

Kerry giggled. 'I wonder who the gay one at Arsenal is? Actually, the big clubs have loads of players and reserve teams. There's probably at least four or five.'

James stood up from the table and boiled over. 'That's not funny,' he shouted. 'There's no such thing as a gay Arsenal player.'

Kerry slammed James' plate on the table in front of him. 'Sit down and eat that,' she said angrily. 'Kyle's your friend, so you better be supportive. If you say anything that upsets him, I'll show you the meaning of uncomfortable.'

12. SUBURBAN

It was Wednesday evening, and James was on his third night making deliveries. His phone went off a couple of times a night; always the same calm female voice on the other end. James had no idea who or where she was, only that she seemed motherly, was happy to give directions and always signed off with the same words: *You be careful out there, young man.*

The deliveries were never more than a few kilometres' ride. The job would be nasty in the winter, but on sunny early autumn evenings it was no hardship. James had imagined his customers would be scraggy-haired women in night clothes holding screaming babies, or wild-eyed men with beards and motorbikes, but it was nothing like that.

*

James was breathless by the time he found the housing estate. The houses were brand new. There was a developer's signpost over the entrance: *LAST FEW HOMES REMAINING – PRICES FROM £245,000*. The houses were neat, with newly planted trees and recent-plate Fords and

Toyotas parked on the driveways. There was no traffic and little kids played outside on skateboards and micro-scooters.

As James freewheeled down a gentle slope, he noticed the streets were named after musical instruments. *Trumpet Close, Cornet Avenue, Bassoon Road.*

He turned into Trombone Villas, the most exclusive street in the development. The grey tarmac became red and the cars on the driveways changed to Range Rovers and Mercedes. He was looking for Stonehaus, and like millions of delivery people before him, James had learned to hate house names. With numbers, you knew that 56 was after 48 and 21 was on the other side of the road. Stonehaus could be anywhere. He found it after a search, the signpost hidden behind a BMW X5 and a Grand Voyager. He wheeled up the driveway and pressed the bell, which sounded off a tinny version of *When The Saints Go Marching In.*

A boy ran down the hallway and opened the door. He was eight or nine, wearing the long grey socks and fancy uniform of a fee-paying school. At this time of day, the kid was in a state, with his bare chest showing under his unbuttoned grey shirt.

'Daddy,' the kid shouted.

A man holding a whisky tumbler hurried down the stairs, while the kid ran back to the TV.

'HEYYYYY there,' the man said, trying to sound cooler than the fat balding man he really was. 'Four grams, wasn't it?'

James nodded. 'Two hundred and forty quid.' He went into his backpack and got the four bags of cocaine. The man peeled five fifties off a roll of notes.

'I don't have change,' James said.

Del had taught James to pretend never to have change. If the customer kicked up a fuss, you miraculously remembered that you had money from a previous delivery in your backpack; but you were hoping the average middle-class coke snorter didn't want to keep a drug dealer hanging about on his doorstep and simply said:

'No worries, son, keep the change for yourself.'

James smiled and tucked the money in his pocket. 'Thanks, mate,' he said. 'Enjoy yourself.'

The man closed the door. James couldn't help smiling. He'd just earned thirty-six pounds commission, plus a ten-pound tip, for a half-hour bike ride.

*

It was gone nine when James got home. Everyone was waiting for him in the living room. Two weeks into the mission, Ewart and Zara wanted a conference to see what everyone was doing and to work out the best way forward.

'Sorry I kept you waiting,' James said. 'But I've got to deliver when I get a call.'

Zara had rearranged the sofas in the living room and brought in kitchen chairs, so everyone could sit facing each other. James squeezed on to a sofa between Kyle and Nicole.

'OK,' Ewart said. 'I want each of you to say what you think you've achieved so far. Keep it short, you've all got to get up for school tomorrow.'

'Nicole,' Zara said, 'why don't you start?'

Nicole cleared her throat. 'You pretty much know. I've been getting on OK with April. She knows what her dad does for a living, but keeps out of it. I've been to Keith

Moore's house a few times doing homework and stuff and I've met him; just exchanging hellos and that.'

'That's a good start,' Ewart nodded. 'Do you think you can carry on getting regular access to the house?'

'Sure,' Nicole said. 'April likes having the girls round and showing off her giant bedroom. She likes to think of herself as the leader of our group. I'm going to a sleepover there this Saturday.'

'Have you had much of a chance to nose around the house?' Zara asked.

'I thought I'd play it safe to start with,' Nicole said. 'You've got all the notes and stuff I copied from the cork board in the kitchen.'

'Do you think you could place mini-cameras and listening devices around the house?'

'Easily,' Nicole nodded. 'The house is big, so if anyone asks what I'm doing, I can pretend I got lost and wandered into the wrong room.'

'Excellent,' Ewart said. 'Could you get a nose inside Keith's office?'

'I doubt it, he's usually in there. The one time he was out, I tried and the door was locked. I suppose I could take my lock gun.'

'No way,' Ewart said. 'If someone sees you with a lock gun, it will put you in serious danger and blow this whole operation.'

'The next best target would be Keith's bedroom,' Zara said. 'He's the kind of guy who gets phone calls at all hours, so you can be sure he takes important calls in bed. Have a good snoop and put in a listening device.'

'Why can't you tap the phones from out in the street?' James asked.

'They've been tapped for years and Keith knows it,' Ewart said. 'A serious villain like Keith Moore uses mobiles or face-to-face meetings. He'll pick up a pay-as-you-go mobile and use it for a day or two, then switch to another one before we know he's got it. He also speaks using code words, and uses something to disguise the sound of his voice, so you could never go into court and prove it was him saying what he said. Our only chance of getting useful information is to have a microphone in the actual room where Keith is talking.'

'So, Nicole,' Zara said. 'That's your target. Get a microphone in Keith's bedroom and maybe a few others around the house. The risks are low, because nobody is going to suspect that a twelve-year-old girl is planting a microphone, but you should still be careful.'

'OK,' Ewart said. 'Good work, Nicole, keep it up. Do you want to go next, James?'

James nodded. 'Me and Junior are top mates, bunking off and going to boxing and stuff.'

'How much do you think Junior knows about his dad's business?'

'He comes out with stuff,' James said. 'He's curious about what his dad does. If any one of Keith's kids knows anything worth knowing, I'd bet on Junior.'

'And the deliveries,' Zara said. 'How are they going?'

'Good,' James said. 'It's mostly nice houses and offices I'm going to. I was worried at first, but it's like having a newspaper round, only with decent wages.'

Ewart spoke. 'The mission briefing mentioned that kids

around here aren't just delivering small amounts of drugs to individuals, but are getting deeper into the organisation and delivering in bulk to dealers from other parts of the country. Have you seen any sign of that?'

James shrugged. 'Some kids are making serious money, so it wouldn't surprise me.'

'Your number one job is to find out how they're making that money,' Zara said. 'Make friends, ask questions and keep pestering until you get an answer. Remember to keep safe when you're out on deliveries. If you think a situation is dangerous, pull out and we'll clean up the mess afterwards. We'd rather abandon the whole mission than risk one of you guys getting hurt.'

'Kyle,' Ewart said. 'Your turn.'

'Ringo's a bust if you ask me,' Kyle said. 'He's a straight-up guy, though he smokes a fair bit of cannabis. I'm getting in with his crowd. There are drug dealers at their parties and plenty of kids using all kinds of drugs. I might get some information from one of them, but I'm not hopeful.'

Ewart and Zara looked at each other.

'Just keep trying, Kyle,' Zara said. 'That's all you can do until we think of something else.'

'So,' Ewart said. 'Last but not least, Kerry.'

'Me and Erin can't stand each other,' Kerry said. 'She's weird and immature and her friends sit in a group and don't talk to anyone else.'

'What did you do to try and get in with them?' Ewart asked.

'We're just so different,' Kerry explained. 'I don't think we'll ever get on.'

'The thing is, Kerry,' Ewart said, 'you've been trained to work out what type of person your target is and then act in a way that makes them your friend. If Erin mucks about and upsets teachers, then that's what you should do, even if you think it's silly and immature. If Erin swears and bunks off, you should do that too. I know you can't guarantee forming a friendship with a target, but I don't ever expect to hear a cherub say they're too different from someone to get along.'

Kerry looked angry. 'You'd need a world-class psychiatrist to work out Erin. She's part of a weird little clique and they shut everyone else out.'

Zara spoke. 'If you haven't hit it off with Erin by now, I doubt it's ever going to happen. I can't see much reason for you to stay on this mission. We can send you back to campus and say you've moved back to live with your real parents, or something.'

Kerry looked close to crying. 'I don't want to be sent back. I'm trying to get involved with someone else, like it says in the briefing.'

'I can't see much point,' Ewart said. 'If you were a boy, you might be recruited as a courier, but that's all done through the boxing club, which is boys only.'

Zara nodded, agreeing with her husband. 'I'm sorry this mission didn't work out, Kerry, but don't be disappointed. Think of it as a learning experience.'

'Let me stay,' Kerry begged. 'There's a boy in my class called Dinesh. I'm getting friendly with him and I think he knows something.'

James put his wrist up to his lips and made a loud smooching noise.

'Grow up, James,' Zara said wearily. 'Kerry, what is it you think Dinesh might know?'

'His dad runs a company that makes microwave meals for supermarkets. When I was talking to him about Erin, he mentioned that his father has dealings with Keith Moore.'

Zara didn't look too impressed. 'Keith is a wealthy man, Kerry. He has business dealings with lots of people.'

'But it's the way Dinesh said it,' Kerry explained. 'It's like Dinesh had a bad taste in his mouth. It might be nothing, but I'd like a chance to dig deeper.'

Ewart and Zara looked at each other.

'*Please* don't send me back to campus,' Kerry grovelled. 'Just give me a few more days.'

'You're fond of this boy Dinesh, aren't you?' Zara said. 'Is that the real reason you're so keen to stay?'

'I'm a professional,' Kerry stormed. 'It's not because I've fallen for some boy. I've got a hunch and I'm asking you guys to show faith in me.'

'OK, Kerry,' Zara said gently. 'There's no need to get upset. Ewart and I will postpone our decision on sending you back to campus until next week. How does that sound?'

Kerry nodded. 'Thank you.'

'Anything else, before we all go off to bed?' Ewart asked.

'Yeah,' James said. 'It's Lauren's birthday this weekend, is it still OK if she visits?'

'No problem,' Zara said. 'If she meets up with any of the local kids, you'll have to tell them she's your cousin. It'll seem weird if you suddenly have a sister popping out of nowhere.'

'If that's everything,' Ewart said, 'let's all get some shut-eye.'

With only one bathroom, there was a scrum over the toothbrushes. Kerry stayed on the couch sulking and James thought he'd give the others a few minutes to fight it out.

'You're really good at this,' Kerry said, looking at James.

'What?' he asked.

'Missions. You go into a room and everyone likes you. Good old James, even the baby likes you. I study hard and I get some of the best marks on campus, but I'm rubbish out on missions where it really counts.'

'Come on, Kerry,' James said. 'You're being way too hard on yourself. This is your first important mission. Nobody expects you to be brilliant.'

'And it'll be my last big mission, after this disaster,' Kerry said. 'I'll probably spend the rest of my CHERUB career doing mundane security tests and recruitment work.'

James moved across to the other couch, next to Kerry. 'I've been meaning to talk to you,' he said.

'Talk about what?'

'We haven't been getting on that well since this mission started,' James said. 'But you still like me, don't you?'

'Of course I like you, James,' Kerry said, breaking into a smile. 'You're one of my best friends.'

James decided to be bold and put his arm around Kerry's back. She smiled and rested her head against his shoulder.

'You've done all you can on this mission,' he said. 'And there's no way they're not gonna give you another shot at a big mission. With your fighting skills and the five billion languages you speak, who'll be able to turn you down?'

Kerry smiled. 'For someone who acts like a moron half the time, you can be a really nice guy sometimes.'

'Thanks,' James grinned.

He thought about starting the speech he had prepared in his head, telling Kerry how kissing Nicole was a one-off and how he liked her a hundred times more than any other girl and wanted to be her boyfriend. But Kerry still looked upset. It wasn't the right moment.

13. VISIT

One of the CHERUB staff dropped Lauren off on Saturday morning. James was barely out of bed when he heard the doorbell.

'Happy birthday,' he said, giving his sister a hug. 'You made double figures, the big one zero.'

Lauren smiled. 'I missed you, James . . . for some strange reason.'

They walked inside. Everyone was wandering between the kitchen and living-room, munching on triangles of toast. Joshua was shuffling down the hallway on his bum. Lauren had never seen him before.

'OOOH,' she said. 'Aren't you cute? What's your name?'

Joshua gave Lauren an odd look, as if to say, *Oh god, not another kid*, and started bawling for Zara.

'Hey, Ewart,' James shouted, 'there goes your theory that Joshua likes anyone with blond hair.'

Lauren wandered into the living-room, threw off her bomber jacket and sat on the couch. Kerry and Kyle wished her happy birthday.

'So,' Lauren asked, 'where's all my prezzies?'

'Actually,' James said, 'I haven't got you one yet.'

'Typical,' Lauren huffed.

'Now I'm a bona-fide drug delivery boy, I thought you might like to spend my ill-gotten gains.' James burrowed down his jeans, pulled out a fistful of scrunched-up bank notes and dumped them in Lauren's lap.

Lauren grinned. 'How much is this?' She straightened out the notes and started counting. 'Twenty, forty, sixty, eighty, a hundred, and ten, fifteen. Wow . . . How long did it take you to make a hundred and fifteen pounds?'

'Four nights,' James said. 'The only thing is, if you want me to take you shopping you'll have to pay my bus fare. I've only got sixty pence left.'

'Is there a Gap near here?' Lauren asked eagerly. 'I want some new jeans. And a Claire's Accessories? If there is, I can get those cool black hair scrunchies like Bethany's got.'

'Can't you just use an elastic band?' James asked.

Lauren ignored her brother and glanced at her watch. 'What time do the shops open?'

'Calm down, you idiot,' James said. 'The money's still gonna be there in a couple of hours. Why don't you go in the kitchen, get some toast and say hello to Zara and the others.'

'Whatever,' Lauren said. 'But let's go early. The shops get really busy on a Saturday.'

*

Zara dropped the kids at the Reeve Centre. James hoped none of the security guards remembered him.

'Why are you wearing those sunglasses?' Lauren asked.

James shrugged. 'Am I? I forgot to take them off.'

'You look a right twit,' Kerry said.

'It doesn't have anything to do with the five Playstation games you've got stuffed under your bed, does it?' Kyle asked.

'What were you doing spying under my bed?' James asked indignantly.

'Remember Monday, before school?' Kyle asked.

'No.'

Kyle mocked James' voice. '*I can't find my PE shirt, Kyle. Will you help us look for it?*'

'Oh yeah,' James said, 'that.'

'So let me guess,' Kyle said. 'You don't want to go anywhere too near Gameworld either.'

'But if he stole them as part of a mission, he's allowed, isn't he?' Lauren asked.

'He's supposed to give the proceeds of any crime to charity,' Kerry explained.

'Well he should give them to charity then,' Lauren said. 'You're not on this mission to make a profit, James.'

'Does that include the birthday money in your pocket?' James asked.

'Oh,' Lauren gasped.

'Yeah,' James giggled. 'That shut you up, didn't it?'

Normally, going around the girly shops would have driven James mad, but being the big brother treating his sister felt good. Lauren, who wouldn't be seen dead in a skirt, got two hooded sweatshirts in Gap, a pair of faded jeans and some silver stud earrings. She treated everyone to lunch in the food court and even got James a pair of novelty socks as a thank you. He was never going to wear the ghastly things, but it was a nice moment when she gave them to him.

After lunch, Kerry went off to meet Dinesh. She told James to give Zara a message that she wouldn't be back until after dinner. Kerry being with Dinesh pissed James off, but he didn't want to spoil Lauren's birthday, so he tried not to think about it.

When they got home, Zara had ordered a fancy cake. The icing was camouflage green and there was a miniature assault course built out of marzipan, with a climbing tower, a water jump and toy soldiers running around. The iced message around the edge said, *Happy Birthday, Lauren & Good Luck in Training.*

Joshua thought the cake was a toy and kept lunging out of Ewart's lap towards it. After Lauren had blown out her candles, everyone sat around the table, cracking up at the huge mess Joshua made with his tiny piece of cake.

*

Lauren was tired out by half-nine and James decided to go up to bed with her. She started off in a sleeping bag on the floor, but she decided it was uncomfortable and climbed in with James. She'd always got into his bed when they were little, but they'd grown since those days.

'This is ridiculous,' James said, wriggling up to the wall so she had more room.

'I'm still scared about training,' Lauren said quietly. 'I don't even see the point of it.'

'You'll understand after you've done it,' James said. 'Training's horrible, so when something tough happens on a mission, instead of being scared, you remember that you've been through worse and you can handle it.'

'Sometimes,' Lauren said, 'just thinking about it makes me feel like puking.'

'The fear is worse before training starts,' James said. 'Once you're there, you're too worn out to think.'

There was a knock on the door.

'Yeah,' James shouted. 'We're awake.'

Zara pushed the door open and stuck her head in.

'James, when Kerry left you earlier, did she say if she was going anywhere after she left Dinesh's?'

'No,' James said.

'I rang their house,' Zara said. 'Dinesh said Kerry left before eight. She ought to be home by now.'

'Did you try her mobile?' James asked.

'That's the first thing I did. I even sent a text.'

'Maybe we should go out looking,' Lauren said.

'I wouldn't panic yet,' Zara said. 'She'll probably turn up. You two get some sleep and try not to worry.'

*

A mobile woke James up. He'd forgotten Lauren was asleep next to him and bumped into her as he sat up.

'That's your tasteless ring tone,' he said, giving her a kick. 'I bet it's that idiot Bethany.'

Lauren got out of bed, flicked on the light and found her phone inside her jacket. James looked at his clock. It was gone midnight.

'Hello?' Lauren answered. 'Kerry, *wow*. Everyone's looking for you . . . Hang on, yeah, James is here.'

James snatched the Nokia off Lauren.

'Kerry?'

'Oh, thank god,' Kerry said. 'Why did you switch your phone off?'

'It's probably gone flat,' James said.

'I couldn't get an answer from Kyle, or Nicole either. I tried Lauren as a last resort.'

'Where the hell are you?' James asked. 'Zara's going frantic. She's sitting downstairs waiting for you to get in.'

'I'm outside Thunderfoods. I need a huge favour.'

'What's Thunderfoods?' James asked.

'Dinesh's dad's company,' Kerry explained. 'I think I'm on to something, but I need you and one of the others to ride out here and give me a hand breaking in.'

'Why don't you explain everything to Ewart or Zara?' James said. 'They'll know what to do.'

'Because if I'm wrong, I'll look like an idiot and they'll boot me back to campus.'

James couldn't refuse. After all, he spent half his life telling Kerry to be more relaxed about rules.

'OK,' he said. 'What is it you want?'

'I'd like Nicole or Kyle to come as well,' Kerry said.

'Nicole's at her sleepover. Kyle's out partying.'

'But I'm here,' Lauren said, sounding excited.

James looked at his sister. 'No way, you're not trained.'

'It's better if there's three of us to search,' Kerry said. 'But two is OK. I need you to bring some stuff: torches, your lock gun, your digital camera and some beer.'

'Where the hell can I get beer at this time of night? Even if there *was* somewhere, I'm too young to buy it.'

'There's a few cans in the bottom of our fridge,' Kerry said. 'Sneak one out.'

'What do you need beer for, anyway?' James asked.

'James,' Kerry snapped, 'I don't have time for two hundred questions. Get the stuff, get on a bike and ride your butt out here.'

James took down directions and ended the call.

'What's happening?' Lauren asked.

'God knows why,' James said, 'but Kerry wants to break into some food factory. She doesn't want Ewart or Zara to know what she's doing in case she's wrong about whatever it is she thinks is going on.'

He stepped into some tracksuit bottoms and trainers.

'I'll go get the beer for you,' Lauren said.

'Thanks.'

Lauren crept down to the kitchen, while James churned through the mess under his bed and got his lock gun and camera. He grabbed Kyle's camera in case they needed two and took Lauren's phone because his was flat.

Lauren came back with the cold beer.

'Thanks,' James said. 'It's gonna be well hard, sneaking my bike out of the garage without Ewart or Zara noticing.'

Lauren started putting on clothes.

'What do you think you're doing?' James asked. 'You're not coming. No way.'

'Kerry asked for a third person.'

'You're not trained.'

'I'll ride along,' Lauren said. 'If Kerry doesn't want me, I'll look after the bikes.'

James knew how stubborn Lauren could be. He didn't have the time or energy to argue.

'Fine,' he said. 'But don't think I'm taking the rap for you if we get in trouble.'

'I'm ten years old,' Lauren said proudly. 'I can make my own decisions.'

14. CURRY

There wasn't much traffic, but what there was drove dangerously fast. It took twenty minutes to ride across to the industrial park. Thunderfoods had a full car park and lights on everywhere. The factory worked 24/7, sending out truckloads of chilled pastas and curries to supermarkets.

Kerry led them into an alleyway between two warehouses.

'Are you sure you want to do this, Lauren?' she asked. 'We could get in serious trouble if we're caught.'

'If you want me to help, I'm up for it,' Lauren said.

'So what's this about?' James asked.

'I got more information from Dinesh,' Kerry explained. 'It's amazing what you can wheedle out of a boy if he thinks you're up for a snog.'

'Did you snog him?' Lauren asked.

Kerry laughed. 'No chance.'

James was relieved. It was worth being dragged out of bed at midnight just to hear that.

'Anyway,' Kerry said, 'Dinesh doesn't get on with his dad. He reckons Mr Singh is a hypocrite when he tells him to behave and do his homework, when he's a crook himself. So I go: *How is your dad a crook?* And Dinesh starts explaining how his dad nearly went bankrupt and KMG bailed him out. I said I didn't believe him. Dinesh tells me there's a storage building at the back of Thunderfoods' production plant. He says he's been inside and seen bags of cocaine. Security seems pretty lax: I've already sneaked right up to the warehouse door, but I can't get inside without my lock gun.'

'What if there's a security system?' James asked.

'There is,' Kerry said smugly. 'You need a swipe card.'

She pulled a plastic card out of her shorts. 'I nicked this one off Mr Singh.'

'And what about the beer?' Lauren asked.

'We need a cover story,' Kerry explained. 'If we get caught, we act like kids who got drunk and decided to cause some mischief.'

Kerry took the beer off Lauren. She pulled the tab and swallowed a few mouthfuls, then dribbled some down her T-shirt.

'It's more believable if we've got the smell of drink on our clothes and breath.'

James took the can off Kerry and did the same. Lauren hated the taste and spat hers in the gravel. 'I don't want to get beer on my new top,' she said.

'Give us,' James said.

He snatched the can off Lauren, poured most of it on the floor and splashed the dregs over her hair.

'OK,' Kerry said. 'Don't forget to act drunk.'

They staggered through the Thunderfoods car park,

keeping behind the cars. Then it was over a stretch of lawn to the side door of the warehouse. James handed Kerry his lock gun.

'You're quicker than me,' he said.

Kerry fiddled with the lock, while James and Lauren sat in the grass yawning. It was an eight-lever deadlock, one of the trickiest kinds to pick.

'You want me to try?' James asked.

Kerry sounded edgy. 'You won't do it. It needs a different attachment.'

She unscrewed the back of James' lock gun. There were nine different-shaped picks inside and it was tough to tell them apart in the dark.

'This one or bust,' Kerry said, clicking a different pick on to the gun.

She rattled about for another half minute.

'Finally,' she sighed, pushing the door open.

The alarm pipped until she swiped the security card. They couldn't turn the light on in case someone saw it through the windows. It felt spooky, shining their torch beams around the cavernous black space. The racks of metal shelving were filled with sacks and tins of ingredients for the factory next door.

'Maybe that's how they get the cocaine into the country,' James whispered. 'Disguised as curry powder or something.'

'No,' Kerry said. 'Dinesh described clear bags filled with white powder. And he said KMG people came and did something with it upstairs.'

'Kerry,' James said, 'I hate to say this, but maybe your

little boyfriend is just trying to impress you. This building doesn't even have an upstairs.'

'We should split up,' Kerry said, deliberately ignoring James. 'There's a lot of shelving to cover.'

They each took a row of shelves and started working along, searching for the white powder. The shelves went up ten metres. You'd need a forklift to access the higher bays.

Lauren whispered to Kerry between the rows of shelves, 'Come look at this.'

Kerry dashed over. Lauren's torch shone on a few clear polythene sacks filled with white powder.

'Borax,' Lauren said. 'It's what you mix with pure cocaine to make the weaker stuff they sell on the street.'

'How do *you* know that, Miss Smarty-Pants?' James asked.

'I read your mission briefing,' Lauren said casually.

James tutted. 'Lauren, do you know how much trouble you could have got in if you'd been caught reading someone else's mission briefing?'

Lauren laughed. 'Less than the amount you'd have been in for leaving a secret briefing lying on your bathroom floor.'

'James,' Kerry gasped, 'you're not even supposed to take briefings out of the mission preparation rooms.'

'I know,' James said, shrugging. 'But I usually smuggle a few bits out to read while I'm on the toilet.'

Kerry took photos of the borax.

'So, Keith Moore stores his borax here,' James said. 'There's nothing illegal about borax. Mr Singh will just say they use it as disinfectant.'

'There must be more to it,' Kerry said. 'Keith wouldn't

bail out a company this size in return for shelf space. Dinesh said about upstairs.'

'I hate to keep saying it,' James said, 'but there *is* no upstairs.'

'Yes, there is,' Lauren said. 'This building has a pointed roof, but the ceiling in here is flat.'

'Good thinking, Lauren,' Kerry said. 'You obviously got all the brains in your family. There must be a loft up there.'

The three of them pointed their torches at the ceiling. The beams got dim over such a distance, but they eventually spotted a hatch that had to lead into the loft.

'How can we get up there?' Kerry asked.

'Easy,' James said. 'It's like a computer game. If you look, the shelves in some bays are closer together. You can use them like a ladder.'

'And we thought all those hours on the Playstation were wasted,' Kerry said, smiling. 'Lauren, you stay down here and keep lookout. Me and James will climb up.'

Lauren nodded. James doubted she'd have been so agreeable if he'd been giving the orders. They clambered up the closely spaced shelves, feeling their way with their hands. They walked along the shelves, stepping over sacks and tins until they came to the next easy-to-climb section. Lauren shone her torch on them, lighting their path as best she could.

The top level was fifteen metres above ground, but the shelves were three metres deep, so it felt safe. There was a wooden pole with a hook on the end for undoing the loft hatch. Kerry pulled it open. James shone his torch into the hole while she pulled out the ladder. It clattered down, banging against the metal sheet on which they stood. The hundreds of fluorescent tubes in the ceiling a few centimetres from their heads started plinking to life. James and Kerry dived down and shielded their faces while their eyes adjusted to the light.

'What the hell did that?' James whispered.

'Someone must have come in,' Kerry said. 'They'll never see us up here, but where's Lauren?'

They crawled to the edge of the shelves on their bellies. James leaned over one side, Kerry over the other.

'I can't see her,' Kerry said. 'It looks like she's had the sense to get out of sight.'

There were two sets of footsteps, accompanied by women's voices. James caught a glance of them. They were both fat, wearing hairnets and dark blue overalls.

'Bay forty-six,' one woman said.

They walked slowly, reading the numbers printed on the shelves.

'Potassium carbonate,' the woman said, leaning into the bay. 'This is it, in the blue drums.'

Something whumped against the floor, echoing around the warehouse. James peeked over the side. A sack of orange powder had exploded on the ground, almost directly below them. Lauren must have knocked it off a shelf.

The two women started walking towards the spill.

'I better see if Lauren's OK,' James said.

Kerry nodded. 'Be careful. Keep out of sight.'

But when he turned around, Lauren was crawling along the metal towards them.

'Why didn't you hide behind something?' James whispered angrily.

'Sorry,' Lauren said, looking ashamed of herself. 'I wanted to be with you guys.'

Even though it was tense, James couldn't help smiling. 'Now you know why you need training: so you don't get scared so easily.'

'I wasn't scared,' Lauren said defensively. 'Just . . .'

Kerry anxiously shushed the pair of them. 'You're making too much noise.'

Down at ground level, the two women were standing by the burst sack, hands on hips, staring up at the ceiling.

'We must have a ghost,' one woman grinned.

The other one laughed. 'I'm not sticking around to see if he chucks another one at us and it's not gonna be muggins here who cleans that mess up, either.'

The women picked up their boxes and switched out the lights as they left. The three kids kept still, making sure the women were gone and letting their eyes readjust to blackness. Kerry lit her torch and shone it up the metal ladder.

'Bet you a pound there's nothing up there,' James said.

Kerry didn't find him funny. 'There better be after all this messing about.'

She went up the ladder first. There were no windows in the loft, so it was safe to switch on the lights. Even before James got up the ladder, he could tell they'd found something good from the grin on Kerry's face.

*

Kyle woke up at 3.30 a.m., in a smoky room snarled up with

sleeping bodies. He didn't know if he'd passed out or fallen asleep, or what the stain on his trousers was, but he remembered it was the wildest party of his young life. The host would be grounded for a year when her parents got back from the Lake District.

Kyle had hammered himself with alcohol and thumping music. Now he was suffering. Anyone else would have crashed back to sleep, but Kyle wanted to get home, have a shower and put his clothes in to soak. He'd always been neat. One of his earliest memories was of chucking a tantrum over going on to a beach with a load of other kids because he didn't like getting sand on his clothes.

It took Kyle a while to find the room where he'd dumped his sweatshirt. He got abused when he trod on some naked guy's ankle in the dark. He stepped over more kids crashed out on the front lawn as he went out of the front gate towards the bus stop. He waited forty minutes for the night bus, which dropped him on the wrong side of Thornton estate at half-four in the morning. Everything looked wrong as he stumbled towards the house: all the lights were on and there was a grey Toyota he didn't recognise parked on the drive.

Nicole wasn't home, but everyone else was in the living room. Lauren had dropped to sleep on the couch. Ewart had his laptop computer on the coffee table. A balding man in a suit and tie sat next to him.

'What's going on?' Kyle asked. 'Did I miss something good?'

'Yeah,' James grinned. 'It turns out bringing Kerry on this mission wasn't a dumb waste of time after all.'

Kerry gave James a look, but she was too full of herself to get offended.

Zara introduced Kyle to the stranger. 'This is John Jones. He's in charge of the MI5 taskforce that's targeting KMG, so we called him over to look at the pictures.'

John Jones reached over and shook Kyle's hand before speaking. 'You kids are amazing,' he grinned. 'When Dr McAfferty offered me a CHERUB unit, I thought it was some kind of joke.'

James looked surprised. 'You must have heard about missions where cherubs have done a good job.'

John shook his head. 'I'd been an MI5 agent for eighteen years without ever hearing of CHERUB.'

Zara explained. 'Thousands of people work for MI5, but only the most senior ones know about CHERUB. People like John only find out if they have to work with us.'

'Even then,' John said, 'there are forty-three MI5 agents working on Operation Snort and I'm the only one who knows about you kids.'

'So what's happened?' Kyle croaked, his throat raw from the smoke at the party.

'Come and look at the pictures James and Kerry took,' Zara said.

Kyle leaned over the laptop screen while John Jones explained what had been photographed.

'KMG smuggles in cocaine at a very high purity, ninety per cent or more. The stuff that gets sold on the street is between thirty and fifty per cent pure. What you see in these pictures is a production plant. The pure cocaine gets mixed with borax and some other stuff in those aluminium vats. Then . . .'

John Jones clicked on the mouse, changing to a different picture.

'The machine in this picture is a real beauty. It must have cost over fifty thousand pounds. It's designed to package seasonings, like soy sauce or pepper. You turn it on, load up a roll of polyurethane bags and tip your powder or liquid in the top. This one has been set up to package one gram bags of cocaine.'

'So did you find much coke?' Kyle asked.

'None at all,' Kerry said.

'There could be drugs hidden in the warehouse,' John said. 'Or somewhere else on the Thunderfoods site, but I doubt it. Most probably, a couple of guys turn up with a few kilos of cocaine, spend a few hours mixing and bagging it and then take it away with them when they leave.'

'So,' Kyle asked, 'are you gonna bust this place up?'

'No,' John said. 'We're going to put it under surveillance. We'll get an undercover team to rig the loft up with video cameras and microphones. We'll watch who comes and goes and where they're coming from and going to. Hopefully, we can track the drugs that are processed at Thunderfoods back to wherever they're being smuggled in.'

'So it's really only the beginning,' James said.

'You kids have got our foot in the door,' John said. 'That's not the same as bringing down KMG, but it's going to be a lot easier now we know where their cocaine is being processed.'

John shook everyone's hand before he left. The sun was on its way up and Lauren was the only one who'd managed any sleep.

*

It was three in the afternoon when James surfaced from under his duvet. He was busting for a pee, but Kerry was in the shower, merrily singing her head off. Lauren had left a note on the kitchen table.

> *James*
> *U looked peaceful! Didn't want 2 wake U up.*
> *CU soon.*
> *Lauren.*
> *XXX*

James was miffed. He'd wanted to say a proper goodbye and wish Lauren luck in training. He sprinted back upstairs as soon as he heard Kerry unlock the bathroom.

'What took you so long?' James gasped, lifting the toilet seat and starting to pee without bothering to close the door behind him.

'Sorry,' Kerry said, towelling her hair. 'Have you seen Ewart or Zara?'

'Not yet. They're at the supermarket.'

'They want a word with us later on,' Kerry said.

'You think we're in trouble for not asking before we broke in?' James asked.

'Lauren got a blasting from Ewart before she left.'

'Was she upset or anything?'

Kerry shook her head. 'She seemed to handle it OK.'

'So, what do you reckon they'll do to us?'

'Kyle overheard Ewart and Zara talking,' Kerry said. 'Apparently we've landed ourselves washing-up duty for the rest of the mission.'

James shrugged. 'We could have got worse, I suppose.'

15. CONTENDER

Not much happened in the three weeks after they broke into Thunderfoods. That's how undercover missions usually work: you find a few things out quickly, then it starts getting tougher. You have to be patient, slowly winning the confidence of your targets and working your way deeper in to an organisation.

Meryl Spencer sent James an e-mail to say Lauren had completed her first week of training and was coping well.

Nicole had put listening devices and miniature cameras around Keith Moore's house. James still liked Nicole, but he hadn't kissed her after the first time because he was more interested in Kerry.

Kerry had wired Mr Singh's house with microphones and was spending a lot of time with Dinesh, trying to squeeze out more information. James still hadn't found the right moment to tell Kerry how he felt about her. At least, that's what he told Kyle. There had been loads of opportunities, but James always chickened out.

Kyle had given up targeting Ringo Moore and was helping a couple of Year Ten kids make deliveries for KMG on weekends. James still couldn't get his head around Kyle being gay, but it hadn't changed anything in their day-to-day lives.

Some days, James almost forgot he was on a mission. It was like being a normal kid: getting up and playing with Joshua, going to school, sitting through boring lessons or bunking off, coming home and eating whatever frozen delight Zara had warmed in the oven, then going out making deliveries.

It wasn't a bad life. There was a hundred a week in drug money to spend. James had got new jeans and tracksuit tops, video games and the dearest Nike trainers he could find. School was a doss and Junior and James always messed around and had a laugh. The two boys had loads in common: they both supported Arsenal, hated school, liked Playstation and had similar tastes in music and girls.

*

James hadn't been in a proper three-round fight yet, but he'd done some sparring and loved the buzz you got in the boxing ring. As soon as you get punched, the chemicals in your body rise up and make you mad, like somebody plugged you into the electricity. Your bad side takes over and you're not scared of anything.

James couldn't manage Ken's target of a hundred and fifty skips a minute, but he'd got well past the stage where the other boys pissed themselves laughing every time he picked up a rope. He stopped skipping and mopped the sweat off his face when Kelvin called him to ringside.

'One round sparring with Del,' Kelvin said.

Del had a longer reach and seven fights under his belt, but James wasn't worried as he stepped through the ropes wearing gloves and a head guard. James was built for boxing: solid arms, big shoulders and strong enough to take a punch.

'Touch gloves,' Kelvin said, stepping back from the two fighters.

James charged forward on the bell. Del landed the first hit, a glancing blow on the side of James' head guard. James hit Del's head harder, sunk another punch in Del's guts and then covered his face, blocking Del's jabs while spying for an opening through the crack between his gloves. When it came, James pounced forward and landed his glove in Del's face. The next punch caught Del off balance, sprawling him out over the canvas.

James wanted Del to get up so he could thump him again, but Del waved his gloves in front of his face and crawled to the ropes. James was disgusted. He spat out his mouth guard before tugging off his glove and hurling it at Del's back.

'Call that a fight?' he shouted. 'Come back for some more, you little wimp.'

Kelvin grabbed James by his shoulders and pulled him backwards. 'Cool it, tiger,' he grinned. 'Try and remember this is amateur boxing. You win on the number of clean punches you land, not on how hard you punch or even how many times you knock the other guy down.'

'I wanna fight somebody really good next time.'

Kelvin laughed. 'You're a strong lad, James, but you need to work on your speed, so don't start getting cocky.'

James unbuckled his head guard and jumped out of the ring. Junior was walking towards him.

'You almost look good enough to fight me,' Junior said, smiling.

'I'd fight you now if they'd let me.'

Del had staggered around from the other side of the ring. His hair was soaked in sweat where it had been trapped under his head guard.

'You're too strong for me,' Del gasped.

'Sorry I called you a wimp,' James said. 'I got carried away.'

Del and James gave each other a sweaty hug. It was always the same: in the ring you wanted to kill someone, but once you got out you were mates again. As James walked over to his training pals, Kelvin called him back.

'I hear you've been a reliable delivery boy since you started,' Kelvin said. 'Don't think it's gone unnoticed.'

'Cheers,' James said, his mind still fixed inside the ring.

'You fancy a little train ride tomorrow evening?'

'How far?' James asked.

'We need a package delivered down St Albans way. You up for it?'

'Sure.'

'There's twelve kilos of coke split into four bricks. Get someone you can rely on to help you carry it. You'll earn forty pounds each.'

'Sounds fair,' James said. 'Where do I pick the stuff up?'

'You know Costas?'

James nodded. 'I've seen him around.'

'He'll meet you in the Thornton playground at about six o'clock. Bring your mate so we can check him out.'

*

Kyle was on another delivery, so James offered the job to Kerry.

'It's fifteen minutes' ride on the train,' James said, 'and we'll be earning twenty pounds each.'

Kerry shrugged. 'I was gonna do homework with Dinesh after school, but I'm not getting anything new out of him.'

It was a drizzly night, so nobody else was in the playground. Costas was a burly sixteen-year-old who'd dropped out of school the year before. His face was a mass of zits and he didn't like the look of Kerry.

'Are you kidding me?' he asked. 'You weren't supposed to bring your girlfriend. You need someone with a bit of presence in case there's trouble.'

'This was arranged at short notice,' James said. 'Kerry's all I could get and she's well up to the job.'

Costas looked at Kerry. 'No offence, babe, but we don't use little girls.'

Unless you were a very large person, preferably armed with a baseball bat, calling Kerry *babe* was a seriously bad idea.

'I'm not your babe,' Kerry sniffed. 'And I'm quite capable of defending myself.'

'I'm sure you are, sweetie,' Costas sniggered. 'Sorry, James, but this is not gonna happen. Bringing a chick on a delivery, man . . . What are you thinking?'

'Give us those drugs,' Kerry said furiously. 'Or you're in deep trouble.'

James smiled at her. 'Kerry, calm down. I'll make a couple of phone calls and smooth this out.'

'No,' Kerry said. 'I'm not letting this bag of pus talk to me like that.'

Costas snorted noisily.

'What you gonna do, baby cakes, pull my hair?'

Kerry lunged forward, slamming a Karate chop into the front of Costas' neck and sweeping his legs away as he stumbled backwards. Costas was on the ground with Kerry's knee crushing his windpipe before he even realised the fight had started.

'Baby cakes?' Kerry shouted, pressing her knee in harder as Costas gasped for breath. 'Nobody calls me baby cakes.'

'OK,' Costas gurgled. 'I'm sorry. You can go with James.'

Kerry stood up and let Costas sit still while his face returned to its normal colour.

'You surprised me,' Costas said angrily, as he got to his feet. 'But you better not try anything like that again or I'll seriously hurt you.'

Kerry couldn't help grinning. 'I'll try to keep that in mind.'

Costas made sure nobody was around before unzipping his backpack. Kerry and James each grabbed two plastic-wrapped bricks of white powder and tucked them in their backpacks. James started walking away.

'Hang on,' Costas said. 'Unless you want me to keep the eighty quid.'

Kerry snatched the money out of Costas' hand.

'Pleasure doing business,' she said.

She started jogging after James.

'Eighty quid, James?' Kerry said angrily. 'I can't believe

you tried to rip me off when you've got a roll of twenties in your pocket and I'm only getting pocket money.'

'It was a mistake,' James lied. 'You can have half, of course.'

'I'm keeping the lot,' Kerry said, tucking the money into her jeans. 'Unless you want to fight me for it.'

16. LOST

James and Kerry stepped off the train on to the platform at St Albans.

'It's a shame we couldn't have got here earlier in the day,' Kerry said. 'St Albans is really historic. There's Roman ruins and mosaics and stuff.'

'Tragic,' James said sarcastically. 'Nothing gets my pulse racing like a good mosaic. We're not going into town anyway. We've got to get out to some housing estate.'

Taxis were lined up outside the station. The driver wanted to see James' money before he'd take them anywhere. The ride took them past farms and some seriously expensive houses, then from nowhere they found themselves surrounded by graffiti and concrete. It was like an alien spaceship had sucked a housing estate out the middle of London, then decided it didn't like the look of it and dumped it in the middle of nowhere.

The cab pulled up outside a shopping arcade. Everything was boarded up, except a pub that had been converted into a snooker club. It had a reinforced metal door and bars over the slits of glass that passed for windows.

Kerry looked around nervously as the cab pulled away. It was already turning dark.

'It must be the pits living in a place like this,' James said. 'Thornton may be a dump, but at least it's near to town. Out here you've got nothing.'

It turned out the shops were the high point of the area. Beyond them were eight low-rise housing blocks. Three were boarded up, with CONDEMNED BUILDING notices and signs warning people not to go inside without masks to protect them against asbestos dust. There was a pack of dogs roaming around, druggies in dark corners and the only normal-looking people you saw walked fast, like they were afraid of being mugged.

James got the directions out of his pocket.

'Twenty-two, third floor, Mullion House.'

They found Mullion House, then walked up a foul-smelling staircase and along the third-floor balcony. The door numbers ended at twenty. James rang the bell and an Eastern-European-sounding woman shouted out of the letterbox in bad English.

'What is you like?'

'Do you know where number twenty-two is?' James asked.

'What?' she shouted.

'Number twenty-two?'

'Wait. I fetch my son.'

The kid who came to the letterbox was about ten. His English was perfect.

'There's no number twenty-two,' he explained. 'I think all the floors are the same. It only goes up to twenty.'

'Cheers,' James said miserably, turning away from the letterbox. 'Sorry to bother you.'

'What do we do now?' Kerry asked.

'There's obviously a mistake with the address,' James said. 'I'll call the lady who rings my deliveries through. She'll sort us out.'

James pulled his mobile out of his tracksuit and dialled. The phone made a bleep and a message flashed on the display: *No Signal.* Kerry tried hers and got the same.

'Crap,' James said. 'You really know you're in the middle of nowhere when you can't get a mobile signal.'

Kerry looked down off the balcony towards the shops.

'There's a phone box by the bus stop,' she said.

James looked down. 'I'd put the odds of it working at something like a million to one.'

They didn't have any other choice, so they went to take a look. The phone wasn't so much vandalised as annihilated. There was no glass, no handset and no buttons; just a burned-up mess.

'This place is giving me the creeps,' Kerry said. 'Do you think they'd let us phone from inside the snooker club?'

'I wouldn't chance it,' James said. 'It looks like the kind of place where you'd get your throat cut.'

'So what then?' Kerry asked.

'Let's get the hell out of here. There's no way to call another cab, so we'll wait for the bus. Our phones will work once we get into town. I'll make some calls and sort this shambles out.'

They wandered across to the bus stop. Kerry glanced at the timetable.

'There's only one bus an hour,' she said. 'I think we just missed one.'

There was hardly any traffic about. They sat on the pavement near the bus stop with their feet in the gutter. Kerry picked a dandelion from a crack in the tarmac and twirled it between her fingers.

'Do you think you'll get in trouble with KMG for this?' she asked.

'I've got the bit of paper with the address written in Kelvin's writing, so they can hardly blame me.'

'It's pretty incredible,' Kerry said.

James nodded. 'Especially when you think what these drugs are worth.'

'How much?' Kerry asked.

'There's twelve kilos. I sell coke for sixty a gram and there's a thousand grams in a kilo. So each kilo is worth sixty thousand pounds. That's . . . seven hundred and twenty thousand altogether.'

'*Wow*,' Kerry gasped. 'That makes our eighty-pound delivery fee look a lot less generous.'

'Course, that's the street price and this is being sold wholesale, but I'd still bet KMG isn't shifting this lot for any less than three hundred grand.'

'You could buy a nice house with that sort of money.'

James giggled. 'Maybe we should do a runner.'

'You know, it's cool the way you can do those sums in your head.'

'I've been able to do it since nursery,' James said. 'Before my mum died, she ran this huge shoplifting gang and she got me to work out her sums; like, who owed how much and who was due what wages.'

'Did she ever get busted?' Kerry asked.

James shook his head. 'Nope. But when I was little, I used to have nightmares where the police came and took Mum and Lauren away. Junior made some comment the other day about his dad ending up in prison. He acted like it was a joke, but I could tell it worries him. I remembered how I used to be, and it made me feel really shitty about us using him to help put his dad in jail.'

'I suppose every bad guy has someone who loves them,' Kerry said.

They watched the sunset as the minutes dragged by. When the streetlights flicked on, James looked at his watch.

'The bus shouldn't be long now,' Kerry said.

Three lads came out of the snooker club and started walking towards them. One was a big guy in his twenties, with a beard and curly brown hair down his back. The other two were skinheads in their late teens. Probably brothers, with ghostly complexions and spindly limbs. They weren't the first people who'd passed by, but something about them put Kerry and James on edge.

The taller skinhead stopped by Kerry.

'Waiting for a bus?' he asked.

'Yes,' Kerry said, standing up. 'That's what people usually do at bus stops.'

'I thought you might be waiting for a hunk like me to come by and sweep you off your feet.'

The shorter one gave James a shove. 'You her boyfriend, blondie?'

'Piss off,' James said, shoving him back.

'Got any money?' Shorty said, eyeballing James. 'Not for very long you won't have.'

Both skinheads pulled knives out of their pockets. CHERUB training teaches you to make an instant decision when you see a knife: either grab the assailant's wrist before the blade is in a threatening position, or back away if you don't have time. James and Kerry went for the first option, grabbing the two skinny wrists and yanking their arms behind their backs. Kerry twisted the tall one's thumb until his knife dropped on to the pavement, then smacked his head against the concrete bus stop. After freeing the other knife, James punched Shorty in the back of the head, before ducking down and picking both blades off the floor. He handed one to Kerry.

'We don't want trouble,' Kerry said, waving the knife. 'We're just waiting for the bus.'

The two skinheads didn't back off, but they didn't look confident either. The guy with the long hair had waited in the background the whole time. He moved up between the skinheads and smiled.

'You two seem to know some pretty fancy moves,' he said, breaking into a grin. 'You got any that will stop one of these?'

He slid a sawn-off shotgun out of his jacket and pointed it at them. James looked at Kerry, hoping she had some smart move up her sleeve, but she looked as scared as he felt.

'This is a twelve gauge,' the guy with the big hair explained. 'One shot will blow the pair of you to smithereens. So, if you want to live beyond the next few minutes, you're going to do exactly what I say. OK?'

James and Kerry both nodded.

'First of all, pass the knives back to their owners, handles first.'

The skinheads took the knives.

'Now put your hands on your heads.'

Once their hands were on their heads, the skinheads rummaged through James' and Kerry's pockets, taking their money, keys, train tickets and phones. Then they stripped off their watches.

'Now, lose the backpacks.'

'You know you'll be in serious trouble if you take those packs?' James said. 'You've no idea what's in them.'

'I know exactly what's in them,' the hairball laughed. 'And you can tell Keith Moore that if he sends any more grubby little brats down here, we'll give them a lot worse than the beating we're about to give you.'

Shorty looked back at the gunman. 'Can I have his trainers before we batter them?'

'Eh?'

Shorty pointed at James' trainers. 'You said we could keep whatever we nicked off them. Those trainers are a hundred and nineteen ninety-nine. My little brother would love 'em.'

The gunman shook his head in disbelief. 'Go on, then.'

James looked mortified as he surrendered his almost-new Air Max.

'Now,' the gunman said, smiling sweetly, 'after we go, you're gonna walk or crawl the hell out of here. If I ever see you again, I'll be the last thing you ever see. And I wouldn't bother waiting for the bus. Kids kept chucking bricks through the windscreen, so they stopped running them after dark.'

The gunman made James and Kerry lie flat on the ground with their hands behind their heads, then he told the skinheads to give them a good going-over.

17. CRAZY

Kerry and James crawled out of the road and lay in the grass verge behind the bus stop, catching their breath. As kickings go, it hadn't been bad, but they'd have plenty of bruises in the morning.

'I guess they wanted us fit enough to walk home and give Keith his message,' Kerry said.

'How's your knee?' James asked.

'I'm OK. Your lip's bleeding.'

'You feel up to walking, or do you want to rest for a minute?'

'I can walk,' Kerry said. 'What are we gonna do?'

'Exactly what the man with the gun told us to do,' James said. 'It'll take at least an hour to get into town. Or if we pass a phone box that works, we can call home and reverse the charges.'

'This will ruin the mission,' Kerry said.

'Nah. I'll just explain what happened to Kelvin. It's obvious we've been set up.'

'What if they think you were in on it?' Kerry asked. 'There's plenty of delivery boys. If there's any doubt, KMG will just dump you and use someone else.'

James realised she was right. 'They're not exactly gonna be happy about me losing three hundred grand's worth of coke, are they?'

'They'll check all of us out,' Kerry said. 'Not just you and me. Kyle, Nicole, Ewart and Zara will be under the spotlight as well. The whole mission will be down the toilet.'

'I don't see how we can get the drugs back,' James said. 'That guy had a gun. I don't even have trainers.'

'He was small-time,' Kerry said.

'What makes you say that?'

'You heard what the skinhead said when he took your trainers. That hairball was paying them by letting them keep our stuff. That's hardly the modus of a big shot.'

'OK,' James said. 'He's small-time, but he's still got a gun.'

'He won't kill us in a million years,' Kerry said. 'He's been paid a few hundred quid to scare us, grab the drugs and send a message to Keith Moore. There's a huge difference between that and murdering two kids.'

'Supposing you're right,' James said. 'How do we find this guy?'

'I think there's only one road in and out of this chunk of paradise and we haven't seen him leave. We're looking for a tall, fat drug dealer with tons of curly hair and a beard. I bet one of the scumbags hanging around here will be able to put a name to a description like that.'

'And we just walk up and they'll tell us?'

Kerry shrugged. 'We'll make some excuse why we need to find him.'

'The thing is,' James said, 'if you've just ripped off KMG

for three hundred grand, you won't be hanging around here for long.'

'I know,' Kerry said. 'But he doesn't think KMG will know what's happened until we get into town. He'll be off his guard for the next hour or so.'

'You're serious, aren't you?' James smiled. 'I'm really gonna go chasing after some gun-toting drug dealer in my socks?'

'I think it's worth the risk, but I'm not forcing you. If you're not up for it, we'll head home.'

James thought for a second as he dabbed his bloody lip on the bottom of his T-shirt. He didn't fancy their chances. If it had been anyone but Kerry, he would have said no.

'Let's go and get shot,' he said, climbing to his feet and taking his first painful steps since the beating.

They cut around the back of the shops, dodging the snooker club in case anyone inside spotted them. They found a couple of skinny women at the bottom of a staircase and got blank stares when they described the hairball. They got lucky on their second attempt, when Kerry described him to a group of teenagers.

'Was it some kind of heavy metal T-shirt?'

'Yeah,' Kerry said. 'Do you know where we could find him? He dropped his keys outside the snooker club and we picked them up.'

'Sounds like Crazy Joe,' one kid said. 'He lives in Alhambra House. You want to be careful, he's a serious lunatic and he's drugged-up half the time.'

'You know where exactly?' James asked.

'What do I look like?' the kid laughed. 'Directory enquiries? Try the second or third floor.'

'Cheers,' James said.

'Nice socks,' the kid replied.

Alhambra House was the furthermost block. There were twenty flats on each floor, but finding the right one was easier than they expected. Loads were boarded up and most of the others didn't look the part: old-person-style wallpaper in the hallways, or ethnic names written under the doorbells. Joe's flat turned out to be a giveaway: the front door was painted black with a devil's-head knocker and underneath the word *Joe's* was written in Tippex. They peered through the glass. There was an Aerosmith poster pinned to the kitchen wall and all the lights were on.

James and Kerry didn't have their lock guns or anything with them. They couldn't get in, so they had to lure Crazy Joe out.

'Check he's at home first,' Kerry said. 'Ring the bell and run.'

James pressed the buzzer and they sprinted to the end of the balcony and hid in the stairwell. Crazy Joe waddled on to his doorstep in his T-shirt and boxers and looked down the balcony. He swore about *bloody kids* and went back inside.

'So now what?' James asked. 'If he's half undressed, he's probably home alone.'

'There might be a girlfriend in there as well.'

'I don't reckon any woman lives in that house,' James said.

'Based on what?' Kerry asked.

'Did you see the filthy sink and cutlery piled up on the draining board?' James asked. 'That's a single man's kitchen if ever I saw one.'

'There's something messed-up about this,' Kerry said.

'You'd think he'd be running or driving some place in a hurry, not sitting around in his underwear.'

'None of this makes any sense,' James said. 'Everything else I've done for KMG has run like clockwork.'

'Joe might have friends nearby,' Kerry said. 'We need to take him down quickly and without making a noise.'

Five minutes later, Crazy Joe emerged from his flat a second time to find James grinning at him.

'I warned you,' Joe sneered.

As Joe lunged for James, Kerry landed her hardest punch into the side of his head. It hit the sweet spot above the eye socket where the skull is thinnest, giving Joe's brain a good rattling. All his muscles went limp and James had to dodge out of the way as he slumped across the balcony.

'Get moving,' Kerry said anxiously, looking at James. 'He'll start coming around in no time and I don't want to have to knock him out twice.'

James stepped over Joe and ran into the flat, checking inside every room to make sure nobody else was home. There were pizza boxes and rubbish everywhere. The smell of stale cigarette smoke made his eyes water. Once he knew the flat was empty, he helped Kerry drag the semi-conscious Joe through to the living-room.

'Find something to tie him up with,' Kerry shouted.

James ripped the electric cables out of the back of the video and the satellite box. Joe struggled a bit, but they managed to knot the flex tightly around his wrists and ankles.

'Where's our drugs, Joe?' Kerry asked, bunching her fist in the air above him.

'How old are you guys?' Joe grinned. 'Thirteen, fourteen?'

'Nearly thirteen,' James said.

'I've seen it all now,' Joe said. 'You guys were supposed to get scared and run home to Mummy.'

'Shut it,' Kerry said in a firm voice. 'From now on, you talk when I say so and you better make sure I like the answer. So, for the second time, Joe, where are our drugs?'

'Found 'em,' James said, spotting the two backpacks beside the couch.

He unzipped them, making sure the stuff was still inside.

'Look for the gun, and anything else you don't want him coming after us with,' Kerry said. She kept Joe under control while James searched the flat. The shotgun was inside Joe's leather jacket, hanging up by the front door. James found a pistol and more drugs under the bed. It was cocaine in one-gram bags, identical to what James delivered most nights.

He'd been trained where to look for hidden stuff and an uneven piece of skirting was a dead giveaway. James pulled it off and found two supermarket carrier bags stuffed with more cocaine, and a few thousand pounds in scrunched-up cash. James stuffed the drugs into the carrier bags on top of the money and carried the lot into the living-room.

'Shall we take all this?' James asked.

'Why not?' Kerry said, smiling. 'He made us suffer.'

'We better not hang around here,' James said.

'You kids are in way over your heads,' Joe gasped.

Kerry bunched up her fist. 'Did I ask for your opinion?'

She grabbed a wad of serviettes out of a greasy pizza box and forced them into Joe's mouth.

'Are we gonna call a cab, or what?' James asked.

Kerry pointed at a picture on the wall. 'Is that parked around here somewhere?'

James looked over his shoulder at a framed photo of a slimmer, younger Joe, standing in front of an American car. It was a fancy two-seater, with mad-looking air scoops on the bonnet and a two-tone orange paint job. James read the little gold plaque stuck on the frame: *1971 Ford Mustang Mach 1. Tuned to 496 Horsepower.*

'They look like car keys on the coffee table,' Kerry said.

Joe wriggled his arms and furiously tried to shout something through the serviettes plugging his mouth.

James grinned as he picked up the keys. 'Sure beats hanging around for a mini-cab to turn up. Where's it parked?'

'You wouldn't leave that on the street around here. It must be in one of the garages out the back.' Kerry pulled the soggy wad of tissue out of Joe's mouth. 'What's your garage number?'

'If you *touch* my car,' Joe gasped, spitting bits of white fluff off his tongue, 'you're both dead.'

Kerry smashed her trainer into Joe's guts.

'Next time it'll be your balls . . .' Kerry shouted, as Joe groaned in agony. 'What's your garage number?'

'No way,' Joe grunted.

'James,' Kerry said sweetly, 'hand me the gun, please.'

James passed it across. Kerry pulled down on the stock to load it and pointed the sawn-off barrel at Joe's knees.

'The next word out of your mouth had better be a garage number,' Kerry snarled. 'Or it's gonna take a miracle to get the bloodstain out of this carpet.'

James knew Kerry wouldn't pull the trigger, but she put on a good act and Joe wasn't so confident.

'Forty-two,' Joe said.

'How hard was that?' Kerry said. 'And if you're lying, I'll come back here in a minute and blow off your foot before I ask again.'

'OK, OK,' Joe gasped. 'I lied . . . It's in number eighteen. Why don't you call a cab? It's a very powerful car. Do you kids even know how to drive?'

'Don't you worry yourself about that,' James said.

All CHERUB agents are taught to drive. It's essential to be able to escape on wheels if things turn nasty.

'Why don't you take a pair of Joe's trainers?' Kerry asked.

'Too big,' James said. 'They'll be like clown shoes on me.'

'We better rip the phones out,' Kerry said. 'We don't want him calling his pals before we're well on our way.'

She pulled the phone out and kicked the socket off the wall with her heel. James pocketed Joe's mobile and demolished the extension in the bedroom.

Kerry grabbed both backpacks.

'Ready to go?' she asked.

James got the carrier bags with the money, pistol and Joe's drugs. They went out of the front door and walked briskly along the balcony, down the stairs and around to the garages at the back. Kerry's head was spinning so fast, she never noticed that she still had the shotgun in her hand.

The padlock sprang open and James noisily rolled up the metal door of garage number eighteen. The Mustang looked better than the day it had come out of the showroom, thirty-five years earlier. Crazy Joe had spent serious money on it.

'Bags I'm driving,' James said, unlocking the driver's door and lowering himself into the leather seat. Kerry didn't care, she wasn't into cars.

James moved the seat as far forward as it would go so he could reach the pedals. He'd learned on the private roads around campus in a little car with an engine the size of a thimble. He wasn't prepared for the thunderstorm when the tuned V8 blasted to life, juddering through the pedals into his socked feet.

'Hoooooooly mother,' James grinned, searching for the headlight control.

The road ahead lit up and the dials on the dashboard turned electric blue. James put the automatic gearbox in drive and rolled the gargling beast out of its pen.

The first couple of kilometres were dodgy. The car had big acceleration, but the brakes had much less bite than on a modern car. It caught James out when he nearly went into the back of someone at the first set of traffic lights. Once they were a few kilometres clear, he parked. Kerry found a road atlas under her seat and worked out the route home. By the time they got on to the motorway, James was feeling confident. When the road ahead was clear, he couldn't resist slamming the accelerator and taking it up to 110mph.

The trim inside the car started to shake and Kerry started going bananas.

'Really sensible, James,' she shouted. 'Two kids in a stolen car carrying guns and drugs. I tell you what: why don't we attract lots of attention by slaughtering the speed limit?'

After seeing the way she'd dealt with Joe, James decided it might be best if he slowed down.

*

They parked the stolen Mustang at the back of a DIY store about a kilometre from Thornton. It was gone eleven o'clock and, now the adrenalin rush had worn off, James and Kerry felt like they could sleep for twenty hours.

'We could leave the keys in the door and someone will nick it,' James said.

'It's got our fingerprints all over,' Kerry said. 'Joyriders usually burn cars out. If we don't want it to look suspicious, that's what we'll have to do.'

James gave the car an admiring glance. 'Seems a shame to kill it.'

Kerry leaned inside and flipped open the glove box. She found Joe's cigarettes and lighter, then tore pages out of the road atlas and screwed them up into loose balls. When there was a mound of paper on the passenger seat, she flicked the lighter and set the edges alight. They left the passenger door open so the fire could breathe, then ducked into some trees and waited until they were sure the flames had taken hold.

The front seats were quickly ablaze. Once the roof lining caught, the flames flashed into the back. The whole interior glowed orange and smoke started curling out from under the hood.

'Better run,' James said. 'There's bound to be a security guard round here somewhere.'

They'd only gone a hundred metres when the heat blew out one of the back tyres. A few seconds later, the fuel caught and the back end of the car went up in a fireball.

It was less than a kilometre home, but they were feeling their injuries and the walk seemed to take for ever. James had a pounding headache. When they staggered through to the kitchen, Ewart jumped up from the table, surprised by the state they were in. He made them both hot drinks and sandwiches while Zara and Nicole cleaned up their cuts and bruises.

'Shower and go to bed,' Zara said, after they'd explained what had happened. 'Don't bother getting up for school in the morning. You both need a good day's rest.'

'I better ring Kelvin first,' James said.

'OK,' Ewart said. 'Do that while Kerry's in the shower, then go straight to bed.'

18. RISKS

James was out as soon as he hit the pillow and the next thing he knew it was 10 a.m. the following morning. He had six huge bruises, a couple of grazes and a giant scab on his bottom lip. When he stood up, his thigh muscle felt tight and he could only manage short steps.

Down in the kitchen, Joshua was on the floor playing with some magnets he'd pulled off the fridge door and Kerry was at the table in her nightshirt. She looked shell-shocked.

'Sleep OK?' James asked.

'Not bad,' Kerry said. 'Zara just made a pot of tea if you want some.'

James poured a mug and got a bowl of cereal.

'I can't believe all we went through last night,' Kerry grinned. 'If I didn't hurt in ten places, I might believe it was all a dream.'

'Same here,' James smiled. 'You were so tough on Crazy Joe when you had him tied up. I know you've got a temper, but I've never seen you juiced-up like that before.'

'I was so angry,' Kerry said. 'I mean, what kind of scuzzball pays skinheads to beat up kids?'

'At least Kelvin seemed cool when I explained how we got the drugs back; and we saved the mission.'

Zara stepped in from the garden and threw an empty laundry basket down beside the washing machine. She'd heard James' last line.

'You know,' she said, 'sometimes a mission isn't worth saving.'

'What?' James gasped.

Kerry looked surprised as well.

'I respect what you two did last night,' Zara said. 'You made a decision under tricky circumstances and it came off. But Ewart and I both feel you should have come home. It was an unacceptable risk going up against a man with a gun.'

James and Kerry both looked wounded.

'There's no need for those faces,' Zara said.

She picked Joshua off the floor and sat him on her lap at the table.

'CHERUB is one of the most secret organisations in the world,' Zara explained. 'Only two people in the British government know it exists: the Intelligence Minister and the Prime Minister. When politicians first find out about CHERUB, they're usually queasy about putting kids in danger. Then Mac explains about all the useful work cherubs do and the lengths we go to to make you guys safe.

'Imagine if you two had been hurt, or even killed, last night. Mac would have had to go to London to explain the facts: two kids got mugged and went chasing after an armed drug dealer. At the least, Mac and the senior people within

CHERUB would be sacked for letting something so irresponsible happen. The politicians might even decide they can't stomach what CHERUB does and shut the whole show down.'

Kerry nodded. 'When you put it like that, I can see it wasn't worth it.'

'Sorry,' James said.

'You've got nothing to be sorry for,' Zara smiled. 'Just try to be less gung-ho from now on.'

*

Kelvin rang James' mobile around midday.

'I've been making calls about what happened,' he said. 'Can you meet us down here at the boxing club and bring everything you got off Crazy Joe with you?'

'I'm not in shit, am I?' James asked.

'No, no way,' Kelvin said. 'I just want you to fetch the stuff down and we'll see you right. And that bird you had with you.'

'Kerry,' James said.

'Yeah, bring her as well.'

*

Kerry had never been up to the boxing club. The gym was quiet at this time of day; just a few of the more serious boxers putting themselves through punishing workouts. Ken, as always, sat in his chair holding a mug of tea and watching everything that happened.

'They're using my office,' he said. 'Knock before you go in.'

A gigantic man in a suit and tie stood guard at the door of the dingy office. James did a double take when he got inside.

Crazy Joe was leaning against the back wall; he had a bloodstained dressing over a cut in his forehead. Kelvin sat on a cabinet off to one side and the big cheese himself was in the cracked leather chair at the desk.

'Take a seat,' Keith Moore said.

He didn't look like anyone special. A smallish man, with cropped brown hair. He wore Levis and a white polo shirt. The only conspicuous sign of wealth was a chunky gold ring.

'I haven't had the pleasure before,' Keith said, reaching over and shaking James' and Kerry's hands. 'Have you brought everything you took off Joe?'

James rattled the carrier bags between his legs.

'It's all in there.'

'I take it you know who I am?' Keith asked.

'Yeah,' James said. 'I've seen you at your house. I was on the Playstation with Junior.'

'My business runs itself these days,' Keith said. 'People go off to South America to buy stock, stock arrives, stock gets distributed.'

James noticed that he never referred to drugs or cocaine, in case the room was bugged.

Keith continued, 'Sometimes I go for weeks hearing the same message: *all the usual problems, boss, but nothing we can't handle.* Then, just when you think nothing is ever going to excite you, something turns up like what you two did last night.'

'It was a test, wasn't it?' Kerry asked.

'That's right,' Keith smiled. 'You won't last long in business without loyal people. The best way to find what they're made of is to give them some fake merchandise and put them in a situation like we put you two in last night. Some people get scared and turn hysterical. Those are the ones who'll cause problems if they get busted. We have to kick them out. Some people are sorry for losing the merchandise, but they tough it out and beg for another chance. That's what we're hoping for: guts and determination. Until last night, though, nobody ever showed enough guts to hunt down and get revenge on the guys we paid to rob them. What you two did was very impressive.'

James and Kerry both smiled.

'This is all nice and cosy,' Crazy Joe said bitterly. 'But what about my stuff?'

'Yes,' Keith said. 'You'll have to return what you took from Joe.'

'What about us?' James said. 'I've lost my best trainers. We both lost our watches and mobiles and stuff.'

'Joe can return them,' Keith said.

Joe cleared his throat. 'Actually, I said the two guys who duffed them up could keep what they took.'

'OK,' Keith said. 'Take five hundred quid out of Joe's money, that'll cover it.'

'That's a bit steep,' Joe said tersely. 'It's not my fault the brat was wearing expensive trainers.'

Keith repeated himself. 'Take five hundred quid out of Joe's money, that'll cover it.'

He didn't change his tone or anything, but Joe knew his place and didn't push the argument. James took five hundred pounds and split it with Kerry. After that, he slid the carrier bags over to Joe.

'Is that everything you took?' Keith asked.

James nodded. 'Everything.'

'Where's my Mustang parked?' Joe asked.

James and Kerry looked awkwardly at each other.

'We were scared you'd report it stolen and our fingerprints were all over the inside,' James said.

'You didn't clean them off with white spirit, did you?' Joe asked. 'White spirit dries out the leather.'

'No, we didn't,' James said. 'We, erm . . .'

He didn't have the bottle to say it.

'We burned the car out,' Kerry blurted.

'You did *what?*' Crazy Joe shouted, lunging over the desk and grabbing James by his T-shirt.

'Let him go,' Keith said, firmly.

'I'll kill these little pricks,' Joe shouted, dragging James across the desk and trying to get his hands around his throat. James thrashed about, trying to push Joe off.

Joe had ignored Keith's order, so Keith gave Kelvin the nod. Joe was no match for the powerfully built boxer; Kelvin picked up the fat man like he weighed nothing, banged him against the wall and slapped him around the face. Joe let out a high-pitched yowl that could have come from an eight-year-old girl.

'That car was my baby,' he sobbed. 'I spent months working on her.'

Kelvin backed off with a stunned look on his face. Joe dabbed up tears with the end of his beard.

'Wasn't it insured?' Keith asked.

'That's not the point,' Joe sniffled. 'I invested love in that car. You'll never get that back.'

Keith was killing himself laughing. 'Joe, it's only a car. Get a grip on yourself.'

'Those kids should pay damages, or something. They shouldn't get away with it.'

'Joe,' Keith said, looking a little angry. 'It's not my fault you let yourself get outwitted by two twelve-year-olds. I've done what you wanted, now get out of here before I ask my minder to step inside and knock your head through the wall.'

Joe grabbed his carrier bags and stumbled out of the office. He looked such a shambles James almost felt sorry for him. Keith got up from behind the desk, shaking his head.

'You know,' Keith said, as Kelvin helped him into his overcoat, 'if you two kids stay loyal and work hard, you're gonna make a lot of money.'

James and Kerry both grinned. The bruises were worth it if they'd earned Keith Moore's respect.

'Actually,' Kerry said, 'I came along as a favour to James. All your deliveries are done by boys.'

'I thought girls were soft until I met you,' Keith said.

'I can set her up, if you like,' Kelvin said.

'These two are really special,' Keith said, grinning. 'They've got brains and balls. Keep them busy and make sure they're properly rewarded.'

'Thanks,' Kerry said.

'And James,' Keith said. 'If you're over my house with Junior any time, be sure to stick your snout into my office and say hello.'

Keith left with his minder like he was in a hurry. James looked at Kelvin, who was shaking his head in disbelief.

'I'm gonna have to treat you two right,' Kelvin said. 'With Keith singing your praises, I might just end up calling one of you boss some day.'

19. THIRTEEN

Friday before school, Kerry knocked on the boys' bedroom door.

'Are you decent in there?'

'I'm still in bed,' James groaned, sounding knackered. 'Come in if you want.'

He'd been up until nearly midnight having a Playstation competition with Kyle and a couple of Thornton kids. Kerry came through the door with Joshua in her arms and dumped him on James' bed.

'He wanted to wish you Happy Birthday,' she said.

James pulled his duvet over his face. Joshua tugged it back and giggled when James made a loud quacking noise.

'How come you didn't scream your head off when Kerry picked you up?' James asked.

'I think he's finally got used to me,' Kerry smiled. 'Can I leave him here while I get my books ready for school?'

Kerry went out. Joshua crawled up the bed and burrowed under a loose pillow near James' face. James moved in to blow a raspberry on Joshua's arm, but as he got close he recoiled from a powerful smell.

'Jeeeeeeesus,' James shouted, covering his nose with his arm. 'You smelly little . . .'

James jumped out of bed and picked up Joshua, holding him out at arm's length. He walked into the hallway, where Kerry and Nicole were wetting themselves laughing.

'I wondered when you'd smell it,' Kerry said.

'You're evil,' James grinned. 'I'll get you two for this.'

James carried Joshua downstairs to the kitchen. Zara was cooking a pan of sausages.

'Morning, teenager,' Zara said. 'There's presents and stuff on the table.'

'This little monster filled his nappy,' James said.

Zara grinned. 'You know where the changing table is, James.'

'Yes, I do, but you're not getting me anywhere near it.'

'Think of it as a learning experience,' Zara said. 'An introduction to life as a young adult.'

James knew Zara wasn't serious.

'Actually,' he said, 'a better introduction to young adulthood would be a crate of beer and some hot chicks.'

Zara smiled. 'I don't think so, somehow.'

Ewart walked in behind James.

'You want to be careful,' Ewart said, taking Joshua out of James' arms. 'You start off with the hot chicks and before you know it you're leaning over a changing table with one of these little beasts peeing on you.'

Ewart tickled his son's belly before taking him outside for a nappy change.

James sat at the table and started ripping into his cards. Because cherubs never have family, except brothers and sisters, they make a point of exchanging cards, even when they're away on missions. James had over thirty, including some with foreign postmarks redirected from campus. Gabrielle had sent one from South Africa. James' old training pals Callum and Connor had posted one from Texas and Amy had sent a postcard with a picture of a giant pineapple on it from Australia. The tackiest-looking card was from Lauren.

'Here, Zara,' James laughed. 'Listen to what Lauren wrote. *Dearest brother, you are an idiot. Sometimes you make me puke. I'll be in training by the time you read this and I wish you were doing it instead of me. PS Happy thirteenth birthday, I love U.* Then she's done a row of kisses.'

James left opening his presents until Kyle and the girls had come down. The biggest box was from Ewart and Zara: a replacement for his stolen trainers. Nicole and Kerry had clubbed together and bought him a T-shirt he'd looked at the last time they went to the Reeve Centre. He got a kiss from each of them when he said thanks. Kyle got him a pack of trendy men's toiletries. It included shampoo, conditioner and a little bottle of aftershave. The label read, *Please use these regularly.*

'This is all cool,' James grinned. 'Cheers.'

He put his goodies aside and grabbed a sausage sandwich from the plate in the middle of the table. His mind wandered back a year to his twelfth birthday, just after his mum had died. He'd been living in a council home and wasn't allowed to see Lauren. It had been about the most desperate day of his life.

Then he thought about other birthdays, back when his mum was alive. Charging down the stairs to stacks of shoplifted toys and clothes, then racing to unwrap everything before school. When Lauren was tiny, she'd had to have a present as well, or she'd chuck a jealous fit.

Thinking back made James feel emotional and his eyes started glazing over. He didn't want to start bawling in front of everyone, so he scraped back his chair and bolted towards the stairs.

'Are you OK?' Zara shouted after him.

'Busting to pee,' James lied.

He locked himself in the bathroom. He wasn't really miserable, it was just that thinking about his mum always made him feel empty. Even though there was loads of interesting stuff going on in his life, James often wished he could go back in time and spend a night in front of the TV with his mum.

After washing his eyes, James stared in the mirror at the same kid who'd been there the night before, only now he was a teenager. It didn't really make any difference, but it was a buzz all the same.

*

James, Junior, Nicole and April arranged to meet at lunchtime, to bunk off and go to the cinema. They swapped uniform for casual clothes as soon as they got out of the school gate. James had loads of money, so he paid for tickets and popcorn and stuff.

It was a stupid thriller. Nicole started giggling every time this American actor spoke in a fake-sounding London accent. James and Junior started putting two fingers in their mouths and whistling noisily every time this fit actress came into shot.

The only other people in the cinema were a few pensioners. One bloke kept shushing them until Nicole turned back and waved her fist at him.

'Shut it, you old git.'

The old man toddled off to make a complaint. The cinema manager came in and told them all to behave or else he'd chuck them out. James settled down to the film. He got a shock when he noticed Nicole and Junior had their arms around each other and an even bigger one a minute later when they started snogging.

They were all over each other. Nicole's leg was up in the air and James kept getting kicked. He got up and moved down two seats so he was sitting on the opposite side of April, away from any flailing limbs.

'They're getting on well,' April grinned.

She grinned for a long time. James watched half a minute of the film and she was still grinning at him. He realised the girls had planned an ambush. Nicole already knew Junior fancied her because he'd asked her out before. James felt like he'd been hooked on a line and reeled in, but he checked April out and realised that as traps go, it wasn't a bad one.

April was decent-looking, with long brown hair and fit legs. James slid his hand under the armrest and put it on top of April's. She twisted in her seat, so she could rest her head on James' shoulder. James turned around, breathed April's smell and kissed her on the cheek while she grabbed a few of his Maltesers.

They stayed that way for a couple of minutes, until April moved away and blew chocolate breath over him.

'So,' she whispered. 'Are you gonna snog me or what?'

James figured *what the hell, it's my birthday*. They snogged for ten minutes, breaking up when the movie got near the end and turned into a big car chase and punch-up that was actually worth watching.

Nicole and Junior started messing around. They poured the dregs and melted ice from the Coke into one cup, then spat in chewed-up chocolate and bits of popcorn off the carpet. Nicole held the cup between James and April.

'Gob in that,' Nicole said.

James and April obediently spat into the cup.

'That better not end up anywhere near me,' James said.

Nicole grinned. 'Don't you worry.'

As soon as the titles came up, Nicole and Junior dashed over and caught up with the old man as he doddered up the aisle.

'Excuse me,' Nicole said politely.

The old man turned suspiciously.

'What is it?'

'I just wanted to apologise for disturbing you,' Nicole said. 'I realise it was dreadfully inconsiderate of us.'

The old man smiled. 'That's OK, I suppose. Just don't do it again.'

'Yeah,' Junior said. 'It's people like you that fought in hundreds of wars so that kids like us could be here today.'

'We'd like you to have this as a token of our appreciation,' Nicole giggled.

She chucked the contents of the cup at the old man, who wheezed in shock as the foul liquid drizzled inside his clothes. His jumper had massive stains and bits of popcorn stuck down the front.

'That'll teach you to be a grass,' Nicole shouted.

James looked stunned as Nicole and Junior broke into a run. He and April chased after them, knowing they'd get into trouble if they stuck around. When they got to the foyer, Junior launched himself into a rack of peanuts and snacks, spilling them over the floor. None of the cinema staff earned enough money to bother going after them.

They ran a few hundred metres from the cinema and cut into a side street. James was livid.

'Are you two retards or something?' he shouted. 'What the hell did you do that for?'

'Who put a bug up your arse?' Nicole grinned.

Junior was laughing so hard he couldn't stand up straight.

'He was an old man,' James stormed. 'That was totally out of order. You could have busted his hip or something.'

April didn't say anything, but she stood beside James, showing she was on his side.

'I hope he *has* broken his hip,' Nicole shouted bitterly. 'I hope he drops dead.'

'Nice,' April said.

'I can't stand old people,' Nicole said bluntly.

'You'll be old one day,' James said.

'Nah,' Nicole said. 'Live fast, die young, that's my motto.'

'Where are we going now?' Junior giggled. 'Shall we get something to eat? I'm starving.'

Being friends with Junior was part of James' mission, but sometimes your emotions take over no matter how hard you try.

'I'm going home,' James said shortly. 'I feel like a shower.'

'You're not throwing a major strop, are you?' Junior asked. 'You're still coming down the youth club tonight?'

'Sure,' James said, half-heartedly. 'Everyone's gonna be there.'

'I'm smuggling some of my dad's beers in,' Junior said. 'Let's all get totally smashed.'

Junior and Nicole wandered off towards a burger place with their arms around each other. James waited at the bus stop with April. When her bus came, he gave her a quick kiss.

'I'll see you at the youth club tonight,' April said. 'Don't let those two idiots spoil your birthday.'

'I won't,' James said.

But he couldn't help feeling it all the way home. There's a difference between mucking around and being nasty to someone. The thing with the old man had left a bad taste in his mouth.

20. CELEBRATION

The incident with Crazy Joe was supposed to be kept quiet, but it was the kind of story that travels fast and gets wilder every time it's told. The story, combined with Keith Moore's seal of approval, had made James into a well-respected face.

He got a good vibe when he walked into the youth centre alongside Kerry and Dinesh. Waves and smiles came from all directions. He sat at a table with Junior and Nicole, who looked like they'd already downed a few of the beers that were stashed under the table. Junior was in a good mood and James didn't want to make a big deal about what had happened at the cinema earlier.

'Beer?' Junior said, passing a can across the table.

Drinking was banned, but the youth club supervisor always just sat in the corner translating books into German. If there was a punch-up, he'd phone upstairs and get a couple of guys from the boxing club to sort it out; apart from that, you could get away with anything.

'Cheers,' James said, cracking the can open.

April pulled up a chair next to James and they kissed. He felt awkward doing it with Kerry sitting a few metres away.

The next couple of hours passed in a blur. Kids came and went. Everyone was taking the mickey out of everyone else and drinking. Kerry and Dinesh only took sips, James and April had a couple of beers, while Nicole and Junior got completely trashed. One time, Nicole got the giggles so badly she fell off her chair.

*

The youth club closed at ten and James thought he'd better have a slash before they headed home. He was in a grand mood as he drifted downstairs to the foul-smelling basement toilets.

'You forgive me, don't you?'

James turned around and realised Junior was peeing beside him.

'For the old man?' Junior slurred. 'Nicole's got a thing about old people. We got carried away.'

'Course I forgive you,' James said. 'Don't sweat it.'

'I've got something for you,' Junior said. 'Come outside.'

They went into the space at the bottom of the stairs between the boys' and girls' toilets. Junior pulled a pillbox out of his jeans and popped off the lid. There was a stubby metal straw inside and a thin layer of white powder in the bottom.

'How long have you been snorting coke for?' James gasped.

'Since the cinema.'

'No wonder you two have been acting like nutters,' James said. He knew that coke gave you a high, but he'd never realised that it could make you act totally crazy.

'Give it a whirl,' Junior said.

James had packets of cocaine in his locker at school and

under his bed at home. He'd been tempted a couple of times, but it had never seemed quite this easy: a few centimetres from his face with a mate urging him to test it out.

'I'm not sure I want to get into that stuff,' James said.

'You tart,' Junior laughed. 'What harm's one snort gonna do?'

Nicole came out of the girls' toilet and looked at James.

'The birthday boy doesn't want any,' Junior giggled.

'Good,' Nicole said. 'More for me.'

She shoved the metal straw up her nostril and vacuumed up half the coke left in the pot. Her head shot backwards and she wiped a tear off her cheek.

'You've *got* to, James,' Nicole rasped, sounding like she was pinching her nose.

'It's not gonna blow your mind or nothing,' Junior said. 'It just makes the world seem like a nicer place.'

'Except inside your nose,' Nicole giggled. 'That goes like a chunk of rubber.'

James looked into the dish. There was only a tiny bit left and he was curious to try it, just once. Nicole gave him the straw. James pushed it up his nose and leaned towards the white powder.

'Come on, you guys,' Kelvin shouted. 'I'm locking up.'

He was at the top of the stairs. Junior pulled the coke out of sight before James had time to sniff. James spun around, hiding the metal straw in his hand.

'Give us a second,' Junior shouted.

'*Now*,' Kelvin shouted. 'Don't mess me about.'

The three of them staggered upstairs, through the

youth club and on to the pavement out front. The nights were starting to turn cold. Kerry, April and a big bunch of other kids were standing around shivering. James found April.

'You want to come round to our house?' James asked. 'It's only ten minutes' walk.'

April shook her head. 'Kelvin's giving me, Junior and Dinesh a lift home. I'll have to smuggle Junior in round the back. If our dad sees him in that state, he'll go bonkers.'

'OK,' James said, leaning forward and giving April a kiss. 'I'll speak to you tomorrow. Maybe we can go to the Reeve Centre or something.'

'Cool,' April smiled. 'It looks like you've got your own set of problems over there.'

James turned around in time to see Nicole hurl up in the gutter.

*

Kerry went in first and checked the coast was clear. Ewart and Zara had gone up to bed early, which was a relief. James and Kyle dragged Nicole into the kitchen and draped her over a dining chair.

'I'm gonna die,' Nicole sobbed, resting her elbows on the dining table. 'I feel so ill.'

Kerry ran her a glass of water. 'Drink that,' she said. 'Alcohol dehydrates you. The water will stop you getting a hangover.'

James hadn't drunk anywhere near as much as Nicole, but he decided a drop of water would do no harm and ran a glass for himself.

'I think I'm gonna be sick again,' Nicole moaned.

Kyle got one of the buckets from under the sink and stood it on the table. Nicole leaned into it, her sobs echoing into the plastic.

'Get us a tissue,' she groaned. 'My nose is running.'

James ripped off a square of kitchen towel and handed it over. When Nicole took the bucket away from her face, they all saw her nose was bleeding.

'Oh, my god,' Kerry gasped. 'I think we should wake Zara up.'

'No,' Nicole begged. 'I'll get into trouble. Take me to bed and I'll sleep it off.'

Kerry grabbed the roll of kitchen towel and the bucket and took them upstairs to the girls' bedroom. James and Kyle each wrapped one of Nicole's arms around their back, picked her off the chair and helped her stumble along the hallway.

'Nicole,' Kyle said firmly. 'We're at the bottom of the stairs. Lift up your legs.'

Nicole's head slumped forward and her legs gave way. A fresh wave of blood began streaking out of her nose.

'*Oh, Jesus,*' Kyle said desperately. 'Put her down.'

Kerry was coming back down the stairs to help them. When she saw Nicole's limp body on the hallway carpet, she spun around and burst into Ewart and Zara's room. Ewart raced downstairs in his boxers. Kyle was taking Nicole's pulse.

'Her heartbeat's all over the place,' Kyle said.

'Shall I call 999?' James asked.

'There's no point hanging around for an ambulance,' Ewart said. 'I'll drive her.'

Zara was running downstairs in her dressing-gown, carrying clothes and trainers for Ewart. Ewart stepped into the clothes before scooping Nicole off the floor. Out on the driveway, Kyle had opened up the people carrier.

'She's taken some cocaine,' James blurted.

He didn't want to grass, but it might save her life if the doctors knew what was in her system.

'Christ almighty,' Ewart shouted, as Kyle helped him lay Nicole across the back seat. 'That's all we need.'

Ewart climbed into the driver's seat and slammed the door so hard James thought the glass might break. When the car was out of sight, James closed the front door and turned around to face Kerry and Zara, who were both in tears.

'I hope she's OK,' Kerry sniffed.

'You're absolutely sure she took cocaine?' Zara asked.

James nodded, feeling a lump forming in his throat. 'I saw it.'

'Why didn't you stop her?' Kerry asked angrily.

'I tried to,' James lied. 'She wouldn't listen to me.'

'What about you, James?' Zara asked. 'Did you take any?'

'No way,' James said. 'I'd never go near it.'

'That's a relief,' Zara said. 'If they find traces of cocaine in Nicole's urine, they'll expel her from CHERUB.'

'Is that for certain?' James asked.

'You both know the rules,' Zara said. 'There's zero tolerance for class A drugs. We even put the reminder at the bottom of the mission briefing where you guys signed your names, in case you considered anything silly.'

'Are you two going up to bed?' Kerry asked anxiously.

'I suppose,' Zara said. 'Unless you want a drink or something first.'

'I don't think I'll sleep,' Kerry said. 'I don't want to be on my own wondering what's happening with Nicole.'

Zara pulled Kerry into her chest and gave her a hug. 'I'll sit up with you for a while,' she said. 'Don't worry.'

James thought about Nicole. Imagining her being wheeled into hospital and having tubes pushed down her throat and needles under her skin. He wondered what it would be like to go into a coma and realised he didn't feel like being on his own either.

*

James and Kerry got their duvets and sat together in the living-room with their feet on the coffee table. It was a weird feeling; anxious for news, being exhausted but not able to sleep. The hands on the clock seemed to be frozen.

Zara had to go upstairs to sort out Joshua when he started bawling.

'Did you really snort any coke?' Kerry whispered.

'No,' James said indignantly. 'I already told you.'

'In front of Zara,' Kerry said. 'What about just between you and me?'

'I saw them doing it and got offered a snort, but I said no.'

'I'm glad,' Kerry smiled. 'I'd have bet my life savings that if something as dumb as that was going down on your birthday, you'd be into it.'

'I'm not a complete moron, you know,' James said.

Kerry's mobile started ringing. James had changed her ring tone to the national anthem for a joke while she was in the toilet at the youth centre, but that didn't matter now.

'Dinesh,' Kerry said, surprised. 'Are you crying? Calm down . . . Tell me what the matter is. What the hell are you doing at the police station?'

21. BRAINDEAD

Three hours earlier, Dinesh had hitched a lift home in Kelvin's car with April and Junior. He lived with his mum and dad in a flash house a few doors down from Keith Moore. Mr Singh was in his study, working on his laptop. Dinesh wasn't surprised to find him there, even though it was past eleven.

'Good time at the youth club?'

'Nothing very exciting,' Dinesh said. 'Did Mum ring up?'

'She asked me to make sure you washed behind your ears and changed your underpants.'

'Very funny, Dad,' Dinesh said, grinning. 'I'm off to bed. Don't sit up working all night.'

Dinesh had brushed his teeth and was getting into bed when he heard a saloon car pull on to the driveway. Sometimes cars used the drive to turn around, but this one stopped and Dinesh watched two doors open. Another car stopped behind. It was white, with blue lights and cop markings on the roof.

'Dad,' Dinesh shouted.

The two cops from the first car were in plain clothes. The

three out of the second wore uniform and carried rifles. Two cops split off and jogged around the house, covering the back exit. Dinesh quickly slid on his tracksuit bottoms and ran on to the landing.

'Dad,' Dinesh shouted again, nervously. 'The police are outside.'

The front door exploded into the hallway. Police never ring the doorbell when it's a drug bust, because it gives the suspect a chance to destroy evidence. Dinesh had never seen a gun outside of a museum before. Now two were aimed at his head.

'On the floor,' the cop barked. 'Hands where I can see 'em.'

They ran up the stairs towards Dinesh, who was trying to stop himself shaking.

'Don't be frightened, son,' the cop said. 'Where's your old man?'

Mr Singh opened the door of his study. The guns swung towards him.

'Hands in the air.'

One of the plain-clothes cops bounded up the stairs. He pushed Mr Singh against the wall and locked on handcuffs.

'You have the right to remain silent. Anything you do say can be taken down and used in evidence against you . . .'

The armed cop looked down at Dinesh.

'Who else is home?'

'Nobody,' Dinesh said.

'Where's your mum?'

'Barcelona. She's back tomorrow.'

'How old are you?'

'Twelve.'

'We can't leave you here on your own,' the cop said. 'You'll have to come with us.'

*

A police car pulled up on the driveway. Dinesh looked nervous when Zara opened the door.

'You don't mind me staying, do you?' Dinesh asked. 'They asked me to think of somewhere I could go until Mum gets home. Kerry was the first person I thought of.'

'Don't worry,' Zara said, putting her hand on Dinesh's shoulder. 'There are so many kids coming in and out of this house, one more won't make any difference.'

The cop gave Zara a custody form to sign, while Dinesh wandered into the living-room. Kerry stood up and gave him a hug.

'I'm so sorry about your dad,' Kerry said.

'I told you he was a crook,' Dinesh said angrily. 'It was bound to happen sooner or later.' He looked at the duvets and pillows scattered around the living-room.

'We couldn't sleep,' Kerry explained. 'They had to take Nicole to the hospital.'

'Is it serious?'

'Kyle called from the hospital. They gave her an adrenalin shot to bring her round. Then they pumped her stomach.'

'I saw that on TV once,' Dinesh said. 'It's so nasty. They force a rubber tube down your throat and right down into your stomach.'

'They'll keep her in under observation for a few hours,' James said. 'But they reckon she'll be OK.'

Dinesh managed a smile. 'I wouldn't want to be in her shoes when she gets home.'

It was gone 3 a.m. when a cab dropped Kyle home from the hospital. Zara told them all to go upstairs and try to get some rest. Dinesh slept on Nicole's bed.

*

While the mission was going smoothly, Ewart had been acting calm, but when he shook James awake at eleven o'clock that Saturday morning, he looked rabid.

'In the bathroom, *now*,' Ewart barked.

'Uh?' James said, still half-asleep.

Ewart grabbed James by his wrist and practically dislocated his shoulder as he yanked him out of bed. He shoved James towards the bathroom, bolted the door and bundled him up to the wall.

'We've got to keep the noise down while Dinesh is in the house,' Ewart whispered. 'But you better start giving me straight answers about last night, or I'm gonna make you sorry.'

'I haven't done anything,' James said.

'So what's *this* then?' Ewart asked, producing the metal straw that had come out of Junior's cocaine. There were still specks of white powder stuck on one end.

'It's not mine,' James said.

'Liar,' Ewart snarled. 'I was checking inside the pockets before I put the washing on. It was in your jeans.'

James realised he must have pocketed it when Kelvin had surprised them.

'I swear I never took coke,' James said frantically. 'That belongs to Junior. I must have picked it up by mistake.'

Ewart opened the medicine cabinet and took out a plastic sample bottle.

'We'll see, won't we? I got three of these at the hospital last night,' Ewart said. 'Pee in that. I'm gonna have your, Kyle's and Kerry's urine samples tested and if there's cocaine in there, you'll be out on your arse with Nicole.'

James was pleased to see the sample bottle. The test would clear up any argument.

'Give it here,' he said, smirking confidently. 'How much do you want to bet that I'm clean? Fifty quid, a hundred?'

'Cut the smart mouth,' Ewart said. 'And piss.'

James angrily snatched the bottle off Ewart, flipped up the plastic lid and stood over the toilet. He was usually busting when he woke up, but he couldn't go with Ewart standing behind him.

'Can't you wait outside?' James asked.

'You might tamper with it,' Ewart said. 'Try thinking about waterfalls or something.'

When he'd finished, James handed the bottle to Ewart.

'Any money you like,' he said cockily.

His air of confidence had taken the edge off Ewart's anger. 'Go back to your room and tell Kyle to get over here.'

After Kyle had gone, James slumped on his bed feeling pleased with himself. Ewart would look an idiot when the drug test came back. Then he had a horrible thought: if Kelvin had called down the stairs a couple of seconds later . . .

James relived the drunken instant when the dish of white powder was just centimetres from his face. He felt sick when he realised how close he'd come to snorting a dangerous drug – and getting himself booted out of CHERUB.

22. NICOLE

Junior called James on his mobile.

'Dude.'

'You sound happy,' James said. 'What's up?'

'It's pandemonium here,' Junior said. 'I've got a killer hangover and the pigs arrested over eighty KMG people last night. My dad thinks he's about to get busted. He keeps running up to the curtain every time a bird flies past the window.'

'Mr Singh got nabbed,' James said. 'Dinesh spent the night here. Ewart's taken him to the airport to meet his mum.'

'They nicked Uncle George and Uncle Pete,' Junior said. 'They're not my real uncles, but they've been working for Dad since before I was born.'

'So how come you're in a good mood?' James asked.

'Nicole, of course,' Junior said. 'I had my hands *everywhere*. No offence, James, I know she's your sister and everything.'

'She's in hospital,' James said. 'The coke did her in.'

'No way,' Junior gasped. 'That explains why I couldn't get her mobile. Is she OK?'

'Yeah, but I wouldn't get your hopes up about seeing her any time soon. She overdosed once before,' James said, repeating Zara's latest cover story. 'Ewart and Zara are terrified that she's gonna end up killing herself. They've arranged for her to go back to a care home in London for a psychiatric assessment.'

'Oh, my god,' Junior blurted. 'I'm really sorry, man. I'd never have offered her coke if I'd known she had a problem. How long will she be gone for?'

'Um,' James said, scratching for an answer, 'it all depends on the assessment, I suppose . . . She might not be back at all . . . Anyway, I just heard Zara pulling up with a carload of shopping. She goes loopy if I don't help her unload.'

'I'll see you then,' Junior said. 'April asked if you fancied coming round for Sunday lunch?'

'Maybe,' James said. 'I don't know what's going on at the moment, with Nicole and that. I'll ring you later.'

James ended the call. There really was a car pulling up, but it was John Jones. Zara made tea while John Jones explained what had been going on over the last twenty-four hours.

'It all came out of the production facility you kids found at Thunderfoods. KMG imports and distributes cocaine through lots of different channels, but you guys uncovered the weakest link in the chain. Almost every gram was being packaged in the automated plant at Thunderfoods.

'We wired the place with cameras and bugs and watched everybody who came and went through binoculars. I've been on drug investigations where you go months without finding a good lead. Once we had Thunderfoods under surveillance, we started getting so much information we had to bring in extra staff to handle it.

'You'd get a couple of guys coming in to mix and package a few kilos of coke. It's boring work, so they'd usually start gossiping. They were off guard and the quality of the information was unbelievable. Names, dates, phone numbers, flight numbers. *What are you doing next week? Where's your next shipment coming in? What deal is old so-and-so working on at the moment?*

'We've made a hundred arrests already, but we're not even scratching the surface. We're sending information to police stations all over the country and another two or three hundred guys are gonna get pulled over the next few days. By the time we're done, KMG will be lucky if it can sell a bag of sweets in a school playground.'

'I just spoke to Junior,' James said. 'Keith Moore still hasn't been arrested.'

'That's politics,' John said. 'Us MI5 guys wanted to keep the undercover work going until we had enough evidence to get Keith, but the police wouldn't hold out. They've got hundreds of people working on Operation Snort. Not just police officers, but the administration and back-up staff that go with them. It's costing over a million pounds a month and there was talk of shutting it down if they didn't start getting results.'

'So Keith Moore might get off?' Kerry asked.

John smiled uneasily. 'I hope not, Kerry. I'd say out of the top ten people in KMG, we've got enough evidence to put eight in prison. We're gonna try and flip a couple of those guys. We're offering total immunity from prosecution. Given a choice between twenty years in prison and walking home to your wife and kids, we reckon a few people might start tattling on Keith Moore.'

'So is there anything special we should be looking out for?' Kyle asked.

'I'd be amazed if you kids make another breakthrough to match the one you've made already,' John said. 'Just keep in with the bad guys and we'll see if anything else turns up.'

'Actually, kids,' Zara said, 'I had to phone Mac and explain what happened with Nicole. He seems to think we've achieved most of what we set out to do. He's not impressed by what happened to Nicole and he wants the rest of you out of harm's way. I expect we'll be heading back to campus in a few weeks, so you might want to start dropping hints to your friends. Suggest that Ewart has gone for a job interview and there's a chance you might be moving back to London.'

John Jones did his routine of shaking everyone's hands before he left.

'Of course,' he said, holding on to Kerry's hand after he'd shaken it, 'this young lady is the biggest hero of the lot.'

Kerry still had an ear-to-ear grin five minutes after John Jones had driven away. James got sick of looking at it and chucked Joshua's furry cement mixer at her head. Kerry chucked it back and they ended up chasing each other around the dining table, along the hallway and into the living-room.

'I'm a hero,' Kerry sang as she ran. 'Hero, hero, hero. Hero, hero, hero.'

James chucked a couple of sofa cushions at her. Kerry

bundled James on to the floor and pinned him down. She grabbed his ankle and started tickling the bottom of his foot. It was James' weakest spot. Within thirty seconds she'd reduced him to a drooling wreck.

'OK,' James gasped. 'You're a hero. You're a hero.'

Kerry stood up sharply and straightened her expression. Ewart and Nicole stood in the doorway, stone-faced. James got off the floor and wiped his lips on his sleeve.

'They tested your samples at the hospital,' Ewart said. 'You two are both clean for drugs, though they found higher levels of alcohol than I'd like to have seen, especially you, James. I know you're allowed to drink if you're in a situation where the kids around you are drinking, but that's not a licence to go crazy.'

'So you're glad you didn't bet me fifty quid?' James grinned.

Ewart gave James a vicious look. He definitely wasn't in the mood for joking.

'Go help Nicole pack and say your goodbyes,' Ewart said. 'I'm driving her back to campus in half an hour. Where's Kyle?'

'He's in the kitchen,' Kerry said.

'Right,' Ewart said angrily. 'Let's go and sort him out.'

Ewart stormed off and slammed the kitchen door.

'What's Kyle done?' Kerry asked, looking at Nicole.

'Don't know, don't care,' Nicole said bitterly. 'I suppose he failed his drug test.'

'No way,' James said.

'He wasn't doing coke with me and Junior,' Nicole said. 'But he's been going to loads of parties. Who knows what he gets up to?'

'Oh, my god,' Kerry said, cupping her hands over her face. 'This is so sad.'

Nicole started up the stairs. Kerry and James followed her.

'How do you feel?' Kerry asked.

'Not bad, except my stomach's agony and I feel like I've got an elephant standing on my head.'

'I'm really sorry about what happened to you,' James said, as they stepped into the girls' bedroom. 'It could have been any one of us.'

Nicole smiled, 'By the skin of your teeth, James.'

'How's that?' Kerry asked.

'He was ready to snort a line,' Nicole explained. 'But he got distracted.'

'You moron,' Kerry said, giving James a shove. 'You told me you tried to stop Nicole.'

'That's not what I said,' James squirmed.

'That's *exactly* what you said, James.'

'So, anyone who takes drugs is a moron?' Nicole asked. 'Eh, Kerry?'

'Nicole,' Kerry said angrily, 'if you'd passed out when you were in bed instead of on the stairs, nobody would have realised until morning. You might have *died*.'

'You're so sly, Kerry,' Nicole stormed. 'You and your prissy *I'm a good girl* act.'

'What do you want me to do?' Kerry asked. 'Congratulate you on getting expelled?'

'I don't care about any of this CHERUB stuff,' Nicole said defiantly. 'It's just a bunch of dumb kids getting hot under the collar over who wears what colour T-shirt and what stupid missions they've been on. Who cares about any of that anyway? They're gonna set me up with a foster family and a place in a nice public school. I can have a boyfriend, chill out and lead a normal life.'

'Don't you get it, dumbo?' Kerry said, tapping her head with her finger. 'You nearly died last night.'

'You don't know what you're talking about,' Nicole said, shoving Kerry backwards.

'Don't dare touch me,' Kerry said, rearing up on the balls of her feet. 'I could kick your butt so easily, but you're such a worthless tramp I can't even be bothered.'

Kerry spun around and stormed towards the door. James went to follow her, but Nicole called him back.

'Stay and help me pack, James.'

There was a desperate touch in Nicole's voice that made him turn back.

'Go ahead, help her,' Kerry said. 'You can make sure she doesn't rip off my stuff.'

Kerry banged the door and stomped downstairs to the living-room. Nicole dragged a sports bag from under her bed and started filling it.

'You know, James,' Nicole said, 'you're a good laugh, you don't belong at CHERUB either.'

'You've no idea how badly I need CHERUB,' James said. 'Sometimes all the work and training does my head in, but my life was a nightmare before I came here. I was in some crummy council home and I kept getting in trouble. If CHERUB hadn't picked me, I probably would have ended up in prison.'

'I'm glad I'm out of it,' Nicole said, zipping up her bag. 'As long as my new foster parents don't turn out to be old farts.'

'What is it you've got against old people?' James asked.

Nicole sat on the edge of her bed. 'You know my family died in a car crash?'

'I'd heard.'

'They were crossing a road in broad daylight. This stupid old fool sailed his car through a red light and smashed into them. They tested his eyes after the accident and it turned out he could barely see past the end of his own nose.'

'That's so bad,' James said. 'I'm sorry.'

'If it had been a young guy, they would at least have locked him away. But no, because it was some old fart, they took pity and let him off. My mum, my dad and my little brothers were killed and he totally got away with it. Then everyone goes around telling me I should have respect for old people. Well, they can shove that idea right up their arse.'

Ewart leaned in the door and looked at Nicole.

'Are you packed?'

'Just finishing off,' Nicole said.

'OK,' Ewart said. 'I'm going to the toilet. I'll see you at the bottom of the stairs in five minutes.'

'Wish me luck?' Nicole asked, looking at James.

'Sure,' James said, wrapping his arms around her and giving her a squeeze. She had a tear rolling down her cheek.

James carried one of Nicole's bags out to the people carrier. Kerry stood in the living-room doorway with folded arms and a frosty expression. James thought it was a shame Kerry and Nicole had fallen out. They'd got on well up to now.

Zara came out from the kitchen, gave Nicole a hug and

wished her good luck with whatever life she chose to lead. When the car started pulling off the driveway, Kerry had a change of heart and ran on to the doorstep. She stood between James and Zara and waved Nicole off.

'I hope she sorts herself out,' Kerry said.

'We'll set her up with a good family,' Zara said. 'I think she'll be better off in the long run. Not everyone is cut out to be a cherub.'

'Oh,' James said, suddenly remembering, 'what happened with Kyle?'

'It's his business,' Zara said. 'It's up to him whether he wants you guys to know or not.'

James and Kerry found Kyle face down on his bunk, having a sulk.

'Why was Ewart having a go at you?' James asked.

'They found traces of cannabis in my urine sample,' Kyle said. 'Almost every drug you could name passes through your body in day or so. Unfortunately for me, cannabis lingers in your system for up to three weeks.'

'But you *did* take some?' Kerry said, sounding outraged.

'It's not some massive deal, Kerry,' Kyle said defensively. 'I had a few puffs of a joint that was going around at some kid's house two Saturdays ago.'

'So how come you're not expelled?' Kerry asked.

'Cannabis is a class C drug,' Kyle explained. 'I would have been sent back to campus, but they could hardly send me and Nicole away on the same day without it looking suspicious.'

'So you're gonna get your botty spanked when we go back to campus?' James grinned.

'That's how it looks,' Kyle said. 'Probably a few weeks scrubbing floors, followed by a few months suspended from missions.'

23. LUCK

Sunday morning, James was in the living-room on his Playstation. Ewart came in and pushed his feet off the coffee table.

'You just gonna sit around doing nothing all day?' he asked.

'That was plan A,' James grinned. He'd missed a lot of sleep over the last couple of weeks. It was nice to bum around indoors for a change.

'What about deliveries?' Ewart asked.

'Kelvin called me,' James said, reluctantly pausing his game. 'The nice lady who calls me with my deliveries has been busted. Not that it matters, because there aren't any customers. Everyone's heard about the arrests and they're scared that if they ring up for a drug delivery, they'll have PC Plod turning up on their doorstep rather than the likes of me.'

'Does Kelvin think KMG is ruined?'

'He says it'll take at least a month to get new supplies of coke and set up distribution. Even then, customers will be wary. Other gangs will move in and snatch a lot of the business, but Kelvin thinks KMG has the clout to get back on top of things, provided Keith Moore doesn't get nicked.'

'What about Junior and April? Have you heard from them?'

'I've spoken to both of them. I got invited to lunch, but I can't be arsed.'

Ewart sounded slightly annoyed. 'Why aren't you going?'

'What's the point?' James shrugged. 'The mission's as good as over. We'll all be back at campus in a week or two.'

'James, the mission carries on either until Keith Moore is caught, or we officially get told to come home. You're our closest link to the Moore kids now Nicole is gone. I'd be interested to know what Keith is up to at the moment.'

James reached forward and switched off the Playstation, looking thoroughly put-out.

'Fine,' he huffed. 'I'll call Junior and re-invite myself.'

*

Ewart left James at the Moore house, then drove on a few hundred metres to drop Kerry at Dinesh's.

James thought there might be a bad atmosphere, but when Keith opened the door he was in swimming shorts with a big grin on his face. The house was huge and even though they had a cleaner, you could tell four kids lived there the second you walked through the door. There were trainers and cushions chucked everywhere, dirty cups and plates. James thought it was cool. He hated it when you go round some kid's house and the mother goes hysterical when you put your cup down in the wrong place.

'Come in,' Keith said, dripping over the floor tiles. 'April and Junior are swimming.'

'I never realised you'd be in the pool.'

'Don't worry. Go up to Junior's room. He's got about ten pairs of swimming shorts in his middle drawer.'

'Cheers,' James said.

Junior had a massive room with a big screen TV and video, a wardrobe full of decent clothes and a gumball machine. It wasn't a bad spread for a kid who claimed to be hard done by.

James stripped off and came down in a pair of orange shorts with seahorses on. The indoor pool was about fifteen metres long, with palms and flowerbeds along one side. Ringo and Keith were swimming laps. April and Junior were at the far end in a whirlpool tub. James stepped into the steaming water, gave April a kiss and sat beside her. She looked fit in her swimming costume.

Once he was in the tub, James was glad Ewart had made him get out of the house. The warm jets of water made him feel relaxed and having April cuddled up close was a bonus. He took his hand off her back when Keith wandered up.

'I'm ordering takeaway,' Keith said, raising his voice above the bubbling water. 'What do you guys want?'

'Indian,' April said.

'Pizza,' Junior said.

Keith looked at James. 'Deadlock. The guest gets the casting vote.'

James didn't like Indian much, but April had a cute grin on her face and she started sliding her toes up his leg.

'Indian,' he said.

'Traitor,' Junior said, slicing his hand through the water and giving James a soaking.

James, Junior and April had a splashing battle, then towelled off and put on robes before the food arrived. Ringo and Keith sat on the sofa while James, April and Junior arranged themselves on cushions around the coffee table with all the boxes of food on it.

Keith found the remote between two sofa cushions and switched the TV hanging on the wall to News 24. They all concentrated on stuffing their faces until the TV cut to a policeman. The title up on screen said: *Superintendent Carlisle, Operation Snort.* He started speaking to the camera.

'We've made over one hundred and fifty arrests in the last three days and believe we have taken a major step against illegal drugs in this country . . .'

A lump of prawn vindaloo smacked Superintendent Carlisle in the forehead and began sliding down the screen.

'. . . This represents a giant stride forward in our war against illegal drugs in the UK . . .'

'Try and catch me, Superintendent,' Keith shouted, chucking another prawn.

Keith's kids joined in, hurling lumps of curry and handfuls of rice until the screen was a blurry mess. Everyone laughed, but it had a hollow ring, like they were really scared by the arrests.

Junior turned around and looked at his dad. 'Did you ask James about Miami?'

'No,' Keith said.

'Miami?' James asked.

'I usually take the boys to my place in Miami for half-term,' Keith explained. 'But Ringo says he's got a lot of homework and doesn't want to go this year.'

'He's having a party,' April explained. 'I expect we'll come home and find this house razed to the ground.'

'Who says I'm having a party?' Ringo said defensively.

'It'll be boring without Ringo,' Junior said. 'And the plane ticket's paid for, so Dad suggested I take a mate.'

'Cool,' James said, bursting into a grin. 'I'll have to check with my parents, but it should be OK. Are you going, April?'

'No,' April said. 'Me and Erin are skiing with our mum.'

'It's a family tradition,' Keith explained. 'We all used to go on holiday together, but I'd always be strangling my wife, Junior and April usually end up rolling around the floor if they're together for more than a few hours, and Erin . . .'

'We think the real Erin was abducted at birth and replaced by an alien from Neptune,' Junior explained.

'I've been here about ten times and I've still never met Erin,' James said.

Keith shook his head and smiled. 'That girl may be my daughter, but I haven't got a clue what goes on inside that little head of hers.'

'You'll love Miami,' Junior said. 'It's boiling hot and our house is right on the beach. You can crawl out of bed, run down the beach and be in the sea within thirty seconds.'

'I'll ring Zara up now,' James said.

'Is Kyle home?' Ringo asked.

'Probably,' James said. 'Did you want a word with him?'

Ringo gave his dad a mischievous grin as he spoke. 'Just tell Kyle there's a big party going down here, Friday after next.'

Keith burst out laughing. James thought Keith was a really cool dad, especially considering the stress he was under.

'You can have your party,' Keith said. 'But Kelvin and a couple of other guys from the boxing club are gonna chaperone it, in case any of your pals decide to start peeing on the carpets or stubbing out ciggies on my Egyptian rug.'

'What?' Ringo gasped. 'I don't want some crew of muscle-heads bossing my mates around. I'll be totally embarrassed.'

'Don't worry,' Keith said. 'I'll tell them to keep a low profile.'

James gave Zara a call. She was surprised, but she said it was OK to travel.

*

It was already turning dark when James got home. He recognised John Jones' Toyota on the driveway. He was in the living-room, with Zara, Ewart, Kerry and Kyle.

'What's this in aid of?' James asked.

John Jones explained. 'As soon as Zara heard about your little holiday, she contacted me and I rushed over here.'

'Why is me going on holiday such a big deal?' James asked.

'Miami is the centre of the world drug trade,' John explained. 'It's no coincidence that Keith Moore has a home there. The saying goes: *If you want a gram of cocaine, stand on any street corner. If you want a ton of cocaine, stand on any street corner in Miami.*

'There are twenty smaller gangs snapping at the heels of KMG. Keith has to get his hands on fresh supplies of cocaine and get KMG working again. A lot of his top people have been arrested and he won't know who he can trust, so he'll be brokering the deal himself.'

'So what can I do?' James asked.

'We know KMG has a long-standing relationship with a Peruvian drug cartel called Lambayeke,' John explained. 'To pay Lambayeke, Keith will have to transfer millions from his overseas bank accounts. If we can find out what bank and country Keith's money is coming from, we'll have a lead that could help us unravel the whole financial structure of KMG and maybe even Lambayeke as well.

'Keith can't keep every detail of his business in his head. He'll be going to Miami carrying some piece of information that links him to his money. It might be a bank account number, or the phone number of a bank, or a file on the hard drive of his laptop. Whatever it is, you're going to be in Keith Moore's house for seven days. You're never going to get a better opportunity to grab information than that.'

James smiled. 'So much for bumming around on the beach all day.'

'As soon as this meeting is over, I'm driving you back to campus for two days' emergency training,' Ewart said. 'There's a lot you need to learn, but we don't want you away from the Moore family for more than a few days.'

'What excuse will we use for me not being at school?'

'We'll tell everyone you were planning to visit your aunt and cousin Lauren during half-term, but we brought it forward because of your trip to Miami.'

24. FACTS

James slept better than he had for ages. His bed in Luton was cramped and had springs that jammed in your back; plus on campus there was no Kyle squirming in the top bunk and no 300-seater jets whizzing overhead. The plumbing worked better as well. James put on a Metallica CD and rocked out in his shower, without having to worry about getting scalded every time someone touched the tap in the kitchen.

When he was clean, he put on CHERUB uniform. The rooms and corridors in the main building reminded James of a hotel. As he waited for the lift down to the dining-room, he reflected that the only thing lacking was room service.

He loaded up a plate with bacon and hash brown and ate bits with his fingers while one of the staff cooked him a mushroom omelette. Most kids had gone off to first lesson, but Amy was sitting at a table dipping a finger of toast into a soft-boiled egg.

'You're wearing a white T-shirt,' James said, taken aback. You got the white shirt when you retired as a cherub.

'My undercover days are over,' Amy said.

James looked sad. 'But . . .'

'I'm seventeen, James,' Amy said. 'I took my A-levels in the summer. I'm working here as an assistant dogsbody to earn some cash, then I'm off to see the world before I start university in January.'

'Where are you going?'

'Cairns, in Australia. My big brother lives there.'

'That's the other side of the world,' James said miserably. 'I'll probably never see you again.'

'You've only got to hop on an aeroplane. My brother set up a diving school when he finished university. He took me up to the Great Barrier Reef a couple of weeks ago. It's so beautiful there.'

'So you're training me up for my Miami trip?' James asked.

Amy nodded. 'And you better behave. Now I'm staff, I'm allowed to dish out punishments.'

'Cool,' James grinned. 'Who have you nailed?'

'Only one kid,' Amy said. 'I was covering for one of the Judo instructors. This horrible little red-shirt boy kept giving me lip. He got a week cleaning up the changing room near the cross country trail.'

'It always gets really muddy in there,' James smiled. 'How old was this kid?'

'Eight,' Amy said. 'He started bawling his eyes out, but I didn't back down. After that, all I got from the other kids in the class was, *Yes Miss, No Miss, Of course Miss.*'

'So what have I got?' James asked.

Amy slid a heap of books across the table. They were all weighty. One was called *The Ultimate Hackers' Reference* and was over ten centimetres thick.

'It's gonna be a busy couple of days,' Amy said. 'I'll try and get you through techniques for hacking Keith's computer by this afternoon. Then we'll make a start on international banking.'

'What's that in aid of?' James asked.

'Suppose Keith was on the telephone and he mentioned a euro CD and an order party. Unless you know about banking, you wouldn't be able to tell whether Keith is on the phone to a Russian money laundering syndicate, or organising a disco.'

'Sounds like this is gonna be a real riot,' James said, flipping through one of the giant books as he tucked in a fork-load of bacon.

Amy ignored him. 'MI5 are preparing a dossier on the Lambayeke cartel. They'll e-mail it here and we'll work on that tomorrow morning. Tomorrow afternoon we'll finish up by testing out your hacking skills on real computers.'

*

James and Amy studied into the evening. You normally got at least two weeks on the background material for a mission, but everything had to be crammed into a couple of days. When it got to eight o'clock, Amy finally let him off.

'I feel like a swim,' she said. 'Coming?'

CHERUB had four pools. The learners' pool was the smallest and least attractive, but Amy had taught James to swim there the year before and they both wanted to go back for old times' sake. There was nobody else around. Most kids preferred using the main pool, which had diving boards and water slides.

They had a ten-lap race. James kept up with Amy until they made the last turn, when she blasted off into the distance. They got out and sat on the edge. James felt like his lungs were about to burst.

'You're getting stronger,' Amy grinned, not even short of breath. 'You might be able to give me a real race when you grow a bit bigger and shed the puppy fat.'

James' heart sank when he realised Amy had been toying with him.

'I'll definitely come and visit you in Australia when I'm older,' he said, circling his big toe through the water. 'If that's all right.'

Amy smiled. 'Of course it's all right. My brother has mates from his CHERUB days turning up all the time.'

'It's weird,' James said. 'I never even think about the kids I knew before I came to CHERUB, but I feel really close to the kids I know here.'

'It's a defined psychological phenomenon,' Amy said.

James looked mystified. 'You what?'

'All humans have a basic need to share their lives with someone,' Amy explained. 'Children with their parents, adults with their wives, husbands, or whoever. Because the kids at CHERUB have no parents, they make very strong bonds with each other. There's a big reunion on campus every couple of years. You'd be amazed how many cherubs end up marrying each other.'

'Sometimes it really gets on my nerves how smart-assed everyone at CHERUB is,' James grinned. 'I mean, how come you know stuff like that?'

'I'm doing psychology at university,' Amy said. 'They gave

us a list of books to read before the course starts. Besides, James, you're not exactly dumb yourself. CHERUB wouldn't even sniff at a kid who wasn't way above average.'

'When I'm at a normal school, I'm always one of the cleverest,' James said. 'But I'm just kind of ordinary here.'

'So anyway,' Amy said. 'When you arrived at CHERUB a few months after your mum died, it was natural that you formed a strong attachment to any girl who played a big part in your life.'

'Like you, because you were teaching me to swim.'

Amy nodded. 'And Kerry, because she was your partner in basic training. Have you asked her out yet?'

'God! Don't you start,' James moaned. 'It's bad enough Kyle always going on about it.'

'But you and Kerry are always *so* sweet together. I love the way you two pick at one another like some old married couple.'

James didn't want to hear it. He slipped off the side of the pool and began swimming towards the deep end.

*

The dossier that arrived from MI5 on the Lambayeke cartel ran to over three hundred pages, though a lot of it was photos and maps. James and Amy spent Tuesday morning in one of the mission preparation rooms, skimming through the chapters and marking the most relevant stuff with highlighter pens. James could take the books on computer-hacking back to Luton for study, but the Lambayeke dossier wasn't allowed off campus.

After they'd worked through the dossier, Amy got five laptop PCs out of a storage room and lined them up on a desk. She set an ancient wind-up timing clock to count down from fifteen minutes.

'Each one of these PCs has a list of stolen credit card numbers hidden on the hard drive,' Amy explained. 'You've got to hack each one inside the time limit, without leaving any footprints behind.'

'Which one first?' James asked.

'Doesn't matter,' Amy said, leaning over and starting the timer. 'Go.'

James had a mini heart attack before grabbing a laptop, flipping up the screen and tapping a couple of keys.

'What do I do?' he said to himself, drumming his hands on the desk in front of him.

'Turning it on would be a good start,' Amy smirked. 'Don't forget to read the BIOS screen before Windows starts.'

James read the figures aloud. 'Two-fifty-six meg of memory. Windows ME. The hard drive isn't partitioned. If it's ME it uses a FAT32 file system, so if I press F8 and enter DOS, I'll be able to open any file, even if it's password-protected.'

James hunted around the desk for a floppy disk. He waved it at Amy.

'This is the disk with the utility on that lists every file on the PC, isn't it?'

Amy nodded. 'I'm not supposed to be helping you.'

James looked around the side of the PC for somewhere to slot the floppy disk.

'Oh . . . This bloody thing doesn't have a floppy drive. Is there an external drive for this somewhere?'

Amy shook her head.

'Well, what do I do?'

Amy shrugged and looked at the timer. 'You've got twelve minutes left to figure it out.'

James fiddled hopelessly with the laptop for another three minutes. He could happily have chucked the clicking timer out the window.

'Nine minutes left.'

'Tell us, Amy,' James begged. 'I'm totally stuck. How can I get this floppy running?'

'The computer has a network interface on the back,' Amy said. 'You could wire it up to one of the other laptops that has a floppy drive. Then you could go into the network properties on the second laptop and change it to a networkable floppy drive. Then the floppy drive on the second PC will work as if it's attached to the first one.'

'I'm never gonna get all that done in nine minutes,' James gasped.

'You might if you hurried. But why not try something much simpler?'

'Like what?' James asked.

'What's the first thing I taught you about computer hacking? The first golden rule?'

'The weakest link is the human link,' James said.

Amy nodded. 'You're trying to find a back door into the operating system before you've tried the front door. Never assume the information you're looking for is encrypted or hidden. For all you know, you can open the document you want just by clicking on it.'

'You're telling me I've just wasted six minutes?'

'Nearer to seven now,' Amy said, smirking.

James switched off the computer and started from scratch.

The computer only had a few programs installed and the documents were all in one folder. James opened up the list and spotted one called *Card Numbers*. He double-clicked the mouse to open the file. A single line of text popped up on the screen: *You didn't think it was going to be that easy, did you?*

James was in too much of a state to see the funny side. He looked at the long list of documents on the screen in front of him. There wasn't time to open every one, but James realised he was looking for a list of numbers, which meant the file would be fairly small. He changed the view, so the computer showed him the size and format of each file. He skipped down the list, opening any text file that looked likely to be the list of numbers.

'Three minutes left,' Amy said. 'Better get your skates on, cowboy.'

James started opening up files as fast as he could. A few demanded a password before they'd open. James dragged these into a separate folder. When he ran out of documents that didn't need a password, he decided to try and guess the password of the encrypted ones.

A password can be any combination of letters and numbers, but James knew the second golden rule of computer hacking: *Over 75% of passwords are easily guessed.* He started working down the list of the most commonly used passwords that Amy had made him memorise the day before. Things like *password*, *open* and *security*.

After these failed, James tried to find personal details about the man who owned the laptop. He remembered that one of the documents he'd opened had been a letter to a school. He clicked on the file and skimmed through it. It was signed off by a man called Julian Stipe and mentioned the names of his three children. James tried the name *Julian* in the password box, then *Stipe*. Then *Julian Stipe* with and without a space in between.

'Ninety seconds,' Amy said.

He started trying the names of Mr Stipe's kids and hit the jackpot when he typed *Jennifer*. The document opened, only it wasn't the credit card numbers. The other protected documents opened with the same password and James got a massive rush when a sheet of sixteen-digit credit card numbers popped up on screen.

'Bingo,' James shouted.

'Fifteen seconds,' Amy said.

'I've got them,' James said. 'What are you on about?'

'Time's up,' Amy said. 'Better luck next time.'

'But I got them,' James said tetchily.

'I know,' Amy said. 'But you weren't supposed to leave any traces behind. It was a good idea to move the password-protected documents, but you should have put them all back where they belonged and deleted the new folder you created . . . Ready for the next one?'

'My head's spinning,' James said. 'Can't I have five minutes' break?'

Amy gave him an evil grin. 'You don't deserve a break after that sorry performance.'

She tapped the reset button on top of the clock, then flipped up the lever to set it ticking.

25. DIGGING

James made such a hash of the laptop-hacking test, Amy kept him upstairs in the mission preparation room until gone nine o'clock for extra tuition. He got ratty with her as his brain stubbornly refused to accept any more information.

When they got downstairs to the dining hall, the kitchen had finished serving. There was a fridge stocked up with sandwiches and microwave meals, but James had been looking forward to a proper dinner before his return to Luton and Zara's dodgy cooking.

James slammed the door of his bedroom. He was in a stinking mood. He packed his hacking textbooks and some odd bits in a backpack, then stripped to his boxers and went to take a pee before getting in bed. There was a muggy smell as he got near his bathroom, like the smell trainers get after a couple of hours on a muddy football field. It spooked him a bit. His imagination toyed with dead rats and leaking sewage as he leaned in warily and flipped on the light.

'What the hell . . .'

It was Lauren, propped on the toilet lid in her filthy

training kit. Her hair was cropped, she had a nasty scab down her face and all the cuts and bruises you'd expect after a month of basic training.

'What's going on?' James asked.

'I messed up,' Lauren said miserably. 'And I'm in so much trouble,'

She did a massive sniff, followed by a howling noise. Then she broke into five minutes of the most desperate bawling James had ever heard. He tried to give her a hug, but she wouldn't let him anywhere near her.

'Lauren,' James pleaded, 'I want to help you, but I can't until you tell me what's happened.'

Lauren seemed to see the sense in this and looked up from the floor.

'I . . . I . . . hit,' she sniffled, unable to control herself.

She stood up and draped her filthy arms around James' back. Her kit stank of mud and sweat.

'Calm down and sit on my bed,' James said gently, rubbing his sister's back.

He stepped backwards out of his bathroom, with Lauren flopped over him. It felt like dancing with a drunk. When he got near his bed, James peeled off Lauren's arms and she slumped on to the corner of his mattress.

'I hit him,' Lauren sniffed.

'Who?' James asked.

'Mr Large.'

James sat down beside her. 'I doubt he even felt it, Lauren. He's ten times your size.'

'He felt it all right,' Lauren said, salvaging a touch of composure.

James reached over to his bedside table and got her a tissue.

'Bethany injured her back yesterday morning,' Lauren explained. 'We were on the assault course. I was helping her as much as I could, but she was still slow. We finished the course miles behind the other kids. Mr Large started shouting his head off! *You two are worthless. You're not fit to be cherubs. You're not even fit to eat your own puke.* He got two spades and told us to start digging our own graves.'

It was a standard torture from Mr Large's repertoire. James and Kerry had got it a couple of times when they were in basic training. Large made you dig a massive hole, then fill it in. If he decided you weren't fast enough, he'd make you do it again.

'It's so tough,' Lauren said. 'I managed, but my back and shoulders were killing me. Bethany had a bad back to start with, so you can imagine how she was after two hours' digging. Large made me stand to attention at the edge of my grave until Bethany was finished. She kept slowing down, until she could barely drag her shovel. She begged Mr Large for a drink, so he got that massive fire hose and drenched her with it. By the time he'd finished, the water was up to her knees. She was crying and sobbing, covered from head to toe in really thick mud. Then he started kicking the mud she'd already dug up back into the hole.

'It was hitting her in the face and he screamed at the top of his voice: *You're too weak, little girl. You'll never make it. Why don't you quit?* It made me so angry. I was so sick of his stupid voice. I just got this urge to make him shut up. Then

547

I realised I still had my spade on the ground, right in front of me.'

'You didn't,' James gasped.

'When Mr Large turned around, I took this massive swing with it and whacked him behind the knees to knock him over. The first time only made him go wobbly. He started turning towards me and I was *so* scared. I thought he was gonna kill me, so I whacked him again. As he went down, he caught his head on a rock and got knocked out.'

James couldn't help smiling. 'You knocked out Mr Large! That's pure class.'

'It's not funny, James,' Lauren moped. 'I'm probably gonna get expelled. I thought I'd killed him for a minute. There was all blood coming out of his head. I was so afraid, I ran out of the training compound and didn't stop. I wanted to speak to you before anyone else, so I went to my room and phoned you. Zara said you were on campus, but I'm not allowed upstairs to mission preparation, so I waited for you in here.'

James pondered for a few moments.

'First things first,' he said. 'You better wash up, then we'll have to find Mac and sort this whole mess out.'

'Do you think they'll boot me out?' Lauren asked.

'I hope not,' James shrugged. 'But laying out a teacher . . . Let's just say it's not gonna go down too well.'

*

James found some of his smaller clothes for Lauren to wear after she got out of the shower. When they got down to the ground floor, Mac's office was locked. They asked the receptionist on the front desk.

'Mac usually heads home at about eight,' he explained. 'But one of the training instructors got injured and I think he's still over at the medical unit. I can ring his mobile if it's urgent.'

'I think you'd better,' James said.

The receptionist had a short conversation before putting down the receiver.

'Mac's coming over ASAP,' the receptionist said. 'I don't know what you two have done, but judging by the tone of his voice, I wouldn't want to switch shoes with you at the moment.'

A few minutes later, Mac rolled up the gravel driveway outside in one of the golf buggies the staff used to move around campus.

'This way,' he said stiffly, striding through reception.

He pulled a great bunch of keys out of his jacket and unlocked his door.

'Sit at the desk.'

James nervously sank into one of the leather chairs at the big oak desk. Lauren looked ready to start crying again.

'So, young lady,' Mac snapped. 'Would you be so kind as to tell me why my senior training instructor is lying in the medical unit with a serious concussion and eight stitches in the side of his head?'

'I'm really, really sorry,' Lauren grovelled. 'He made me so mad. Poor Bethany could hardly stand up and Mr Large wouldn't leave her alone.'

'If Bethany was injured, she should have quit,' Mac said. 'It wasn't your business to interfere.'

'So what are you gonna do to her?' James asked.

'I don't like expelling people,' Mac said. 'But if I don't expel a cherub for a serious assault on a member of staff, then what exactly *do* you get expelled for?'

'I know what Lauren did is wrong,' James said. 'But it's not like she walked into a classroom and belted a teacher for no reason. She was knackered and she was watching one of her friends get tortured by a raving lunatic. Everyone wants to take a swing at Mr Large at some point during basic training. It's just unlucky Lauren happened to have a spade nearby when the thought crossed her mind.'

'Hmm,' Mac said, covering a tiny smile with his fingers. 'I suppose there's an element of truth in that. If I did expel Lauren, though, we'd send her to a good school and set her up with a foster family near campus so that you could visit her at weekends.'

'I don't care if she only lives across the street,' James said. 'If she goes, I'm going with her. We were separated after our mum died and I don't ever want that again.'

'Recruiting cherubs is tricky,' Mac said, 'and I don't want to lose either of you two. But if I allow Lauren to stay, she'll have to accept a stiff punishment; otherwise, we'll have every kid on campus taking pot shots at the training staff.'

'Please let me stay,' Lauren begged. 'I'll do whatever you want and I'll be so good, I swear.'

'James,' Mac said. 'Do you have any thoughts on how we should make Lauren suffer?'

James looked uneasily at his sister.

'It's obviously got to be the worst punishment going,' he said. 'And it'll have to last the whole two and a bit months until she can restart basic training.'

'Agreed,' Mac nodded.

'What about cleaning toilets and changing rooms?' James said. 'Everyone always says that's really horrible.'

'Not hard enough,' Mac said, sweeping the idea away with his hand. 'Kids get toilets and changing rooms for swearing or skipping lessons. It's unpleasant, but all it boils down to is pushing a mop and squirting disinfectant.'

'Worse than toilets, then,' James said, trying to work out how Mac had twisted the situation around so that he was trying to think up some awful punishment for the person he was supposed to be helping out.

'Well,' Mac grinned. 'It just so happens, I did have an idea. There's a drainage problem in the wooded area on the far side of campus. The fields keep flooding because the ditches have gradually become blocked up with silt. I reckon someone Lauren's size would take a couple of months to clean them all out. She'll have to work hard, every day before and after school, plus all day on Saturdays and Sundays. How do you like the sound of that, Lauren?'

'I've got to be punished,' Lauren said, nodding meekly. 'If that's what you want, I'll do it.'

'Ditches it is,' Mac said, clapping his hands together. 'And I'll be putting you on final warning, Lauren. That means if you do one more thing wrong, you'll get kicked out. And I mean *every* tiny thing. Run in the corridor, you're out. Miss a homework assignment, you're out. Get to class late, you're out. For the next three months, you're walking on eggshells. Your behaviour must be immaculate. Is that understood?'

Lauren nodded.

'And there's one more condition,' Mac said. 'For you, James.'

'For me?' James gasped.

Mac nodded. 'You've talked me into giving Lauren a final chance. In return, I want something from you. If Lauren breaches her final warning, I want you to promise that you'll stay at CHERUB.'

James thought for a couple of seconds. 'But you'll put her with a family nearby so I can still see her when I'm not on missions?'

Mac nodded. 'That seems reasonable.'

'I suppose, then,' James said.

It seemed pretty convenient, the way Mac had found the perfect punishment for Lauren. James suspected Mac had worked everything out in advance. The expulsion threat was a ploy to make him and Lauren squirm.

'And of course, Lauren,' Mac grinned, 'once you've cleaned out those ditches and start your second attempt at basic training, I'm sure Mr Large will wreak his own special revenge.'

*

Lauren slept in James' room. The bed was a double, but the two of them still cuddled up in the middle. Lauren woke early and didn't seem too miserable, considering that the next five months of her life looked like being a living hell.

'Have you got a diary?' she asked.

'It's in my desk,' James said, still buried under his duvet.

Lauren used the diary to work out that it was one hundred and seventy-four days until she finished her punishment and basic training. She took a sheet of paper and began writing the numbers from 174 down to zero in her neatest writing.

James poked his head out of his covers. 'What are you doing, Lauren?'

'Making a countdown chart. For the next hundred and seventy-four days, I'm not gonna whinge or cry about anything. I'll take this piece of paper everywhere I go. However bad it gets, all I'm going to think about is how many hours it is until I can tick off the next number. In one hundred and seventy-four days I *will* pass basic training. I swear it, on our mum's grave.'

James scrambled out of bed.

'No way,' he said angrily. 'You can't swear something like that on Mum's grave. Some things are out of your control. What if you get injured, or sick?'

'I won't,' Lauren said sternly. 'If something hurts, I'll close my eyes and think about the piece of paper in my pocket.'

'It's a good idea to focus your mind,' James said, sliding his legs into a pair of tracksuit bottoms. 'But try and be realistic. There are quite a few kids who've taken three or more attempts to get through basic training. You could be setting yourself up for a big disappointment.'

Lauren stood in front of James and barked an order. 'Slap my face.'

'Yeah, I'm really gonna hit you,' James said, shaking his head with contempt.

'I'll show you I can take it,' Lauren said. 'As hard as you like.'

'Give us a break, Lauren. You realise we could have lain in bed for at least another half hour?'

Lauren lunged forward, grabbed hold of James' nipple and gave it a savage twist. James rolled backwards on to his bed, howling in pain.

'What the *hell* did you do that for?' he shouted.

'Slap my damn face,' Lauren shouted back.

'You really want to see how tough you are?' James raged. 'Fine. Maybe I'll knock some sense into you.'

There was a sharp *crack* as his hand hit her face. It was more painful than Lauren had expected, but she stifled her groan and toughed it out with a thin-lipped smile.

'One hundred and seventy-four days,' Lauren said. 'Believe it.'

James grinned. 'Will you be coming down to breakfast with me, or are you too tough for food as well?'

*

There were about sixty cherubs in the dining-hall when James and Lauren arrived. It took a couple of seconds for the room to go quiet, then chairs grated backwards and everyone stood up and started clapping and banging cutlery on the table. There were shouts of *Lauren* and whistles as well.

Shakeel was standing nearby; James looked over at him.

'What's this all about?'

'Your sister,' he said, as if James was some kind of idiot. 'She's the biggest hero in the history of CHERUB. Everyone dreams of getting revenge on Mr Large, but I never imagined any kid would really have the guts to do it.'

Kids piled in from all directions, until Lauren stood in an ocean of hugs and handshakes. A couple of stocky teenage boys hoisted Lauren off the ground, balanced her on their shoulders and took her on a victory parade around the dining-room. She had a mix of emotions on her face; happy, freaked out and afraid of getting her head smacked on a light fitting. As Lauren was galloped around the room, the kids at the dining tables were all pledging to help her dig.

'Dig what?' James asked.

'We heard Lauren's got to clean out the ditches at the back end of campus,' Shakeel explained. 'Everyone is putting on their wellies and going up there Saturday morning to help her out. We reckon with a hundred or more kids on the job, we'll get the whole lot cleared out in a day.'

'Cool,' James said. 'That's really great of everyone.'

'It's what she deserves,' Shakeel said. 'I wish I'd belted Mr Large one. There's a collection going around as well. Everyone's putting money in and we're gonna get her something from that shop in town that does trophies.'

Amy came up to James as Lauren was on her third circuit of the dining-room.

'We had a whip round up on my floor,' Amy said. 'We got seventy quid. What's Lauren's favourite shop?'

'She gets a lot of stuff from Gap Kids,' James said. 'Why?'

'There's already more than enough for the engraved tankard,' Amy explained. 'We were thinking of getting her some gift vouchers, or maybe a humongous teddy bear . . .'

26. SOCKS

'You're such a jammy little git,' Kerry said. 'You realise me and Kyle are stuck here on Thornton until this mission is finished?'

It was Friday night. They were in the boys' bedroom and James was packing a hold-all for his flight to Miami in the morning.

'That's the wrong attitude,' James said, grinning. 'We're all equally important members of a team. It's just that my role is toasting on some beach in Florida, while you get to spend half-term here. If you're lucky, someone might start a fire and you can watch one of the derelict houses burn out.'

'You're *such* a funny guy,' Kerry sneered.

'How many socks do you reckon?' James asked.

'At least one pair for each day.'

James looked in his underwear drawer and realised he only had two clean pairs. He started hunting around the floor and balling odd socks together.

'Aren't those dirty?' Kerry asked.

'A bit,' James said. 'But I've only worn most of them once.

They don't smell that bad.' He put one of them under Kerry's nose. 'See.'

'For *god's* sake,' Kerry said angrily, pushing James' arm away. 'They're appalling.'

James gave them a sniff.

'*Phew*,' he gasped. 'Those ones are a bit ripe. I think they're what I wore to boxing club last night. But most of these are OK.'

Kerry shook her head. 'You're an animal, James.'

She slid off the bed and walked across the hallway to her own room. James' mobile rang.

'Hey, April,' James said. 'Where are you?'

'I'm at the airport with Erin and my mum,' April said. 'We're sitting here waiting to board the plane and I thought I'd say hi.'

'I only saw you a few hours ago,' James said.

'Don't you want to talk to me?' April said, with a hint of acid in her voice.

'Of course I want to talk to you,' James lied. 'It's just . . . I'm really busy, packing and stuff.'

'I'm wearing your Nike watch,' April giggled. 'So I can think about you whenever I look at the time.'

'Don't forget to give that back,' James said. 'It's my only good one.'

'Blow me a kiss,' April said.

James shook his head before doing a couple of quick smooches into his phone.

'I think Zara's calling me downstairs, April. I've got to hang up. Have a wonderful trip, bye.'

'James. I—'

'Gotta go, April, sorry.'

James ended the call and tutted. Kerry had walked back in behind him. She was holding four pairs of clean sports socks.

'Girl trouble?' she inquired.

'Don't ask,' James said.

'Borrow these,' Kerry said. 'My feet aren't much smaller than yours. Just make sure you wash them before you give them back.'

'Cheers,' James said, tucking the socks into his hold-all. 'You know, April's driving me round the bend.'

'Why?' Kerry asked. 'She seems like a really nice girl.'

'She is,' James said. 'But she's too intense. She phones me *all* the time. She follows me everywhere at school and starts putting her arm around me. If I'm talking to someone else, she pulls me away and whispers stuff in my ear.'

'She's got a crush on you,' Kerry said. 'You should be flattered.'

'It's more than a crush,' James said. 'I bet she's already picked out the wedding dress, and now she's working out the names of our kids.'

'Typical man,' Kerry said indignantly. 'You like having a girl draped off your arm, but only so you can snog her and impress your stupid mates.'

'Give over,' James said. 'It's just, April is a lot keener on me than I am on her. It's not my fault girls can't resist me.'

'In your dreams,' Kerry grinned. 'I suppose you'll dump April and leave her in a state, like you did with Nicole.'

'Nicole?' James said, looking mystified. 'I only kissed her once, for about two seconds.'

'Nicole asked if you liked her,' Kerry said. 'So you snogged her, then you dumped her.'

'I just didn't snog her again,' James said. 'I don't know why you're turning it into some big deal.'

'But you didn't have the decency to face her. You just skulked around the house avoiding her for the next couple of days. Nicole was really upset.'

'Well . . .' James said. 'I didn't mean to hurt her feelings.'

'Yeah, right.'

'Look, Kerry, I don't deliberately treat girls like that. To tell the truth, there's someone else I really like.'

'You mean Amy?' Kerry said. 'You can practically see the drool run out your mouth every time she comes near you, but get over it, she's seventeen years old.'

'That shows how much you know,' James said tersely. 'Every boy on campus fancies Amy, but it's not her I'm talking about.'

'Who is it then?'

'None of your business.'

'Huh,' Kerry sneered. 'You're making it up so I don't think you're a pig.'

'No,' James said.

'Do I know her?' Kerry asked.

'Yes.'

'It's not Gabrielle, is it?'

James laughed. 'No.'

'You're such a plonker,' Kerry said. 'I don't know why I'm even bothering to talk to you.'

James loved the way she reared up on the balls of her feet whenever she got ratty.

'You really want to know who I like?' James said.

'I don't care,' Kerry said, folding her arms.

'Fine, I won't tell you then.'

But James had piqued Kerry's curiosity and she quickly changed her tack. 'Oh . . . go on then.'

James toyed with the idea of making someone up, or saying something stupid, but he realised he was never going to have a better opportunity to tell Kerry how he really felt. He couldn't carry on bottling it for the rest of his life. He took a deep breath.

'I . . .'

His mouth dried up. He felt like his head was about to explode.

Kerry shook her head. 'I knew you were lying.'

'No, I like *you*,' James blurted.

He stared at Kerry for what felt like a trillion years, studying her face for some kind of reaction.

'Are you winding me up?' Kerry asked, suspiciously.

'Ever since basic training,' James rambled. 'Even when we were covered in mud doing combat practice and you were battering me, there was something about you that I really liked. I mean . . . We're always really good together, because you're kind of stuffy and do everything by the book and I'm kind of . . . Well . . . I suppose you could say I'm an idiot at times.'

'You really like me?' Kerry grinned.

James felt like he wanted to die. 'Yes.'

'So you're serious?' Kerry asked. 'Because if you're messing with me, I'll punch every single tooth out of your dumb head.'

'I swear,' James said. 'So, you know . . . Am I wasting my time? . . . Or?'

Kerry smiled a bit. 'Everyone we know has been going on about us having a thing for each other. I never thought you really liked me though. You're always going on about tits and I've hardly got any.'

'Yeah, well,' James said. 'I'm not perfect either. But you do like me?'

Kerry nodded. 'When you're not driving me insane, you're just about my favourite boy on campus.'

James leaned forward to kiss her, but the hold-all was stuck in the middle of the tiny room and they had to shuffle around it. It was a only quick peck on the lips, but James got a massive rush.

'I wish you were coming to Miami with me,' he said.

'It's only a week,' Kerry smiled. 'And there's one condition if I'm gonna be your girlfriend.'

'What?' James asked.

'From now on, your underwear only gets worn once.'

27. MIAMI

James and Junior touched down in Miami on Saturday evening. Keith had changed his plans and flown out a couple of days earlier with his minder, George. The beefy ex-heavyweight met the boys at immigration and drove them to Keith's house in a Range Rover.

James spent the whole drive with his face stuck up against the window like a five-year-old. He loved the little differences that make you know you're in a different country: traffic lights strung over the road on wires, billboards with prices marked in dollars, the huge double-trailer trucks that looked like they'd roll over your car without the man in the cab feeling so much as a jolt.

Automatic gates parted obediently when the car got near Keith's house. The pastel-blue building sprawled out behind a mass of palm trees. There were two storeys, with balconies overlooking the ocean and lush terraces planted with palm trees and flowering cacti.

'Your dad is *so* loaded,' James said as he stepped out of the car, shaking his head in disbelief.

'Come and check out his cars,' Junior said.

There was a separate garage, the size of which reminded James of a fire station. The boys wandered in as George dealt with their bags. There was a row of everyday modern BMWs and Mercedes, but the exciting stuff was parked behind: the outlines of seven Porsches, clad in protective blankets. Junior pulled up a corner of one, revealing a headlamp.

'This ran in the Le Mans twenty-four-hour race,' Junior said. 'My dad had it taken up to Daytona for a track day. He got it up to three hundred kph on the straight.'

'Class,' James said.

'Like my motors, James?' Keith asked.

James turned around to see Keith standing in the doorway, wearing pool shoes and an unbuttoned Hawaiian shirt.

'You've got a different Porsche for every day of the week,' James grinned.

'I'll take you for a cruise down South Beach in one of them tomorrow night,' Keith said. 'It's all lit up with neon signs after dark and there's heaps of great restaurants. Did you see anything else you wanted to do in that guidebook?'

'Is it too far to go up to Orlando?' James asked. 'Junior said Universal Studios is cool.'

'It's a few hundred kilometres,' Keith said. 'But it's no hassle driving out there. We can stay overnight and get a couple of theme parks in if you want. I've got some business to sort out, but that should be wrapped up in a day or two. Was there anywhere else?'

James shrugged. 'I dunno, don't put yourself out or anything. Me and Junior can hang out on the beach, go shopping and stuff.'

'The fan boats over the everglades are good fun,' Keith said. 'And how are you set for spending money?' He pulled a roll of dollars from the back of his shorts.

'I can't take money off you as well,' James said. 'You've already paid for my flight and everything.'

Keith handed James three hundred-dollar bills and gave the same to Junior.

'Buy something for April at the mall,' Keith said. 'She's sweet on you.'

'Cheers,' James said. 'Is it all right if I use the phone to tell Zara I've arrived?'

'Sure,' Keith said, spreading his arms out wide. 'With a house this size, the phone bill is the least of my worries.'

After a quick call home, the two boys stripped to their boxers, jumped off the wooden decking at back of the house and sprinted across the deserted white beach towards the ocean. James was feeling grotty after eight hours crammed on an aeroplane, but all that washed away as he curled his toes in the mushy sand and let the sea water spew over his chest.

'I'm so glad you came instead of Ringo,' Junior said, raising his voice above the waves. 'This week is gonna be such a laugh.'

*

James slept in one of the guest bedrooms. He had a four-poster bed, plus an en-suite bathroom with a giant marble tub. When he woke up, he slid on shorts and a T-shirt and opened up a set of glass doors that led on to a balcony overlooking the ocean. He took some of lungfuls of sea air and leaned against the metal railing, letting the sun toast his skin.

The coastline was dotted with yachts and motor launches out for a Sunday morning cruise. An elderly Hispanic gardener was hosing the terraces below. The man nodded politely when their eyes met. It made James wonder where he'd end up in life. Would he have the $10 million ocean-front house, or would he be like the crinkled old guy who watered the flowers?

'Yo,' Junior shouted.

He came strolling through James' bedroom and stepped on to the balcony.

'What you doing out here?' Junior asked.

James shrugged. 'Just thinking.'

'Dumb idea,' Junior said. 'Thinking wears out your brain. My dad wants us downstairs. We're going to IHOP for breakfast.'

'You what?'

'It's a pancake place,' Junior explained. 'I'm getting a stack of strawberry whipped cream pancakes. They give you so many you can barely move when you finish. Dad and George are going into town for some business meeting, so they're dropping us at the mega-mall. It's about twenty times the size of the Reeve Centre. We can spill some dosh on shopping, then there's a sixteen-screen cinema and a rollercoaster if we get bored.'

'Sounds good,' James grinned.

*

James bought himself new jeans and swimming shorts and a couple of CDs, including one as a present for Kerry; then they caught a movie and waited around until George arrived to collect them. It was mid-afternoon when they got back to the house.

'How was the meeting?' James asked.

'Good,' Keith grinned. 'Very, very good.'

'Does that mean I'll be able to go back to making money from deliveries?'

'I don't know about that,' Keith said awkwardly. 'Everything is gonna be different. Do you fancy going for a swim now the sun's lower?'

'Actually,' James said, 'do you mind if I use your laptop to e-mail my family?'

'No worries,' Keith said.

George, Keith and Junior put on swimming shorts and walked down to the sea. Once they were out of sight, James raced up to his room and got a couple of USB memory sticks and a hacker's toolkit CD-ROM out of the bottom of his bag. He climbed on to one of the metal stools at the breakfast bar in the kitchen, turned on Keith's laptop and connected to the internet.

James clicked on Hotmail and checked the e-mails, in an account he'd set up for his James Beckett alias. He had three messages from April, including one that contained a blurry photo of April and Erin in their ski suits with the message *Miss U already, April, XXX.* James replied insincerely with *Miss U2,* before writing a longer message to Kerry, gloating about the weather and the beautiful house he was staying in.

When he'd finished typing his e-mails, James stood up and peeked out the window, making sure Keith, George and Junior were well clear of the house. As he flipped confidently through the files on the laptop, he realised that his marathon training sessions with Amy had been worth the brain-ache.

He clicked on Keith's documents folder. There were a couple of hundred files inside. Most had a little padlock symbol next to them, meaning they were encrypted. James decided it was too risky trying to read stuff with Keith just down on the beach. Instead, he plugged a memory card into the USB socket on the side of the laptop. The card was only the size of a pen top, but it held as much data as six CDs.

A grey box popped up on the screen: *New USB device detected*. James checked the size of Keith's documents folder and realised there was enough space on the memory card to copy the whole lot over. He waited a couple of anxious minutes while the computer copied Keith's files. Then he switched off the laptop and walked back to his bedroom. He got his mobile out of his luggage and set it to search for an American network. When it found a connection, James speed-dialled the number of a local Drug Enforcement Agency office he'd been given before he left.

John Jones answered. 'James?'

'Hi.'

'Settled in OK?' John asked.

'Not bad,' James said. 'You?'

'My flight was fine, but the heat out here does me in. I'm more of a fish-and-chip-supper-on-a-cold-winter-night kind of guy.'

'I can't talk for long,' James said. 'But I've been through Keith's laptop.'

'Anything exciting?'

'Dunno,' James said. 'I checked for fancy stuff, like hidden partitions on the hard drive, but there's none of that. All Keith's documents are encrypted. I didn't want to fiddle about trying to open them. I've copied the whole lot on to a memory card for you guys to deal with.'

'Good work,' John said.

'The only thing is, how do I get the card to you?'

'We can arrange an unscheduled rubbish collection for this evening. Have you got something you want to throw out that you can hide the memory card inside?'

James looked around the room.

'There's a half-eaten box of Milk Duds I got at the cinema,' he said. 'I can stick the memory card inside that then throw it out.'

'Perfect,' John said. 'Scrunch the box up, so the card doesn't fall out. Then make sure you put your rubbish in the main bins out by the road. We'll send a dustcart along to pick them up.'

'Will you guys be able to break the encryption?' James asked.

'Depends what software Keith's using,' John said. 'But probably. Is there anything else you'd like to report?'

'One thing Keith said struck me as odd,' James said. 'I asked him when I'd be able to go back to making deliveries. Keith goes, *I don't know, everything's gonna be different.*'

'Hmm,' John said. 'I've no idea why he'd say that, but it's certainly interesting.'

'I better go anyway,' James said. 'They'll be wondering what I'm doing.'

'OK then,' John said. 'Keep up the good work and watch out for yourself.'

28. ORLANDO

James was having one of the best weeks of his life. Monday he went out on a fishing boat with Junior. He'd never fished out in the ocean, but the crew showed him the basics and helped him reel his first catch.

He called John Jones from the beach that evening with some snippets he'd picked up from Keith's telephone conversations. John told James that American drug enforcement agents had retrieved his Milk Duds box and MI5 specialists had managed to read most of the files. They contained details of several foreign bank accounts with transactions linking Keith to a money-laundering operation whose speciality was collecting your cash, bouncing it around the world banking system until it was untraceable and finally depositing it in an anonymous foreign bank account – minus their 25% commission.

John didn't think it was enough information to get Keith convicted, but he reckoned it was a useful piece of the jigsaw.

The next day, James, Junior and Keith set off early for the 350-kilometre drive up to Orlando. It was low season, so the boys had a great time at Islands of Adventure, scaring themselves witless on all the rollercoasters and simulator rides, without wasting too much time queuing. James went nuts in the gift shop, buying T-shirts for Kyle and Kerry and a little bib and shorts for Joshua. When he went to pay at the till, Keith put the whole lot on his credit card.

By mid-afternoon, they were all knackered and sunburnt, so they checked into a hotel and showered before heading down to the restaurant. They got an outdoor table at the edge of a man-made lake with ducks and fountains in the middle. Keith ordered tagliatelle, while James and Junior got half-pound burgers and fries. The waitress brought walnut bread and olive oil to the table while they waited for their food.

'I think I'm safe to talk here,' Keith said. 'Unless a bunch of cops followed me up here and they're pointing a parabolic microphone at me from the other side of the lake.'

James looked away from the ducks, which were scrapping over a handful of bread he'd thrown into the pond a second before he noticed the *Please Do Not Feed The Ducks* sign.

'Talk about what?' Junior asked.

'Anything,' Keith said.

'Do you think the cops are listening to you most of the time?' James asked.

'The cops have got microphones everywhere,' Keith said. 'The house in Luton, the house in Miami, my cars, my offices. I don't even know what people I can trust any more. I've even got the secret service after me.'

'MI5?' James asked.

'They've been after me ever since the corruption allegations inside Operation Snort,' Keith nodded. 'One of my better sources told me George is working for the cops. I don't think it's true, but you can never be sure. He's a family man with a couple of kids. If the cops threatened him with a long stretch in prison, who knows what he'd be prepared to do?'

'Are you gonna have him whacked?' Junior asked.

Keith burst out laughing. 'Son, if I had somebody killed every time I heard a rumour about an informant, I'd be a mass murderer. The cops plant most of these rumours, hoping it will create friction inside KMG. We get our own back by dropping rumours that straight cops are taking bribes.'

'Have you ever had anyone killed?' Junior asked.

'I get problems and I tell people to make them go away,' Keith said. 'It's not my business to know whether they tickle the guy's feet until he promises to be a good boy, or chuck him off a tenth-floor balcony.'

'Cool,' Junior said, grinning.

'You know that scene in the movies, where the car's heading for the edge of the cliff, and the cop cars are chasing?' Keith asked. 'That's where everyone thinks I'm at, but the cops don't realise something.'

'What?' Junior said.

'I've bailed out of the car,' Keith said. 'Everyone thinks I'm out here buying drugs, trying to get KMG up and running again. I've made a few noises in that direction, but all I'm really doing is settling debts and sorting out finances. I'll be staying in America for a few months, until things die down back home, then I'm gonna rest on my laurels. How many millions does a man need anyway?'

'That's cool, Dad,' Junior smiled. 'I don't ever want you going to prison.'

'What will happen to KMG without you?' James asked.

'I expect it'll break into a thousand pieces,' Keith said. 'Some people will go to prison. Some of the ones left on the outside will make contacts with my overseas suppliers and start importing cocaine themselves. In a year or two, nobody will even remember me. The same guys will be making deliveries and selling coke on the street; it'll just be new faces supplying them and stacking the big money into foreign bank accounts. Give it four or five years and you'll probably find one group has become dominant; a new KMG. The police will set up another Operation Snort type deal; they'll break it up. Then the whole cycle will start again.'

'Stopping KMG must have some effect on the cocaine trade,' James said.

'The police have budget cuts and efficiency targets, the drug dealers have got billions of pounds,' Keith said. 'It's like the weediest kid in Year Seven picking a fight with the entire Year Twelve rugby team. The police might land the odd punch, but they're always gonna get their arses kicked at the end of the day.'

'Do you think you'll stay out of prison?' James asked.

'I'm shelling out enough in bribes and legal fees,' Keith said. 'So let's hope for the best, eh?'

The waitress came over with the three plates of food.

'Anyway,' Keith said, shovelling down his first mouthful of pasta, 'all this serious talk's gonna spoil my appetite. You boys want to go see a movie or something tonight?'

*

James waited until Junior was asleep before slipping out of the hotel room. He made his nightly call to John Jones from an alcove down the corridor that had an ice dispenser and a couple of Pepsi machines in it. James explained about Keith's retirement plans.

'We've tracked down more of Keith's money with the information you copied off the computer,' John said. 'I was starting to suspect Keith wasn't in Miami to do a drug deal and what you said confirms that. But I still don't think he's told you the whole truth.'

'Why's that?' James asked.

'We traced a transaction from one of Keith's bank accounts in Trinidad. Keith just purchased half a million dollars worth of US treasury bonds in the name of Erin Moore. We contacted the bank and asked for details. Keith Moore has handed the bonds over to the bank, with instructions to sell them on Erin Moore's eighteenth birthday and pay her the money. Keith has made similar transactions for Junior, April and Ringo. He's also set up a trust fund for his ex-wife. He's paid off the mortgages for the two houses in England and sold the house in Miami for a lot less than it's worth, to raise fast cash.'

'But Keith told me he's planning to stay in Miami until the heat dies down back in England.'

'There's a new owner moving into the Miami house in three weeks,' John said. 'And we can't find any trace of the eleven million dollars he got from the sale.'

'Do you think he's using the money to buy drugs?' James asked.

'I don't think so.'

'What then?'

'How many boats have you seen since you got to Miami?' John asked.

'Millions,' James said. 'They're everywhere.'

'Once he's set up the arrangements to provide for his family, I think Keith is going to sneak out of the house, climb aboard one of those boats and vanish like a puff of smoke.'

'How come?' James said.

'Keith can feel the net closing in. He has informants inside Operation Snort, so he knows we're close to having enough evidence to put him behind bars for a seriously long stretch.'

'Where will he go?' James asked.

'Eleven million bucks will go a long way in South America. My money would be on Brazil. It's easy to disappear in a country with two hundred million people. He can buy a new identity off some corrupt government official, maybe even have a spot of plastic surgery to change his appearance.'

'What about his kids and stuff?'

'They'll be set for life financially,' John said. 'Keith will have made double sure that the money set aside for his family can never be traced back to drug dealing.'

'But he'll never be able to see them again.'

'He won't see much of them from inside a jail cell, either,' John said. 'You keep telling me Keith is in a good mood, but that's all front. He's got to make decisions and none of his options are easy.'

'So what are you doing to stop him disappearing?' James asked.

'We have a big problem. We've asked the Americans to

put a twenty-four-hour watch on Keith, but they're only prepared to spare us one DEA agent. We've even offered to pay their costs, but they're short-staffed and they've got their own bad guys to catch. We're having more meetings with the Yanks to try and sort out a deal, but for at least the next few days, there's nothing to stop Keith Moore slipping off into the night.'

'Except me,' James said.

'Remember you're undercover,' John said. 'And you're supposed to be a regular kid, so don't interfere. All you can do is call me if you think he's about to leg it.'

James heard someone coming along the corridor and quickly hung up his phone. It was Keith, wearing a hotel gown and carrying the ice bucket from his room. James was in a T-shirt and boxers, so he had nowhere to hide his phone.

'Trouble sleeping?' Keith asked. 'Who are you ringing at this time of night?'

CHERUB training teaches you to always have an excuse ready.

'Zara,' James said. 'It's morning back home and Joshua always wakes her up early.'

'Most mobiles don't work in America,' Keith said. 'You must have a tri-band.'

James' mobile phone had been modified by the intelligence service so it worked on just about any network in the world, but he couldn't tell Keith that.

'I've got no idea,' James said, shrugging. 'I just turned the thing on and it worked. I stepped out here because I didn't want to wake Junior up.'

'You know it's about four quid a minute using your mobile from America?' Keith said.

'Is it?' James gasped, acting like he was really worried. 'Ewart will murder me when he gets the bill.'

Keith filled his ice bucket from the dispenser and put quarters in the Pepsi machine.

'I must have got dehydrated walking about in the sun all day,' he said. 'I woke up with a raging thirst. Do you want one?'

James nodded. 'Yeah, I wouldn't mind.'

Keith fed in more quarters until a second can dropped out of the machine. He handed it to James and they both pulled back the tabs and swallowed a couple of gassy mouthfuls.

'I'm really grateful you brought me out here on holiday,' James said. 'Ewart and Zara could never afford to take me abroad.'

'That's OK,' Keith said, smiling. 'When Ringo dropped out, it was me who suggested you came instead.'

'Really?' James said. 'Why?'

'You're the only one of Junior's mates I thought I could rely on to look after him if something bad happens,' Keith said.

'Bad like what?' James asked.

'They could arrest me at any time, James. I know Junior likes to think he's the big man, but he's led a pretty sheltered life and I'm a lot happier knowing there's a guy like you with him.'

'You've got George back in Miami,' James said.

'George is good for two things,' Keith laughed. 'Breaking heads and polishing cars. I've known the man since infant school and I love him, but frankly, it's a miracle he can tie his own shoe laces.'

'Who knows?' James said. 'Maybe you'll never get arrested.'

'Life is certainly full of surprises,' Keith said. 'I'll tell you that for nothing.'

He ripped off a monster belch that echoed down the corridor. James giggled and responded with a tiny burp.

'Pathetic,' Keith said. 'Check this out.'

Keith tipped back his head to drain his can, then rolled out the longest, loudest belch James had ever heard. An elderly American was toddling along the corridor. She had giant rectangular sunglasses and the wrinkled face of somebody who'd spent too much of her life in the sun.

'Why don't you mind your damn manners?' she said furiously.

'Don't worry, ma'am,' Keith said, giggling as he gently cuffed James around the back of the head. 'I'll make sure the boy doesn't do it again.'

'It wasn't me,' James gasped, struggling to keep a straight face.

The woman shuffled a few more steps and stopped outside her room. As she rummaged through her handbag for the plastic card that unlocked her door, Keith stepped into the corridor and belched again. It wasn't as big as the first two, but it was still loud. James couldn't control himself and started howling with laughter. The woman scowled so hard, he half expected a laser beam to shoot out of her eyes.

'This hotel used to attract decent people,' she shouted. 'Why don't you act your age?'

Her door slammed. James and Keith stood there laughing for about ten minutes. James got it so bad his sides started hurting.

Keith looked at his watch. 'You better get back to bed, it's gone midnight and we're doing another theme park tomorrow.'

James crept back into his room, being careful not to wake up Junior. He took a quick pee before sliding between his sheets. He was tired, but his brain kept churning over as he lay awake, listening to Junior's gentle breathing.

James wondered if Keith really was planning to do a runner. It seemed sad that a guy who'd been showing him the time of his life was facing a choice between twenty years in prison and running off and never seeing his family again. James asked himself what he'd do if he saw Keith making a run for it. Would he grab his mobile the second he realised, or give Keith time to get away?

*

They left the hotel early next morning and went to Disneyworld, then spent the afternoon cooling off at a water park. It was getting dark by the time they left Orlando for the five-hour drive back to Miami.

James woke up late Thursday morning on his four-poster bed in the Miami house. He was on top of his duvet, wearing the trainers and clothes he'd had on the day before. The last thing he could remember was falling asleep in the back seat of the car. He needed a shower and his mouth tasted like a sewer, but before any of that, he scrambled downstairs to see if Keith was still around.

George, Keith and Junior sat at the breakfast bar in the

kitchen, wearing swimming shorts and watching a daytime talk show.

'Here's sleeping beauty,' Keith said.

Junior started to laugh.

'What?' James asked.

'I pinched your cheek and everything,' Keith said, 'but you didn't bat an eyelid. I had to get George to carry you upstairs and dump you on your bed.'

'All red-faced and tired-out,' Junior giggled. 'You looked like a little angel.'

'I can't remember a thing,' James gasped. 'God . . . That's so embarrassing.'

'It's all those midnight phone calls,' Keith said. 'You're not getting enough sleep.'

James had a mental jolt. He'd missed his nightly call and John Jones might be worried.

'I better go freshen up,' James said.

As soon as he got to his room, he found the overnight bag he'd taken to Orlando and grabbed his mobile. He tried to switch it on, but the battery was dead. He hunted around the room until he found his charger and his American socket adaptor. The phone bleeped to life as soon as it was plugged in.

'Rip Van Winkle,' John Jones said. 'How you feeling?'

'Don't you start,' James said. 'How did you know about that?'

'When it got to one in the morning and I still hadn't heard from you, I got worried. We got a track on your mobile phone signal and realised you were driving back from Orlando. Then your mobile stopped transmitting.'

'It went flat,' James explained. 'I forgot to take my charger with me.'

'Pretty basic operational mistake, James,' John said, tutting. 'But I guess we have to make allowances for the fact you're thirteen years old.'

'I'm glad *you* make allowances at MI5,' James laughed. 'Nobody from CHERUB ever does.'

'Anyway, I thought I'd better check you were OK, so I hid in the bushes out back and watched George carry you out of the car. You looked like you were six years old, all bundled up in his big fat arms.'

'I'm never gonna live this down,' James said. 'So, apart from me making an idiot of myself, nothing much happened yesterday. What about your end?'

'The Yanks want to help us watch Keith, but they don't have the manpower. We think we've got enough evidence to convict Keith on tax evasion and money-laundering charges, but that's only worth a two- to five-year sentence. We wanted to wait until we could bust him on drugs charges, but with no twenty-four-hour surveillance and the risk of Keith running off for good, we've decided to move now.'

'Extradition?' James said.

'That's right, James. Bedfordshire police will be contacting the DEA later today, asking them to arrest Keith on money-laundering charges and send him back to Britain. We have to present our evidence to an American judge before they issue an arrest warrant. It'll take a day or so to get the paperwork together and organise the hearing.'

'So you're hoping Keith doesn't leg it in the meantime.'

'Exactly,' John said. 'And one final thing. I got a message from Zara. Dr McAfferty has decided to pull the CHERUB side of this operation whether or not Keith Moore is in jail. Tell Junior and Keith that Ewart's been offered a better job and you're all moving back to London.'

29. NIGHT

That night James ended up in Junior's room watching a horror film on DVD. James got up to go back to his room when it finished.

'That sofa pulls out,' Junior said. 'You can sleep in here if you want.'

James smiled. 'Scared of being on your own? Think that guy with the bloody axe might come bursting through your window?'

'No,' Junior said defensively. 'I just thought we could talk and stuff.'

James fetched his duvet and pillows while Junior pulled out the sofa bed. They switched the light off and lay in the dark talking. *If you could have any car in the world, what would it be? What if you could live anywhere you wanted?*

'Would you stick your tongue up a dog's arse for a million pounds?' Junior asked.

James thought for a couple of seconds. 'Yes.'

Junior started rolling about laughing. 'EUGHH, James. You filthy animal.'

'It's OK for you,' James said, laughing. 'Your dad's loaded already. But a million pounds would change my life. I'd never have to go to work. I could have a decent house and a cool car and stuff.'

'What if you had to do it on TV and everyone knew about it?'

'Doesn't make any difference,' James said. 'A million would set you up for life.'

'OK,' Junior said. 'What's the *least* amount? Would you do it for ten thousand?'

'No way.'

'What then?'

'I dunno,' James said. 'Half a million, maybe . . .'

An arc of light burst into the room and Keith's head appeared in the doorway.

'Come on, guys,' Keith said. 'Be sensible. It's one in the morning. We're going out early tomorrow and you two are gonna be wasted. Calm down and go to sleep.'

Both boys struggled to stop laughing.

'Goodnight, Dad,' Junior said.

'Get some sleep,' Keith said firmly.

He closed the door. The boys waited until they were fairly sure Keith was in his bedroom.

Junior sounded sad. 'You know,' he whispered, 'if you're moving back to London, I'll probably never see you or Nicole again.'

'I'll miss you as well,' James said. 'You're one of the best mates I've ever had.'

'Maybe we could visit each other in the holidays,' Junior said.

'Maybe,' James said, although he knew it could never happen. 'It's only half an hour on the train to London. You know what else?'

'What?' Junior asked.

'I was looking forward to boxing against you.'

Junior thought for a second. 'Do you want to fight now?'

'Your dad will go psycho,' James said.

'There's gloves that go with the punchbag downstairs in the gym. We can fight on the beach in the moonlight. You can't see from the house if you stay down near the sea.'

'OK,' James said, sitting up on the sofa bed and smiling. 'Just don't start bawling to Daddy when I punch the snot out of you.'

Junior sneered. 'You talk pretty big for someone who's only ever done sparring.'

Junior flicked on the lamp beside his bed and put on his watch. Both boys slipped on shorts and trainers. They sneaked downstairs and got the gloves. James was surprised when he saw how small they were.

'These are pro-weight,' Junior whispered. 'Much less padding than for amateur boxing. You really feel a sting if you get hit with one of these.'

'Are there head guards?' James asked.

'We're fighting like men,' Junior said. 'No finger tape, no head guards, no gum shields, pro-gloves. Not chicken, are you?'

James was starting to wonder if fighting was a good idea. The CHERUB staff wouldn't be impressed if he got himself injured in an unnecessary midnight boxing match, but he was too proud to back down.

They walked through to the living-room and got a fright when George let out a loud snore. He'd fallen asleep in front of the TV. Junior quietly slid one of the French doors open and they jumped off the decking on to the beach.

The tide was on its way out. The moon was bright and the wet sand near the sea squelched under their trainers. Junior used a stick to draw the outline of a lopsided boxing ring, before setting his watch to do a three-minute countdown.

'Three rounds, lasting three minutes each,' Junior said. 'If you go down three times you're out of the fight.'

James felt nervous as he pulled his second glove on with his teeth.

'Go to your corner,' Junior said.

When Junior's stopwatch bleeped, the two boys charged forward and started throwing punches. With amateur gloves, even a full-force punch barely hurts, but Junior's first barrage with the professional gloves connected hard. One punch knocked James off balance. He couldn't catch his breath as he stumbled backwards. Junior sunk a blow below the elastic of James' shorts, doubling him over. Junior's next punch caught James in the side of the head. He splattered helplessly into the damp sand.

'Low blow,' James wheezed, clutching his abdomen.

The fight had only been going a few seconds, but it was a warm night and both boys were pouring sweat.

'It wasn't low,' Junior said. 'That counts as my first knockdown.'

James clambered to his feet. He usually loved the rush you got during a fight, but Junior was fast and strong. James had a nasty feeling he'd bitten off more than he could chew.

'So we're fighting dirty, are we?' he said, holding back a burst of anger. 'That's fine by me.'

He threw a fast punch. Junior wasn't ready and the thinly padded glove smashed into his nose. James' next shot was an uppercut that snapped back Junior's head.

'Stop,' Junior shouted, groaning in pain as he wrapped his arms over his face. 'Jesus Christ . . . You idiot.'

'What?' James asked.

'You've got sand on your gloves. It's gone in my eye.'

Junior tore off a glove and started rubbing his eye.

'Sorry,' James said. 'I never realised. Are you OK?'

Junior broke into an uneasy smile as he blinked out the sand.

'You know what?' he said. 'I blame the idiot who thought up this stupid idea in the first place.'

James laughed. 'That would be you.'

'Call it a draw, eh, James?'

'Fair enough,' James said. 'Now we know why they don't have beach boxing.'

'I'm going for a swim,' Junior said, kicking off his trainers. 'I need to wash all this sweat off.'

James thought he heard a banging sound as he pulled off his gloves.

'Did you hear that?'

'What?' Junior asked.

'I thought I heard something up in the house.'

Junior smiled. 'Maybe George woke up and fell off the sofa.'

'Yeah,' James laughed. 'Either that or they've set loose the axe-wielding maniac from that movie.'

Junior waded into the sea and dived forward, turning a somersault underwater. James pushed off backwards and let a wave wash him back towards the beach.

'You ever had a nightmare after watching a scary movie?' Junior asked.

'You know the film *Seven*?' James asked, as he bobbed in the surf.

'I love that movie,' Junior said. 'It's totally sick.'

'When my mum was alive, I showed off until she let me watch the video. I woke up in a state and climbed in her bed. My sister, Lauren, heard about it and didn't stop ribbing me for about a week.'

'Your sister?' Junior said, surprised.

'I mean cousin,' James said, nervously covering his mistake. 'It was the summer holidays and Lauren was staying at our house.'

'Ringo used to tease me when I was little,' Junior said. 'I'd ask him to put on my *Pingu* video and he'd stick on *The Terminator* to scare me.'

'We better go to bed,' James said, as he picked his boxing gloves off the sand and slid his wet feet inside his trainers. 'I'm looking forward to the air-boat ride tomorrow.'

'We never usually do half the cool stuff we've done this week,' Junior said. 'My dad really likes you for some reason.'

James thought Keith was spoiling them because he was planning to disappear in a few days and would most likely never see Junior again. As they walked towards the house in their dripping shorts, Junior turned around and started walking backwards, staring at the moonlit sea.

'Just think,' he said, spreading his arms out wide. 'If you count the time difference between here and London, in less than three days' time we'll be getting up for another miserable Monday at Grey Park school.'

'Cheer us up, why don't you?' James said. 'Is your eye OK now?'

'Stings a bit,' Junior said. 'I wish we could have had a proper fight.'

James clambered on to the wooden decking at the back of the house and put his foot inside the sliding door. His trainer slipped in something wet. He rested his palm on the wall to steady himself. The light was on in the kitchen and George's body had rolled off the sofa on the floor.

'Something's going on,' James said edgily.

Junior grinned. 'What is it, the axe murderer?'

'I'm serious,' James said, lifting his trainer out of the sticky liquid.

He felt like his head was going to explode when he realised it was blood.

'Give over, James,' Junior said. 'You're not scaring me.'

Junior stepped through the door and noticed George on the floor.

'He really did fall off the sofa,' Junior laughed.

James crouched down and clicked on a table lamp. Junior saw George was dead, realised his trainers were planted in a puddle of blood and let out a massive scream.

30. BODY

James was still haunted by the cold touch of his mother's fingers the night he found her dead in front of the TV. George's body didn't affect him the same way, though the sight was more horrible. There was blood seeping from a bullet wound under his shirt. It was draining down a hanging arm and along the joins in the floor tiles, creating a grid of red lines leading to the pool of blood by the sliding doors.

James felt like everything was happening in slow motion. He could feel every vibration in Junior's screams and watch the droplets of saliva spraying out of his mouth.

James had a theory: Keith had shot George for betraying him, then disappeared. But the theory sprang apart as he crept across the room and stared down the hallway through the half-open kitchen door. Three armed men had Keith Moore pinned on a stool at the breakfast bar. It looked like they'd roughed him up.

'Leave the boys,' Keith shouted when he heard Junior scream. 'I'll tell you everything.'

James knew he only had milliseconds before one of the men beating up Keith came out of the kitchen pointing a gun at him and Junior. He turned back to Junior, who stood rigid in the doorway, staring at George's body.

'Run,' James shouted. 'Get help.'

Junior snapped out of his panic long enough to hear the order. He jumped off the wooden decking and began sprinting down the beach. James hoped he'd have the sense to run to one of the neighbouring houses and call the police.

James planned to follow Junior, but a thuggish-looking guy emerged from the kitchen before he got the chance. James could see tattoos through the sweat-drenched vest clinging to his skin.

'Get here, kid,' he shouted, sliding out the pistol tucked into his jeans.

James burst through the nearest door, into the front living-room where Keith kept his hi-fi and record collection.

'Hey,' the man shouted furiously. 'You wanna mess with me? I'll kill you before you reach the door.'

He sounded Mexican or something. James didn't know what the men wanted from Keith, but they'd shown they were prepared to kill and he didn't fancy being their next victim. He thought about climbing out of the window, but the room only had a long narrow window up near the ceiling. He'd never get through before the man shot him.

There was a key inside the door. Turning the lock bought James a few seconds. He pushed an armchair against the door as the gunman rattled the handle on the outside. James desperately needed some kind of weapon.

'Unlock this or I'll shoot you to pieces,' the man shouted, as he pounded the door with his fist.

James slid one of Keith's LPs off its rack. He'd learned in weapons training that you can make a dagger by shattering any object made out of hard plastic. He leaned the record sleeve against the wall and stamped on it with his bloody trainer.

The gunman shoulder-charged the door.

One of his colleagues shouted after him from the kitchen. 'You need a hand?'

The gunman didn't sound worried. 'It's just some smartass kid who's gonna be feeling a lot of pain real soon.'

Three deafening shots fired into the door, blasting away the lock. James tipped the pieces of the album out of its sleeve and grabbed the longest shard of what, until a few moments earlier, had been a valuable purple vinyl edition of Led Zeppelin IV.

The gunman kicked the door twice, barging the armchair out of the way. James backed up to the wall beside the door, with the shard of purple vinyl clutched tightly in his hand. His heart drummed like it was set to burst. If he got this wrong, he'd end up with a bullet through his head.

The second he saw the pistol coming through the door, James grabbed the muzzle with one hand while plunging the sharp piece of plastic into the gunman's wrist. The man screamed out. His fingers sprang apart and James snatched the gun, before backing up to the opposite wall and turning it around so that his finger was on the trigger.

The man tugged the plastic out of his arm as he stumbled over the armchair. He faced James off with a self-assured grin.

'Big gun for a little boy, eh?' he said, showing off a rack of yellow teeth. 'Are you really gonna shoot me?'

Some sort of commotion broke out in the kitchen. Keith Moore screamed in pain.

'Get on your knees and put your hands on your head,' James stuttered.

The man edged closer. James remembered his firearms training: from a safe position you can shoot to wound, but if you're in mortal danger you can't risk missing. You have to aim for the biggest target: the chest.

'Don't make me shoot you,' James said desperately.

The gun weighed a billion tons in his trembling hands. The man ignored the threat and kept moving closer. James didn't want to shoot, but what choice was there? He held his breath to steady the gun.

'You ain't gonna kill *noooooo*body,' the man sneered, as he lifted his shoe off the carpet, preparing to take a step that would bring James into reach.

A shockwave ripped through the room. The bullet slammed into the gunman's chest from less than two metres. His feet lifted off the floor as his body crashed backwards into the upturned armchair. Stunned by the fact that he'd just fired a bullet into a real human being, James felt sick as he scrambled over his bleeding victim and out into the hallway.

James ran into the back living-room, planning to escape via the beach, but another gunman was frogmarching Junior across the sand towards the house. He ducked back into the hallway, hoping the man walking up the beach hadn't spotted him. It could only be a matter of seconds before the men in the kitchen came out to investigate the gunshot. The only way out the front of the house was by walking past the kitchen door, which would be suicidal. That only left one option.

Still holding the pistol, James ran upstairs. He went into his room, grabbed his mobile phone off the bedside table and called John Jones. A woman answered.

'Is John Jones there?'

'I'm Beverly Shapiro,' the woman said. 'Is that James Beckett?'

'Yeah,' James said. 'Where's John?'

'He's in the restroom. You sound worried, James. You can talk to me. I'm the Drug Enforcement Agency officer working with John.'

James gasped with relief. 'Thank god. Listen, I'm at Keith Moore's house. There's a whole bunch of gunmen downstairs. They're beating Keith up, trying to get some kind of information out of him.'

'I'll call the local cops out,' Beverly said. 'Can you make it out of the house?'

'They caught Junior running down the beach. I think they've got guys watching outside.'

'I'm calling the cops right now,' Beverly said. 'You find yourself a good place to hide and keep this line open.'

James thought about hiding, but he didn't think he'd be safe for more than a few minutes. The cops would take longer than that to arrive and even when they did, they'd be unlikely to come charging straight into the house and risk getting shot. James considered hiding out at the top of the stairs and shooting at anyone who tried to come up. It might have worked in a house with one staircase, but Keith's Miami home had three. Four if you counted the metal walkway that led across to the garage.

The garage.

James realised that was his best chance. He leaned out into the corridor as Beverly said something into the phone.

'What?' James asked.

'I said, the police are on their way. Have you found a safe place to hide?'

'I don't think it's safe up here,' James said. 'Someone's gonna come up looking for me any second.'

'I *told* you to hide,' Beverly said stiffly. 'Keep calm and wait for the police.'

'No way,' James said. 'I've got to bust out.'

He tucked the phone into the waistband of his soggy shorts, without ending the call. He sprinted down the hallway to the master bedroom and found Keith's trousers on the floor. He grabbed a bunch of keys from the pocket and rapidly flipped through them. There were keys to a couple of the Porsches and a Mercedes, but James thought the huge four-wheel-drive Range Rover would give him his best chance of escape.

When he got back into the hallway, he heard footsteps on the staircase. He fired a shot towards the stairs, knowing it would make the men stay back for a minute or two.

James cautiously opened the door at the end of the hallway. He checked no one was around outside, before stepping on to the metal steps that linked the house to the garage. He opened the door into the garage and walked down a set of spiral stairs to ground level, before unlocking the Range Rover and sliding on to the driver's seat.

594

He put the key in the steering column and started the engine. Clipping on his seatbelt to cut off the annoying bing-bong noise, he pressed the button on the dashboard that opened the garage doors and the iron gates at the front of the house.

The wooden doors, less than a metre from the front of the car, began parting slowly. James knew someone would hear them if he just sat waiting. He put the car in drive, floored the accelerator pedal and ploughed through. He had to slam on the brake to avoid a brick wall as chunks of wood sprayed in all directions around the car.

As he put on full steering lock and turned towards the gate, James' heart sank. The front gates were still closed. The button on the dashboard hadn't worked. James realised the gunmen must have short-circuited the automatic gate when they broke into the house. The Range Rover might have been able to break them open, but the gunmen had their two cars parked in front of the gates, ready for a quick getaway.

As James looked around, frantically trying to work out an alternative escape, a bullet came out of a first-floor window, ripping through the roof of the car and punching a neat hole through the front passenger seat. James floored the accelerator and spun the car around. He pointed the Range Rover at the thickly planted terraces around the house, hoping the car was powerful enough to punch through a hundred metres of trees and plants. If it was, he'd be able to escape on to the beach at the back of the house.

The chunky front tyres reared on to a set of narrow steps. The car crawled up a gentle slope, rocking from side to side as it trampled bushes and tore a couple of small trees out of the ground. Chunks of stone and wood clattered against the underside of the car, then it hit a massive palm tree and ground to a halt.

The car slipped backwards as a second bullet ripped through the tailgate. The noise made James' eardrums pop. He thought he might have to bail out and run for it, but the car's automatic gearbox slipped into its lowest ratio. The rear tyres dug into the soft ground. James dabbed the accelerator. After a touch of wheelspin, the car toppled the palm tree and bounced over its thick trunk.

At the top of the slope, the ground levelled off on to a tiled patio. James swerved around Keith's brick barbecue and picked up speed as he rolled downhill. It was much easier navigating through the low bushes and flowerbeds on the windswept ocean side of the house. At the bottom, James swerved to avoid Keith's fishpond, then floored the accelerator. He needed to pick up speed to break through the fence at the back of the house.

A thin concrete post shattered as the front of the car ripped a hole through a tangle of plastic mesh and barbed wire. The car nose-dived off a metre-high wall. The back wheels spun in free air until the front wheels burrowed into the soft sand and pulled the front of the car forward. Once all four wheels were firmly planted on level ground, James hit the accelerator and began tearing along the sand, dragging a ten-metre section of chain link fence behind him. He nudged the steering wheel from left to right until the wire disentangled itself from the rear bumper.

Once the wire was gone, everything seemed eerily calm; just the gentle whoosh of the air-conditioning and a few hundred metres of level sand lit up by the headlamps. James looked back in the mirror. Nobody seemed to be coming after him. He reached into his shorts and grabbed his mobile.

'Beverly, are you still there?'

'What the hell was that noise?' John Jones asked, sounding like he was in a bit of a state. 'Did I hear gunshots? Are you OK?'

'I'm OK, but I might have just killed some maniac and now they've got hold of Junior. I'm driving along the beach in Keith's Range Rover. When I see a gap between the houses, I'm gonna pull up on to the road.'

'OK,' John said. 'You're sure nobody's following?'

'Not so far as I can tell.'

'Do you know how to drive to the IHOP from where you are at the moment?'

'Sure,' James said. 'It's only a couple of kilometres.'

'I'll meet you there in fifteen minutes. Beverly will be with me. She knows you're my informant, but she doesn't know anything about CHERUB, so watch what you say.'

'No worries,' James said.

'Get off the beach as quickly as you can and drive sensibly. You don't want to get picked up by the cops.'

*

The pancake place was closed, so they ended up in a twenty-four-hour McDonald's across the street. John sat across the table from James, while Beverly got apple pies and coffees at the counter. James looked between his legs at his blood-stained trainers.

'A hundred and nineteen ninety-nine,' James said bitterly. 'The first lot got stolen, now this lot are ruined.'

John Jones laughed. 'Maybe it's god's way of telling you that a hundred and twenty pounds is an obscene amount of money to pay for a pair of plimsolls.'

Beverly put the tray of coffees on the table and squeezed up next to James on the plastic bench. She was small, about twenty-five, with long chestnut hair and freckles. She didn't look hard enough to be a drug enforcement agent.

'I spoke to the local units,' Beverly said. 'The bad guys got rattled when you escaped. They tried to take Keith Moore away in their car. The police spotted them and there was a shoot-out. Keith Moore took a bullet through his shoulder. It's early days, but they think he'll be OK.'

'What about Junior?' James asked.

'The guys knocked him around quite badly. He's been taken to hospital, but it's too early to say what kind of state he's in.'

'I hope he's OK,' James said anxiously. He took a sip from his steaming polystyrene cup. 'So who were those guys? What did they want with Keith?'

'They're probably linked to the Lambayeke cartel,' John said. 'I'd bet my last dollar bill that they were after the numbers of Keith's secret bank accounts.'

'I thought Keith dealt with Lambayeke,' James said. 'Weren't they friendly?'

'Keith dealt with the Lambayeke cartel for twenty years,' John said. 'But they're not the kind of people you invite round to your house for a dinner party. As long as Keith was buying drugs from Lambayeke and making them money, they left him alone. Then KMG collapsed around Keith's ears. He's not going to buy any more drugs, he doesn't know who he can trust and he's sitting on a big pile of money.'

'So they decided to rob him?' James said.

'That's right,' John nodded. 'Keith Moore has millions stashed away in illegal bank accounts. So they send some thugs in to take Keith hostage and smack him around until he gives them all the bank account details and transfers all his money over to them.'

'Keith would have had no comeback,' Beverly added. 'You can hardly go to your local precinct and complain that the money you made selling illegal drugs that's stashed away in illegal overseas bank accounts has been stolen.'

'It's almost the perfect crime,' John said. 'Except the guys they sent in were so incompetent they forgot to check upstairs and get you and Junior out of bed.'

'Actually,' James said, 'we weren't in bed. Me and Junior sneaked out and went down the beach for a midnight swim.'

He thought it was best not to mention the boxing match.

'Well, it's a good job you did,' John said, breaking into a smile. 'Otherwise you'd have woken up with a gun pointing at your head.'

31. CATCH

James grabbed a few hours' sleep in Beverly Shapiro's office at the DEA's Miami headquarters. She woke him up at ten the following morning and dumped clean clothes and trainers on the desk in front of him.

'We got those from the house,' Beverly said. 'There are showers down the hall if you want to clean up. We're going to speak to Keith Moore in about forty minutes. John said you can sit in the observation room and watch if you want to.'

'I thought Keith had been shot,' James said.

'Only in the shoulder. It'll heal up.'

'How's Junior?' James asked.

Beverly sighed. 'The bad guys didn't think Keith was telling them everything about his bank accounts, so they stopped hurting Keith and started on Junior. He's got a broken nose, broken collar bone and some serious internal injuries.'

James felt sick when he tried to imagine what Junior must have gone through. 'I should have done something to help him,' he said.

'What could you have done against eight armed men?' Beverly asked, smiling sympathetically.

'So is Junior going to be OK?'

'He won't be able to fly home for a while. He's asked to see you, but you don't exist any more.'

'What do you mean?' James asked.

'The United States has no immigration record for James Beckett. You're booked on a flight to London this evening. We want you to disappear before people start asking questions about you and the guy you shot in the chest.'

'Oh,' James said. 'I kept having these creepy dreams about the gun going off and the room where it happened. Is he dead?'

'Yes.'

'He wouldn't stop coming closer,' James said, feeling tense as he replayed the scene in his mind. 'I tried getting him to back down. I thought about shooting him in the leg, but I was taught to go straight for the chest.'

'I would have done the same,' Beverly said. 'You can't take chances, especially when it's not your own weapon. You didn't know how many bullets you had, or if the gun was some rusty piece of junk that'd jam up the second the barrel gets hot.'

'I just can't believe I killed someone.'

*

James showered in the men's locker room. There was paraphernalia everywhere – police radios, holsters, body armour. James stared at his hands while the water rushed over his body, studying the finger that had killed someone a few hours earlier. He didn't exactly feel guilty about killing a

man who was going to kill him, but it did make him a bit
sad. The guy probably had a mother, or a kid, or something.

'Hey, boy, what you doing?'

James looked up to see a couple of muscular cops stripping
off their kit.

'Beverly Shapiro said it was OK to clean up in here.'

'You sound English.'

James nodded. 'I'm from London.'

'Cool,' the cop said. 'You ever met one of the royal family?'

'Sure,' James said, laughing. 'I hang out with them all the
time.'

James stepped out of the shower and started towelling off.
He looked at the cops' guns lying on the slatted wooden
bench and wondered if they'd ever been used to kill anyone.
Then he wondered what it would be like to die. He hadn't
given it a thought while he was trying to escape, but there
were two bullet holes in the Range Rover, less than a metre
from where he'd sat.

Beverly took James to the canteen. She told him to put his
bacon and scrambled eggs in a polystyrene box so he could
eat it in the observation suite. It was a narrow room, with a
row of plastic chairs and black and white monitors. There
was a giant one-way mirror in one wall that looked into an
interrogation room. Keith Moore was in there. He stared
into space, nervously drumming his fingers on the table in
front of him. His T-shirt was bulked out by the dressing
wrapped around his shoulder.

'You'll have to keep quiet in here,' Beverly said. 'It's quite
a thin partition.'

She walked out, leaving James with the eerie sound of

Keith's breathing, amplified through the tinny loudspeakers in the ceiling.

Seconds later, Beverly walked into the interrogation room behind John Jones.

'Good morning,' John said, pulling out a chair opposite Keith and sitting down. 'My name is John Jones. I'm here to help you out.'

'I want a lawyer,' Keith said. 'I've been shot. I've had no sleep. You can't question me like this.'

'I'm with British Intelligence,' John smiled. 'I have no authority here in the United States. All we're doing is having an informal chat.'

'I don't care if you're the grand wizard of the Ku Klux Klan,' Keith said. 'I'm not saying one word until I see a lawyer.'

'The local cops found a deceased member of the Lambayeke cartel and a bunch of unlicensed firearms in your house,' John said. 'Somebody killed him, and unless the bad guys decided to start shooting one another, you're the main suspect.'

'I want a lawyer,' Keith said sourly.

John turned and looked at Beverly. 'What's the standard sentence for a drug-related murder in Florida?' he asked.

'Life without parole, on a good day,' Beverly said, smiling. 'Though if the judge doesn't like the look of you, he might bump that up to death by lethal injection.'

'What if Keith claims self-defence and puts in a guilty plea to a charge of manslaughter?' John asked.

'Between twenty and fifty years in prison,' Beverly said.

'Man,' John Jones laughed. 'They're certainly tough down

here in Florida. Keith Moore, I believe you're in a big heap of trouble.'

'I've got money,' Keith said, trying to sound confident. 'I can afford a very smart lawyer.'

'You reckon this case will ever make it anywhere near a courtroom?' John asked.

'Why shouldn't it?' Keith asked.

'You'll be charged with murdering a member of the Lambayeke cartel,' John said. 'You're a foreign citizen on a murder charge, so there's not a hope in hell you'll get bail. You'll be banged up on remand, awaiting trial, in a Florida prison stuffed with members of the Lambayeke cartel. How long do think you'll last before one of them sticks a knife in your back?'

Keith looked a lot less sure of himself when he thought about this. John theatrically slammed his mobile phone on the desk.

'There's my phone, Keith. Go ahead, call your big-shot lawyer if you want to. The Florida legal system will take you under its wing and you'll be a dead man by Christmas.'

'So what's my alternative?' Keith asked.

'You'll have to sign a deal,' John explained. 'The DEA will grant you immunity from prosecution in the United States, if you give a full and accurate account of your dealings with the Lambayeke cartel over the last twenty-whatever years. And you'll have to agree never to set foot in the United States again.

'The DEA will pass all the information you give to the British police. I'm sure you'll have given them enough to prosecute you. You'll face the full weight of British justice, which will probably be a twenty to twenty-five year prison sentence. With remission for good behaviour, you could be a free man inside fifteen years.'

'Why not leave me out here to rot?' Keith asked.

'This deal makes everyone happy,' John said. 'The Americans get lots of valuable information on the Lambayeke cartel, rather than a big bill for prosecuting you and trying to keep you alive in prison. Back in Britain, the Home Secretary gets to stand up in parliament and mouth off about the success of Operation Snort and his big crackdown on drugs. And most importantly, you'll still be alive this time next year.'

'What if the Lambayeke cartel comes after me in Britain?' Keith asked.

'They might try to get at you,' John said, shrugging. 'But Lambayeke members are thin on the ground in British prisons, whereas you'll be on home turf. I expect a man with your resources will be able to find plenty of friends to protect you.'

'You've got it all worked out,' Keith said, shifting uneasily in his chair.

'This is a once in a lifetime deal,' John said. 'There won't be any negotiation. You've got one hour to make a decision.'

Keith leaned back in his chair and ran a hand through his sweaty hair. 'You know what?' he said. 'I reckon I've been in business long enough to know when someone's got you by the balls.'

He reached his arm across the table to shake John Jones by the hand.

'I think you've got yourself a deal, Mr Jones.'

When the interview was over, James went back to Beverly's office and called the house in Luton.

'Kyle?' James asked. 'Is that you?'

'James, what's happening?'

'John Jones just nailed Keith Moore,' James said. 'They arrested him last night and he's cut a deal to save his butt.'

'Excellent,' Kyle said. 'We're just packing up here. We've had to tell everyone we're moving back to London.'

'How was half-term?'

'Ringo's party was nuts. Kids were smashing up furniture, puking on the stairs. I met this cool guy called Dave, he's really cute and—'

'Stop, stop, *stop*,' James said sharply. 'I can just about get my head around you being gay, Kyle. That doesn't mean I want graphic details . . . What about Kelvin and that? I thought they were supposed to be looking after Keith's house.'

'Didn't you hear?' Kyle said. 'The police raided the boxing club on Tuesday night. They arrested Kelvin, Marcus, Ken and that tall kid in your class.'

'Del?'

'Yeah, Del, and loads of other guys. The cops found the contact diary of the woman who used to organise the deliveries. They nabbed all the young couriers. You probably would have got busted if you'd been there.'

'So is Kerry in?' James asked. 'Can I have a quick word?'

'She's with Max Power.'

'Who?' James gasped.

'This new kid turned up in her class on Monday. They're all over each other, snogging morning, noon and night.'

James realised it was a wind-up. 'Yeah, right, Kyle.'

'I had you going for a second,' Kyle giggled. 'Kerry . . . it's your new beau. He wants to talk to you.'

Kerry came to the phone.

'We busted Keith,' James said. 'He's looking at twenty-five years.'

Kerry let out a big shriek. James had to move the phone away from his ear.

'Brilliant,' she said. 'We're heading back to campus tomorrow morning. When will you be home?'

'I'm flying out of here this evening,' James said. 'I'll probably get to campus about the same time as you guys.'

'You *were* serious about the boyfriend–girlfriend thing, weren't you?' Kerry asked.

James smiled. 'Oh, yeah. I can't wait to see you.'

32. LAST

James walked into Meryl Spencer's office, which overlooked the athletics track on CHERUB campus. Even though the window was open, you still got a hint of the damp smell from the changing room across the hallway.

'Ewart is impressed,' Meryl said. 'Zara's impressed and even Mr Jones from MI5 is impressed. I have to say it, James, *I'm* impressed.'

James smiled at his handler as he placed a black bin liner on the desk and sat down opposite her. Meryl tipped out the contents. There were clothes, trainers, CDs, an envelope with over five hundred pounds in cash and the five Playstation games he'd stolen from the Reeve Centre.

'I trust there's nothing else hidden up in your room?' Meryl asked.

'No,' James said. 'That's everything I either stole, or earned from selling drugs. Except money I spent on food and going out, some presents I got for Joshua, and Lauren's birthday money.'

'Which charity do you want to give it to?'

'Me and Kerry looked on the internet. She found this

hostel near Luton that helps young people with drug problems. Gets them off drugs, finds them jobs and gets them places at college and stuff.'

'That sounds excellent,' Meryl said. 'You're due over thirty pounds' pocket money for the time you were away, and the clothes won't go for much in charity shops. If you want, I'll put the pocket money in the envelope and you can keep the clothes and trainers.'

'Cool,' James said. 'I'll go for that.'

'You know, James,' Meryl said. 'It must be Kerry's influence, I could almost mistake you for a reformed character.'

James couldn't help smiling at the compliment. 'I've been at CHERUB for exactly a year,' he said. 'I reckon I've spent too much of that time scrubbing corridors, peeling vegetables and running punishment laps to mess you around any more.'

Meryl burst out laughing. 'That's what I like to hear,' she giggled, 'total obedience . . . But seriously, James, your performance on this mission shows that the training and hard work have paid off. When Keith Moore was being held hostage a few nights ago, you kept your head in a very nasty situation and thought your way out of it. If you'd found yourself in that position before you came here, I'm sure your reaction would have been very different.'

James nodded. 'I probably would have freaked out, like Junior did.'

'And the close bond you made with Keith Moore was tremendous.'

'Keith's a really nice guy,' James said. 'I know he's a drug dealer, but I almost feel sad that he's gonna go to prison.'

'Well, *don't*,' Meryl said sharply. 'Keith had enough money and power to keep his distance from the nasty side of the drug business. He might have spent his days swanning around his pool acting like a cool guy, but he knew what was going on. KMG was a ruthless organisation that didn't hesitate to use violence and intimidation to get what it wanted. For every person KMG made rich, there's probably a thousand more who messed their lives up with drugs. Either by taking them, or getting caught selling them.'

'Keith said breaking up KMG wouldn't even make a difference to the amount of cocaine being sold on the streets.'

'Maybe there's some truth in that,' Meryl said. 'But you can't stop fighting against something just because it's difficult. That's like saying there's no point having doctors and hospitals because everyone eventually dies.'

'So when's my next mission?' James asked.

'Ah,' Meryl said, 'bad news on that score, I'm afraid. You've been on two long missions already this year and you've missed a lot of school. We're not looking to send you off campus again until the new year.'

'That's not so bad, actually,' James said. 'Missions are hard work. It'll be nice to go a few months without waking up every morning wondering what my name is and if I'm gonna get shot at.'

'I heard about the man you killed. We do all we can to keep our agents out of situations like this, but it's an unfortunate fact that drug dealers and guns are inextricably linked. Have you thought about it at all since you got back?'

'A bit,' James said. 'But I get more freaked-out wondering what would have happened if me and Junior hadn't decided to go down the beach for a boxing– erm . . . For a swim, that night.'

'Have you had trouble sleeping, or nightmares?'

'I was lying awake thinking about the car chase on the plane home,' James said. 'The woman sitting next to me said I looked pale. She got me a little tub of mineral water.'

'I'll arrange some sessions with a counsellor,' Meryl said. 'You've been through a traumatic experience and it's important that you talk about your feelings with someone.'

*

Kerry was sitting on a bench by the athletics track waiting for James when he got out of Meryl's office. He gave her a quick kiss and sat next to her.

'How many punishment laps did Meryl give you?' Kerry asked.

'None,' James said.

'That's got to be a first.'

'I didn't do anything bad.'

Kerry started giggling. 'Another first.'

'They don't want to send me on another mission until the new year. It'll be cool if we can just chill out on campus together. Watch movies, do homework and stuff.'

'That's OK for you to say, James. You've already fluked into the lead role on two major missions and earned your navy T-shirt. I'm still a nobody.'

'It's not such a big deal,' James said casually. 'It's just a T-shirt.'

Kerry huffed. 'If there's one thing I really hate, it's people who have something and say that it doesn't matter. It's like those rock stars on MTV who go on about how their millions of dollars and supermodel girlfriends haven't made them any happier. But you never see them giving it all away and going back to live in Mummy's trailer home, do you?'

James thought it was best to change the subject before Kerry got into one of her moods. 'Do you fancy taking a stroll over to the back of campus?'

'That would be nice,' Kerry said, breaking into a smile. 'The leaves are pretty colours at this time of year. I never thought you had a romantic side, James.'

'Actually, Kyle and Lauren are up there cleaning out ditches. I thought we could go over and wind them up a bit.'

Kerry gave James a gentle shove. 'I might have known you *didn't* have a romantic side . . . What happened about Lauren, anyway? The last I heard, everyone was gonna go up there and help her out.'

'Mac said Lauren had to be punished and that anyone caught helping her dig would have to run thirty laps every day for a month. Everyone's making her life easier in other ways though: doing her laundry, letting her jump the queue in the canteen, copying homework, that kind of stuff.

'It was so funny when Kyle got back from ditch-clearing last night,' James continued. 'You know how he's always immaculate? His uniform was plastered in mud and it smelled *so* bad. A lot of the water in those ditches runs off the farms around here. It's all full of cow and pig manure, and god knows what else.'

'Serves him right for taking drugs,' Kerry said.

'Give over, Kerry, all he did was take a puff on a joint. He would never have got caught if Nicole hadn't collapsed.'

'I don't care,' Kerry said. 'If something's against the law, you shouldn't do it. Especially drugs.'

James started to laugh.

'What's funny?'

'You,' James said. 'You're always *such* a goody two shoes.'

Kerry jabbed a finger in James' ribs.

'What was that for?'

'I'm not a goody two shoes.'

James grinned. 'Little Miss Perfect.'

'Take that back or I'll make you sorry.'

James mocked her voice. 'Take that back or I'll make you sorry.'

'Don't start repeating what I say.'

'Don't start repeating what I say.'

'That's *it*, James,' Kerry said angrily.

'That's *it*, James.' James leaned forward and planted a cheeky kiss on Kerry's face. She broke into a smile.

'I knew you weren't really mad at me,' James giggled. 'I'm too delightful.'

He stopped giggling when he realised it wasn't Kerry's nice smile. It was her evil smile. She jabbed James in the ribs again, then used the moment while he was in spasm to wrap her arm around the back of his neck and wedge him into a headlock under her arm.

'Still goody two shoes, am I?' Kerry grinned as she tightened her grip.

'No,' James croaked.

'Quite sure?'

'You're not a goody, Kerry,' James squirmed. 'Just . . . Please . . . Let me go.'

Kerry let James loose. As he straightened up, James couldn't help but see the funny side of being effortlessly humiliated by a twelve-year-old girl wearing pink and white striped socks with penguins embroidered over the ankle.

Kerry got off the bench.

'Where are you going?' James asked.

'Romantic stroll,' she explained, as she marched towards the trees. 'Are you coming or not?'

*

After their walk, James, Kerry and a big bunch of other kids spent Sunday evening at the bowling alley in the nearest town. They got beaten three games to two by the identical twins, Callum and Connor. James and Kerry had a total laugh. James had never felt so relaxed with a girl before. Now he'd asked Kerry out, it seemed dumb that he'd spent so long finding excuses not to.

James lay awake until gone midnight. His body was still running on Miami time and it was early evening over there. He tucked his hands under his head and stared at the shadows on the ceiling.

He wondered how Junior was doing in hospital and got pissed off when he remembered that April still had his Nike watch. But the KMG mission already felt distant, like part of some other kid's life. James Beckett was no more. James Adams felt warm and comfortable under his duvet. He realised he was the happiest he'd been since his mum died.

James thought about life on campus. He knew the quickest routes around every building. He knew everyone's names. Which kids not to start a conversation with in the lift because they'd bore you to tears. Which teachers would have a laugh with you and which ones would hammer you for the tiniest little thing.

James knew there would always be mornings when he woke up and didn't want to get out of bed for two hours' combat training, or a brain-numbing double history lesson. But when he pulled on his uniform and walked down to breakfast, he knew most other kids looked at him with respect. Whenever James got to the dining-room and looked around for a seat, there were always a few tables where he could sit amongst friends, spreading the latest gossip and winding each other up.

A year earlier, CHERUB campus had been a bunch of strange faces, winding corridors and scary teachers. Now it felt like home.

EPILOGUE

KELVIN HOLMES was sentenced to three years' youth custody for conspiracy to supply drugs. Most of the younger boys who worked as delivery riders for KMG got off with police cautions and supervision orders. A few who had previous drug convictions received 3-6 months in youth custody.

Without funding from Keith Moore, the JT Martin youth centre and boxing club closed its doors for the final time after the 2004 Christmas party. No charges were brought against KEN FOWLER, who died of a heart attack a few months later.

MADELINE BURROWS, the nice lady who called James with his deliveries, got a five-year prison sentence, as did her younger brother JOSEPH BURROWS (Crazy Joe). Over 130 other members of KMG received prison sentences as a direct result of the MI5 surveillance operation on Thunderfoods.

Dinesh's dad, PARVINDER SINGH, received a twelve-year prison sentence. DINESH SINGH and his mother moved away, to live near relatives in south London.

KEITH MOORE spent over a week being interviewed by DEA officials at their headquarters in Washington DC. Keith was bitter about the Lambayeke cartel's brutal attempt to steal his money and provided a mass of information that led to the immediate seizure of $130 million in drug money and the arrest of several senior figures within the Lambayeke organisation.

Keith was later flown back to Britain, where he pleaded guilty to numerous charges relating to money-laundering and drug-trafficking. The judge sentenced Keith to eighteen years in prison and recommended that he should not be considered for early release until he had served at least ten.

The police have uncovered £12 million of Keith's personal fortune, but he is still believed to have at least another £40 million in secret bank accounts.

JUNIOR MOORE fully recovered from his injuries and flew back to Britain. Shortly afterwards, he was expelled from Grey Park school for persistent truancy. His mother said she was 'sick of his behaviour' and didn't want him ending up like his father. She found him a place at a tough boarding school that specialises in dealing with difficult boys.

APRIL MOORE quickly grew tired of James Beckett not responding to her text messages and e-mails. She returned

James' best watch to the address where the Beckett family had supposedly moved and it was eventually forwarded to CHERUB campus. When James opened the envelope, he found his watch had been hammered into a dozen pieces. It was accompanied by a note reading: '*You could at least have had the decency to dump me to my face. Hope you die slowly, April.*'

JOHN JONES announced he was leaving MI5 after nineteen years' service. He has accepted a new job as a CHERUB mission controller.

EWART & ZARA ASKER are expecting their second child in April 2005.

NICOLE EDDISON now lives with two retired cherubs on a farm in Shropshire. She has two young stepbrothers who she adores and a boyfriend called James. She attends twice-weekly counselling sessions and is slowly coming to terms with the loss of her family.

Dr McAfferty's beloved mission preparation building is on schedule to be completed in February 2005. He conducted a review of Nicole's recruitment to CHERUB, to see if any mistakes had been made. His report reached the following conclusion:

'*If anything, the tests Nicole Eddison completed before being asked to join CHERUB show that she had an above average chance of becoming a successful agent. Unfortunately, no recruitment test yet devised can account for all the complexities of human nature. It seems likely that a small number of unsuitable candidates will be recruited into CHERUB for as long as the organisation exists. All we can do is remain vigilant and try to keep this number to a minimum.'*

A few weeks after James returned from Miami, AMY COLLINS left campus to live with her brother in Australia. James was part of the crowd that waved her through the departure gate at Heathrow airport.

It took KYLE BLUEMAN and LAUREN ADAMS two months to clean out all the ditches at the back of campus. Kyle was suspended from missions for another four months. Lauren re-entered basic training, with her daily countdown paper in her pocket and a grim determination to make it through no matter how tough Mr Large tried to make it.

After a few weeks back on campus, KERRY CHANG was sent to Hong Kong on a mission that looked set to last several months. James and Kerry are exchanging daily e-mails and occasionally speak to each other on the phone.

JAMES ADAMS used his time on campus to catch up on schoolwork. He has recently started studying for GCSE exams in three of his strongest subjects, has begun regular weight training, and narrowly failed a second-dan black belt grading in Karate class. He expects to be assigned to another undercover mission in early 2005.

Read on to find out about how James and the other cherubs prepare for Christmas on campus . . .

1. THE OLD NEIGHBOURHOOD

Friday December 24th 2004, 10:37 a.m.

James knew exactly what he'd see as he turned the corner into Holloway Villas: six-storey housing blocks, built around a courtyard, with a vandalised playground in the centre and the stench of rubbish as you walked past by the giant steel bins.

The only thing James didn't recognise was the graffiti. PIG41 was the new spray can supremo on James' old estate. His bright red tag adorned walls, doors, billboards and even the pavement itself.

'You OK, James?' Bruce asked as the two boys walked side by side.

'Yeah,' James said, swallowing a lump in his throat.

But he wasn't OK. Memories of the night when his mother died fourteen months earlier still had the power to sting.

Bruce handed James a tissue. 'It's a bit crumpled, but there's no snot on it.'

'Ta,' James said, feeling a little embarrassed as he took it and rubbed his eyes. 'I don't know ... I mean ... I just remembered the ambulance men carrying my mum out and Lauren holding my wrist. It all came flooding back.'

'Nothing to be ashamed of,' Bruce said. 'Nobody's gonna get over their mum dying in any sort of hurry.'

The boys headed up a concrete staircase. A bitter gust of wind hit them as they stepped out on to the second-floor balcony. James' sadness was replaced by nostalgia as he remembered his mum yelling down from the balcony with a finger drumming against the face of her watch.

'*Eight o'clock, James. You'll catch hell if I have to come down there and get you.*'

James stopped when he reached the living-room window of his old flat and glanced inside.

'Looks like a young couple moved in,' he said as he peered in. 'It's all been done up. Wood floors and that.'

Bruce nodded. 'Looks pretty smart.'

'It does,' James said. 'But I wouldn't have paid two hundred and twenty grand to live here.'

'How much?' Bruce gasped.

James grinned. 'Property prices round here are insane. Mum owned the flat and her mortgage was paid off by the life insurance when she died. Me and Lauren get to share the loot when we leave CHERUB.'

'You're jammy,' Bruce said. 'My parents died when I was a baby and they owed three grand on their Barclaycard.'

James stepped away from the window and rang the bell of a flat six doors further along the balcony. He waited half a minute, but there was no answer.

'We came all this way and the geezer's out,' Bruce spluttered angrily. 'I'm gonna kick his arse . . .'

'Keep your wig on,' James grinned. 'This isn't Alan's place. My old mate Sam lives here. I was just gonna say *hi*, but it looks like he's out. Alan lives in the one up the end; he'll be waiting for me.'

When the door of Alan's flat opened, James was engulfed in the arms of a grubby-looking man with black body hair down his arms and a giant beer gut.

'Hey, Alan,' James grinned, pleased to be reacquainted with a friend, but slightly less pleased at being hugged into a white vest that smelled of three-tins-for-a-pound body spray from Holloway market.

'You look good,' Alan gasped. 'Quite a handsome young man now. You've got taller and thinned out. Come inside. Where's the little lady?'

'Lauren couldn't come. She's back at our foster home with a stinking cold,' James lied. 'This is my mate, Bruce. He's gonna help me carry all the gear home.'

Alan led them down the hallway. 'That's a shame. I was looking forward to seeing Lauren. I hope being sick doesn't spoil her Christmas.'

'I reckon she's over the worst of it,' James said, as the boys stepped into Alan's living-room.

There was no space to sit because the entire room was stacked up with bags of stolen items. Only the tip of the Christmas tree was visible behind a stack of Xboxes and PS2s.

Alan had been James' mum's number two before she died and now he'd taken over her shoplifting racket. James had grown up around the business and wasn't impressed by what he saw.

'You want to be careful, Alan,' he said, as he spun around

looking at the piles of stolen goods. 'My mum would never have anything freshly nicked in our flat. If the police see all this lot, they'll lock you up and throw away the key.'

'I know, I know,' Alan said defensively, sounding like he'd already heard this advice from other quarters. 'But you know how mental everything gets at this time of year, James. I've got so much coming and going. I've got two lock-ups piled up with stuff. There's nowhere else to put it all.'

James nodded. 'Mum used to tell everyone to get their orders in early, but it still went mad every Christmas.'

'You boys look half-frozen. Would you like a hot drink? All the stuff you ordered is in those three bags over by the door.'

While Alan headed out to make tea, James dragged the bags into the centre of the room to check that everything he'd ordered was there. It wasn't that he didn't trust Alan, but with the place in a state of chaos he could easily have made a mistake.

Bruce read down the list, 'Burnout 3, five copies, Gabrielle's make-up, PDA for Kerry, Lauren's clothes, my extra-large nunchaku, Predator footy boots size six, Dior perfume set for Kerry, FCUK stuff for Bethany, two pairs of . . .'

The bags contained most of the stuff James, Bruce and their pals were getting each other for Christmas.

When Alan came back holding two steaming mugs, James had a roll of fifty-pound notes in his hand.

'Half the shop price for this lot comes to five hundred and eighty quid,' James said. 'It's all there.'

Alan snatched the money and started counting it. Every seat in the room was covered in shoplifted goodies, so

James and Bruce had to squat down on the carpet with their hot tea.

'So, what are you up to over Christmas?' James asked.

Alan shrugged. 'Gonna visit my sister and her 'orrible offspring, same as always.'

'Cool,' James nodded.

Alan held out three hundred from the money James had just handed him. 'There you go, boy, split that lot with your sister.'

James waved his hands in front of his face. 'Don't be daft, Alan. I told you I had the money to pay for this stuff when I rang up. I'm not asking for charity.'

Alan smiled. 'James, your mother was very good to me over the years. She would have wanted me to look out for you and Lauren.'

'No,' James grinned.

But Alan dropped the money in James' lap.

Bruce laughed and made a grab for it. 'I'll have it if you don't want it.'

James reluctantly picked the money off the carpet. 'You're a good geezer, Al,' he grinned. 'My nan always said she couldn't understand how my mum ended up marrying that idiot Ron when you lived just down the balcony.'

Alan burst out laughing. 'Old missus Choke, I haven't thought about her in ages. She was a tough old bird, your grandmother. Didn't stand any nonsense from anyone.'

James clambered off the carpet and reached out to shake Alan's hand. 'I'm gonna take a piss, then we'd better be going back to cam— erm, to our foster home.'

'Oh,' Alan said, sounding a touch disappointed. 'You can

stay a while if you want. I'll take you down the shops and get you both McDonalds or something.'

James shook his head. 'Thanks for the offer, Alan, but we've got a fair journey back and you know how mental the trains get if you leave it till last thing on Christmas Eve.'

2. MUDDY PUPS

12:08

In the main building on CHERUB campus the bell had rung for the end of lessons and the kids were free until the second of January. Some had gone off to the dojo to watch the Christmas Karate Tournament, some had gone out to play football, but most kids headed off to their rooms to dump their schoolbooks and change out of their CHERUB uniform into normal clothes.

Everyone was in high spirits at the prospect of a week-long break, except for eight kids inside the basic training compound and two others who were serving a punishment over on the far side of campus. Kyle Blueman was being punished for smoking cannabis, Lauren Adams for battering CHERUB's head training instructor with a spade.

*

Lauren lost her footing as she clambered up the side of the ditch. Her wellington slid down the muddy embankment and she collapsed forward, unable to save herself because she was holding a bundle of branches in her arms. Kyle ploughed through the thirty-centimetre-deep sludge and put out his hand.

Lauren could feel cold water trickling inside her waterproof trousers as Kyle hauled her up.

'Are you OK?' he asked.

Lauren was a picture of misery as chunks of mud slid down the front of her waterproof jacket. She gathered up the branches she'd dropped around her feet and began lobbing them up on to the embankment a couple at a time.

'I'm so knackered,' she said, breaking into a yawn before glancing at her watch. 'And there's still five hours to go.'

Kyle pulled his shovel out of the slurry. He scooped up a load of soggy leaves and dropped them into a heavy plastic sack.

'At least we've got the next two days off,' he said.

Lauren nodded. 'Yeah, but you can forget about enjoying Christmas. I'm just gonna go to bed and sleep. I don't even care about my presents.'

Kyle felt sorry for Lauren. They'd landed the same punishment, but it was tougher on ten-year-old Lauren than on Kyle, who'd turned fifteen a week earlier.

'We deserve a break,' Kyle said.

'It's not one o'clock yet.'

Kyle turned backwards and looked at the section of cleared ditch behind them. 'I reckon we've done a good morning's graft, don't you? I dug out all those leaves, you stripped down all the branches and chopped up that tree trunk.'

Lauren smiled in agreement. 'Maybe you're right. There's nobody around and we deserve an extra fifteen minutes' lunch after all that.'

They were in a particularly deep section of ditch, so Kyle

clambered up the muddy embankment first, then gave Lauren a hand so that she didn't slip over again. The dining-hall was over a kilometre away and they wouldn't have been allowed in without stripping off their overalls and washing, so packed lunch was their only practical option. Lauren slumped down with her back against a tree, pulled off her gloves and wiped her muddy fingers on a damp flannel.

She grabbed a flask filled with hot soup from her backpack, poured it into the lid and dipped in a hunk of bread. The extra-thick soup was made in the CHERUB kitchens and Lauren was starving. Kyle dunked his soup with a ham and tomato roll as a man's voice came out of the trees.

'What's this then, slacking off?'

Ken Crane was the CHERUB groundskeeper supervising Lauren and Kyle's punishment. Lauren thought about jumping up and pretending to work, but Ken was close by and he was a decent bloke as long as you didn't muck him about.

'Is it early, Ken?' Kyle said weakly. 'My watch must be fast.'

'Must be,' Ken smirked, as he squelched up to the edge of the ditch and looked at what they'd done.

'Not a bad show,' he nodded. 'You two make a good little team. I'll be sorry when your punishments are over.'

Lauren smiled. 'We certainly won't be.'

Ken laughed. 'Anyhow, I came over here to tell you both to scoot off.'

Kyle grinned. 'You serious?'

'Yep. Take your tools back to the shed and hose the mud off your boots and overalls. I'll pick up the branches and sacks of leaves with the tractor later on.'

Lauren interrupted. 'But Dr McAfferty's very strict. He said—'

'Do I look concerned about Dr McAfferty? It's Christmas Eve and *I'm* telling you to buzz off. Go and have a good Christmas and I'll see you back here in a few days.'

Lauren chucked away the last of her soup, screwed the lid back on her flask and stood up, grinning.

'Thank you, Mr Crane. Have a good Christmas yourself.'

3. A FINAL LOOK

12:40

Ancient memories washed over Marcus Thompson as the taxi wound down the road leading to CHERUB campus' single entrance.

In particular, he recalled a summer's day nearly fifty years earlier. Back then he was a newly qualified CHERUB agent, walking along this very stretch of road in plimsolls and cotton shorts, with a couple of young pals for company. They were heading for a nearby lake that was the closest thing CHERUB had to a swimming pool in those days.

Everything, except the twisting outline of the road itself, had changed. The dirt track that got churned into mud every winter had been widened, tarmacked and fitted with street lighting. The small farms that had surrounded campus back then had gradually been bought up. Where Marcus remembered a view over open fields, there was now a ten-metre breeze-block wall, topped with razor wire and CCTV cameras. Every twenty metres there was a yellow warning sign:

DO NOT ENTER
Any attempt to climb this wall
may be met with deadly force.
By Order of the Ministry of Defence.

'Gives me the spooks, this road,' the taxi driver said, as he took a sharp bend slightly too fast, pressing Marcus against the car door. 'It's like the X-Files, or Area 51, or something. Everyone goes on about it in the pubs and that. I even know a couple of ladies who work in the kitchens, but they never say a word about what goes on inside.'

Marcus allowed himself to smile. Fifty years hadn't changed some things: the locals still wanted to know what CHERUB campus was all about.

'It's probably better you don't know,' Marcus said.

The driver laughed. 'You're probably right, old-timer. I'll give you lot one thing though, this place is good for business. The run between here and the station is one of my biggest earners.'

The taxi took another bend uncomfortably fast, and when they were round it the metal gates of CHERUB campus were visible. The cab driver pulled up in front of the gate and walked around to the boot to grab Marcus' suitcase. His elderly passenger was struggling to get out of the car, but turned down an offer of help.

'That's six-eighty, guv.'

As Marcus fumbled in his wallet, the chairman of CHERUB emerged through a riveted door at the side of the main gate. He spread his arms out wide and the two men hugged.

'My god,' Mac shouted. 'Marcus Thompson, I haven't seen you since . . .'

Marcus smiled. 'I was here for the fortieth reunion, back in eighty-six.'

*

13:32

Gabrielle O'Brien knocked on the Chairman's door and got called in immediately.

Dr McAfferty – commonly known as Mac – sat at his fireplace holding a tumbler of whiskey. Gabrielle didn't recognise the black man sitting opposite him. He had a few wisps of grey hair on his head and a can of Heineken in his hand. He turned to Gabrielle and gave her a gap-toothed smile.

'By gum, you're beautiful,' Marcus grinned, standing as quickly as his frail body would allow and kissing the back of Gabrielle's hand. 'Will you marry me?'

Gabrielle backed off uneasily, sensing that the man was a little drunk. 'I think thirteen is a bit young to be getting married.'

'*Thirteen*, but you're a giant,' Marcus smiled. 'You look at least fifteen. Is it me or are you kids getting bigger these days?'

Mac laughed. 'They're bigger. That's why they eat so much and grow through so many clothes. I got a letter from the Intelligence Services Procurement department last week. They wanted to know why I'd spent over sixty thousand pounds on footwear over the last year.'

'Sixty grand,' Marcus spluttered, shocked. 'In our day we had hobnail boots and white plimsolls that were handed down from one kid to the next till the soles wore through.'

'Tell me about it,' Mac grinned. 'The combat boots these kids wear for training are a hundred and twenty pounds a throw. And every kid these days *has* to have designer gear for their casual clothes.'

Gabrielle smiled guiltily. 'Well, kids on the outside wear that stuff and we have to blend in when we're on missions.'

Dr McAfferty nodded. 'Gabrielle, Marcus here is one of my oldest and dearest friends. We were both CHERUB agents together back in the 1950s. He's been living in Barbados for most of the last twenty years, but he's caught the nostalgia bug and asked if he could visit us for Christmas. I'm afraid I have some paperwork to finish up before the holidays, so I'd like you to treat Marcus to the grand tour. Show him all our new buildings and facilities. Access all areas, I think we can trust him.'

Gabrielle would have preferred to hang out with her mates, but Marcus seemed a nice enough old bloke, and you can't really say no when the Chairman asks a favour.

As Marcus walked slowly towards the door, Mac whispered in Gabrielle's ear. 'I appreciate this, Gabrielle. Take Marcus round in one of the golf buggies, he's a very sick man and I'm led to believe that he's only got a few months to live. He just wanted to take a last look at the place where he spent most of his childhood.'

4. GMT + 8

It was past midnight in Tokyo, but Kerry was jet-lagged and couldn't get to sleep. She threw back a corner of her bedding and looked at the digital clock on the bedside table: 00:03, Christmas Day.

It was a miserable feeling, being trapped in a hotel room with only a snoring mission controller for company. Kerry's first big solo mission was a golden opportunity to establish her reputation amongst the elite corps of recently qualified CHERUB agents.

She'd spent weeks polishing her Japanese language skills, hours reading mission briefings and detailed texts on the Yakuza. She wanted to succeed more than anything else in the world; it was just a shame that she couldn't have flown out a couple of days later and spent Christmas with her friends on campus.

Kerry closed her eyes again, but quickly realised that she wasn't even close to feeling sleepy. It might have been dark outside, but as far as her body clock was concerned, it was four in the afternoon. She stepped up to the window and opened a tiny crack in the curtains. The room was fourteen storeys up and the streets below glimmered under a mixture of streetlight and neon signs. Flocks of ant-sized people moved along the pavements and the traffic remained solid, even at this early hour of the morning.

If the room had been larger, Kerry might have flicked on the TV or bedside light to read by, but the two single beds were separated by less than half a metre and she didn't want to disturb her mission controller. Instead, she stepped into the bathroom and pushed the door closed quietly before turning on the light.

The cramped space had a slight disinfectant smell. There was barely enough room between the shower, toilet and sink to take two steps. She sat on the toilet lid and noticed that there was a telephone attached to the wall beside the tissue holder.

*

James had been picked up at the station nearest to campus by mini-bus, along with a bunch of other cherubs who'd managed to wrangle Christmas Eve as a shopping day. He was waiting for the lift up to this sixth-floor room, holding two big bags of presents, when his mobile rang.

He flipped it open. 'James Adams, super stud speaking.'

'Super *what*?' Kerry giggled. 'Super idiot more like.'

'How was the flight?'

'Ten hours, economy class. Two days before Christmas, so you can imagine. Heathrow Airport was a nuthouse, the plane was packed. It's already Christmas Day over here. Well, we're ten minutes into it anyway.'

'I've just been down to London with Bruce,' James explained as he stepped into the lift. 'I'm holding your present in my hands.'

'You know this is a really long mission, James. It's gonna be at least April before I get to open it.'

'I'll tell you what it is if you like.'

Kerry thought for a second. 'No, it'll be a nice surprise when I get back.'

'I just hope *I'm* not on a mission when you do. We could end up not seeing each other for yonks.'

The lift doors opened at the sixth floor and James stepped out.

'Well,' Kerry said, 'I only rang to wish you a happy Christmas and I bet this call is costing a packet. I'd better go.'

James made a kissing noise. 'I wish you were here, Kerry. Christmas is gonna suck without you around.'

'I'll miss you too,' Kerry said sadly. 'Goodbye, James. Tell Gabrielle and everyone else that I wished them a happy Christmas.'

James flipped his phone shut and put the two bags down on the carpet outside his room.

Bruce grinned at James and blew him a kiss. 'Bye bye, Kerry, *smooch*,' he grinned, mocking James' voice. 'I miss you sweetie cakes, *smoochy, smoochy*.'

James tutted as he pulled his room key out of his tracksuit bottoms. 'Shut up. Just 'cos you haven't got a girlfriend. You'd better help us sort out all this shopping. I've got tons of wrapping-up to do.'

As James headed into his room, he heard his name being yelled out from Meryl Spencer's office at the end of the corridor. He knew it couldn't be Meryl herself. She was at a TV studio in London.

He realised it was her assistant, Christine.

'James Adams,' Christine repeated angrily. 'Get your sorry butt down here *right* now!'

'Crap,' James muttered to Bruce under his breath.

'Busted,' Bruce giggled.

'Clearly,' James shrugged. 'I'm just trying to think what I've done.'

He pushed his shopping in to the doorway and headed towards the slender woman standing at the end of the corridor.

'Into the office, James,' Christine said tersely.

James headed in, Christine followed. The door clattered shut as she sat down behind Meryl's desk.

'James, Meryl allowed you to take a Christmas shopping day on the understanding that you were up to date with all of your homework.'

'Yeah,' James nodded. 'I am.'

'I had Mr Grwgoski up here looking for you earlier, James. He doesn't seem to agree with you.'

James looked a little shocked. 'Oh.'

'A short essay, written in Russian, on the history of Moscow. I believe it was due to be handed in more than a week ago.'

'Yeah, um . . . I forgot.'

'James, if I had a pound for every time you've *conveniently* forgotten a homework assignment . . .'

'Sorry, Chris, but I'll do it right after Christmas, I swear.'

Christine slowly shook her head. 'Oh no, you won't. You're going to do it right now.'

'But . . .'

Christine pointed at a small wooden desk in the corner of her office. It was a really old-fashioned one with an inkwell built in and a place for storing your books underneath.

'I took the liberty of going into your room while you were out. I found your Russian books and your pencil case and put them on that desk ready for you to start work.'

'But . . .'

'No ifs, no buts, James. You're going to sit at that desk and complete that homework while I'm sitting here watching you.'

'It's gonna take hours though,' James whined. 'It's Christmas.'

'Then you'd better get a move on. As far as you're concerned, Christmas doesn't start until you've finished that assignment.'

James reluctantly slumped down at the desk. 'So much for the season of goodwill,' he said miserably as he opened his textbook. 'Can I at least watch Meryl when she's on TV later?'

Christine looked at her watch. 'James, her show's not on for another two and a half hours. If you get your act together you'll be finished long before then.'

5. CELEBRITY MADNESS

18:58

It had been more than five years since Meryl Spencer had appeared on television. She'd always been reclusive and rarely made public appearances, even when she was at the pinnacle of her career. She'd told everyone that she'd accepted the offer to appear on the show because it was for charity, but she was also quite flattered that people still remembered her more than six years after she'd retired from athletics.

Meryl felt self-conscious sitting behind a neon-lit counter with two other sports personalities for company. She had a buzzer and bank of small screens in front of her. The hot studio lights made her brow sweat and a young man leaned in and dabbed them away with a cotton-wool ball.

A roar came up from the audience as the warm-up comedian rounded off his spiel.

'Ladies and gentlemen, let's have a big cheer for tonight's host. England's all time number one international goal scorer and winner of three premiership titles, Martin Monroe.'

The balding ex-footballer stepped in from stage left in a

snappy suit as the audience cheered. He signed a couple of autographs, before walking on to the set and taking his seat at the centre of the stage. Meryl heard the director speaking into her earpiece.

'OK people, look happy. Remember, you're going out live to seven million people so let's keep it sweet.'

Meryl's face got another dab with the cotton wool and her glass of water was refilled while the opening titles rolled. The audience went wild as the camera panned in on the host.

'Hello and welcome to this special Christmas charity edition of Sports Quiz. Two teams of three contestants battling it out and, for one night only, every correct answer wins five hundred pounds for charity. Joining our regular team captains Rhys and Susan tonight are four outstanding sports personalities from around the world.'

Meryl stifled a gasp as her face filled up the monitor. *Seven million people.*

Monroe continued. 'Joining us tonight in a rare public appearance, Meryl Spencer.'

The audience broke out into another bout of wild clapping.

'Meryl was the red-hot favourite for a one-hundred-metre gold at the 1992 Olympics in Barcelona but tragically pulled up in her heat. But it all came right in Atlanta in 1996.'

The monitor cut away from Meryl's face to a scene recorded in the Olympic stadium eight years earlier. A close shot opened out to show a line of muscular women on the starting blocks. The pistol fired and the women sprang up. Meryl was first out of the blocks and continued powering away from the field, passing the finish line ten and a half seconds later, three strides clear of the field.

The commentator's voice boomed. '*The Kenyan simply blew the rest of the field away . . .*'

Meryl had seen footage of her victory thousands of times before, but she still looked proud as the director cut back to her face.

'Meryl,' the genial host grinned. 'That run still stands as the Olympic record and as the third fastest one hundred metres ever run by a woman. A truly phenomenal achievement.'

Meryl nodded. 'Thank you, Martin.'

Martin smiled sneakily as the audience clapped. 'And we understand you went to Japan and made some TV commercials shortly after your victory?'

Meryl covered her face with her hands and shrieked with nervous laughter. 'Oh no, you're not going to show *that*.'

Meryl knew they *were* going to show *that*, because they'd done it in rehearsals a few hours earlier. She heard the director's voice in her earpiece.

'That's a great expression, Meryl. You look really shocked, now give the audience a smile just to show that you're not really upset – that's perfect.'

*

There were more than a hundred and fifty kids gathered in the CHERUB dining-hall watching Meryl Spencer, dressed in a chicken suit, being fired out of a cannon while an array of incomprehensible Japanese slogans flashed across the screen.

James was laughing as hard as anyone else. 'Oh my god!' he snorted. 'I wonder how much they paid her to do that.'

Kyle replied, 'Meryl did OK, judging by the gold Rolex and that fancy Mercedes she drives.'

James and Kyle sat around their usual table with Bruce,

Callum, Connor, Gabrielle and Marcus Thompson. The sixty-two-year-old had turned down the opportunity to join Mac in the staff dining-room. He'd downed a bottle of red wine while he struggled through a plate of fish and chips, and entertained the kids with anecdotes from the early days of CHERUB.

Marcus told the kids that he enjoyed their company because they made him feel young. The kids didn't mind because most of the stories were funny and Marcus was happy to dish out dirt on some of CHERUB's most senior staff.

6. LESSONS ABOUT DRIVING AND ALCOHOL

20:00

When Sports Quiz ended, the kids had to clear out of the dining-hall so that the kitchen staff could come in and set everything up for Christmas dinner the next day.

'What are we gonna do now?' Kyle asked. 'Someone upstairs must be having a party or something.'

James shrugged. 'I'd better go back to my room, I've got loads of presents to wrap.'

Gabrielle spoke. 'I'm taking Marcus over to the junior block. The little kids are doing a nativity play.'

'I'm up for that,' Bruce nodded. 'Remember last year when that little shepherdess fell off the stage?'

Kyle nodded. 'I felt sorry for her, but it *was* hilarious.'

Everyone else decided to go over and see the play.

'Come on, James,' Connor said. 'Let's all stick together, it's Christmas Eve.'

'I can't. I've got presents to wrap.'

'Who cares?' Kyle said. 'They're all gonna be unwrapped in a few hours anyway.'

James had bought labels and wrapping paper in town the previous weekend, but the more he thought about it, the more he realised that the prospect of sitting on his floor with scissors and tape wasn't going to be as much fun as hanging out with the gang.

'OK,' James nodded. 'I'm in. Lauren should be over there anyway and I wouldn't mind seeing her for a bit.'

Marcus led the way towards the exit.

'To the Batmobile,' the grey-haired man shouted, taking a swig of rum from a hip flask that had appeared from inside his jacket moments after he'd drained the last of the wine.

As they stepped out into the chilly air, Gabrielle was alarmed to see Marcus taking up the driver's seat of the electric golf buggy she'd been using to shuttle him around campus.

'Marcus,' she said sternly. 'I don't think you're in any fit state—'

Marcus broke into a big grin. 'Hogwash, girl,' he grinned. 'I've been driving all my life and I've not had so much as a scrape. Come on, kids, climb aboard. Next stop the junior block. Have your fares ready to pay the conductor.'

'Shotgun,' James shouted, as he dived into the front passenger seat of the little buggy. Kyle, Bruce and Callum crammed themselves into the back, while Connor and Shakeel had to perch on the small cargo shelf with their legs dangling over the rear of the vehicle.

Gabrielle placed a firm hand on Marcus' shoulder. 'Mr Thompson, I *really* don't think you should be driving.'

Marcus shot her a mischievous grin. 'I don't want to marry you any more, Gabrielle O'Brien. You're starting to sound just like all of my ex-wives.'

Marcus hit the accelerator and the overloaded buggy began whirring away without her.

'Frankly, I'd rather walk,' Gabrielle shouted bitterly after them. She was angry at the way Marcus had treated her after she'd spent half the day chaperoning him around campus.

The little buggies were good for thirty kilometres an hour, but not with seven passengers aboard. Marcus lurched the steering wheel sharply to the right as the buggy edged off the paved path on to the grass verge.

'Watch it, dude,' James yelled.

'I can hardly see where I'm going,' Marcus said, as he pulled back on to the path and began picking up speed.

'It might *help* if you turned the headlamps on,' James said. 'The switch is on your right, below the steering wheel.'

Much to James' alarm, Marcus took his eyes off the road and began looking for the switch. All six passengers simultaneously realised that Gabrielle had been right about their elderly pilot being in no state to drive.

James grabbed the steering wheel as the vehicle lurched off the road. Marcus flipped the headlamps on in time for James to see that they were going *way* too fast to make it around a sharp bend less than twenty metres in front of them.

'Oh my god,' James shouted, wrapping his arms over his face as Marcus hit the brake pedal.

The braking did little to stop them careering off the path into one of the combed gravel beds at the front of the dojo. There was a horrific grinding noise as the buggy ploughed into the loose stones, sending them firing off in all directions.

The battery cut out and the headlamps failed as the buggy nudged a low wall and ground to a halt. James heard the flying gravel settle and breathed a mouthful of dust as they were plunged back into darkness.

'Is everybody OK?' he gasped.

'I think we're gonna live,' Kyle said dryly, as he clambered out the side of the buggy. 'Just.'

Bruce and Connor had both fallen off the back when the buggy juddered over the gravel, but it only seemed to be pride that was hurt as they dusted themselves down.

Marcus Thompson began to giggle drunkenly. 'Perhaps I should have let young Gabrielle drive after all?'

Kyle whispered in James' ear, 'If I didn't know the old soak was already dying, I'd kill him.'

7. GOODNIGHT SWEETHEART

20:48

By the time they'd hauled the golf buggy out of the gravel and reset the fuses to make it run again, James and his friends had missed Mary and Joseph setting off for Bethlehem and Mary was dilated to seven centimetres. All the seats were gone, so they had to stand up at the back of the hall.

'I can see the head,' a seven-year-old Joseph squawked from the gloomily lit stage at the front of the hall.

Mary yelled out in pain as an attentive shepherd mopped her brow.

'Come on, Mary, put your back into it.'

'I can see it,' Joseph screamed as he grabbed a plastic doll off the floor and launched it high above his head. 'It's a boy.'

'We're going to call it Jesus,' Mary said.

James stood up on tiptoes and tried to spot Lauren in the darkened hall. He whispered to Kyle, 'Can you see my sister anywhere?'

Kyle looked at his watch. 'It's gone nine and she looked

pretty beat when we finished digging. Maybe she went to bed early.'

James nodded. 'I'll go check her room.'

He crept out of the hall and passed down a deserted corridor. He knocked gently before sticking his head around the door. The room was dark, but he could make out Lauren's outline rising and falling beneath her duvet. One arm dangled over the side of the bed and her fingertips touched the floor.

James stepped inside and stood watching his sister for a moment. He felt sorry for her, knowing that she faced five more weeks of digging, followed by the horrors of basic training. He wished there was a way he could take some of the burden off his sister, but he knew that the only thing he could do right now was let her sleep.

'Goodnight, sis,' James whispered as he backed out of the room.

At least he knew Lauren would be happy in the morning when she saw what he'd got her for Christmas.

CHERUB: Maximum Security

Over the years, CHERUB has put plenty of criminals behind bars. Now, for the first time ever, they've got to break one out . . .

Under American law, kids convicted of serious crimes can be tried and sentenced as adults. Two hundred and eighty of these child criminals live in the sunbaked desert prison known as Arizona Max.

In one of the most daring CHERUB missions ever, James Adams has to go undercover inside Arizona Max, befriend an inmate and then bust him out.

CHERUB: The Killing

When a small-time crook suddenly has big money on his hands, it's only natural that the police want to know where it came from.

James' latest CHERUB mission looks routine: make friends with the bad guy's children, infiltrate his home and dig up some leads for the cops to investigate.

But the plot James begins to unravel isn't what anyone expected. And it seems like the only person who might know the truth is a reclusive eighteen-year-old boy.

There's just one problem. The boy fell from a rooftop and died more than a year earlier.

CHERUB: Divine Madness

When a team of CHERUB agents uncover a link between eco-terrorist group Help Earth and a wealthy religious cult known as The Survivors, James Adams is sent to Australia on an infiltration mission.

It's his toughest job so far. The Survivors' outback headquarters are completely isolated. It's a thousand kilometres to the nearest town and the cult's brainwashing techniques mean James is under massive pressure to conform.

This time he's not just fighting terrorists. He's got to battle to keep control of his own mind.

CHERUB: Man vs Beast

Every day thousands of animals die in laboratory experiments. Some say these experiments provide essential scientific knowledge, while others will do anything to prevent them.

CHERUB agents James and Lauren Adams are stuck in the middle.

CHERUB: Brigands M.C.

Every CHERUB agent comes from somewhere. Dante Scott still has nightmares about the death of his family, brutally killed by a biker gang.

When Dante joins James Adams on a mission to infiltrate the Brigands Motorcycle Club, he's ready to use everything he's learned to get revenge on the people who killed his family...

Look out for CHERUB: *Brigands* M.C., coming soon from Robert Muchamore and Hodder Children's Books.

And don't miss the rest of the CHERUB series: *Maximum Security*, *The Killing*, *Divine Madness*, *Man vs Beast*, *The Fall*, *Mad Dogs*, *The Sleepwalker* and *The General*.

Summer 1940.

Hitler's army is advancing towards Paris, and millions
of French civilians are on the run.

One of them is a twelve-year-old boy called Marc.
His travelling companion is a British spy named
Charles Henderson.

The very first CHERUB adventure is about to begin.

Henderson's Boys is a major new series from
Robert Muchamore, coming 2009.

Turn the page to read an exclusive preview.

HENDERSON'S BOYS: THE ESCAPE

Charles Henderson didn't feel great about having Marc alongside him. Before joining the Espionage Research Unit he'd been a naval intelligence officer and their training course gave strict instructions never to use kids. The intelligence manual said that children were physically weak, untrustworthy, unable to handle stress and liable to panic or scream.

But Marc was the only help on offer and Henderson wasn't ungrateful for it. He'd slept less than ten hours in the past four days. He hadn't washed or eaten a proper meal and was only keeping himself going with strong black coffee and Benzedrine pills. The worst part was knowing that it wasn't over. If Henderson made it out of Hotel Etalon alive, he'd still have to break through the German and French lines and somehow get to Tours ahead of Potente, who was already on the road.

Henderson drove a small Fiat and the clock on the dashboard told him it was just a few minutes until the eight o'clock curfew, though at this time in June there was still plenty of daylight. The roads were dead, except for the odd truck packed with German troops. Most cars had left the city crammed with refugees, and the few remaining drivers didn't want to risk being made into an example by the newly arrived Germans. Everyone had seen newspaper pictures of the corpses hanging from lampposts in Warsaw.

Marc sat in the passenger seat. The mix of adrenaline and whisky made him feel better, and regular beatings at the orphanage had left him with an unusually high pain threshold. He was worried about Henderson though. Sweat poured down the man's face, his driving was crazy and a couple of times his expression glazed over so badly that Marc thought the car was going to end up ploughing into a wall.

They cruised past Hotel Etalon at just six minutes to eight. The private road leading up to its grand lobby was lined with open-topped Kubelwagens and three of the grand Mercedes saloons used by senior German officers.

'There's four regular soldiers guarding the entrance,' Marc noted, as Henderson turned into a narrow side street and pulled up.

'I saw them,' Henderson said warily.

He stepped out of the tiny car and looked up and down the street. 'We've got to get in there before curfew or we're buggered.'

Henderson took out a duffel bag containing the partially assembled Sten gun and handed it to Marc.

'How do we get inside?' the boy asked, as the weight of the bag practically wrenched his arm from its socket.

'Every posh hotel has a staff entrance. It'll be around the back.'

'But they might be guarding that too,' Marc said. 'And if we get in, how the hell are we going to get away again when the whole city is under a curfew?'

'Good questions,' Henderson said, as they walked briskly towards the back of the hotel. 'I'll let you know the answers just as soon as I think of them.'

A left turn took them on to a concrete ramp, misted with steam curling out of the hotel kitchen and stinking of the rubbish overflowing from giant metal bins. Three kitchen staff stood in an open doorway smoking cigarettes and a bored-looking German guard sat on a step behind them.

'Act as if we do this every night of our lives,' Henderson said to Marc, as they approached the door.

'Evening, gents,' Henderson said brightly, nodding to the smokers.

They looked a touch mystified, but it was a big hotel and they didn't know everyone who worked there. The German stretched out his leg to stop them and spoke in bad French.

'My French not too good,' Henderson said, pointing jovially towards himself. 'I night porter. My son is shoe shine.'

The German didn't seem happy to have drawn guard duty on his first night in Paris and he looked up miserably and pointed into the kitchen with his thumb. 'Go ahead.'

Savage heat blasted Marc as he stepped inside. A filthy corridor took them into the hotel kitchen proper, where three men as rough as any Marc had seen leaving the Dormitory Raquel stood in front of a trough, scrubbing massive pots. Another man barged past, carrying a crate filled with empty champagne bottles.

It seemed impossible that anything could be hotter, but as they reached the centre of the kitchen Marc felt as if the sun had crash landed on his head. It seemed impossible to breathe, let alone work in such heat, but dozens of kitchen staff carted ingredients, chopped, boiled, seared and dragged heavy trays out of ovens.

Marc and Henderson caught a few odd glances, but nobody had time to stop and ask questions. When the waiters passed through the swinging doors leading into the restaurant they were able to glimpse a room filled with black uniforms. At the far end, someone was making a speech to a chorus of drunken laughter.

'It's good if they're pissed,' Henderson said, smiling as he stepped out of the kitchen into a narrow corridor with great clumps of mildew growing on the walls. 'Remember, Marc: confidence is key. Always look like you know where you're going, even if you haven't got a clue.'

Marc was scared and felt slightly woozy, but at least the corridor was merely stifling, rather than unbearable. They walked twenty metres until they came to a wooden staircase that went down to the hotel basement. A door at the bottom led them into a room containing two giant washing machines. Beyond the machines a woman worked flat out, stretching white hotel sheets over a steam-press, then taking off the flattened sheets and folding them into neat squares.

She stared oddly at Marc and Henderson. Clearly she didn't get many visitors.

'Hello,' Henderson said. 'We just started work here. I'm supposed to unblock a toilet for someone called Mannstein.'

The woman raised a single eyebrow. 'How the hell does that bring you down here?'

'I just came along the corridor.'

She looked at Marc. 'And you've brought your son to work?'

'Shoe-shine,' Marc said.

'We've never had that before,' the woman said. 'Night porter does the shoes when reception is quiet.'

'They wanted him special,' Henderson said. 'All those Germans need their boots cleaned.'

'Germans,' the woman said, as she spat on a sheet before folding it. 'I've been having a nice time these last weeks with Paris so quiet. Now they're turning everything upside down. Threw out all our guests, including residents who've lived here for years, then went down to the cellar and dragged up all the best wines and champagne. You can bet they won't be paying their bills and if I don't see my wages I'm out of here.'

'That's the breaks, I guess,' Henderson said uncertainly as he turned towards the door. 'You wouldn't know how I can find out what room Mannstein's in, would you? I don't want to go back upstairs and make myself look stupid.'

The woman tutted with contempt, but pointed towards a telephone on the wall. 'Dial zero, zero for the front desk. They'll give you his room number.'

As Henderson grabbed the phone, the laundress walked over to a clothes rail and grabbed a set of pressed overalls. 'You'd better put them on,' she said. 'If the floor manager catches you in a public area without a uniform he'll go spare.'

Then the woman looked at Marc. 'We've never had a boy shoe-shine before. The only thing I've got that will fit you is a messenger's uniform. But don't go getting polish on it because it'll never come out of white cuffs.'

'Thank you.' Marc nodded to her as he grabbed the hanger. His uniform comprised a white shirt, black trousers and a velvet waistcoat with gold buttons.

'Very fetching,' Henderson teased, as they stepped back into the corridor.

'Did you get the room number from reception?' Marc asked.

'Six-one-two,' Henderson replied. 'Now we need somewhere to put these clothes on.'

They headed back upstairs and passed a janitor's cupboard that was big enough to change in. Henderson closed the door behind them, switched on the light and unzipped the bag, taking out the compact machine gun and showing Marc how to take off the safety catch, fire and reload. On the way out, he grabbed a mop, plunger and bucket.

'Now we've got to find the lift.'

The staff area on the ground floor was a warren and it took several anxious minutes of wandering badly-lit corridors until they found themselves near the hotel's reception desk with the main elevators facing directly towards them.

Several Gestapo officers were returning to their rooms. The lift stopped at the second and fifth floors and on each the departing officers were saluted by two German infantrymen on guard duty.

'Seems they've got this place sealed up pretty tight,' Henderson said.

They were alone for the final ride to the top floor and Henderson used the opportunity to check that his silenced pistol was ready to fire.

'You sure you're OK with the machine gun?' Henderson said. 'Remember to hold it exactly how I showed you or you'll rip your shoulder off.'

The two guards stepped forwards as the lift doors opened.

'State your purpose,' one guard said, in truly awful French.

Henderson began to mumble a convoluted explanation about blocked pipes in room 612 and how the messenger boy's little arms would be needed to reach behind a sink and undo a valve. Of course, the Germans didn't understand a word.

'Blocked toilet,' the German said irritably. 'That's all you need to tell me.'

Henderson nodded apologetically as he walked off with Marc in tow. But after a few steps he realised he'd gone the wrong way and he turned around. Once they'd passed the guards again, one spoke to the other in German.

'Useless bloody French,' he sneered. 'Too much wine. It's no wonder they lost the bloody war.'

Henderson and Marc both thought it best to pretend that they hadn't understood and carried on towards Mannstein's room. Fortunately there were several turns in the corridor and two sets of fire doors.

'As soon as Mannstein opens the door I'm going to shoot him in the face,' Henderson said. 'Stand well back unless you want to get splattered in blood.'

'Right.' Marc nodded, taking a deep breath as he poised his knuckles in front of the door. Henderson dropped his bucket and mop and pulled the silenced pistol.

Marc knocked and waited.

'Who is it?' a German said.

'Messenger boy,' Marc shouted.

Henderson panicked. 'That's not Mannstein,' he gasped.

Marc didn't have time to ask what to do as a Gestapo officer opened the door. 'Message from Oburst Hinze—' he began.

But before Marc knew it, Henderson had fired his shot and a mist of the officer's blood had spattered his face. Marc was stunned as Henderson burst into the room, just in time to hear Mannstein cry out and run for the bathroom. The bolt slid across the door a second before Henderson barged into it.

'I just want to talk, Mr Mannstein,' Henderson lied. 'It's not too late. I can still get you out of France.'

Inside the bathroom, Mannstein was going frantic. Banging against the wall, stamping on the floor and screaming for help. He wasn't a fool and he knew Henderson wasn't here to talk.

'Machine gun,' Henderson shouted, pointing towards the bag.

Marc handed the gun over and Henderson stepped away from the door and let rip. The bullets shredded the door. Henderson used his fist to punch through a large hole and then aimed directly at Mannstein, who'd taken shelter by lying flat in the bath.

A second blast from the Sten gun turned him into red goo, but Mannstein's cries and the gunfire had been heard by the guards down the corridor and by several Gestapo officers in their rooms.

The first black uniform came out of the room directly across the corridor. Marc dived to the floor as the officer took aim with his pistol, but Henderson spun around and annihilated him with the machine gun.

'Shit,' Henderson howled. 'Shit, shit, shit.'

'Never mind shit,' Marc said, as he grabbed the pistol from the dead German's hand. 'What do we do?'

'What do you think we do?' Henderson said as he charged towards the door. 'Run like hell!'

Find out more at:
www.hendersonsboys.com